D1232892

X
17

THOUSAND YARD STARE

a novel

Pierce Kelley

iUniverse, Inc.
New York   Bloomington

Thousand Yard Stare
a novel

iUniverse books may be ordered through booksellers or by contacting:

iUniverse
1663 Liberty Drive
Bloomington, IN 47403
www.iuniverse.com
1-800-Authors (1-800-288-4677)

Because of the dynamic nature of the Internet, any Web addresses or links contained in this book may have changed since publication and may no longer be valid. The views expressed in this work are solely those of the author and do not necessarily reflect the views of the publisher, and the publisher hereby disclaims any responsibility for them.

ISBN: 978-1-4502-2836-7 (sc)
ISBN: 978-1-4502-2837-4 (dj)
ISBN: 978-1-4502-2838-1 (ebook)

Printed in the United States of America

iUniverse rev. date: 04/28/2010

*"To George and all those who have
or have had the 'Thousand Yard Stare.'"*

Other works by Pierce Kelley

Kennedy Homes: An American Tragedy (iUniverse, 2009);
A Foreseeable Risk (iUniverse, 2009);
Asleep at the Wheel (iUniverse, 2009);
A Tinker's Damn! (iUniverse, 2008);
Bocas del Toro (iUniverse, 2007);
A Plenary Indulgence (iUniverse, 2007);
Pieces to the Puzzle (iUniverse, 2007);
Introducing Children to the Game of Tennis (iUniverse, 2007);
A Very Fine Line (iUniverse, 2006);
Fistfight at the L and M Saloon (iUniverse, 2006;
Civil Litigation: A Case Study (Pearson Publications, 2001;
The Parent's Guide to Coaching Tennis (F&W Publications, 1995);
A Parent's Guide to Coaching Tennis (Betterway Publications, 1991)

* * * * * * *

"Both The Pacific and Band of Brothers focus on the horrors of the war and the emotional trauma that a soldier or Marine can endure. P.T.S.D. should be treated with as much seriousness as a gunshot wound. If the president is going to send tens of thousands more troops [into combat], he also needs to consider the emotional payload. With suicide rates up among veterans — accounting for 20 percent* of all suicides among Americans — the government must dedicate more money to support programs for our returning troops."

Former Senator Bill Bradley, March 11, 2010

* * * * * * *

Acknowledgements

I thank those who have supported and encouraged me on this and other projects. I wish to specifically thank Sue Pundt, Paul Christian Sullivan, Pat and Marlene Doherty, Doug Easton, Bob Mason, Tug Miller, Dennis Geagan, Richard Monan and Scott Harrison, who have read drafts and offered their insights into this and other works. In particular, I thank Warren Parkin for providing me with much appreciated editorial assistance and advice, in addition to writing the Foreword to this book.

I also acknowledge and thank Duffy Soto of the Hunter Printing Company in Lake City, Florida, for the graphic design work on the cover.

The photographs were provided to me by my friend, George, the man about whom this book is written and to whom this book is dedicated. I thank George for giving me the insight into his world to make this book as 'real' as I am able to make it. Though this is a work of fiction, and I have departed from what truly happened to George in some material ways, it is based on his life. I hope that by having his story told he can let some of the demons out and diminish the memories of forty years ago which continue to haunt him and, perhaps, help others realize that they are not alone.

Foreword
by Warren Parkin

Thousand Yard Stare provokes thoughts about duty, rage, innocence and understanding. It is a timely novel, particularly relevant to present day as the United States wages war on two fronts, Afghanistan and Iraq, and soldiers return home with unprecedented levels of diagnosable Post Traumatic Stress Disorder.

In this novel Pierce Kelley explores selfless patriotism and the psychological casualties of war through the protagonist George Murphy, who willingly enlists to serve in the Vietnam War. George embodies the countless members of our armed forces who return home with wounds invisible to the naked eye. Not disfigured in any visible way, but scarred in mind and spirit.

Generically named George Murphy is an Everyman, every individual who serves our country and bears the consequences of the service. During his two Vietnam tours George learns to fix all things mechanical – from tanks to choppers – even as he witnesses executions and suicide, sees savagery, and acts as an undertaker for friend and foe alike. George comes home to civilian life only to find that although he is an excellent mechanic, he doesn't possess the skills to fix what is broken inside of him, a dysfunction that causes him to be a stranger to society and himself.

In *Thousand Yard Stare* George goes from victim of war to personhood as the reader comes face to face with the question: Can one legally justify criminal choices due to past suffering?

Unlike the real person this novel is based on, my military experience is strictly vicarious.

Unfortunately, Post Traumatic Stress Disorder is much more familiar to me.

Years of sexual abuse by a ring of pedophiles during childhood and adolescence produced in my first wife a rage and loss so absolute and all encompassing that weeks went by when I didn't know where she was or what physically wounded condition she would return home in. She died young. That was my official introduction to PTSD.

For the past 11 years I have raised a foster daughter (now 21) who also suffers from PTSD. When I met her she was so full of unbridled rage that she was a danger to herself and others. She has multiple disabilities: physical and cerebral alike. She is further disabled by certain cues that trigger an atavistic response to present situations. After more than a decade of love and understanding, past events – neglect, physical and sexual abuse, exploitation and deprivation – continue to haunt her.

Based on my experiences with loved ones, I find the portrayal of PTSD in *Thousand Yard Stare* highly accurate.

In addition to my personal experienced with PTSD, I have spent countless hours listening to veterans' stories of horrors and triumphs in the 20th and 21st centuries.

My grandfather served in the Navy during World War I, my father served as a pilot in World War II, my father-in-law served in Korea, and my brother-in-law served in Vietnam. I've heard their stories and those of others. Complete strangers have shared their experiences with me. Not one of these veterans has talked to me out of self pity. Not one of them spoke to me in defeat. I honor what they told me. And I'll never forget the scars they bear, psychological wounds that don't merit a medal, but are chronic all the same.

A Military Police officer in Saigon during the Tet Offensive watched his buddies sawed in half by machine gun fire while defending the U.S. embassy. He used a Russian AK-47 because it didn't jam like the standard military issue M-16. When fired upon while patrolling the streets of Saigon, he often shot his radio first. "There wasn't any time to ask for permission to return fire," he explained. Rules of engagement jeopardized him and his fellow soldiers.

Only three from his platoon came home. He credited survival with watching the children, readying himself for trouble when they vacated the streets. He told me about living in fear, about seeing an officer, who refused to remove identifying emblems from his uniform, killed after serving a mere 20 minutes in Vietnam. He shared stories for an hour and a half then asked me to never tell his family. He was proud, depressed, bewildered and guilt-ridden by his time in the military. He sleeps in a separate bed now so he doesn't hurt his wife in his sleep. When firecrackers explode, he hits the deck.

A former patrol point man told me that the only reason he got out of Vietnam alive was that he followed the advice of a veteran of the Korean War.

Over moonshine sipped from a jar on a porch in Georgia, his uncle told him to "shoot first and ask questions later."

While waiting for my RV to be worked on I met a former sniper. He entered the military at age 15 and was trained in South America before embarking on years of black ops in Vietnam, Cambodia and Laos before the United States officially declared war – and afterwards. "They would give us the target, drop us in and then it was up to ourselves to make it out." He told me he had killed more than 100 people. "It's sad to say, I have a wife and children and I can't love them. Killing people changes you. It makes loving impossible." He looked into the distance hollow eyed, then left me to check on the progress of his vehicle.

A veteran of Desert Storm cried about a wounded comrade's pleading demand to be killed. He is haunted to this day because he did what his friend asked. To add insult to his injury, once stateside the government demanded repayment of hazard duty wages. It was deemed that his months in the sand were not dangerous enough.

More recently, a veteran of the Iraqi War talked far into the night. Although his training was in maintaining firearms, he was assigned border patrol, recon, discovery and disposal of potential improvised explosive devices. Overweight by Marine standards, he was one of a few strong enough to remove tires from the roadside, common hiding places for bombs. In his seventh year of service at the time, he was not equipped with any explosive protective gear. He showed grisly picture after grisly picture and spoke of how he was diagnosed with PTSD, but now after being stateside for four months, he was over it. Nothing could be further from the truth.

All these soldiers were wounded by war. Not on the outside, but on the inside.

All came home only to find that the comfort of home was unavailable. Home was alien. When one has been part of something bigger than one's self, what is one to do outside the group that gave life meaning? Departure from this group of shared experience leaves the individual adrift. It is in the midst of such chaos that the individual must find a place, try to develop a space of acceptance and understanding. It is this story that Kelley tells through George's eyes.

Thousand Yard Stare is a novel about loss, loss of innocence, loss of relationships, loss of country, loss of sanity, loss of perspective, loss of self. It is a novel that poignantly illustrates the existence of experiences which make us strangers to ourselves. The story of George Murphy resonates today as record numbers of veterans return home damaged. They exhibit no exterior maladies. And yet sadly, when one talks with them, it becomes obvious that they are the walking wounded of our society.

Is it any wonder that veterans disproportionately make up the homeless and the prison populations? This implicit question and others are asked in the novel. There is, however, an explicit question posed in *Thousand Yard Stare*: Does Post Traumatic Stress Disorder exonerate a person who commits a crime? It is the strength of this novel that Pierce Kelley leaves it to the reader to decide.

PROLOGUE

"SHOOT ME!"

I knelt beside him, screaming for a Medic, crying like a baby, even though I knew there was no one around, no one who would help us that is. Minutes before we had been driving down a dirt road on our way back to Pleiku from An Khe, like we had dozens of times before, talking about what we were going to do when we got out of the hell we were in. He was a 'short-timer' with less than thirty days to go. I still had to do another four months. He was my best friend and we had plans to open an auto repair place back home. I would be the mechanic and he'd do the body work.

"Shoot me!" he screamed, louder than before.

I looked again but there was no one in sight in either direction. We had just finished loading a Jeep onto a trailer and were bringing it in for repair. It had slid off the road into a ditch because of the heavy rains we were getting. During monsoon season it didn't take much for a driver of one of those little two-seaters to lose control. We weren't far from base when it happened.

"God damn it, George, shoot me! You promised…"

He was crying uncontrollably now, begging me to shoot him. There was blood everywhere. I was bleeding, too, and I knew I was hurt, but not like Tillie. Both of his legs had been blown off below the knees and blood was everywhere. I had made two makeshift tourniquets as best I could to stop the bleeding, but he had blood coming out from all over his body.

"Hang in there, Tillie! I'm gonna get you to the base as fast as I can, man! Hang in there!"

I was afraid to move him but I knew if I didn't get him some to help, and soon, he was a goner. His eyes were closed. He grabbed my shirt, and begged, "Just shoot me, George…please…"

"Don't die on me, man!" I screamed. "You're gonna make it! I swear!"

His voice was growing softer. It was barely audible now. His grip loosened and his body went limp. I thought about doing CPR but he was breathing alright...too much, in fact. He was panting, breathing real hard and real fast.

We'd hit a mine and it must have been right under him. We both got thrown out of the vehicle but I was able to get up and run over to where he was lying. I pulled him back behind the vehicle. Our truck had burst into flames within seconds after I got us safely away.

He cried, "It hurts so bad, George. I can't feel my legs," he cried. "I don't want to be a cripple...you promised, man..."

I pulled my pistol from its case. I always carried it the entire time I'd been in 'Nam whenever I went off base, but I'd never used it before. As I did, he opened his eyes, looked me straight in the eye and said, "Please, George... please...do it!"

"Wake up! George, wake up! Wake up!"

My wife shook me until I came to.

"Was I making noises again?"

"Yes, you were, and kicking the sheets and flailing your arms. I had to get out of bed to get out of the way, George. I can't go on like this. One of these nights you're gonna hurt me. You're gonna hit me, not on purpose, but you're gonna hit me. I can't sleep anymore in the same bed with you. I'm sorry. I'm not sure I can live in the same house with you any longer."

She got up and started walking out of the room.

"No, you stay. I'll go." I said. "I don't mind sleeping on the couch. I may not be able to get back to sleep at all anyway."

"Was it the same dream, George?"

"It was one of the same ones I've had before."

"Do you want to talk about it?"

"No. You wouldn't want to hear it."

"Maybe I would. Maybe that would help."

"No you wouldn't. Trust me."

"What are we going to do, George?

"I don't know."

"When's it gonna get better?"

"I don't know. I don't know if it ever will."

CHAPTER ONE
Jeannette, Pennsylvania

I GREW UP IN A small town, Jeannette, Pennsylvania, which had about 10,000 people in it at the time. It was a blue-collar, working-man's kind of town, an industrial town. It had a glass factory, a couple of foundries where they made molds for things, and the plant where Penn tennis balls were made. It was about an hour from Pittsburgh, a nice place to grow up.

There wasn't much crime that I can remember and I don't remember there being any kind of problems at all to speak of. Most everybody knew me and I knew them, at least in our neighborhood. I had an older brother and an older sister, but they were several years older than me and out of the house by the time I became a teenager, so it was just me and my folks in the house during those years.

My Dad worked as a mechanic and my Mom stayed at home and took care of us kids, just like everybody else's mom did. I was a happy kid growing up. I liked everybody and everybody seemed to like me well enough. I was an ordinary kid, nothing special. I wasn't a star athlete, but I wasn't the worst, either. I wasn't on the honor roll, or a gifted student, but I always passed. I wasn't the best looking kid in the class, but I wasn't the worst looking one either. I was happy with who and what I was. I didn't ever get into any fights or if I did I don't remember them.

I always had chores to do, just like my friends did. There was always something we had to do, like cut the grass, weed gardens, trim hedges, wash cars, take out the garbage – whatever our parents told us to do, we did it. I think I started playing sports just so I wouldn't have to do chores.

As a kid, I played little league baseball and pee-wee football, like everyone else, but I really didn't like it all that much. I was more interested in cars. Most of the kids were like me and if they weren't the star players by the time they were thirteen, they quit playing. My parents would've let me quit if I wanted to. They didn't push me, but I stuck it out with football through high school. By the time I graduated I was 5 foot 7 and a half inches tall and I weighed less than 165 pounds. I was too small and sat the bench most of the time. I would only get into the game if we were way ahead or way behind.

The most fun I had as a kid was going to the races with my Dad on Saturday nights during the summer months. Jeanette had a little oval track not far from our home and the local men would race each other every week. I used to beg my Dad to stay until all the races were over, and every now and then we would. When I got old enough, my parents let me go to the races by myself as long as a few of my friends were going to be there too.

By the time I was fourteen, I lived at the gas station. My Dad was a mechanic and that's where he worked. I used to just sit there and watch him work. I'd do whatever he'd let me do and watch what was going on.

I really didn't care much about anything else but cars. When there weren't any cars to work on, I'd work on lawnmowers and anything with a gas-powered engine. High school was okay but all I wanted was to get out and work at a gas station, just like my Dad.

When I turned sixteen, my Dad's boss let me work there after school and on weekends. I didn't get paid very much at first, a dollar and a half or something like that, whatever the minimum wage was, but I pumped gas, cleaned windshields, took out the trash and when I had nothing else to do, I watched whatever my Dad and the other two mechanics did and helped them any way I could. In school, they told me that I was "mechanically inclined," and I was happy to hear it. It came naturally to me. I became a pretty good car mechanic at an early age and that's all I could see myself doing for the rest of my life, which would have been fine with me.

There wasn't a whole lot to do in Jeannette for us kids. About the only other thing I can remember doing, other than working, watching sports and car races, was going to the dances at school. We all watched American Bandstand on TV and saw how the kids from Philadelphia danced. I danced more like the kids from Pittsburgh, children of steel workers.

I liked the Beatles, the Rolling Stones, the Beach Boys and a lot of other rock 'n roll bands. That's what I'd listen to on the radio all the time, especially when I was working on cars, but not at the gas station or when my Dad was around. He and his friends didn't like that music at all. It was all country for them. Hank Williams, Charlie Pride, Johnny Cash, Merle Haggard, and Elvis were his favorites. That was the '60s to me. Whatever else was going on in the rest of the country wasn't happening in Jeannette.

My Dad bought me an old fixer-upper my Junior year. It was a 1960

Ford Fairlane with a blown-out engine. We went to the junk yard and found a motor and put it in together. It ran fine and I worked my butt off to make it look as good as I could. That may have been the best time I ever had with my Dad, fixing up that old Ford. I could hardly get it to go fast enough to break the speed limit, but that was okay with me. I was glad to have my own wheels.

I turned eighteen in March of my senior year, a couple of months before graduation. Shortly after I did I received a notice from the Selective Service that I had to report for a physical examination. Although the news about the war in Vietnam was on TV and in the newspapers, I didn't read the papers much and seldom watched the news. The thought of going into the military never entered my mind. Protests against the war had nothing to do with me. All I wanted to do was be a mechanic.

When I got the notice I wasn't too worried about it. I felt like it could happen to somebody else, but not to me. I was pretty naïve. I knew that I didn't want to go to college but I wasn't thinking of it as a way to get out of being drafted, although a lot of my friends went to the local community college just to stay out of the Army. I wasn't that smart and I didn't like school. I didn't want to go into the Army but the more I thought about it, the better it sounded. They told me that I could be a mechanic and that I wouldn't have to march through rice paddies. They told me I would be assigned to work on tanks and trucks and might not have to go to Vietnam at all.

Me and my parents talked it over and since we didn't know, for sure, if I would be drafted or not, we discussed whether or not it was better to wait and see if I got drafted, and hope that I didn't, or join. We figured things would go better for me if I volunteered to go in instead of being drafted, so after talking to the counselors at school and the recruiter a few times, I took a physical, signed all the papers and within a week or two I was all set to go into the Army once I was out of school.

I graduated from high school on June 8, 1968 and two days later I was on a bus headed to Fort Jackson, South Carolina. All I had with me was a duffel bag with a few pairs of pants, a couple of shirts and some pictures of my family. As soon as I got off the bus and walked through the gates to the base, along with hundreds of other kids about my age, things changed. Everybody started yelling at me. I wasn't ready for that. I doubt anybody could be even though everybody knows that's what to expect.

The drill instructors attacked us. They screamed and told us to jump and we jumped. They told us to run and we ran. They pushed and shoved us from one green room to another, yelling and screaming at the top of their lungs. We had to get our uniforms, dog tags, ID cards, blood tests and a whole bunch of other things. They handed us shirts, shoes, socks, pants, most of which didn't fit, but whatever was wrong was our fault and we were called shit-for-brains, pussies and worse.

When it was time to eat we stopped whatever we were doing, put down our equipment and got in line for chow. We were given ten minutes to get our food and ten minutes to eat it. All the time the drill instructors were walking around screaming, yelling, pushing and ridiculing us. When we finished, or when time was up, whichever came first, we were back in line running somewhere.

From the very first night, people were assigned to guard duty. Even though we were on an Army base on U.S. soil, every one of us was assigned to spend an hour that night walking around the building that was our barrack. At 5:00, the lights were on and the drill instructors were yelling at us. We had to be on our feet, standing at attention, ready for inspection immediately after the lights went on. Everybody was up in a matter of seconds.

We were allowed ten minutes for the four 'S's – shit, shine, shower and shave, and then it was off to breakfast, on the run. After breakfast, everybody got 'the' *haircut*. After that was a two-mile training run. Not many of us were ready for that, either. I sure wasn't.

After that we learned to march, in unison, which we practiced endlessly. We learned to stand at attention until an order was given to be 'at ease' or do something else. If we made a mistake, we were punished, mostly immediate physical abuse, and other punishment, which could mean push-ups, kitchen patrol, more guard duty or something else. There was always verbal abuse. Nobody talked back, nobody questioned the authority of the drill instructors. Everybody learned to scream responses back at the top of their lungs.

We were yelled at, beaten, harassed, humiliated, ridiculed and shamed for eight straight weeks. Up at 5:00 and on the go until 8:00 at night, with lights out at ten. But before anyone went to sleep we had to polish and clean our uniforms, boots, buttons, and rifles, all of which would be inspected the next morning.

There were lectures on everything from orientation on the Army's way of doing things, like the Dress Code, the Code of Conduct, the Uniform Code of military justice, plus the evils of Communism and other academic kinds of things. Then there was the training on how to hold a rifle, how to clean it, how to assemble it with your eyes closed, and how to fire it.

We practiced shooting our rifles, M-16s, every day, and occasionally at night, too. We were given moving targets the shape of a human being to shoot at. We were judged by how well we did and harshly criticized if we didn't do well enough. "Lock and load! Fire when ready!"

I was in a platoon of twenty men. All of the guys were about the same age as me. They put us all in the same building, five bunk beds on each side of the room, two guys in each bunk. I was in the top bed.

My bunk mate was a guy from Missouri. His name was Jim Berkshire. He was a kid, just like me, and we got along fine. It was the same with all of the other guys, too. It was us against the drill instructor and his assistants.

Our sergeant was Watson. He was a hard man. I never saw him smile the whole time I was there. He had two corporals with him all the time, one on either side and they'd yell whenever he'd yell and they'd yell the same thing he yelled, as if we couldn't hear him or something. Whenever one of them yelled anything, we had to yell back just as loud or they'd make us repeat it, like they hadn't heard what we said.

Every morning, it was the same thing – cold, rubbery eggs, toast and grits, and a pint of milk made from powder. Lunch was always a cold sandwich of some kind and water. Nobody complained.

Dinners were our only hot meal of the day, unless you count the eggs, which were never warm, let alone hot. Sunday dinners were the best. They worked us hard on Sundays just like every other day, but not quite as long. We got to enjoy Sunday dinners a little while longer.

Everybody ate together at the same table and nobody started to eat until everybody sat down. Nobody got up until everybody was finished. There was never anything left on anyone's plate. If someone didn't eat all he had been served, someone else finished it for him. We did everything as a team.

We'd go to an obstacle course to run over, under, around and through various objects. The hardest part was the rope climb. Everybody had trouble with that, not just me. They taught us how to wrap the rope around your feet, to give yourself a little platform, and then shimmy up the rope. There was no way I could pull myself up at first. After doing it for a while, I got better at it, though I never understood when a mechanic might have to do that.

It was summer time in Georgia and it was hot. We'd be out in the sun all afternoon no matter how hot it was. Guys would be dying for water but nobody drank anything unless the sergeant said so, and nobody drank anything unless everybody drank and we all drank at the same time. By the time we got back to our barracks, we were beat. We had ten minutes to shower, get dressed and get ready for dinner.

Once the lights went out at 10:00 that was it for the night. Everybody went to sleep. Some guys would get up in the middle of the night for guard duty or to go to the bathroom, but other than that, we slept until the lights came on to wake us up, except for the raids they pulled on us every so often during the middle of the night. They'd come in yelling and screaming at us. We'd fall in next to our beds and stand at attention while they searched our bags and everything we had to make sure we didn't have anything we weren't supposed to have, like drugs.

One of the first things we were taught was how to pack our back-packs, which weighed up to seventy pounds. We had to run and walk with our back packs on from then on. There was only one right way to put all of that stuff in the back pack and there was no easy way to do it.

There were always meetings where we were told the rules and regulations about everything from doing laundry to getting mail. There was one way things were done and we had to learn how to do it the right way right from the start, and we did. Sergeant Watson made sure of that.

By the fourth or fifth week, they'd taught us hand-to-hand combat. They'd put a broomstick with a heavy pad on each end and have us fight with each other, acting as if the broomsticks were our rifles.

They taught us how to use grenades, how to use gas masks, rocket launchers, and what to do if we were exposed to chemicals or land mines, and other things, like snake bites. A lot of time was spent on injuries and what to do before the medics got there if we were hurt or a fellow soldier.

By the seventh week, it was time for us to go on maneuvers. They took us out in the woods for two and three days at a time, teaching us how to set up camp, pitch a tent, make a fire, take down a campsite and do all the things we'd have to do if we were on patrol.

That was life in the Army during basic training. Seven days a week, twenty four hours a day. For eight weeks, the twenty of us did whatever we were told to do, no questions asked. When it was over, everybody received an assignment. Some guys went straight from basic to Nam, but most went to someplace else, like Europe, a base in the States or somewhere else in the world.

Because I had signed up to be a mechanic, they sent me for sixteen weeks of training which was at Fort Jackson, as well, so I didn't go anywhere. I was going to be a "wheel and track mechanic" and I was looking forward to it. I was thinking that the sixteen weeks of Advanced Individual Training, or AIT as it was called, would be different from what I had gone through in basic but I was wrong. We were all soldiers, first, and we had to keep our boots polished, our uniforms clean and our mouths shut, just like before. We still had to do all of the things every other soldier had to do in the military, like march and drill, and the lights came on at the same time every day, and lights went out at the same time too.

Most of the days were spent learning how to work on tanks and armored personnel carriers, which were called APCs. They wanted me to know how to fix everything, though, so I also learned how to work on trucks and jeeps, too.

When I finished the training, I was assigned to the Wheels and Tracks Division of the 128th Engineering Battalion. Tracks were vehicles like tanks and some road equipment, like graders, that didn't have wheels and ran on revolving treads. My unit was assigned to go overseas. In early December of 1968, we boarded a U.S. Army transport plane in Fort Dix, New Jersey and headed for Camp Echborn, near Frankfurt.

I was stationed in Germany for the next nine months and I can honestly say that I didn't like it there at all, not one little bit. We stayed together as a unit all the time. We were in the barracks five days out of seven. We were given passes to leave the base on weekends and when we went out, we went as a group.

We did more of the same training, the same marching on the same schedules, but I became a better mechanic during those months. That's what I did all day every day. The food was better, the barracks were better and most everything else was better than it had been at Fort Jackson, but there wasn't much going on in Germany at the time. We were there to watch the Russians and they were there to watch us. The war was in Vietnam and that's all anybody wanted to talk about.

Most of the guys were in the infantry divisions and they went out on overnight camping trips called bivouacs. They'd go into the woods on long hikes, pitch tents and set up a camp site. Sometimes we'd meet them there, bringing in supplies and things. While we were there, all of us took turns being sentry or night watchman.

Once we stayed in the woods for four nights and then came back to base. I think we did two or three camping trips like that. I thought of myself as a mechanic, not a soldier, but as far as the Army was concerned, I was a soldier first and foremost.

It seemed like we were just in Germany to make sure that the Russians didn't invade. We were on one side of the line between East and West Germany and they were on the other. It was the same throughout the whole country between East and West Germany but the only wall was in Berlin. Nothing ever happened, but thousands and thousands of us soldiers were there just in case something ever did.

The guys in my platoon became the best of friends. We did everything together – eat, sleep, shower, shave – everything. There were guys from all over the country. Everybody was different but they were all pretty much like me – just young kids becoming men.

Most everybody had graduated high school. I don't remember anybody who hadn't. Nobody had been to college. A few were a little older than me and some a little younger, but we were all about the same age. We were all eighteen or nineteen, just out of high school. There were a couple of guys from

Kansas, a few from Texas, one from Louisiana, two from Florida, some from Michigan, Ohio and Wisconsin, several from California and one was even from Alaska. About a third of the guys were African-Americans, some were Mexican-Americans, but most were like me, white and Christian. Everybody had a different accent. Some talked real fast and some talked real slow. I was about in the middle.

In Pennsylvania and South Carolina, the only other places I had ever been, the drinking age was twenty one. In Germany it was eighteen. On the first weekend we had a pass, which was a month or so after we got there, we all went to a place called the Hofbrau Haus. There were beautiful women dressed in German clothing from a hundred years or so before serving ice-cold beer out of huge containers called steins.

It wasn't too long before we were all as drunk as we could be. I wasn't the only one who had never been drunk before. I got sick in the streets and have no recollection of how I got home that night. A few of the guys either didn't drink or didn't drink too much and they took care of the rest of us. We were as sick as dogs the next morning.

All that next week, that's all we talked about and the next Saturday night we did the same thing, except we didn't drink quite as much. Not long after that, one of the guys found out where the prostitutes were and that's where we all went. It was legal and most of the patrons there were U.S. soldiers, like us, going in and out of the buildings. A group of us, including me most of the time, stayed outside while a few of the other guys went in. For $10 we could get laid. Before we left Germany, all of us had been in there at least once. That was the first experience with sex for most of us. It was for me. That, like drinking, was part of the process of growing up. Drugs wasn't a part of that, yet, but it would be.

In Germany, soccer was the only sport they cared about. None of us cared much for soccer back then and I still don't, but all the guys would watch football every chance they got, rooting for their home teams. The Green Bay Packers with Bart Starr, Paul Hornung, Ray Nietschke and many other star players were the best back then and the Dallas Cowboys with Don Meredith and Lee Roy Jordan were the next best. I didn't care about any of it all that much but if I heard the Steelers were playing, I'd root for them. They weren't all that good back then but I still wanted to see them win.

All of the guys had their favorite pro team, same thing for college football. Penn State and Pittsburgh were good at the time, especially Penn State. I'd root for them against anybody else except for Pittsburgh. I cared more about football when I was out of the country than I did when I was living there.

Because of the time difference between Germany and the U.S. we'd be watching games ten hours later in the day, and for late afternoon or night games in the U.S. it would be the next day for us. Some guys would stay up halfway through the night to watch a game, but not me.

After nine months in Germany, we received orders that we were going to Vietnam. I'd been in the Army for a year and two months. I was five months past my nineteenth birthday. As crazy as it sounds, I was glad when I received that order. I was happy to be leaving Germany and didn't ever want to go back. Still don't.

CHAPTER TWO
Vietnam

W<small>E</small> LEFT GERMANY IN the pre-dawn hours on a Sunday morning during the first week in August of 1969. It was raining and the wind was blowing hard as we walked for the last time out of our barracks and loaded onto a bus that would take us to the plane. The temperature might have been in the low fifties when we left. We had our heavy jackets on over our uniforms and wore our helmets with the insulated lining. We boarded a giant C-5A Galaxy. There were no windows and no flight attendants.

Some sixteen hours later, we arrived at the airport at Cam Ranh Bay. When they opened the doors, we got hit with a wave of heat that about knocked us down. We looked in one direction and saw hundreds of ships in port. We looked another way and saw what seemed like thousands of planes. We turned around and saw thousands of Army-green tents. The Navy, the Army and the Air Force all had tens of thousands of men there.

The sun was shining and the temperature was over a hundred degrees. Within minutes, we were all down to our t-shirts, but we still had on baggy pants, heavy boots and those 70 pound packs on our backs.

Our barracks were way out at the end of that huge complex and we marched for almost an hour to get there. We were alongside one of the many long runways. The naval base and all the ships were on the other side of the base from where we were but we could see them off in the distance. Platoons and platoons of men just like us marched or ran in formation, hollering as they went, all day long.

I remember thinking what an incredible display of military strength it was. I remember saying to myself that there was no way the Vietnamese could stand up to that kind of military might. We'd fought the Germans and Japanese, and we were ready to fight the Russians. The Vietnamese? What kind of army could they possibly have to stand up to us? I knew nothing about what I was in for and who we were fighting.

The whole place was fenced in and there was another fence around that. Our leaders were still hollering orders to us and we were obeying them just as if we were still at Ft. Jackson in basic training. It was all still spit and polish where we were.

That first night, the officers sat our platoon and the other new arrivals down and told us that we'd be taking the fight to the Viet Cong. It was a "seek and destroy" policy that had been General Westmoreland's strategy for years. We were told that it was working. The infantry divisions would be moving out soon and the APCs would be taking them. 'Tracks' would go with many of them. Our division wasn't going anywhere.

Our shop was on base and our job was to fix vehicles when they broke down. We were to do regular maintenance on all vehicles and make sure they were running good. We were told that most of the time Chinooks, huge helicopters with two enormous rotors, would deliver the tanks and trucks to us. Other times they'd be towed in to be fixed, but there would be times when we might be called upon to go out in the field to fix a damaged vehicle. It sounded good to us. We were ready to go to work. Our barracks weren't far from our shop.

That night, our first night in Vietnam, our barracks got shelled. We didn't actually get hit, but a few bombs and mortar shells landed not far from us and when they did, all hell broke loose. There was heavy artillery all over the base, especially along the perimeter, as well as tanks that were parked close by, so when shells came our way, about a thousand times more shells went back at the enemy. Our guys would try to get a fix on where the incoming rockets came from and pound the hell out of that target until someone told them to stop. The noise was deafening.

Although I was exhausted, I didn't get any sleep that first night. Some of us had guard duty and I was one of them. I was so tired I didn't know how I could do it, but I took my turn and I found out real quick. My post was a wooden shack about ten feet up in the air and I was to watch out for everything. Those were my instructions, the only instructions I received.

I heard the artillery, the noise of the helicopters coming and going, the machine gun fire, the mortars, the planes, and the rest, but it was the other noises that scared me the most. The sound of small arms firing nearby was bad, but the sound of twigs breaking in the jungle just past my line of sight was even worse. Was it a VC attack? Was it a suicide squad of Sappers trying to infiltrate? I didn't know, nobody had told me what to do and what not to do. I had no trouble staying awake.

Every now and then one of the other guards would send up a flare which would parachute down and illuminate the area. As I watched each come down I looked for any sign of movement. I had my hands on my rifle the whole time. That's all I had, my rifle, a helmet, a flak jacket and some spare clips. I had no idea what I would have done if it had been a full-scale assault.

I had heard about Tet. We all had. Every January the Vietnamese recognize their New Year just like we do except their calendar, like China's and that of many other countries, is based on the cycles of the moon. It's called a lunar new year. Tet was their new year celebration The festival lasts several days.

In January 1968 at the beginning of the holiday, the Viet Cong had attacked hundreds of targets all across South Vietnam, all at the same time. In Saigon, they seized government offices for a period of time. Some places were over-run and whole units were massacred. In other places the fighting went on for days, weeks and in some cases months. They'd even attacked Cam Ranh Bay, the base where I was. We all knew about it and we all knew it could happen again.

Before that the United States didn't think that the Viet Cong or the North Vietnamese Army would ever attack us. Everybody thought that they'd continue to use a defensive, hit and run type strategy. That changed after Tet of '68. I arrived in the Republic of South Vietnam a year and eight months after that but the shock waves still hadn't died down.

It was hard for me to believe that the Viet Cong had attacked Cam Ranh Bay because of how big it was, but they had. We were told to be alert and expect anything. I was and I did. Fortunately, nothing happened. That was the longest night of my life, up to then.

Sergeant Wilson was my platoon leader. I had become a corporal in Germany so I was in the chain of command in our unit. He was a hard-nosed kind of guy but as long as we did our job, and we did, he treated us decent, not like the drill sergeants did. When we were working it was more about being a good mechanic than it was about being in the military.

That day, our first day of work as mechanics in Viet Nam, we worked on everything. There were hundreds of other mechanics in the area but our platoon was assigned to one building which was off by itself. We had mostly earth-moving and road-building heavy machinery in our shop. There were other things too, like tanks, armored personnel carriers, four-seat jeeps, flat-bed trucks and a whole lot of everything, too, and we worked on whatever we were told to do. As a corporal, I had to supervise the work of other soldiers and I picked and chose what I worked on.

That second night was more of the same. That night and every night after it we'd get some shells come our way and every night we'd respond with the big guns, the tanks, the planes and the rest. It was like that every night for the entire time I was in Cam Ranh Bay.

There was no noise I had ever heard that could compare to the sound of heavy artillery firing. The noise at a race track on a Saturday night back in Jeanette when I could hardly hear my Dad talking to me while he was sitting right next to me couldn't hold a candle to any of the nights I was at Cam Ranh Bay. When cannons and tanks started firing, you'd have thought the whole world was going to explode. It sounded as if they were going off right next to our barracks, even when they were a mile away, and they kept firing for a long time, too.

The worst part was when the enemies' bombs got close to us. We'd get a warning to get out of bed and hit the bunkers we'd dug. They were just holes in the ground deep enough for us to jump into, with sand bags around the top. It would take a direct hit right on top of the hole to get us, or at least that was what we were told.

When it rained, as it did most every day during the rainy season, our bunkers would fill up with water. If we had to get in them we'd be soaked up to our shoulders. Our clothes never seemed to get completely dry. If it wasn't rain, it was sweat. We didn't have much to change into so we wore the same stuff every day. A lot of guys got rashes and sores that lasted for months.

I had never seen anybody from Vietnam before I got there except in a photograph and neither had anybody else in my battalion. When we finally went off base, after a month or so, the first thing I noticed was how small the Vietnamese were. Other things I noticed were that for the most part they didn't wear shoes and seemed to carry everything they owned on their backs or on a bicycle or two-wheeled wagon. Most wore black clothes that looked like pajamas with large, cone-shaped straw hats on their heads. They kept their heads down. People wouldn't look at us, but when they did, they immediately turned their heads. We didn't see many smiling faces.

When I heard people talking, I couldn't understand a word they said. In fact, I never did understand a word they said in all the time I was there. I didn't see anybody who was overweight, like they had been eating too much, but I saw a whole lot of people who looked like they hadn't had anything to eat in a while. Most looked like they hadn't eaten in weeks.

Most of the time, I stayed on base, but whenever I went into Saigon and saw adult Vietnamese, they'd walk right past us, not saying a word. But the Vietnamese children always came running up to us and begged for money. I usually gave them whatever change I had and so did most of other guys.

If we went into a bar or a restaurant, there were always plenty of women wherever we were. They wanted our money, too. I didn't like going into Saigon. Guys were always getting into trouble when they did, whether it was a fight, drugs, getting drunk, some kind of venereal disease, or all four at the same time, it was always trouble.

After six months at Cam Ranh Bay, we received orders that our unit was being transferred up to Pleiku. I was glad to hear it. I figured it had to be better. I was hoping that I could get some more sleep. It seemed like I was always awake, even when my eyes were closed. I expected a shell to land right on our barracks at any moment or else get an order to get up and hit the bunkers. Everyone said it would be much cooler in Pleiku. I hoped so. As hot as I remembered Ft. Jackson to be, it was nothing compared to Cam Ranh Bay.

We rode out of camp in Armored Personnel Carriers with steel meshing on the windows so tight you could hardly put a finger through one of the holes. Once we were a few miles from base we were off asphalt and concrete and on dirt roads. Most of the roads had been worked on by us and they'd been widened and improved, but the roads weren't safe. There were patrols on the roads all the time and no one was allowed on the roads before 10 o'clock in the morning or after 6 o'clock at night.

Minesweeps would go up and down the roads to make sure no bombs had been planted. Vehicles kept in the middle of the road if they could so as not to get too close to the sides. We left as soon as we were allowed and it took us most of the day to get there. We had to be off the road before curfew, just like everyone else.

Pleiku was in the Highlands where mountains get up over 10,000 feet. We knew that we'd be seeing soldiers from the North Vietnamese Army, who would be in uniform, in that part of the country. In the south, around Saigon and in the Mekong Delta, it was almost entirely the Viet Cong. During the Tet offensive, the NVA attacked our bases in the northern part of the Republic of South Vietnam and the VC attacked us in the south.

Our base was at the foot of the mountains. It was tiny compared to Cam Ranh Bay. There were dozens of large tents, all with dirt floors. We had no running water, no inside bathrooms and no electricity.

I was hoping that it wouldn't be as noisy but I was wrong. What heavy artillery we had was much closer to us and it was inside the perimeter fence, not far from our tents. We had almost as many helicopters in Pleiku as in Cam Ranh Bay, but no planes, except for a couple of two seaters. Although it might not have been as loud at Pleiku because there weren't near as many huge guns on the base, or near as many tanks, but it seemed just as loud because things were much closer.

The worst part about Pleiku was that we had to do things other than be mechanics and we were required to leave base and go out into the jungle. We were often ordered to ride as passengers on flat-bed trucks being used to transport supplies. At Cam Ranh Bay, there were always cargo planes and supply ships landing and unloading at the base. It was the source of food and materials for all of the other bases across that part of the country.

At Pleiku, we were inland by a couple of hours and our base was used to transport troops, equipment and supplies mostly by trucks to various smaller camp sites, or other bases anywhere close by. We'd go to Quinhon, which was on the coast just south of the Gulf of Tonkin on the South China Sea, since that was the closest place ships could unload supplies, to pick up supplies. That was the biggest base in that part of the country.

Mechanics would also ride with the motorcades to make sure there were no mechanical problems on the way. When we did we carried our rifles in case there was any trouble. We were expected to fight if necessary. At Cam Ranh Bay I hadn't ever left base except on a weekend pass.

We also had to go out and either fix a broken down vehicle or tank or bring it back to be fixed. When we did have to leave base, there were many times when we had to stay at the camps, called fire bases, with the infantry. They weren't nearly as safe as the bases. There were always much fewer soldiers and many times no tanks or artillery. They still had bombs coming in at night like we did on base but they also had the much bigger threat of being attacked by the enemy.

When mortars hit, sometimes there was no response at all, so as not to give away a position. Other times they'd call for air support, which could be helicopter gunships, jet fighters, bombers or some other type of plane. What also would happen when a fire base got bombed, mortared or hit with light arms attacks is that the coordinates would be called in and the artillery from some far off place would respond.

A night didn't go by when there wasn't gunfire, mortars and bombs exploding. I'll never forget the mortars. They were constant. You could hear them coming, never knowing where they might land. I don't think I'll ever be able to forget that feeling of helplessness, knowing that the next one might have my name on it.

The first time I had to go out of camp was with a convoy of trucks headed to a fire base in the La Drang valley, not too far from Pleiku, to the south and towards the border with Laos. Our guys needed ammunition and supplies. I was told we'd be bringing back some dead and wounded.

We were on a dirt road with heavy jungle on both sides. I was riding shotgun with a rifle in my lap and tools under my feet. It was raining hard and the driver had the windshield wipers going full speed. We were about the twentieth vehicle back, just keeping up with the truck in front of us. We were in a deuce-and-a-half, or a two-and-a-half ton truck. It was sagging because of the heavy load we were carrying which consisted of guns and explosives in thick wooden containers.

Since it was the first time I had been off the base, I was leery about everything but fascinated by it too. We passed ragged Vietnamese with crude wooden carts pulled by water buffalo. They could have been VC for all we knew. We just flew on by them.

We came across a group of people that looked like our American Indians walking along the side of the road. The young children had no clothes on and the adults wore brightly colored clothing. They were Montagnards. I'd heard of them but never seen them before. They were supposedly hated by the Vietnamese, North and South, because they weren't natives of Vietnam. I was told that they weren't even allowed into the military, North or South, because they weren't considered citizens. Apparently, they lived in the jungles and wandered from place to place but when they fought, and they did, they fought with us. They were 'friendlies.'

We passed through many small villages, little more than a group of straw and mud huts with animals all over the place, and little children running around. I didn't see many young men, just women and old men taking care of the children.

The women walked with large baskets of rice, fruits and vegetables on their backs with shoulder poles that swayed as they moved. They were all in black pajamas and large straw hats shaped like a cone. They all kept their heads down, just like the other Vietnamese I'd seen. No one waved to us as if to say thanks for being there to help us rid the country of communists. It was as if they wanted to pretend that we weren't there or else they really didn't like us and didn't want us there. I didn't know which.

The driver was telling me about hunting Elk in Montana, where he was from, when all of a sudden there was an explosion and a flash of light followed by a wall of hitting the windshield. My ears were ringing and I couldn't see anything. I was frozen. I didn't know what to do, stay where I was or jump out.

The driver yelled "Mine! Hold on!" and jerked the wheel to the left and headed off the road into the jungle, taking down trees and brushes and everything in the way. When we came to a stop I was thrown violently forward, hitting the dashboard with my helmet, and then backwards against the rear window of the vehicle.

I had a death grip on my rifle but I couldn't see anyone to shoot at. I had dirt and mud in my eyes and struggled to find something to wipe my face so I could see. I knew I was bleeding but I didn't know where it was from or how bad it was.

The driver, whose name was Reno, grabbed my shoulder and asked if I was okay. Though I wasn't, I told him I was. We got out and ran over to where the guys in the truck behind us were standing, everyone with guns at the ready, looking around. Nobody was doing any shooting. The truck in front of us was completely destroyed as were the occupants. There was nothing left of anyone and nothing we could do about it.

The officer in charge came running up and told us that it was a land mine which probably had been detonated from some remote location. He said there was no telling where they might be now but that we didn't want to sit around and wait for them. He ordered some soldiers to pick up the boots and whatever else was left from the men in the bombed truck and get the vehicle off the road as fast as possible so that the convoy could get moving again. There was nothing else that could've been done. The trucks in front of us waited for the road to be cleared so that we'd all move out together.

Reno told me that a lot of soldiers would put a dog tag in their boots because sometimes that's all that would be left if a guy got blown up like those guys had been. There wasn't much left of those guys that could've been saved but the Army kept whatever it could find. That truck and everyone in it was obliterated. All that was left was a smoldering metal frame, and some boots.

My head hurt and mud and dirt was on my face, in my hair and all over my clothes and body. I felt my ears to make sure they were still there. My head was ringing. Then it started to rain, slowly at first, then harder and harder. We stood around, weapons in hand, waiting to be shot at or attacked while the road was being cleared.

After what seemed like an hour or so, one of the big tracks pushed the burned heap off to the other side, smoothed out the road and pulled us back onto it. Our truck started right up and we kept on going, never laying eyes on the people who had done that to us.

The truck in front of us was carrying explosives just like we were and when it hit the mine, the explosives went off. We were lucky the cargo didn't cause damage to any other of our vehicles.

An increase in the noise level let us know that we were approaching the firebase. There was artillery fire and helicopters were circling overhead. Trucks were coming towards us, on their way back to Pleiku. They were in the convoy that had left before us that morning.

We slowed and pulled off to the side to let them get by. I watched as they did. I saw men's bodies thrown in the back of some of the flatbeds, not stacked, just arms and legs dangling in every direction – those were soldiers, our soldiers. The drivers had grim expressions on their faces, no hint of a greeting or exchange of any kind. They were on their way out and we were on our way in.

We rolled into the makeshift camp and followed the trucks to the place where our cargo would be unloaded. Men on forklifts started to unload us. We wanted to get out of there as fast as we could.

When we were unloaded, Reno was ordered to take the truck to another location and make a pick up. There were mortars and bombs exploding all around us. Our artillery was sending back round after round, non-stop.

Before we got loaded up to leave, we received word that because we arrived so late in the day, due to the land mine, we'd be spending the night. Nobody drove in the jungle at night. Our unit of drivers and trucks, plus one wheel and track mechanic, me, parked our trucks, gathered together and awaited instructions.

We were told to pitch our tent in a certain location and we did. We each had our own sleeping bags in our packs that went with us wherever we went. We were given one huge tent in which all of us, some twenty or thirty of us, or more, could sleep. There were large tents scattered all over the firebase and an even bigger one where food was usually served. Tonight nobody would be doing any cooking. It would be C-rations for everyone.

Everybody was in motion and doing what they were told to do. A couple of platoons acted as look-outs for the rest and they were prepared for an attack. This wasn't a camping trip like the ones we took in Germany or back at Ft. Jackson. This was war. The enemy I'd heard so much about and had yet to see was close, real close.

Once our tents were up we were told to take our rifles and spread out over our southern perimeter. We took over defensive positions so that the soldiers at the base were able to get some relief. Though we'd been on the road all day, we were at our post for half the night.

No fires were lit. Nobody was shouting any orders. Any orders given were in a muffled voice and passed down from man to man. There was no laughing or idle chatter. In all the time I'd been in the Army, I had been a lot of things – exhausted, weak, sad, angry and I'd felt like crying and going home but I'd never been scared before, really scared. That night, I was scared.

While I was lying in my bag, trying to sleep, it rained. When it finally was time to get up, we put our tents away, had canned meat of some kind for breakfast, loaded up and waited until the road was supposedly cleared of land mines and we could head back to Pleiku. Mortars were still coming in and we were under fire as we drove out. We came across the body of a soldier in the road. Somebody jumped out, tied a rope to his feet and to the back of the truck and jumped back in. The truck pulled him a mile down the road until it was safe enough to stop and put him in the back of an empty flat bed. I wasn't the only one who was scared that day.

When we made it back to Pleiku, we had a lot to talk about. Few of the other mechanics had seen anything like what I'd seen the day before. One of the guys had brought back an entire platoon, twenty guys, on his truck, all dead. Some had their heads cut off. He said when he got there the bodies were lying on the ground side by side, ready to be transported home, and he and another guy had to load them up, one by one. It was hard for me to imagine what that must have been like.

After I heard that, I never could get that image out of my mind. Still can't, even though I never saw it myself. Sometimes things other guys told me about was enough to give me the willies. There were lots of those kinds of stories, stories I wish I never heard.

At Cam Ranh Bay, there was the constant sound of planes, artillery, guns, tanks and other noises due to the war going on. I can still hear those sounds. I don't remember the sounds of birds, or seeing butterflies, and there weren't too many insects or vermin, either.

At Pleiku, we had to use mosquito nets around our beds or we couldn't sleep at all. Rats and snakes and other creatures snuck into our tents most every night. That we got used to, but anytime you heard anything, like a tree falling or an animal running through the brush, or a twig snapping – anything – it made you jump. That didn't happen at Cam Ranh Bay.

Because there weren't near as many mechanics at Pleiku as there were at Cam Ranh Bay we were called upon to do a whole lot of things other than work on vehicles. Since we had more helicopters on our base than anything else we worked on them too. We weren't asked to do that at Cam Ranh Bay. They were always short on people to work on helicopters and the pilots ended up doing a lot of their own maintenance work. That was because there was a high mortality rate for helicopter crews.

I started helping out with the helicopters at our base by doing the nightly maintenance stuff at first, but I learned how to work on the rotors before too long. If it had anything to do with an engine I usually caught on quick and I did with helicopters. It got to the point where I was spending more time working on helicopters than I did on the other stuff.

I got to be friendly with the pilots and the crews, too. The crew for a Huey, which was what most of the helicopters were, included a pilot, a co-pilot, a crew chief and a gunner on each side. The crew chief was basically a mechanic. He didn't know how to fly the aircraft, but he could fix it. They asked me to go along for a ride every once in a while, like when they were transporting someone important from one place to another, or carrying supplies. I did a few times, and I liked it.

When a soldier gets close to the time when his tour of duty is up, the Army does things to try to get the soldier to stay in the war zone. They offer promotions, increased pay, change of duty and other things. When I got to be a short-timer with less than 60 days to go, they offered me a promotion, a lot more money, and a chance to be a crew chief on a Chinook. I took them up on the offer.

CHAPTER THREE
Crew Chief on a Chinook

AFTER THE PROMOTION, I was a Motor Pool Sergeant. I was still assigned to the 128th Engineering Battalion and our unit was still stationed in Pleiku, so not much changed other than my MOS. I was now assigned to be a crew chief on a Chinook helicopter. I wouldn't be with the general pool of mechanics, as I had been, anymore.

I remember the first full day I spent with the helicopter units. It was late in the day and we heard the sound of helicopters approaching. Ten minutes after we first heard them, a couple of big transport helicopters landed. I happened to be about fifty feet away and I had to turn my back and shield my eyes because of the wind they made. The helicopters were carrying dead and dying soldiers. Para-medics jumped out and started taking the wounded to medical tents. Other men went around removing dog tags and other things off dead soldiers. Then they put the men in body bags to be taken back to the States.

I cried as I watched the men zip up the bags. The ones whose heads had been cut off had already been covered up. Me and some other guys carried the bags to other helicopters and laid them where they told us. We all stood and watched the helicopters fly away until they were out of sight. Most of the dead were my age or younger.

I heard that the average age of the soldiers in Vietnam was nineteen. That meant that there were a whole lot of eighteen year olds in the Army. I was still a kid, or at least I still felt like one. I heard that the average age of soldiers in World War II was twenty six. That's a big difference. I turned twenty one in March of 1971 in Pleiku. At that point, I was one of the older guys.

One night, while we were sitting around the camp site waiting for dinner, a helicopter landed not far from us, bringing cigarettes and beer and fresh supplies of meat. We couldn't believe it. That didn't happen very often, just every now and then. It never happened when I was at Cam Ranh Bay because all of that was readily accessible any day of the week.

One of the biggest problems we faced, among many, was suicide missions by the VC. Guys were saying that they were doing that because of what Ho Chi Minh had supposedly said years earlier, "You can kill ten of my men for every one I kill of yours. But even at those odds, you will lose and I will win." He had warned the French of the same thing in the early 1950s before a peace was declared at a conference in Geneva in 1954, which was about when the French got out and the U.S. somehow became involved under Eisenhower. In 1961, President Kennedy sent in troops, too, military advisors who carried no weapons.

The first combat troops arrived in Vietnam in 1965 under orders from President Johnson, but the first U.S. casualties came in July 1959 when a Major and a Master Sergeant, who were watching a movie with some South Vietnamese soldiers at Bienhoa, an air base twenty miles north of Saigon, were ambushed and killed. I didn't ever fully understand when and how we got there or why, other than to fight the spread of communism, and prevent what was called the "Domino Theory" from taking place. Years later those two soldiers, Dale R. Buis and Chester M. Ovnand, were the first two names listed on the Vietnam Memorial in Washington, D.C.

Chemical warfare units, the big bombers, used herbicides to take the leaves off all the trees in the forest. We didn't have any planes that big. Our runways weren't big enough. When they dropped those bombs anywhere near us, we'd get the smell for days. The herbicides did their job. None of us had any idea what the after-effects would be. We didn't even think about it. We didn't find out about that until many years later.

Vietnam is shaped like an 'S' and is about six hundred miles long, but only thirty miles wide at its narrowest point. We'd fly way past the Laos and Cambodian borders all the time, turning north through the mountains usually, and then head back the way we came. In the rainy season, we could see the rivers swell in the north through the mountains and become enormous deltas in the south.

The countryside to the north of Pleiku was mostly mountainous with forests, but the trees weren't like what I was used to seeing back home. There were no pine trees or many of the types of trees I was used to seeing. We saw a lot of Teak, Mahogany and Ironwood trees, among others. The terrain was so different in Vietnam from one place to the next. It could go from flat land with nothing but rice paddies as far as the eye could see to some of the highest mountains I'd ever seen, plus there were the jungles, and then there was the rain, which could last for months. The typhoon season went from July to November.

The countryside to the south of Cam Ranh Bay was almost completely flat. We'd fly over it whenever we went flew to Saigon and gave some officer or high-ranking official a tour of the area every now and then. To the south and west was the Mekong Delta. Flying across it, I saw miles and miles of rice paddies, which would be bone-dry in the dry season.

The highlight was seeing a crocodile while crossing one of the streams. In the mountains you might see an occasional elephant by a river, or tiger, or even a leopard, but that was usually after it had been captured or killed. There were also monkeys and orangutans, as well as bears and deer.

Occasionally, we'd have to transport wounded prisoners, but mostly all we did was transport our soldiers and soldiers from the South Vietnamese Army to and from places where the enemy might be or where a battle had been or was about to take place. We took enemy fire on a daily basis. I heard that the casualty rate for helicopter pilots and crew was higher than for any other units in the military, even the infantry in the jungles. We were flying targets.

One day as we were sitting around our helicopter after dropping off a squadron or our guys, waiting to for another squadron of our guys to arrive so we could take them back to camp, the squadron we were to pick up came walking up just as the squadron we were dropping off was getting off. That made everybody lighten up. U.S. soldiers were always glad to see each other.

As they walked by, everybody had something to say. Nobody stopped walking, but everybody said something and most smiled. It was good to see friendly faces. It made me feel as if we were strong, too, as if we were ready for a fight and could win any battle we fought. The problem was finding the people to get into a fight with. Most of the time it was them lying in bushes, waiting to ambush us and then us responding. Usually they'd turn and run after killing however many they could. It was never like what we'd heard WWII was all about with the Germans, or even with the Japanese, or with Korea either.

The soldiers were always glad to have us take them back. Once they were back, first thing they'd do was take a hot shower. After that, they'd put on some clean clothes, if they had any, and have a hot meal. Most of the time they had to wash what they had and put it back on. Sometimes after a day or two they'd have to turn around and go right back out to the jungle.

At Cam Ranh Bay reville woke us up every day. We marched, checked our rifles and went on a run. At Pleiku, we never heard reville. In many ways, life at Cam Ranh Bay wasn't bad while we were on base. It had everything you could possibly want as far as clothes, tape recorders, transistor radios and all sorts of things to buy, including shampoos, deodorants and other things we couldn't get out in the woods, like condoms. Women were all over the place in all directions anywhere near any of our bases and, if that wasn't enough, Saigon wasn't too far away for a weekend pass.

Pleiku didn't have anything like what was at Cam Ranh Bay, but guys didn't have any trouble finding women off base, because there were always little villages nearby. Even though guys knew about the diseases they might contract, there was no stopping them. I was told that the French had an official brothel on their bases when they were in Vietnam. The women even traveled with the troops in some cases, I heard, but the American Army would have none of that.

It was just an accepted fact of life that guys were going to go to restaurants, bars, nightclubs, massage parlors, shacks or huts and any other place where women would be. A woman could supposedly make more in a week than her father, husband or brother made in a year. From what I was told everybody's daughter, wife or sister became whores. Half of them were probably VC, too. They loved us for our money and hated us for what they had to do to get it.

During the rainy season, there were flash floods. Soldiers in the jungles or in the mountains would have to hold onto trees or bushes to keep from being swept away by the water. The jungles were infested with leeches and other bugs that swarmed all over them. They had to cross deep rivers and streams. The mountains, some as high as 10,000 feet, were sometimes swallowed up by the clouds. It was difficult for the helicopters to climb at those altitudes because the air would get thin but we went wherever the soldiers were, if we could, and took them wherever they told us.

Those guys had to carry fifty to seventy pounds of equipment on their backs, and it was tough going in the heavily wooded areas, especially in the mountains because of the climbing they had to do. They'd have to pull themselves along from one tree branch to the next and they needed help doing it sometimes. Usually, there were some squads assigned to flank the main column and protect it, but sometimes it was single file, with no flank support at all.

No one wanted to be on flanking squads. They had the highest casualty rates in the infantry, but they told us that there were times when they wouldn't see any sight of the enemy for days or weeks. Then there were other times when the enemy decided to fight back, but that was only by way of a hit and run attack or an ambush, and then they'd run off and hide.

Most of the time we'd drop off the soldiers at a clearing, in places where the enemy wasn't around. Sometimes, though, we'd drop them off near a village. When we did, it was usually before dawn, before the VC could get up and out, at least that was the plan. Guys would jump out, run into the village, start kicking down doors, scream, fire shots into the air, and make all of the people who lived in those huts get out and into an area in the middle of the village. There would usually be at least one South Vietnamese soldier or police officer with us and an American interrogator, who would question everyone about the Vietcong.

Of course, they could have heard us coming for miles away and got up and out before we got there. The ones found in the tents could have been Vietcong and we wouldn't have known it. Even if they weren't VC, our guys would think they were. We stayed near our helicopters and watched when we could. We saw people get beaten up pretty badly lots of times by our interrogators, more often than I care to remember. It was never pretty.

If there was ever a sign of trouble in a village, some mortar fire or heavy small arms fire, sometimes the bombers would be called in. When that happened, whole villages would be totally destroyed. I saw it happen more than a few times. People would be running around screaming and yelling while the huts that had been their homes were burning to the ground.

When our guys found an underground shelter, and most of the huts had one as protection against the bombing even if they weren't Vietcong, soldiers would drop a grenade in and blow it up. I'd see this happen and wonder who we were helping. We'd destroy entire villages and never know for sure if they were VC or friendlies.

One day, after we dropped troops at the outskirts of the city of Hue', which was reportedly secured, we got out and walked around a little before heading back. Just as we neared a Buddhist temple at the center of town, we saw a woman dressed in robes of a Buddhist nun, who seemed to be in her mid-fifties, sit down in the lotus position. We watched from about a hundred yards away as her two friends doused her with gasoline. Before anyone could do anything, the woman lit a match, and immediately exploded into flame. The two friends poured peppermint oil on the fire to cover up the stench of burning flesh.

As we walked by, we could see that her burning body was still erect, her hands still clasped in prayer. We heard that there were many of those suicides, all by Buddhist monks who wanted both the Americans and the Communists out of Vietnam. That was the only one I saw. That was enough. That was another sight I couldn't forget.

After a year in the helicopters, after more close calls and near-death experiences and seeing all the things I'd seen, when I got to be a short-timer a second time, I decided I'd had enough. I was ready to go home. It had been so long since I'd had a good sleep that I couldn't remember the last time I had slept in. Even when I went on "R and R" for a few days I couldn't sleep.

I don't think I ever had a night when I slept well enough to actually have a dream, let alone a nightmare, while I was in Viet Nam. I don't think I fell completely asleep. I might pass out from sheer exhaustion, and that happened most nights, but I always felt like something was about to happen, and it usually did. At the end, I felt as though the next bomb was going to have my name on it. If not, the next tracer was going to find my chopper. It was time to go. My luck was about to run out. I was sure of it.

CHAPTER FOUR
Back Home

I ARRIVED BACK IN THE States on June 19, 1972. I had served two tours of duty in Vietnam and had my fill of that, but I liked being in the military and I wasn't ready to get out of the Army. I planned to stay in the military for a full twenty years and retire with a pension, or so I thought.

I was assigned to be a Motor Sergeant at Ft. Eustis, Virginia. It was a desk job. My responsibility was going to be preparing "readiness reports" and letting the higher-ups know how many machines were ready to be sent at a moment's notice to wherever they were needed, usually Vietnam. The ready items included mechanical things like generators, air conditioners and refrigerators in addition to jeeps, trucks, motor vehicles and other things. It sounded like a job I would have no trouble doing, none at all.

Even though I was safely in the United States, inside an Army base, I still didn't sleep well. I slept better, but I kept waking up at night, not once or twice, more like every hour or so. A few times soldiers found me on the floor or under my bed screaming. I didn't know how to explain it to them. Most of them had never been to Vietnam. If they had, I wouldn't have had to explain it at all.

It got to the point where I had to see the counselor on Post about it. He wasn't a doctor but he gave me some pills and told me not to worry about it. He said that the nightmares and bad dreams would go away after I'd been back in the States for a while longer. I kept waiting for it to happen but it never did.

I thought it was going to be a pretty cushy job and it was. But after about two years, I had to get out. It was too boring for me. After what had been about five and a half years of service, I was tired of being in the military. I'd done enough, seen enough, been enough places that I was ready to go back home to Jeannette, become a civilian and be a mechanic, just like I'd planned so many years before.

Once the decision was made, before I knew it it was time to go. I wore my uniform one last time as I left the base to catch the bus for Jeanette late one night. It was a funny feeling for me, since I'd been in the military so long. It felt funny being in the civilian population wearing the uniform. People looked at me like I was still a soldier. They didn't know and they didn't want to know that I was out. The bus ride was pretty uneventful and I arrived in Jeanette early the next morning. My parents were there to meet me.

It was 1974 and the war was still raging in Vietnam. There wasn't any parade or welcome when I got home. No articles in the newspaper about me. Not long after I got home I put all of my military gear in a closet. I swore I wouldn't wear it again, not even on Memorial Day or Veteran's Day. It wasn't that I wasn't proud of what I had done, it was more like whenever I wore anything I had from the Army, a t-shirt, a hat – anything – it would cause some kind of commotion, discussion, argument or something. It was never good, so I decided just not to wear any of that stuff at all.

I didn't talk too much about what I'd been through, either. When I did, people looked at me funny, like I had done something wrong, or with some peculiar look on their faces. Nobody ever wanted to hear what I thought about it all. They had their own ideas about Vietnam and they wanted to let me know what they thought. These were people who knew me, too, the same ones who had encouraged me to join the Army back when I was in high school. I let my hair grow, so it was as long as everyone else's, wore old blue jeans, plain t-shirts, and a Steelers cap. Things got better for me when I did.

I lived with my parents for a while. It was strange being back home with them. They seemed to me to be exactly what they were like when I left and they treated me like I was the same person I had been. I didn't tell them much about what I'd seen or done, but they knew something was wrong when I started waking them up at night. That began pretty soon after I got home.

I was having a whole bunch of nightmares at the time. I still remember them all. There were many. I remember the one that I had at Ft. Eustis, not long after getting back to the States, when I woke the whole barrack up.

I see myself riding in an APC going down a dirt road, with the jungle tight on both sides of us. I listen as the driver, my old buddy, Reno, tells me about fishing in mountain streams of Montana, like he did many times. I never did know his real name. He was born in Nevada, that's why he was called Reno. He liked the nickname. Anyway, I see us pull into a Firebase and I hear the Sergeant tell us to pick up some dead Vietnamese and take them back to camp. He points to a tent at the back of camp and tells us there will be some soldiers there to help us load the bodies.

We go to where he sent us but there's only one soldier there, and he leaves as soon as we get there. Reno opens the flap to the tent and we see dozens of bodies on the ground. Reno and I look at each other, hold our noses to fight back the stench and think about getting back in the truck and leaving. But that's not an option.

We start picking up the bodies, one at a time. They're all women and children. Some of the kids couldn't have been older than three or four. Some might have been as old as nine or ten, none of them old enough to fight. The women were all ages…young, old and in-between. Reno gets one end and I get the other. We throw the bodies into the back of the truck.

After a while, we start moving faster. We want to get out of there as fast as we can. Then, after what seems like an hour, we finally get the last dead body in the truck. Just when we go to close up, one falls out, still alive. It was one of the older children. She gets up and runs off into the jungle before we can say or do anything. That's when I'd wake up and find myself sitting bolt upright, panting like I just ran a four minute mile or something.

My heart was always pounding like it was gonna come right out of my chest whenever I had that or any of the other dreams. Whenever I had a nightmare at my home, my folks would come running into the room, asking if I was okay. They'd tell me I had screamed and must've awakened the whole neighborhood. I'd tell them I was fine, I just had a bad dream. They'd ask if they could get me something, milk or anything. I'd tell them no, I'd be alright. They'd go back to bed and I'd lay there, sweating, my heart still pounding.

That dream about toting the dead Vietnamese was just one of many, but it wasn't the worst, not by a long shot. It was one I had many times over the years, though, and it created a big stir several times. Most of the time I was the only one who knew what had happened and I'd lay awake, alone, unable to sleep. I started having them pretty regular. It got so I wasn't able to go to sleep too easily. I thought it was because I was afraid I'd have another nightmare and cause a scene again.

I started drinking more and more beer, then vodka and the hard stuff to help get me to sleep. Then I started taking pills, hoping it would be enough so I wouldn't wake up in the middle of another bad dream. I never did get into drugs much, other than those kinds of drugs, though I saw plenty of guys who did. I smoked marijuana while I was in Pleiku every now and then, never in Cam Ranh Bay, but that was it. I never did anything else and didn't do much of it after I got out, either. The pills and the booze were enough to mess me up. I didn't need more.

After a while, my night-time antics got to wearing on my folks. A few months into it, they kind of suggested that I look for another place to live, though they never came right out and said it. I started looking around for an apartment or a house to rent.

I didn't work for several months. I had some money saved up and I was just taking things easy, half-heartedly looking around for a job. Deep down, I really wasn't sure that I wanted to be a mechanic down at the gas station in town like I had always planned before I went to Nam. But that was about the only thing I knew, so when I was ready, that's what I did.

Things were better after I went back to work. I was a good mechanic. I had learned a lot in the military, but I was the new kid on the block at the gas station. Everybody was a lot older than me and had been there for years so I was given most of the easy stuff – oil changes, flat tires, things like that – which was fine with me, for a while.

I was just trying to fit in and adjust to being a civilian, with nobody yelling at me anymore. I was tired of taking orders and saying "Yes, sir!" and "No, sir!" all the time. I had known most of our regular customers since I was a kid and I started to get together with some friends I grew up with who were still around. I started feeling like I fit in.

I was still drinking too much and taking too many pills and I knew it. There wasn't much I could do about it. If I didn't, I couldn't fall asleep for hours and hours and when I did fall asleep I kept having bad dreams. I started going down to the local bar to watch football games or whatever was on television. If I wasn't working, I was at a bar.

I was still having nightmares, though, even with the pills and the booze. The combination of alcohol and narcotics didn't take them away, it just delayed them for a while or numbed me to the point where I didn't, or couldn't, think anymore. I tried to find a way so that I could get some sleep but not have the bad dreams, but I couldn't ever do that. Nothing I did worked.

Some of my nightmares were about what happened to me and what I actually saw. Some were about what other guys told me, and others were my fears playing with my mind, just my imagination playing tricks on me.

Another of the recurring nightmares was about a time when I was on guard duty one night when we stayed at a fire-base overnight because of the weather or some VC activity in the area, I can't remember which. I never did like doing guard duty. I never considered myself a regular soldier, though the Army always did. I was a mechanic. I fixed things. I never felt all that comfortable with a rifle on my shoulder. But when I was on guard duty, I was a soldier and my job was to protect all the other soldiers who were sleeping or trying to get some sleep.

This one dream has me coming back into my tent dead tired after being on guard duty for three hours. I'm being as quiet as I can be, not making any noise so as not to wake anyone up when I kick something. I flick my lighter to see what it is and I see that it's the head of one of my buddies. I light the lantern and see that everybody's head has been cut off. I wake up screaming when I have that dream. That never happened to me but I'd seen men beheaded and it left a mark on me, especially when I saw the faces of the guys in my platoon in my dreams, as I always did when I had that dream.

I found myself a little apartment in a small complex. It wasn't too fancy but it was enough for me. I would get up and go to work in the morning, come home, shower up, get something to eat and watch television until it was time to go to sleep, or try to go to sleep. I couldn't watch shows that had anything to do with the War.

Nixon was bombing Hanoi and the North much more than Johnson ever did, but he was reducing troop levels, too, so the country wasn't sure what to think. Was the war escalating? Was it winding down? Was it ever going to end? Were we ever going to win? That's the one that made me laugh, but only to myself. I don't think I ever told anybody how I really felt.

The way I saw it, the only way we would have won that war was if we killed every man, woman and child in Vietnam. I don't doubt that there were many in South Vietnam who, for their own personal reasons, wanted to see a democratic state and to see us be successful in that effort. For that matter, I'm sure there were people in North Vietnam who would have liked to see Vietnam re-united as a democratic country. But we didn't know who was who and what was what and many times we killed people without ever knowing the truth about who they were and what they believed. I kept all of that to myself, deep inside. I swore I wasn't going to tell anybody about the things I saw and did and what I thought about it all.

I didn't have many friends outside of work and I was pretty lonely and unhappy. The only people I talked to were people at work and at bars. I wasn't meeting any women except the regulars at the bars.

One of the customers at the gas station had a daughter about my age and she came to the station every now and then with him. When she did, I couldn't keep my eyes off of her. I'd catch her looking back at me every so often. After a while, when I'd look over at her I saw a little spark in her eyes, like we knew each other, even though we hadn't actually met yet. We exchanged small talk back and forth like 'hello, how are you' and, well, one thing just led to another. After several weeks of that, I asked her out on a date. Her name was Joanna, Joanna Wright.

Back then, taking a girl out to dinner and to the movies was about the best thing a guy could do – and that's what we did. I'd been with prostitutes in Germany, Vietnam and a few other places but I hadn't been on a date since high school. I wasn't sure how to act. We started holding hands on the first date, kissing on the second date, had sex on about the third date and were married about three months later. I guess you could say it was a whirlwind courtship. You could also say that I was young and immature, and both of those things were true, but I figured that marriage had to be better than the way I was living, and it was.

We never did live together or spend a night together before we got married. She was still living at home and her parents wouldn't have approved of it. That was part of the reason we got married so quick. We had a small wedding, just me and my folks and her and her folks and a few others. My brother was my best man and one of her high school friends was her maid of honor. We spent the weekend in a cabin in the Poconos, not far away. It was the happiest I'd been in my whole life.

I really didn't know all that much about her, and she really didn't know much about me, either. We spent the first few weeks just getting to know each other better. She was several years younger than me and kind of shy. She was about average height, not too heavy, with medium length brown hair, brown eyes and a pretty smile. She was very nice. She was also very religious, which I wasn't, or at least I hadn't been in a long time. She got me to go to church with her on Sundays. I hadn't been to church or worn a coat and tie since before I went in the service, when I was a kid and my mother made me.

We rented a nice little house and were doing all the things a young married couple was supposed to do. I was hoping that marriage and being happy would help get rid of my nightmares, and it did for a while, though I slept lightly, so afraid I'd have a nightmare and scare her.

I was doing good, better than I had in a long time. She didn't drink and wouldn't let me drink in the house, so I was losing weight and feeling better. We'd go over to my folks' house for Sunday dinner one week and then to her folks' house the next week. I was working six days a week at the time and Sunday was our day to do things together. On Sunday afternoons we'd go for a ride out in the country and have a picnic. The War in Vietnam, which wasn't over yet, was as far from my mind as I could get it.

During the first few months we were married, we got along about as good as was possible. I'd come home every night right after work and we'd go for walks in the park or to a movie. She had led a somewhat sheltered life and her mother had done most of the cooking for her. Since she was just learning how to cook we went out to dinner a lot.

About three months after we'd been married, I had my first nightmare, and it scared her. She cried for a while and I had to comfort her. I was the one who'd had the nightmare but she was more upset than I was. She finally settled down and was able to go back to sleep, but I wasn't.

I had another nightmare a week or so later. This was one of the really bad ones. I had gone along as crew chief in a Huey, which I rarely did, to pick up a Captain who was in a remote camp to visit with some troops.

We thought it was going to be a routine fly in-fly out kind of deal. I sat in the back with the gunners as usual. We landed with no problem and there was no apparent danger at all. When we got out of the chopper we saw a woman tied to the ground, a Vietnamese translator kneeling beside her. Soldiers were standing around and we walked towards them. The Captain was in the middle, watching.

When we got to within about thirty feet of where he was standing, we heard him say, "Tell her that we will shoot her if she doesn't tell us who did this to Tommy."

The translator yelled something at the woman in Vietnamese but the woman didn't respond.

"Take your gun and point it at her and tell her you will shoot her in the head if she doesn't talk."

Again, the translator did as he was commanded, but again the woman wouldn't talk.

"Take your gun, put it next to her head, pull back the hammer, and tell her again that you will shoot."

Again, the translator did as he was commanded.

We were standing by our helicopter, not saying a word. This was a Captain, the man we were to pick up, I assumed. I was sure it was just a threat. We turned and started to back to our chopper. We'd seen enough. We were ready to go.

The next sound I heard was a gunshot.

The Captain walked over to us and said, "I'm sorry you all have to see this, but this is the way things are out here in the jungle. Tommy was last seen last night with this woman. This morning, we found him tied to a tree with stab wounds all over him. We haven't found his head yet, and she knows where it is and where the men are who did this to him. She wouldn't tell us so I did what I had to do. Maybe the next one will tell us."

I stood there, frozen, unable to believe what had just happened in a span of a few short seconds.

"Let's go, men," he told us. "In case you are asked, this didn't happen, you hear?"

"Yes, sir," the pilot mumbled.

"The Cong will get the message, and we'll get the men who did this before too long. I just wish I was here when we do."

As he stepped into the chopper, he yelled back over his shoulder, "Carry on, men. You get those bastards who did that to Tommy, you hear?"

"Yes, sir!" the men yelled back in unison. Then I woke up, bolt upright in the bed, eyes wide open, heart racing. Joanna woke up and started to cry again. This time I got up and went into the shower, pretending to be sick. When she asked if I'd had a nightmare, I said it must have been something I ate, hoping I hadn't screamed or flailed around. It scared her more than it did me, I think. I didn't want to lose her.

While things were good on the home front, except for the bad dreams, I ran into trouble at work. It had been building up over a period of time but, though I can't say it was a surprise, I wasn't expecting it. I'd always been a guy who could get along with anybody and didn't complain much but after six months of doing oil changes and all of the little crappy work, I got tired of it. I said something about it to the head mechanic, but I could tell that he really didn't want to hear it. He told me he'd see what he could do about giving me some of the better jobs like changing transmissions or doing complete engine overhauls, and that satisfied me, but it never happened.

Plus, after that, he started watching over me closer and became more critical. I mean, if it was something as simple as taking out five bolts to do a tire change, he'd find a way to say I should've done it differently.

In the Army I'd worked on the biggest vehicles the military could throw at me, not to mention the helicopters, and I was more than able to work on any of the mechanical problems that shop would ever have to handle. I was as good or better than anyone else in there, even though they were older than me and had more experience. After a few more months of the same shit, I couldn't take it anymore. I decided that I just couldn't work with the guy and I did my best just to stay away from him.

One day it all came to a head. He told me to change the tires on an old Chevy truck. It was the fourth tire change I'd done that day. I asked him why he didn't make one of the other guys do it and he said they had more important things to do. That made me mad. I don't know what I said to him or what he said back but the next thing you know we were jaw to jaw and I was ready to tear his head off. I'd never been so mad in my life. Before it came to blows, somebody stepped in between us. We were still yelling back and forth at each other. They sent me home for the rest of the day. I never went back.

As I look back on things, that was the first sign of me having a temper. I never knew I had one. I thought it was just that guy, and I still do, but it made me so mad that I was ready to kill him. Fortunately for me, and for him, I walked away.

It took me a while to find another job. While I was out of work, I guess I was a little difficult to live with at the time, probably more than a little difficult. My wife wasn't working, either, and with me just sitting around the house with her, we just started to get on each other's nerves. We'd never had a cross word up until then.

After a month or so, I went to the big boss who owned the gas station. He was a nice guy. He collected the money, but the other guy ran the business. The owner didn't really pay all that much attention to what went on with the mechanics who actually did the work and he didn't want to tell the manager how to do his job. Since I'd always done good work for him as a mechanic and he'd known me most of my life, when I asked him for some help finding a job, he said he'd see what he could do. A couple of weeks later he found me one.

It was in the same line of work, automotive that is. I drove a truck for a parts supply place out of Pittsburgh. I worked five days a week. I'd leave the house about six in the morning and get back about seven at night. I drove all over the place, mostly within a hundred mile radius of Jeannette. I knew all the roads, so it was an easy job for me in that respect. I was tired all the time, but things were better between me and Joanna while I was working. I'd be happy to see her when I got home and she was happy to see me.

I learned more about cars and parts on that job because somebody was always asking me a question about something I didn't know and I'd have to find out. I knew the answers to most of the questions but there were a lot of things I didn't know, too. It wasn't a bad job but when the economy took a little nose-dive I got laid off. It had nothing to do with what I did or didn't do and I didn't have any problems there, but after a year and a half of working there I needed to find a new job.

My old boss found me another job driving truck again, but this time it was long-distance driving. I was driving an eighteen-wheeler all over the country. I was gone for weeks at a time, sleeping in the cab and eating at rest stops. That was when things got bad for me on the home front.

When I came home after being out on the road the fourth or fifth time, things started to change. I figured that was because we hadn't seen each other in so long. It would take a few days of being around each other for us to warm up to one another. That's the way it had been the first time or two. I'd be in town for a week or so and then gone for a month. It was hard to keep a relationship going that way but that's what we had to do. It was the only job I had. We'd only been married for a couple of years and we were both still in our twenties.

The nightmares just made things worse. On one of my trips home I had another nightmare. This one was while I was about something that had happened to me while I was in Pleiku and it was the one I hated having the most. My dreams were always in full color and very much like the way it happened. It was like I was re-living the event. It starts with Tillie screaming at me,

"Shoot me!"

I knelt beside him, screaming for a Medic, crying like a baby, even though I knew there was no one around, no one who would help us that is. Minutes before we had been driving down a dirt road on our way back to Pleiku from An Khe, like we had dozens of times before, talking about what we were going to do when we got out of the hell we were in. He was a 'short-timer,' with less than thirty days to go. I still had to do another four months. He was my best friend and we had plans to open an auto repair place back home. I would be the mechanic and he'd do the body work.

"Shoot me!" he screamed, louder than before.

I looked again but there was no one in sight in either direction. We had just finished loading a Jeep onto a trailer and were bringing it in for repair. It had slid off the road into a ditch because off the heavy rains we were getting. During monsoon season it didn't take much for a driver of one of those little two-seaters to lose control. We weren't far from base when it happened.

"God damn it, George, shoot me! You promised..."

He was crying uncontrollably now, begging me to shoot him. There was blood everywhere. I was bleeding, too, and I knew I was hurt, but not like Tillie. Both of his legs had been blown off below the knees and blood was everywhere. I had made makeshift tourniquets for both legs as best I could to stop the bleeding, but he had blood coming out from all over his body.

"Hang in there, Tillie! I'm gonna get you to the base as fast as I can, man! Hang in there!"

I was afraid to move him but I knew if I didn't get him some to help, and soon, he was a goner. His eyes were closed. He grabbed my shirt, and begged, "Just shoot me, George...please..."

"Don't die on me, man!" I screamed. "You're gonna make it! I swear!"

His voice was growing softer. It was barely audible now. His grip loosened and his body went limp. I thought about doing CPR but he was breathing alright...too much, in fact. He was panting, breathing real hard and real fast.

We'd hit a mine and it must have been right under him. We both got thrown out of the vehicle but I was able to get up and run over to where he was lying and pull him back behind the vehicle before our truck had burst into flames. The heat from the flames burned my face.

He cried, "It hurts so bad, George. I can't feel my legs. I don't want to be a cripple...you promised, man..."

I pulled my pistol from its case. I always carried it the entire time I'd been in 'Nam, whenever I went off base, but I'd never used it before. As I did, he opened his eyes, looked me straight in the eye and said, "Please, George… please…do it!"

"Wake up! George, wake up! Wake up!"

Joanna shook me until I came to.

"Was I making noises again?"

"Yes, you were, and kicking the sheets off us and flailing your arms. I had to get out of bed to get out of the way, George. I can't go on like this. One of these nights you're gonna hurt me. You're gonna hit me, not on purpose, but you're gonna hit me. I can't sleep anymore in the same bed with you. I'm sorry. I'm not sure I can live in the same house with you any longer."

She got up and started walking out of the room.

"No, you stay. I'll go." I said. "I don't mind sleeping on the couch. I may not be able to get back to sleep at all anyway."

"Was it the same dream, George?"

"It was one of the ones I've had before."

"Do you want to talk about it?"

"No. You wouldn't want to hear it."

"Maybe I would."

"No you wouldn't. Trust me."

"What are we going to do, George?"

"I don't know."

"When's it gonna get better?"

"I don't know. I don't know if it ever will."

Between me being on the road too long and the nightmares, it was the beginning of the end for us. I stopped going to church with her when I was home on Sundays, which wasn't all that often, saying I was too tired. We stopped going over to our parents' houses for dinner, too. Our marriage was falling apart.

A few months later, I found out my wife was running around on me from the wife of one of the guys she was running around with. This other woman and I had gone to the same high school, though I was a couple of years older. We weren't friends, but she knew me and I knew who she was. I happened to see her at the grocery store one day and she pulled me aside and said something like she knew I was out of town a lot and she thought I should know what was going on while I was gone. Basically, she said that if I didn't put a stop to it she was going to. She was a big ole country girl and she told me she was going to put a whipping on my wife if I didn't keep her away from her husband.

When I confronted my wife about it, she cried and cried and said it wasn't true. She told me that she loved me. She wanted to know who it was she was supposedly with but I didn't want to tell her and I didn't. I did tell her that she should be careful because if the man was married or had a girl friend she could get hurt. I let her think it was just a rumor I'd heard. I figured that it would just cause more problems if I told her the truth.

She knew who it was anyhow. She just wanted me to tell her what I knew. Maybe there was more than one, I didn't know. Plus, I wanted to know if it was still going on after I left on the next trip. I figured that if she thought that I knew who it was then she might stay away from him, but if she thought I didn't know who it was, then she might go back to seeing him while I was gone. I wanted to believe her, I really did. I didn't want my marriage to fail but that put the seeds of doubt in my mind about what was going on while I was out on the road. That played with my mind on those long, lonely nights in the cab of the truck, trying to get some sleep.

Things went downhill from there. When I came back from my next trip, we never did really warm up to each other. By the end of the third or fourth trip, she had moved back in with her parents and had gone to see a lawyer. Fortunately, we didn't have any kids together and we hadn't been married long enough for me to have to pay her any alimony. There was hardly any property to divide, so other than the lawyers and the court costs and all, it wasn't too bad. It still cost me several thousand dollars, a lot of money at the time, but it could have been worse.

I started drinking a lot more. I didn't drink much at all while I was on the road, but when I came home to an empty apartment after being on the road for a month, I started to go back to the local bars. Between the bad food I was eating on the road and the beer I was drinking at home, what with me not doing any exercises or anything, I started to put on weight and the nightmares got worse. Living alone, I didn't have anyone to worry about bothering and that didn't make things better.

I was depressed and that made my nightmares even worse. I was having more of them. Another was from my days as a crew chief on the Chinook. We were always going to pick up soldiers or drop them off and we carried many different platoons. Sometimes we carried cargo and sometimes we carried the wounded or the dead. The Chinooks could carry over fifty men. On the Hueys, anything over six was too many.

During the years when the United States Army was so concerned about body counts, soldiers were required to actually bring back the bodies of dead Viet Cong so they could be counted. One time, they loaded up our Chinook with over a hundred dead Viet Cong and, after they were counted, we were ordered to fly them over to where we knew the VC had a strong presence and drop them. I watched as they hit the ground. That was a bad memory and a bad nightmare.

Another one was about ears. Some of the guys we picked up said that there were platoon leaders who gave three day passes to soldiers who cut off the ears of the dead Vietnamese to prove the kills they had made. I didn't believe it. The story was that for six ears, or three pair of ears, a soldier would get three days of R & R, one day for each pair. A soldier had to have three pairs to get the days off. I remember when I first saw a soldier wearing about a dozen ears around his neck on a chain and realizing it must be true. He was proud of himself, bragging about what he'd done. He told me he was on his way for six days of R & R in Bangkok. I didn't know what to say to him so I didn't say anything.

In my dreams, the ears would come to life, and the dead people would grow back the rest of their bodies, like the science fiction movie the Blob starring Steve McQueen. It was the strangest of all my strange dreams because I knew it couldn't really happen, but the nightmare kept coming back.

When I graduated from high school, I weighed a hundred and sixty five pounds. When I got out of the Army, I was up to a hundred and eighty five. After a year of driving truck, I weighed two hundred and twenty five pounds, and I was miserable.

The best I ever felt was in the morning after shaving, taking a hot shower and putting on some clean clothes. After that it was all downhill. Finally, after driving two years, I quit. I couldn't take it anymore. I had become extremely irritable and the littlest things would set me off, like other drivers cutting in front of me, or tail-gaiting me, even a bad meal or a rude waitress. I couldn't go on like that. A bad accident was waiting to happen and I knew it. Worst of all, it probably would have been my fault if it did. I had become a dangerous driver because of my attitude.

I had a hard time finding another job. I knew I didn't want to drive a truck anymore and I didn't want to be on the road either, so I figured I'd go back to being a mechanic. I'd learned a lot about taking care of an eighteen-wheeler while driving as long as I did. I'd done just about everything there was to do as far as auto mechanics was concerned. I figured I could find a job somewhere.

I wasn't in a good place in my head during that time in my life. I wasn't happy with myself but I didn't understand why. All my life I'd gotten along with most people pretty well but I didn't have many friends during that stretch. I thought it was them. I guess it was me. Everything that went wrong bothered me for a long time. I'd think and think about things that really weren't all that important and couldn't get them out of my mind. I figured I needed to meet someone and that would make things better.

The problem was that the only people I was meeting were at the local bars and they all had problems of their own. We weren't helping each other. I was in a rut and couldn't figure out how to get out. I was twenty seven, living in a dumpy one-bedroom apartment not far from where my parents lived, going nowhere. I needed a big-time change in my life and I knew it. I just didn't know how to make it happen.

CHAPTER FIVE
Deep Creek Lake

Pittsburgh IS IN THE western part of Pennsylvania and Jeanette is about an hour east of it. The Maryland line is about an hour south of Jeanette. West Virginia, up near Morgantown, isn't too far away, about the same distance as Pittsburgh. If I didn't have anything else to do, which was most of the time since I wasn't working, I'd take drives in one direction or another just to see places I'd never been to before.

One of my favorite places to visit was the Amish country. There are lots of pockets of the Amish, or the Mennonites, which aren't much different, all over Pennsylvania. One of the biggest areas where they can be found is around the little town of Grantsville, which is in Maryland, not too far from Cumberland.

I especially liked to be there on Saturday mornings because that was when the Amish went to church. I'd find a spot where I could sit and watch as they drove by in their buggies, one by one. The horses were always as calm as could be, walking along the side of the road as cars zoomed by them at fifty and sixty miles an hour.

I loved just sitting and watching them go by. I might see a hundred of the buggies go by in a line, following behind the leader. Nobody was ever late, at least it didn't seem so. I never saw anybody trying to make their horses go faster like they were late and had to catch up.

Most of the buggies were open and the people would be sitting so I could see them. They all dressed the same – dark clothes, dark dresses, dark hats and white shirts. The men all had long beards, most wore glasses, and the women all had their hair tucked up underneath some kind of fish-net thing so you couldn't see their hair at all. The kids, usually small ones, and lots of them, would be in the back on top of one another, dressed just like their parents.

Even the horses were the same. I never saw a paint or a palomino, and not too many grays, either. They were all bays – dark brown with black tails and black manes, all good horses, too.

Some of the buggies were closed, especially in the winter months and they had doors on them with windows in the front and on the sides. I couldn't see the people inside those buggies. Those buggies were like the Cadillacs of cars. From what I could tell, only the men drove the buggies, or if women did, too, I never saw a woman drive one.

The best part was when they got to church and parked their buggies. There was an open field next to the church and they lined the buggies up, side by side, got out, let the reins loose, and walked into church. They didn't tie up the horses or leave someone to watch over them. The horses would just stand there for an hour or more and not move around or wander at all. It was amazing.

I'd sit and watch for hours, until the last buggy had left church. I guess it reminded me of the way things used to be, before cars were invented. I thought about how for centuries and centuries, all the way back as far as thousands of years before Christ, human beings had been riding horses. The wheel was one of the biggest discoveries ever, followed by wagons pulled by horses. It fascinated me. Still does.

I liked to go to Grantsville on days when they weren't going to church, too. I wouldn't see as many horse and buggy outfits but I could go to their farms and shops, talk to them and buy things. Here were these people who looked like they came from a different century, dressed up in outfits like none I'd ever seen anyone wear before, talking just like regular people talk. Although when they talked among themselves, when no outsiders were around, they spoke German.

For me, it was just a different experience. I'd always come back home thinking thoughts I hadn't had before I left. I loved their food, too. I'd buy their jams, pies and breads, especially the raspberries and blueberry pies when the berries were in season. I'd usually eat them in a day or two, which was one reason why I couldn't get my weight down under two hundred and forty five pounds for a while.

I had a few friends up in Jeanette who had horses and they would go to the Amish people to get their saddles repaired and to buy bridles and things. They said the Amish were the best craftsmen around. They still did it all by hand.

Not too far past Grantsville, heading south, is a big lake they call Deep Creek. I'd heard of it before, but I'd never been there and I didn't know too much about it, other than it was supposedly the biggest body of water in Maryland, other than Chesapeake Bay.

One Saturday in early May, after watching the last buggy leave church and go down the road out of sight, I headed south out of Grantsville on State Road 219 another hour to a little town called McHenry, which was right on the lake, about 15 miles past Interstate 68 that runs east and west through Pennsylvania.

I didn't know what I was going to find and didn't really expect much. It was a beautiful spring day with temperatures in the mid-sixties, blue skies and sunshine. It was a nice drive through farms, though I had to pass over some mountains to get there. I was having a good day.

I got into town a little after noon, parked my car on the main road next to the Lake and walked around town. After passing a few stores, I found a little marine shop with a sign out front that said Bill's Marine Service. It was right on the lake. I read the sign on the window and saw where they stored boats, fixed boats and rented them, too. I asked the girl at the counter about renting a little outboard to take a spin on the water. It was ten dollars per hour and I decided to do it.

They had a little deli counter inside, plus a gift shop. I ordered a sandwich and a drink and planned to have a little picnic out on the water. They gave me a map of the lake which showed that there were sixty nine miles of shoreline and it covered over 3900 acres. I wasn't going to go far, but I would be able to get off by myself without much trouble.

I paid my money and was told to walk down to the docks and find Bill, the owner, who would fix me up. Once I got to where the boats were, I saw a couple of guys standing in the back of a nice looking ski-boat with a big Mercury engine on the back.

They were trying to get it started and apparently weren't having much luck. Another guy was standing off to the side, on the dock, watching what was going on, not saying anything. I stood there and watched for a minute or two, waiting for a chance to ask about the boat I was to take out.

The guy standing off to the side was obviously not happy. He had his hands on his hips and I heard him say that he'd just paid a couple of hundred dollars to get it fixed and he'd been there for half an hour and hadn't left the dock.

As I got closer, I noticed a young girl sitting on the dock with her feet dangling in the water. She looked to be about nine or ten.

Then one of the other guys said to him, "I'm real sorry about this, Mr. Sullivan. I'll make it right. If we can't get this started, I'll let you have one of these other boats, no charge."

The third guy was doin' all he could to get that motor to turn over. He was pulling on that starter rope for all he was worth but it wasn't doing any good. The engine just wouldn't fire.

He said, "I don't know what the problem is. I put new spark plugs in myself just this morning. It's got new fuel and I replaced the line from the tank to the motor, too. It should fire right up."

I really hadn't been around boats that much in my life, but I'd been around machines all my life. If that guy had done all the things he said he did, it seemed to me the only thing it could have been was that the spark plugs weren't spaced right, unless there was something really wrong with the engine.

I didn't say anything but after a few more minutes had passed, I got a little impatient and said, "Excuse me, but would you tell me where I can find a man named Bill. I've rented a boat for a couple of hours and I'd like to get on the water if I could."

The taller of the two men standing next to the motor, not the one pulling on the rope, said, "I'm Bill and I'll be right with you. I'd like to get this boat going for Mr. Sullivan here before I do."

I don't know why I did it because it really wasn't like me, but I said, "Well, I've been standing here for five minutes and if you give me a socket wrench I'll get that damn thing running in less than thirty seconds."

So the guy says to me, "Oh, yeah? Well come on down and show me what you can do. That alright with you, Mr. Sullivan?"

"I don't care who fixes it. I'd like to go water-skiing with my daughter before it gets dark."

"Mister, you've got five minutes. You get this thing running and that rental boat is on me. Ernie, give this man whatever he needs."

Now Ernie was not happy about this at all. I had basically told him that he didn't know what he was doing. He was a young kid. He looked to be no more than a teenager. He backed off, leaving his tool box next to the engine. He didn't say anything to me, but it wasn't hard to see that he was frustrated and really didn't know what else to do except pull on the cord and play with the carburetor.

First thing I did was take the spark plug out. I didn't know what it was supposed to be calibrated at, but it was brand new and looked to me that the gap might have been a bit too wide. I adjusted the gap, making it smaller so there was less distance for the current to jump. I put it back in and hand-tightened it. I also drained the line coming out of the gas tank to the motor, just in case there was some air or water in there, then re-attached it.

I closed down the choke completely. I was afraid that the engine was flooded. I didn't know how long they'd been fooling with it.

I pulled the cord and the engine started right up on my third pull. The frowns on people's faces turned to smiles as it sputtered for a few seconds and then picked up some steam and kept on running. I throttled it up a little and it responded just fine. I put it in neutral, stepped back and said, "There you go. Good as new. Now where's that rental boat I'm going out in?"

"Ernie, put this man in the number four boat. No, let's give him an upgrade. Put him in number seven. Thank you very much, Mr...."

"Murphy," I said. "George Murphy."

"Thank you very much, Mr. Murphy. Enjoy your ride."

While Bill was chatting it up with Mr. Sullivan, I told Ernie I was sorry about what had happened, and that I'd been a mechanic all my life. I said I'd made a lucky guess at what it was. He said it was alright. He was planning on going back to school in the fall and was a business major at the local community college. It was just a summer job to him.

They put me in good-sized aluminum boat, about four feet longer than the one I'd paid for, with a bigger engine on it. I had no trouble starting it and I rode off towards the middle of the lake, thinking I was pretty lucky to get the rental for free. It was a beautiful day and I was enjoying myself, not thinking of any of the problems in my life.

Deep Creek Lake is west of the Allegheny Mountains. It was clear enough to allow me to have a good view of them. There were hills to the west with mostly tall trees and a deep forest along the lake. A road ran alongside the lake and I could see cars passing by occasionally but as the town of McHenry got smaller there were fewer signs of civilization.

When I got far enough out, I turned off the motor, opened up the sandwich box and started to eat my lunch. While I was sitting there, Mr. Sullivan and his daughter went by me several times. His daughter was up on two skis. After half an hour or so, just as I was about to start up the engine and take a little tour of the lake, he idled up alongside me and said, "Say, thanks for helping out back there. Our day was going to be completely spoiled if we weren't able to get this boat going."

"No problem at all. Glad to help," I said. "I've been a mechanic all my life and I made a lucky guess at what the problem was."

"Say, would you mind coming on board and steering this thing while I take a turn at skiing?"

"I really haven't handled too many boats before and I..."

"All you have to do is go straight until I tell you to stop. I'll go about ten minutes down that way, turn around and come back. You can leave your boat right here. It won't go anywhere and we'll be right back."

Mr. Sullivan was a tall, thin, distinguished looking man, with glasses and a head of white hair. It was obvious from the boat he was driving that he had some money. He seemed to be a nice enough man so I said, "I don't mind if you don't mind. It sounds like fun. That thing sure goes a lot faster than this one."

It had a Mercury 175 on the back and I knew it would fly. "It looks like that thing will go pretty fast if you want it to. How fast do you want me to go?"

"You can pretty much open it up with me. I've been skiing all my life and I'll tell you whether to slow down or not. My daughter can spot me so all you have to do is keep the wheel straight and watch out for other boats."

So I hopped on his boat while he jumped in the water. His daughter got back into the boat once I was safely aboard. She put on a sweatshirt and told me her name was Colleen. She had long, wavy reddish hair and blue eyes. She said she'd tell me when her dad was ready and thanked me for helping.

"I'm not old enough to drive this," she said. "I think you're supposed to be at least sixteen and I'm only ten. I'm not even supposed to be able to ski without someone else on the boat but my Dad says it's okay. He couldn't go skiing without someone else in the boat besides me, though."

"I'm glad to help," I said. "This is fun for me, too."

Colleen told me he was ready and I gradually pushed the throttle forward. I looked back and saw Mr. Sullivan teetering from side to side, like he was about to fall.

Colleen yelled, "Hit it!"

I pushed the throttle all the way down and the boat shot forward. I looked back again and Mr. Sullivan was leaning back on the one ski and started to go from the middle to one side all the way out so that he was even with the boat. I looked over and he gave me a 'thumbs up' sign.

Then he started back the other way and within a few seconds, he was on the other side of the boat. I kept both hands on the wheel and watched where we were going. Every now and then I turned to watch him ski.

About ten to fifteen minutes later, Colleen said, "You can stop now."

I looked back and saw that Mr. Sullivan wasn't on his ski anymore. I pulled back on the throttle, put it into neutral, and started turning the wheel to my left to turn the boat around, careful not to run over the line.

"Just go real slow until you get past where he is and he'll get the rope and ski back," she told me. I went at idle speed until he had the rope in his hands and was preparing to go again.

When he was ready, I gunned it and he got right up. Fifteen minutes later, we got back to where my boat was and Mr. Sullivan let go of the rope and sunk into the water. I pulled back on the throttle, turned the boat around and we picked him up.

"Man, that was great! Thank you so much, Mr. Murphy. I thought Colleen was going to have all the fun today."

"George is my name. Call me George, please," I said. "I'm happy to do it. It was fun for me, too."

He took me back over to my boat, which had floated away a little bit, not much, and thanked me again. When they drove off, I took a little spin around the lake, but after his boat, mine was like a putt-putt.

I brought the boat back about fifteen minutes early, tied it up, and went into the office to turn in the life-preserver I'd been given. Bill was behind the cash register.

"Say, Mr. Murphy, thanks again for helping out like you did," he said.

"No problem," I replied. "Glad to do it. That Mr. Sullivan and his daughter are nice people. He let me run his boat out there while he skied."

"That's what he said. He appreciated that quite a bit, Mr. Murphy."

Please call me George. Nobody calls me Mr. Murphy."

"Okay, George it is. Say, George, you wouldn't be looking for a job would you? I could use a good mechanic around here."

"Well, as a matter of fact, I am. I haven't worked on boats but I've worked on all kind of engines most of my life. I don't see why I couldn't figure out a boat engine."

"Tell me a little about yourself, George. What experience do you have as a mechanic?"

I told him about my Dad being a mechanic and me growing up around a gas station in Jeanette, about my time in the Army and all the rest, and when I was finished, he seemed satisfied.

"So it sounds like you can work on cars, trucks, tractors, forklifts and things like that while you learn about boats, yes?"

"Oh, yeah. I've worked on some big machines in my day. Those Chinook helicopters have dual rotors and are pretty complicated, as are tanks and armored personnel carriers. I'm sure I can learn to handle an outboard motor."

"When can you start?" he asked.

"Right now," I responded.

"How about Monday morning. Your hours will be 8 to 5 with an hour for lunch. I'll start you out at $7 an hour and see how you do. How does that sound?"

"I'll need to find a place to stay."

"There's a motel down the road about a mile as you're headed north out of town. It's owned by a friend of mine named Matthew. He'll give you a good rate while you look around. The name of the place is the Lakeside Motel. Tell him I sent you. If that's not to your liking, I can give you some other places to look at on a temporary basis."

"I'm sure that will be fine. Thanks a lot."

"We'll see you Monday morning, bright and early. I've got a truck and a forklift that need work right now and I'm tired of paying ole Danny down at the garage. Besides, he's getting so busy with the summer crowd starting to come to town and all he doesn't seem to find the time to do my work anymore. We'll give it a try and see if it works out. I hope it does for both our sakes."

"I think I'm going to like it here," I told him. "I got divorced a while back and I've been needing a change in scenery."

"You'll like this place during the summer months. There's no place I'd rather be," he said.

I drove to the Lakeside Motel and met with Matthew. He showed me a corner room on the second floor I could have for a hundred and fifty per week, since I would be working for Bill. I gave him a hundred dollars and told him I'd be back with my clothes and things the next night. He gave me a key and wished me luck. Just like that, I had a new job and a new life.

CHAPTER SIX
Bill's Marina

IT DIDN'T TAKE LONG to get all my things packed and ready to go. I didn't have much other than my tools, and I had assembled quite a lot of them over the years between the time spent at gas stations, garages, on the road as a trucker, and as a parts salesman/delivery man. Getting them loaded up was the hardest part. Since I wasn't sure that this thing was going to work out, I didn't give up the lease on my apartment and take everything with me that first day.

My parents were glad to hear about what had happened to me down in McHenry. They'd never been to Deep Creek Lake but I think they were just happy see me get on with my life. It wasn't that far from Jeanette and they could come see me if they wanted. Or I could always come back to see them, which was more likely. They were getting up in years and didn't get around near as much as they used to.

I was back in McHenry at the Lakeside Motel by late afternoon the next day, which was Sunday. Everything was closed up by the time I got there, except for some convenience stores. I enjoyed walking the empty streets from the motel down to the marina. The place had a nice feel to it. It was the lake that made it special and I watched the sun set over it that night. I hoped this was going to work out.

I arrived at work fifteen minutes early the next morning. Bill was already there, sitting in his office with a cup of coffee ready for me. He told me that Ernie would be my helper and asked me to teach him what I could about being a mechanic. I was sure that Ernie knew more about boats than I did so I was glad that he would be around. He could help me out with the boats and I could teach him about cars and trucks.

Ernie arrived a few minutes after 8:00 looking a little sheepish. I think that when he saw me standing there he was afraid he was going to get fired. When he found out he still had a job, he was okay with it. Once we started working on the fork lift and the trucks, which is what Bill had us do first, he could see that I knew what I was doing and when I taught him a few things the tension between us vanished.

I spent most of that first week working on things other than boat motors. I kept Ernie busy working on the boats, doing what he knew how to do and I learned by watching him. A motor is a motor and it didn't take me too long to figure boats out. They're still gas combustion engines, no different from what's in a car or a truck.

Now that forklift was a different animal and although I had worked on a few while in the Army, it was an older model and I wasn't familiar with it. I had to pour through the manuals to figure things out, but I did and by the end of the week, after getting a few parts, I had the thing running. I earned my pay and then some when Bill saw that fork lift put the first boat up on the racks. He had a smile from ear to ear. I don't know how much he was paying to have the work done before I got there, but I'm sure it was a whole lot more than what he was paying me.

Bill was a nice guy. He'd lived in the area his whole life and was now in his late fifties. His father had started the business back in the twenties, before Bill was born, not long after the Pennsylvania Electric Company built a dam in 1923 off of a tributary to the Youghiogheny River and put in a hydroelectric facility.

Bill's wife of thirty years had up and left him once his kids were all grown. He was lonesome and liked having someone to talk to. He liked me to tell him stories about Vietnam. It was 1977 and though we were out we were still putting an end to that chapter in the history of our country. It was long over for me, except for the nightmares. Telling him all those stories brought some of it back, a lot of the bad things I really didn't want to remember and those I didn't tell him about.

Thinking about Vietnam dredged up a few more memories that became nightmares before too long. Even though moving to McHenry made me happier, it didn't get rid of the nightmares. Like the time we had to take a whole bunch of people who'd been hit with napalm and burned to a hospital. Most of them were burned beyond recognition and already dead. Some of the ones that were still alive wished they were dead. Many of them died before we got them to the hospital.

The ones who were partially burned, especially the ones with facial burns, haunted me. There were some who knew they had been badly burned but didn't know what it looked like, whose lives would be ruined forever, but they didn't know that just yet. They were still hoping that they'd be okay.

Thinking about them would cause me to wake up in a panic, like all the other nightmares did.

Every night that first week Bill and I would go down to the local diner and have dinner together. We'd talk for a couple of hours then I'd go back to the apartment and get some sleep. We talked about all kinds of things. When we weren't talking about the war or the Steelers, he liked hearing about what it was like to drive an eighteen-wheeler all over the country. He was a Steelers' fan, too. It seemed like I did all the talking. I enjoyed talking to him and it gave me a way to meet people since he knew everybody.

After I fixed the forklift, I went to work on the truck that Bill used to pull boat trailers. It was a big, powerful Chevy with dual axles and a diesel engine. I didn't realize it at first, but that was a big part of his business. Many of his customers would take their boats out of the water every winter and storing them at Bill's facility, which held over a hundred boats up to thirty feet long. Boats over thirty feet weren't allowed on the lake. Some of the owners had us move their boats down south, mostly to Florida, for the winter. The ones that weren't being stored in McHenry had to be moved, by trailer, one at a time to wherever they were going and then brought back again the next spring. There was a lot of boat-moving to be done.

I still held a license as a commercial driver so once I fixed the truck I could drive it to get boats from wherever the owners had them, if they wanted us to. Since it was late spring, most of the boats were already there but more were coming. The truck needed a new engine, and he was pleased when I told him I would be able to put that in for him.

There were all kinds of things for me to do that didn't involve boat motors, like fixing trailers, fixing up the storage facility, powering up batteries and operate the fork-lift and put boats in the water – all kinds of things, plus plenty of motors to repair.

Ernie and I stayed busy from start to finish every weekday, but the weekends were the busiest. As far as Bill was concerned, I could work every day, and since I didn't have anything better to do, I did. On weekends, I'd spend most of my time helping with renting boats, showing people how to operate them and getting boats in and out of the water from the storage facility. Time was spent getting the motors started and showing people how to run the boats, too. A lot of people would flood the engines or pull too hard on the starter cords and break them. Then I'd have to replace them.

After a couple of weeks, over dinner, Bill told me that he was giving me a raise. I was glad to hear it since he was paying me less than Ernie, probably, and he raised my pay to what was a decent hourly rate for a mechanic in that part of the state. When he did, I felt like I was being treated fairly, plus I was enjoying myself. I enjoyed the dinners with Bill as much as anything. I usually had a few beers every night and I was meeting people.

The diner was the biggest restaurant in town. McHenry was a town of about 1500 people and that was at the high point of the season. Most people didn't live there full time. There were a lot of people who had second homes there and they were counted in that population.

Fishbones held about eighty people. There were twenty tables that could seat four. They usually had enough customers to keep four waitresses busy during the week and six on weekends.

One waitress, a local girl a couple of years out of high school, who was going to the Garrett County Vo-Tech to be a medical technician, took a liking to me. It seemed as if she would usually get our table. She was always real friendly to me. Her name was Rebecca. She was about five foot four inches tall with long, brown hair which she usually tied on top of her head, and big brown eyes. She was a little on the heavy side but she had a pretty face and was as friendly as she could be to me.

After a while I looked forward to seeing her a whole lot more than having dinner with Bill. When he missed a day I went there by myself. Dinners with Bill slowed down to maybe once or twice a week when he saw that I was settling in on my own. I kept going in there most every night, just to see Rebecca.

One Saturday, about a month after starting work there, Bill told me to put Mr. Sullivan's boat in the water. I hadn't seen him since that first day. He was a big part of the reason as to why I was there and I looked forward to seeing him.

Just like I did for all other customers, I took his boat down off the racks with the fork lift, cleaned it up, gassed it up, checked the oil and put it in the water for him. I started up the engine and made sure she was running good. He and Colleen arrived at about 11:00. I was standing next to his boat out on the dock as they walked up. He was bigger than I remembered and though he had a head full of white hair he had a baby face that made him look much younger. He must have been at least 6 foot tall and looked to weigh almost as much as I did.

I was still well over two hundred pounds but I was sure that I'd lost at least twenty pounds in the month I was there. I could tell by my clothes. My pants wouldn't fit anymore, they were too loose. There were no more openings on my belt, which was wrapping half way around my side.

"How are you, Mr. Murphy?" he said.

"Fine thanks, Mr. Sullivan," I told him. "And you?"

"Couldn't be better. You remember my daughter, Colleen, don't you?"

"Of course I do. How are you Colleen?"

53

She smiled and muttered something, burying her head behind her father's right arm, looking very sleepy. Mr. Sullivan and I exchanged small talk on this, that and the other.

"So have you found a home here?" he asked.

"I'm just renting for now, but I'm as happy as can be and I have you to thank for that."

"Well, I don't know that I had much to do with it, other than we happened to be having a problem with our boat that day. From what Bill tells me, you're quite the mechanic. I think you've earned this job on your own."

"He's had me doing a lot of work on machinery, trucks, cars and things and that's what I do best. I can work on just about anything with a gas engine. I catch on pretty quick and I'm learning more and more about boat engines every day."

"That's what he said. He also told me you can transport the boats for him too."

"That's right, I do. I spent a year or so on the road behind the wheel of an eighteen wheeler."

"Well, I'm sure that I'll be in need of your services one of these days. I like to take this down to Florida for the winter, plus I have some cars up at the house that need some work."

"I'll be happy to help any way I can," I told him.

"That's great. It looks like you've got us all ready to go, yes?"

"She should start right up for you," I responded.

He pulled on the starter cord and the engine purred like a kitten.

"That's more like it. Thanks, Mr. Murphy."

"George, please."

"Thanks, George, and call me Paul."

They motored off and I went back to taking care of customers with the boat rentals, putting boats in the water and getting the engines started, like I did every weekend.

I saw them coming in several hours later and walked down to the dock to greet them. We exchanged pleasantries and I took the boat and put it away. Mr. Sullivan was obviously pleased with the special attention I gave him and he said so. He offered to give me a tip but I told him that it wasn't necessary.

I didn't see them again for a few weeks, but what he said about working on his cars gave me an idea for things I could do after the season ended, provided it didn't interfere with my work at Bill's. I could see myself at Deep Creek Lake for a long time.

CHAPTER SEVEN
A Winter Job

Things didn't slow down at the marina until Labor Day. I didn't have a day off during the whole summer season. I had moved out of the motel into a small apartment closer to work and I walked most every place. I wasn't sure how long I'd have a job but I was hearing things that made me think I probably wouldn't be able to stick around through the winter with Bill. I hoped that something would turn up because I liked it in McHenry.

I was sleeping better. The long days of hard work and keeping busy were good for me. I didn't have to take the pills and drink to get to sleep. I still had the occasional nightmares, but they were less frequent. I was much happier than I had been and that had something to do with it, too.

Once the kids went back to school, everything changed at Bill's place. Some people started taking boats out of the water and having us prepare them for winter storage right after Labor Day. There was still a good couple of months of boating left before it got too cold, and many boat-owners wanted to be in the water right up until Thanksgiving, but the rental business dropped off dramatically by the third week in October. Bill told me I'd be doing most of the driving for the moving of boats south, which was a good sign that I'd have something to do for a while longer, at least. I took the first boat south on the first of November – to Biloxi, Mississippi.

He gave me the first weekend off after Labor Day and I went back to Jeanette to see my parents. They had come down to visit one Sunday in July but I was so busy I didn't have much time to visit with them. We had lunch together and I showed them a nice spot to sit and enjoy the lake. They walked around the town and did some sightseeing and enjoyed themselves, but mostly they were happy to see that I was happy.

Jeanette hadn't changed any in the months I'd been away. I didn't go to any of my old haunts. There wasn't anything in bars that I was looking for and there wasn't anybody there I wanted to see. I had lost touch with most of my high school buddies. Most were married and had kids. A lot of them were divorced or never married at all, which was even worse when kids were involved. I stayed at home with my folks and watched TV, ate some good meals and left after dinner on Sunday. I was anxious to get back to Deep Creek. That was my new home.

Once school started, Ernie stopped working at Bill's place during the week. He was in his last year at the Community College and had plans to start at State College in January, if he could. He worked weekends though, and that gave me the weekends off.

Things between me and Rebecca were still simmering, though we still hadn't been out on a date yet. That was probably a good thing since it gave us a chance to get to know each other better, not like with Joanna. She worked every Friday and Saturday night because that was when she could make the most money. We had our first date the third Sunday in September.

We went out on the lake. She didn't own a boat and neither did I. Bill let us take one of the rental boats. Rebecca packed a picnic lunch and I scared up a few rods. We planned to make a day of it.

We got on the water mid-morning, drove to a quiet spot far away from the Marina, dropped anchor and put our lines in the water. Neither one of us was much of a fisherman. We got lines tangled several times. We just laughed about it when we did. She wasn't afraid to put the worms on the hooks by herself. I liked that. She was a small-town, country girl and I liked that, too.

We caught a whole bunch of bass and brim. She said that she liked cooking and eating fresh fish, but we decided to just throw them back and save that for another day. We stayed on the water most of the afternoon. After we got back, she came over to my place for pizza and beer. We started seeing each other on a regular basis after that.

Mr. Sullivan and his daughter came back a few times before the season officially ended, which was the week after Thanksgiving. The last time he was there was in mid-October, when the fall colors were at their peak. He made arrangements for us to take his boat south for him, but told us he wouldn't need for it to be done before the middle of December. While there, he asked me to stop by his place first chance. We agreed to meet the following Saturday.

I had no trouble finding his house. It was on top of a hill overlooking Deep Creek Lake, a beautiful spot. I pulled into the driveway and saw a huge garage off to the left, barely visible from the road above. It was still early, not quite 9:00 and Mr. Sullivan was sitting on the back porch drinking a cup of coffee.

He started down the back steps as soon as he saw me coming. He probably heard me before he saw me. There weren't many houses in the neighborhood and there were no other cars on the road at that time of the morning.

"Good morning, George. No trouble finding the place?"

"None at all. The directions were perfect. This is quite a place you have up here, Mr. Sullivan."

"Paul, please. Call me Paul. When you say Mr. Sullivan it makes me think my father is standing next to me."

"It's quite a place you have here, Paul."

"Thanks. It took a lot of years of hard work for me to get this, but it was worth it. It's about the only place I can go to where I can really relax. I don't get up here as often as I'd like but on the weekends when I have Colleen, I like to bring her here. She likes it as much as I do."

"Is she with you now?"

"She's still sleeping. She won't be a teenager for a few years but she's already acting like one. Goes to bed late and sleeps late but whatever makes her happy is fine with me."

"That's quite a garage you have there. It looks like it's big enough to be a good-sized auto-repair shop." I saw six separate bays with a door for each. Mr. Sullivan took a device out of his pocket, clicked it and opened up one of the doors.

"It holds five cars. I could put six in there if I had to but one of the bays has a hydraulic lift and I like to keep that open."

"A hydraulic lift! That's impressive. You don't see that too often at a private home."

"Well, come on over and take a look. I've got a pretty good set of tools and equipment, too, plus oilers, fluids and all the whistles and bells."

The first bay held a blue and white 1957 Chevy Bel Air.

"Wow! I'm impressed. That's one of my favorites. It's a classic." I ran my hand over the finish, barely touching it. There was no dust on it and looked like it was freshly polished.

"I keep them as clean as I can. I wash and vacuum them all at least once a month, and I take each of them out on the road for a spin just about every time I'm here. I put some polish on this one just last week. Colleen can't wait until she's old enough to drive. She has her eyes on that little beauty over there."

I looked down the row and saw an Edsel in the next bay but then my eyes fixed on a black Triumph next to it.

"Is that a '62 Spitfire?"

"Yep."

"That's the first year they were made, wasn't it?"

"Sure was."

"Wow! Now that's a real collector's item."

"She's my pride and joy."

"They called it a Spitfire4 because she has four cylinders, right?"

"That's right and, man, does she take the turns on these country roads! Part of me wants to let her loose and another part of me wants to go slow because I don't want to be too hard on her."

"Wow! That's about all I can say." I ran my hand across the hood. "I feel like I should have gloves on to touch her. She's beautiful!"

"Small, sporty, yet still comfortable for me to sit in. She'll go from zero to sixty in about 17 seconds, which was really good for back when she was built."

"What's her top speed?" I asked.

"I've had her up to eighty five but the manual says she'll do ninety."

"Man o' man! I've just seen pictures of this thing. I've never worked on one."

"Never?" Paul asked.

"Well, I've worked on Triumphs and Spitfires, but never one of these. They stopped making them two years later, right? And then they came out with the MK2 or something like that, as I recall."

"That's right," Paul responded. "They made an MK1, MK2, an MK3, and an MKIV and then they went to the 1500. They called this one a Spitfire, and named it after a fighter plane from WWII."

"She's a beauty, alright. And this is the one Colleen wants, right?"

"That's right."

"I can see why. Are you going to let her have it?"

"I'm not so sure about that. We'll see how things go, but I'll let her drive it when she's old enough. She can't wait."

I looked over at the last bay and saw a Rambler and asked, "Is that an authentic Kenosha Cadillac?"

"That she is."

"The old two-door convertible…man o' man! This is a classic, too. What year is this one? '53? '54? '55? It's somewhere in there, isn't it?

"1954, just before Nash-Kelvinator merged with the Hudson Motor Car Company to form American Motors. I'll bet you didn't know that, did you?"

"No, I didn't. That's before my time. You've got some nice cars here, Paul!"

"Thanks. I take a lot of pride in them and try to keep them in good shape.

It's a full-time job and I don't have enough time for it. I'm hoping you can help me out some."

"What are you thinking?"

"I'd like for you to do some maintenance on these for me. I'm trying to keep them all in as near to their original condition as possible. I think they'll be worth a whole lot more money if I do."

"Do you take them to the antique car shows and all?"

"Not yet but I'd like to some day. Right now, they stay up here and I take them on these country roads as often as I can but some of them need some work and I'm not a mechanic. I can't do the major repair stuff."

"Well, I can help you out with that, for sure," I said.

"The only thing I ask is that you don't do anything that will damage the vehicle or reduce its value, like using anything but original parts. Sometimes that's half the battle, finding original parts and then waiting for them to get here."

"Yeah, I can see where that would be a problem for any of these vehicles," I responded.

"If you don't know how to do something, just tell me and I'll find someone else who can. I don't want you experimenting. I've seen your work and talked to some people about you and I'm sure you can do most everything that needs to be done, but you might run across something that is too much for you. I want you to tell me when you do."

"That's fair. I've got no problem with that."

"And remember, most importantly, use only original issued equipment – nothing that wouldn't have been on it when she rolled off the assembly line."

"I'd be delighted to work on these. It'd be a pleasure."

"And I'll pay you a fair price for doing so."

"When did you want this to be done?" I asked.

"No hurry. There's nothing that needs to be done right away. I'm thinking it will give you something to do in the winter when this place shuts down."

"I don't know what I'm going to do when my work at the Marina comes to an end, or slows down so much I can't pay my bills. I figure I'll be busy moving boats for a while. I'd like to stick around if I can. I like it up here."

"Well, this won't be a full-time job. I'll want to put a limit on the number of hours you can work each week. I expect that I can just about guarantee you a couple of hundred dollars a week for the next several months. How does that sound?"

"It sounds great. That'll be enough to keep me here, I think. When would you like for me to start?"

"Let's say when the first hard snow falls, which will be before you know it. That's about the time the Marina hunkers down for the winter. I think Bill keeps it going by himself after that. He hasn't said anything to you about it yet?"

"Not yet."

"I'll tell you what. You talk to him and find out. As far as I am concerned, you can start work when you want. When you do, I'll want a weekly report. It doesn't have to be too detailed, but I want it in writing, showing me what you did and how many hours you worked and all. I'll need that to pay your bill."

"Sounds great to me. I'm looking forward to it."

The other two vehicles were an old Jeep that looked to be in mint condition and a 1964 Ford Mustang.

We talked about them for a while and as we were walking down towards the last bay where the hydraulic lift and all the tools were, we heard Colleen call out, "Dad! Where are you?"

"I'm down here, Sweetheart. I'll be right there."

He turned to me and asked if I wanted to join them for breakfast but I declined. I walked up to the house with him, said hello to Colleen, and left. Once again, thanks to Mr. Sullivan, it looked like I had found myself a job.

That winter Rebecca and I saw more and more of each other. After we'd been dating for a couple of months she stayed overnight at my place the first time. Next thing I knew, she was there every night, visiting. She'd spend the night with me every now and then. When we were together we laughed often and had no trouble finding things to talk about. We enjoyed being together.

I was so worried about my nightmares and scaring her that I told her about them. No details, just that I had them every now and then and why. She wanted to know what it was like for me in Vietnam. She said that she had taken a class in sociology and they had talked about what it was like for veterans returning home from Vietnam.

I'd read where a lot of guys weren't doing too well. None of us had been welcomed home with open arms and some had been downright ridiculed and made to feel ashamed of what they'd done in the war. Some had gotten into drugs, or crime, or both. I was trying not to think about it, hoping my problems would eventually go away, but when we talked it over, I figured there were a whole lot of guys with bad dreams, not just me.

I wasn't the only one who'd gone through all of that shit and some had it a whole lot worse than me. Those boys in the rice paddies or out on patrols in the jungles for weeks at a time didn't have a fenced in base to work out of like I did, or a helicopter that could take you out of the jungle. Knowing that didn't make things any better for me. I was still afraid of having a nightmare while she was there and freaking her out.

I spent that winter doing odds and ends for Bill around the Marina, hauling a boat every now and then, working on a vehicle or on whatever came along that Bill needed help with, but most of the winter I spent working on Mr. Sullivan's cars. That was great. I wasn't making much money but I wasn't spending much either.

At Paul's place, since there was no one else around, I could play whatever music I wanted as loud as I wanted and I could work whenever I wanted. That gave me as much time to spend with Rebecca as Rebecca was able to spend with me. She was busy with school and work, but when she wasn't doing one of those two things, we were together.

Rebecca and I got along well and the more time we spent together made things even better. She seemed to like me well enough and I liked her a lot. I didn't need to know too much more about her than what I already knew. She seemed happy with me and who I was and I was happy with her. I couldn't think of a reason not to get married so I asked her and she said yes.

She was five years younger than me and this was her first marriage. Her folks wanted her to do it up right and so did she. I could have cared less about any of that. By the middle of February, she started planning a church wedding for June, less than three months away.

After we got engaged, I decided to buy a small house in town not far from the restaurant or the Marina. I was able to get a loan through the VA without putting much money down. Since we had a date set and all, and I'd given her a ring, her parents didn't seem to mind as much when Rebecca began spending even more time with me. Unlike Joanna, she was a really good cook and when she wasn't working we had romantic candlelight dinners in front of the fireplace, with soft music playing. Things were better than they had been in years for me, maybe ever.

A few weeks after she moved some of her clothes and other things in, I had my first nightmare. It was the one where Reno and I had loaded all those Vietnamese bodies in the back of our truck and the one little girl jumped out and ran off. It made me jump and bolt out of bed. She woke up, worried about me. I told her that I'd had one of my nightmares, but I didn't give her any of the details.

I was afraid she'd think less of me or think I was a bad person for doing what I had been ordered to do. Worse yet, I didn't want her to think I was a crazy person. I didn't do anything wrong. I wasn't the ones to cause all those people we put in the back of the truck to die. For all I knew, the VC had killed them.

I'd heard stories all the time from soldiers about how they'd come back through villages after being out on a search and destroy mission and find the head man of the village tied to a pole, hanged by the VC for being too friendly to us. If a villager was friendly with American soldiers, he was killed by the VC. It was that simple. I'd seen plenty of Vietnamese men hanged when we'd picked up soldiers in the Chinook, and that's what I'd been told had happened to them.

Rebecca seemed to understand, though there was no way she could ever really understand, but at least she was willing to listen. I still wasn't ready to tell her, or anyone, everything that was going on inside my head when I had those dreams. I told her more than I ever told Joanna, though. She didn't cry and get all freaked out like Joanna did. That made me feel better but it didn't stop the nightmares.

About six weeks after we started living together full-time I had one of the nightmares that always got to me the most. It was about when I was on guard duty at a Fire base, late at night. In this one, I'm at my post and I hear the sound of a twig snapping. All I have is my rifle, my helmet and a flare. I fire a flare and as it lights up the night sky I see about a dozen VC in their black pajamas coming straight at me, less than twenty feet away. I go to fire my rifle and it backfires. That's when I wake up, shaking like a leaf in a strong wind, and that's what happened this time, too.

Fortunately, that never happened to me, but I'd heard stories about things like that happening to other guys. Rifles malfunctioned all the time. In fact, that's what happened to the French at Dien Bien Phu in 1954, not the part about the rifles back-firing, but about soldiers being over-run. The French were massacred there. A large Battalion sized unit had been ambushed and completely destroyed. That's what supposedly led to the truce and the French getting out of Vietnam. America never thought that it could happen to us. It could happen to the French, but never to us.

Before I went to Vietnam I'd heard stories about how the North Vietnamese Army had over 500 Marines surrounded by 5000 of their soldiers at Khe San up in the North, not far from the de-militarized zone. The NVA had artillery and tanks too, which we did not. The siege at Khe San went on for months. We finally got our guys out of there, but the NVA wanted a massacre and we all knew it.

The only time the NVA would fight us was when they knew they had an enormous numerical advantage. When they did they'd try to over-run the base with a massive assault and kill all of our soldiers. It happened several times while I was there to men in small firebases.

The VC would fight us despite the fact that they rarely had a numerical advantage. They would ambush us, kill as many of us as they could, and then run away and hide, waiting for another opportunity to do it again. There were so many caves and hiding places we never knew about that they managed to escape most of the time, but I'd heard stories of how they had over-run smaller units of soldiers and butchered each and every one of the men.

That was another dream I couldn't tell Rebecca about, and I didn't. Again, she said she understood. She told me that she wouldn't think less of me because of whatever it was that happened to me. That made me worry less about what would happen when I did have another nightmare. Maybe there would come a time when I could tell her about some of them, but not yet. There were others I could never tell her or anyone about, ever.

We got married that June on a Saturday afternoon at the church she had attended since she was a little girl, with all of her family and friends in attendance. My parents, my brother and sister and their families came to the wedding, as did Paul Sullivan and Colleen. They came to the reception we had in Rebecca's back yard, too, though they didn't stay long. Fortunately, the weather was good that day and everything worked out perfect.

We were real busy at the Marina at the time. It was the beginning of the summer season so we couldn't take a long honeymoon then. Rebecca was okay with it, though she would have liked to. I got the weekend off, plus the following Monday and we went to Pittsburgh and stayed at a fancy hotel for three nights. We went out to eat at a couple of expensive restaurants. That wasn't something I would ever have done but that's what Rebecca wanted to do so we did.

I was happier than I'd ever been in my life. Rebecca was talking about finishing her education, having children, and what we would do for the rest of our lives. The nightmares seemed to be slowing down. Even when I had one, it wasn't as big a deal as it had been with my parents or with Joanna, or when I was by myself. Rebecca was good for me. There wasn't any place else I wanted to be or anyone else I wanted to be with. I could see myself being right there in McHenry, with her, for the rest of my life. That was the high-water mark.

Everything changed two months later, on August 21, 1978 to be exact. It was a Tuesday morning, right after our usual coffee and donuts. Bill suffered a massive heart attack, right in front of my eyes. He was dead before the rescue people could even get there.

I did CPR and everything I knew to keep him alive until help arrived but there was nothing that could be done. That's what the paramedics told me. Despite that, I felt horrible, like I should have done more.

The funeral was two days later in the same church where Rebecca and I had married two months before. The whole town turned out. He was buried in the cemetery at the top of the hill with a great big marble headstone.

His children showed up for the funeral. I'd never met them before. Bill really hadn't spoken about them much. His ex-wife didn't make it. I kept working and did my best to keep the Marina up and running until things sorted out as to who was to get what and who would be taking over for Bill at the Marina.

Paul Sullivan, whose law office was in Cumberland, came to the funeral. We spoke briefly and he asked me what was going to happen to the business. I told him that I didn't know but that I'd call him once I did. I'd called him the day Bill had died right after breaking the news to Rebecca. I thought he'd want to know.

Turns out that Bill didn't have a will so his two kids got everything. I don't know if that's the way Bill wanted things to be, but that's the way it was. Problem was, his son, Todd, didn't like me.

He was a few years older than me, in his early thirties, with long blonde hair, tied up in a pony tail. After he found out that I had been in the Army, he told me that he had opposed the war. He had avoided being drafted by getting married right out of high school. That marriage ended in a divorce several years later. He and his father hadn't seen eye-to-eye on a lot of things since he had left home.

When he came back a few days after the funeral, he told me that he'd be taking over the business and that my services were no longer required. He had a few old buddies who were out of work and he was going to give them all jobs. He didn't want me around. Just like that, I was out of a job.

Again, I called Mr. Sullivan, right after breaking the news to Rebecca. Mr. Sullivan was only in his late forties but he had done so well that he was already planning for an early retirement. He had been spending several weeks during the winter months in Ft. Myers for years and had recently bought a condo down there. I'd driven his boat down in the fall then brought it back in May.

When I told him the news, he asked me if I would be interested in moving to Florida if he could find me a job. I told him I'd sure consider it. He said he'd make a phone call to the Marina where he kept his boat during the winter and ask if there were any openings for a mechanic.

He must have said some good things about me because I received a phone call later the same day from the owner asking me about my background. The man asked if I would be willing to come to Florida to meet him. He said he'd split the expenses and, if I got the job, pay them in full. I told him that I'd have to talk to Rebecca first and that I'd call in the morning.

Rebecca and I talked about it but she wasn't too excited about the idea. What would she do while I was working? What schools were around there? Where would we live? How much would it cost? How much would I get paid? What was it like down there? We didn't know anyone and she didn't like hot weather very much, though the thought of escaping the cold Maryland winters appealed to her some.

I didn't have answers to any of her questions. All I knew was I was out of a job and needed to find one. I hadn't looked around but we both knew that there weren't any jobs like the one I had. Mechanic jobs were hard to find. I didn't want to go back to driving truck, especially long-distance, over-the-road kind of driving like I'd done in the past. I wanted to find out more about it.

We talked for most of the night and finally decided that we would go, together, and listen to what the man had to say. She had a week off between classes at the end of the month. If he could wait that long we would do it.

I called the man, Randy, the next morning and we agreed to meet on the following Friday. He wouldn't pay for Rebecca's travel expenses, which was understandable. We talked about going to Disney, which was a three hour drive from where we'd be. She'd never been there and neither had I. We could make it a mini-vacation, or the honeymoon we never had, though it wasn't the best time for it.

CHAPTER EIGHT
The Caloosahatchee River Marina

WE LEFT ON A Thursday afternoon and flew into Tampa on a Southwest Airlines flight out of Baltimore. It was a direct flight and only took us two hours to get there. We rented a small car, the cheapest one we could find, and drove down I-75 for an hour and a half to Ft. Myers.

We found the Holiday Inn where we would be staying with no trouble at all. It was right on the river. Randy had told us it was less than half a mile from his marina. After we checked in, we found out that we could walk across the Caloosahatchee River to get there. The bridge was over a quarter of a mile long. It was a surprisingly big river.

By the time we got settled and changed our clothes, it was only 7:30 and the sun wouldn't be going down for another hour. Rebecca and I walked across the bridge to Randy's place which was, just as Randy had told us, directly across the river from the Holiday Inn. We stopped half way across and saw an island in the middle of the river with boats tied up to a dock. It looked to be a deserted island and there was a nice beach there too. It looked like a nice place to have a picnic, right there in the middle of downtown Ft. Myers. We talked about doing that while we were there, if we could.

We found the place easy enough. It was all locked up but we could see inside. I was able to see the office, the lifts, the storage area for boats, and a big dock. There were several boats tied up at the dock with many more sitting on trailers nearby. There was parking for at least 30 or 40 cars.

The office was a one-story concrete block building with a huge green awning at the entrance. We walked along the outside of the property, which was completely fenced. It looked like a nice place. Even Rebecca said so, and she was pretty skeptical about the whole deal going in.

After we'd seen all that we could see of the Caloosahatchee River Marina we walked back. The river runs from east to west and empties into the Gulf. We could see the sun low in the sky just about to go down. We stopped on the bridge and watched until it disappeared on the horizon.

I had my arms around Rebecca, feeling a cool afternoon breeze on my face. This was a good omen. I wasn't as skeptical as Rebecca, but I was going to cautious about this whole deal. All I knew for sure was that I didn't have a job, I needed a job, and there was a chance that I'd be given a job. So far, we both liked what we saw.

We walked from the Holiday Inn down First Street to a little Italian restaurant with tables and chairs on the sidewalk where we had dinner. Two men were playing music on the corner. They called themselves 'Screamin' and a Cryin'. They played old-time blues on two acoustic guitars.

After dinner we walked a few blocks past the Lee County Courthouse and the city and county buildings to the municipal pier. There were sightseeing boats and a pretty good size harbor. We talked to a few people who kept their boats there and lived on them year-round.

The place was well lit but there wasn't much traffic and not too many people on the street. We could hear music but we couldn't figure out where it was coming from. We walked another block or two and saw that the band was on top of a four-story building, the largest building on the block. We took an elevator up to the top, found a table overlooking the water, the marina, and the pier, and had a couple of beers. It was a romantic, magical kind of night. Everything was new and different and we were doing it together. It was an adventure for us.

I was supposed to meet with Randy first thing in the morning and we didn't want to stay out too late. We walked back to the Holiday Inn and went to sleep, each with our own thoughts, wondering what the next day had in store for us.

I woke up at 6:00 just like always. Bill's place didn't open until 8:00 every day but I'd always get there early. I liked to get there before Bill did and he was always there half an hour before it opened. I'd been used to waking up early ever since my days in the Army and it still felt like I was sleeping in if I slept past 5:00.

I showered, shaved and got ready to go. I left Rebecca still sound asleep. I'd seen a little breakfast place on the walk the night before that was only a block away. I planned to get some coffee and a pastry and walk over the bridge to meet Randy. I had plenty of time.

The place was called April's Eatery. It was run by this older couple who'd been there for years. It was on First Street, tucked in between a restaurant and an old movie theatre where they now put on plays. They made their muffins fresh every morning and I took a hot coffee and a blueberry muffin to go. I sat on a bench next to the water and savored the moment, wondering what the day would bring. I wished Rebecca was with me. She would have enjoyed it, too.

When it was time, I walked across the bridge to meet Randy. I allowed myself enough time so that I arrived fifteen minutes early. When I walked in, I saw a large black man sitting behind the counter. He appeared to be in his mid 40s, tall, thin, a pencil mustache, wearing blue jeans and a white polo shirt with the words 'Caloosahatchee River Marina' embroidered on the front where a pocket would be.

He stood as I entered, extended his hand, smiled and said, "You must be George. I'm Randy Cross. Pleased to meet you."

I was taken aback. Not that I was prejudiced, I'd met too many black men in the Army for that. Several of my sergeants were African-Americans and they were damn fine men. It was just that I rarely saw many black people out on boats, especially up at Deep Creek Lake. There just weren't that many of them who either owned boats or rented boats, that's all, and even fewer were in the business. I smiled, and said, "Thanks for meeting with me."

"Thanks for coming down. While I'm thinking of it, be sure to give me the invoice for your plane trip and the hotel and I'll send you a check for half the bill like I promised. I'll need the invoices for my taxes."

I handed him a copy.

"Of course, if you get the job, I'll pay the whole thing, like I said."

"I'm hoping that will happen," I responded.

"You brought your wife with you, did you?"

"Yes. She's back at the hotel sleeping. We came by last night and saw what we could see. It looks like a nice place you've got here."

"Well, come with me and let me show you around."

Randy proceeded to walk me around the place, introducing me to people as we went.

"I have a couple of staff members who take care of sales and rentals. Mr. Sullivan tells me that's how he met you in the first place, something about you renting a boat up there and ended up with a job."

"That's right. We do quite a bit of rental business in the summer months, small stuff, nothing over sixteen feet, and on weekends I spent a lot of time with the rentals."

"Well, you won't have to do any of that down here and we don't service too many boats under twenty feet."

"Do you sell boats, too?" I asked.

As we talked, we kept walking, through the parking lot and into the main storage area, which was at least 100 feet by 300 feet. It had a V-shaped metal roof and boats were on racks stacked three rows high.

"Nothing new. Lots of our customers are looking to get rid of their boats for one reason or another, plus we have some situations where the owners don't pay and we have to sell them to get our money. The lawyers take care of most of that. Can't do business without a lawyer or two these days, you know."

"Not up where I come from. Mr. Sullivan's about the only lawyer I know to talk to and I don't think Bill had much to do with them, either. I could be wrong. When he died, of course, then the lawyers took over."

Randy laughed and said, "I can't imagine life without lawyers. Maybe I should be going up to where you come from instead of the other way around."

We walked through the back door of the building, towards the far corner of the property. Way in the back, under some trees, away from the water, was the service shop area. It was a concrete block building which I had seen the night before but it was closed up and looked like it might have been a parking garage or a boat storage area. It had four garage doors. They were open and I saw two men under a large awning, with fans blowing at them, busily engaged with outboard motors. The last bay had a huge yacht up on a hydraulic lift and I could see a man standing on the deck of the boat. There was one bay door that was closed. We kept walking as we kept talking.

"It's nice up there. I wouldn't be here if Bill hadn't died like he did."

"Yeah, that's what Mr. Sullivan told me. That's too bad."

"And I swear it happened just about the time I said something to my wife, Rebecca, how I couldn't think of living anywhere but where we did. We'd only been married a couple of months and we'd already bought a house and were talking about having kids."

"Life's like that sometimes. One of my favorite posters is the one with a gorilla sitting in a corner, scratching his head. The caption reads, "Just when I figure out the answers, they change all the questions.""

We laughed. I said, "One of my favorites is the one with the old cowboy, a cigarette hanging from his mouth, weather-beaten, scruffy three day old beard, and a beat-up hat on his head, with the caption, 'There's a lot of things they didn't tell me about this job before I signed on.'"

"I know that one, too. That is a good one. I'll try not to do that. The pay is $10 an hour with full benefits. You'll work a forty hour week, Monday to Friday, 8:00 to 5:00 with an hour lunch. We don't work on Saturdays, at least not in the shop. We're open seven days a week 8:00 to 8:00. I pay eight holidays and I take the whole week off after Christmas, but it's unpaid. You'll get a week of vacation after the first year and two weeks after you've been here two years. I'll have you sign an employment contract and everything will be written down so there won't be any misunderstandings. How does that sound?"

"Sounds good to me. Will I be expected to do anything other than work on engines?"

"Not usually. You definitely won't be working on any motor vehicles any more. We've got more work than we can handle with the boats. You won't be driving trucks and moving boats, except maybe as a forklift operator every now and then. As you can see, I'm missing a man right now. Bay number three is empty. If you like what you see and I like what I see, that will be your spot."

He then introduced me to the three mechanics who raised their heads, smiled, waved and kept on working.

"I like what I see so far," I told him.

"Well, I see that you've dressed nicely to meet me," he said, though all I had on was a polo shirt, slacks and a pair of brown loafers. "I don't expect you to do any work in the clothes you've got on but if you don't mind, I'd like to see you do a little work. We've got a restroom in the back there that has some lockers and a shower. I've put some clothes in there for you and I'd like for you to change and show me what you can do with this thing here," he said, pointing to a Mercury that was sitting on a stand above a barrel full of water in Bay 3.

"What's wrong with it?" I asked.

"Won't start. That's all you need to know. Is that alright with you?"

"Sure," I said. "I don't expect you to hire me just because of some nice things a customer said about me. I'll see what I can do with her."

"I'm going to run back to the office. Take your time and get ready, but don't start working on it until I get back. I want to watch you work. I'll be back in ten minutes."

Randy walked back towards the office and I walked to the back of the building in the direction he had pointed me. I walked past the mechanic in Bay 2 who said, "Taking a test, huh?"

"Yeah, something like that," I responded.

"We all had to do it. Good luck."

I changed into the standard blue mechanic bib-overalls and was standing by the cabinet that held all of the tools for Bay 3, looking them over, when Randy returned.

"Ready to go to work?" he asked.

"I'm ready."

"Okay, she's all yours. I'm going to have a seat over here and watch. I won't say a thing, but if you have any questions, just ask."

Randy sat on a folding chair in a corner and I proceeded to go to work.

Boat engines aren't all that complicated. I'd worked on a bunch of Mercury engines up in Maryland. I pulled off the cover, checked the gas, the oil, the condition of the motor and the cord, all the obvious things first. Other than being a little dirty, like it hadn't been run in a while, I didn't see anything that looked suspicious.

I checked the filters and the lines, and then I took out the spark plug. It was like that old engine I worked on that very first day up at Bill's place in Maryland. The spark plug was fouled and the gap looked a little too big.

"Got any replacement spark plugs," I asked.

"Nope. You're to work with what you've got. We've checked the plug and it's still got life in it."

I cleaned it up as best I could and found the tool to measure the gap. Sure enough, it was too wide. I cleaned it, adjusted the size of the gap and put it back in, hand-tightening it.

I then disconnected the gas line, squeezed the bubble to get any air out of it, reconnected it, pulled out the choke and gave a gentle pull on the starter cord. I could immediately feel that the line had too much play in it. I had to work with it for a minute or two, shortening it so that contact was made at the right spot.

After fifteen to twenty minutes of that, I gave it a good hard pull and she fired, sputtered, and stopped. It seemed as if it was getting a little too much gas. I opened up the carburetor. Maybe should have done that before, I thought to myself. I put a screwdriver on the nut that opens and closes the valve that feeds the mixture of gas and air. I closed down the gas input just a little.

I left the top off the carburetor and gave it another pull. She fired again but began to sputter. I pushed the choke in half way and adjusted the nut with my screwdriver. The engine responded appropriately and, after fifteen to twenty seconds, when I felt that it was running right, I turned to Randy and said, "She sounds pretty good to me. What do you think?"

"Go ahead and close it up if you think it's done, but I'd like for you to fill out that repair order hanging on the wall over there, too. The job isn't over until the paper work is done. I want to see you do that too." he said."

I looked over and saw a clip board with some paper on it.

"Will do."

I found a rag, cleaned up the engine, like I would if we were giving it back to a customer, closed the lid, cleaned up the top, then looked over at Randy, who said, "There's a cart over there. Our mechanics are required to walk the engines over to the service desk right behind the office and turn in the paperwork. For now, just put this on a cart, if you don't mind."

"No problem," I said, and I lifted the machine out of the tub of water and put it on one of the carts. I then filled out the paperwork, explaining the problem and what I had done to fix it.

"You shouldn't have any contact with our customers. Our people at the service desk will take care of all of that. All you will do is fix engines. Go ahead and get cleaned up then come see me in the office. The test is over."

"So how'd I do?"

"We'll talk about it in my office, but I'd say you passed. There is a towel and a new bar of soap in there if you want to take a shower," he offered.

It was hot. Even at 8:30 in the morning it was much hotter than it ever got in Deep Creek in the middle of a hot summer day, but Deep Creek was in the mountains. The temperatures were supposed to be in the 90s that day and even though I hadn't done that much I had worked up a sweat. This was going to get some getting used to, I thought to myself.

"I think I'll take you up on that. It's a little hotter down here than what I'm used to," I responded.

"Yeah, I'll bet Deep Creek Lake is a great place to be in the summer time."

"It is."

"You'll like our winters," he responded.

"That's what I've heard."

Randy turned and started walking back to the office. "Take your time. I have a few things to get ready before you get there."

When I was showered and changed, I walked back to the office and found Randy sitting at a desk overlooking the water with his head down, writing. I knocked. He looked up and said, "Come in. Have a seat."

I sat down.

"I like what I see and I'm prepared to offer you a job." He handed me a file folder with several sheets of paper inside. "This is a formal employment contract and it has all the information you'll need, I think. It explains our benefits package and our rules and regulations. So there is no misunderstanding, I don't tolerate habitual tardiness and I won't tolerate any drinking on the job or during the lunch break, or anyone coming to work who still has the effects of drinking from the night before. Other than that, you come to work, do your job and you'll do just fine here.

"Occasionally we have some personnel problems, like when guys just don't get along with one another and they can't work together. That doesn't happen too often, but if it does, we should find that out fairly soon. You'll be on probation for 90 days. I should think that any problems you have with us or we have with you will come to the surface in that time. How does that sound?"

"I'd like to have some time to look these over and talk things over with my wife," I said.

"No problem. I wouldn't expect anything else. Do you think you can get back to me by this afternoon or will you need more time?"

"I'll go back to the hotel, talk to my wife, and get back to you before noon with a response. How's that?"

"I usually eat my lunch at my desk, but today I've got an appointment out of the office from 11:30 until 1:00. How about you come back to see me at 1:00?"

"Will do," I said.

We stood, shook hands, and I left.

When I got back to the Holiday Inn it was 9:00. Rebecca was up, showered, dressed, and ready for breakfast. I had noticed a French bakery a few blocks down First Street, just past April's Eatery, called Barra Bread, and we went there. She had some coffee and a pastry and listened attentively as I told her everything that had happened while she'd been sleeping. She immediately took the folder and began reading it as I spoke.

After about ten minutes, she looked up from the paperwork and said, "So you really want to take this job, don't you, George?"

"I'd much rather be working and living with you in Maryland in the house we own but that doesn't seem to be an option. This is the only option I have right now."

"But you haven't even looked around for another job yet," she said.

"You know the job market up there as well as I do. Don't forget, I was out of work for a while before I got to McHenry. Besides, there's nothing else like what I had up there with Bill in McHenry or anywhere close by. I'd have to drive at least an hour, maybe more, to find work, especially during the winter months."

"There are other things that you can do," she pleaded.

"Yeah, I'm sure there are but I'm a mechanic. I always have been and I expect I always will be," I responded.

"But what about me?"

"You mean, what about us?"

"Yes, that's what I mean. You know what I mean."

"I don't want to do this without you. If you're not sure this is the right thing to do I'll tell him that we'll need a little more time to decide, but I'd like to give this a lot of thought before I turn it down."

"You really think this is that good of a job, George?"

"Yes, I do. Don't you?"

"It all looks good on paper. I haven't met this man so I have to trust you on that part."

"You want to meet him?"

"No, that's not the part that worries me."

"What does?"

"Everything else…leaving Maryland, leaving my family, leaving my job, my school, my friends…everything."

She started to sob a little. I put my arms around her and said that I thought we ought to give it a try. If we didn't like it, we could always move back. I felt it was better to have a job and be looking for another one than not to have any job at all.

We talked about her schooling and how all that would work. There was a Community College in Ft. Myers she could look into. We also talked about what we could do with the house and where we would live. I didn't have all the answers. I didn't have any of the answers but I was as sure as I could be that this was better than what I'd be doing up there. I remembered those years of working in a gas station, driving a delivery truck and being on the road for weeks at a time driving an eighteen wheeler. This was a whole lot better than anything I'd seen up that way. I liked working around the water. It beat a hot, sweaty gas station any day.

We sat there talking for almost three hours. I must have been pretty persuasive because, finally, she agreed with me that it would be best for us if I accepted the job. Her exact words were, "Do whatever you think is best."

We agreed that she'd stay up in Maryland until I could find us a place to live and that she'd stay in school for the time being. That meant we'd be apart for several months but I couldn't see any alternative. I didn't want that, and neither did she. We agreed that she would look around and do her best to find me a job up there that was as good, or even anywhere close to as good as the one I'd been offered.

We walked down to the park and along the water. The sightseeing boats were out on their morning tours and wouldn't be back until after lunch. I still had over an hour before Randy would be back. We talked about driving over to Orlando and Disney later that afternoon, as we had planned, but she said she wanted to look around Ft. Myers for a place for us to live since it looked like it was going to be our new home.

We got in the car and started to drive around. When we drove a few blocks south on U.S. 41 out of the downtown area, we came to a tourist attraction about Thomas Edison and Henry Ford. We stopped to have a look. Both men had huge estates on Deep Creek Lake but we hadn't known that they also had winter homes in Ft. Myers.

Sometime during the 1920s they had built themselves large houses on the water, right next to each other, no more than a mile outside of downtown as a place to come during the winter. The houses weren't extravagant. They each had gardens and had a few out-buildings where they worked on various projects. The Edison mansion and grounds had been given to the city of Ft.

Myers and was the tour. The Ford family still owned Henry's property and that was off-limits. We walked through the Edison house and cottages and saw all the beautiful flowers and plants.

There were twenty acres of tropical plants and bushes. There were five hundred unique species of plants. Supposedly, the men worked on those things together and created some hybrids and new species. Some of the trees had been planted by the men way back when.

After we finished the tour it was almost 1:00. Rebecca came with me to meet Randy. She promised to keep a positive attitude towards the whole deal, at least in front of him.

Randy was glad to hear that I'd be coming to work with him, and wanted to know when I could start. I told him that we were flying back on Sunday and that I'd pack up, turn around and be back by Tuesday if he wanted me to. He told me to take my time and that I could start the following Monday.

I asked about places to rent and he gave us a few suggestions. We couldn't buy a house until we sold the one we had. Rebecca wasn't ready to make that bold a move anyway. I needed to find a place where I could rent on a short-term basis, if possible.

Rebecca and I found a restaurant on the water about a mile from the Marina called Hurricane Bob's. We bought a paper and started looking for a place to stay over a fresh grouper sandwich.

We looked at a few places and then stumbled on a small apartment complex with some vacancies late in the afternoon. It wasn't far from the Holiday Inn or from where I would be working. It was going to be torn down in six months and people were already starting to move out. I signed a month-to-month lease with the understanding that I'd have to vacate in six months but I could leave at any time.

We had dinner at a French restaurant a few doors down from the Italian place we had eaten at the night before. We liked being able to walk places. It was a bit somber as Rebecca wasn't happy with the prospect of living apart for a while and neither was I. We'd only been married a few months and everything was still new to us. The honeymoon hadn't ended, but it was about to.

We spent the next morning driving around neighborhoods and taking flyers from mailboxes to see what things cost. In the afternoon, we ended up in a beautiful area called Sanibel Island, about half an hour from where we were staying. It was fifteen miles of beaches. At the end of the island was another one called Captiva Island, but we didn't go that far. We walked a long way, stopping every few yards to look at unusual shells.

Neither of us was used to the August sun in Florida and we were burned before we knew it. We bought hats, long-sleeved shirts and Coppertone at one of the many novelty stores but it was too late. We had to go back to the room and get out of the sun.

We checked out of our room the next morning a little later than we planned and drove back to Tampa. Our flight didn't leave until late in the afternoon and we spent a few hours at a Marine Aquarium in the downtown area, not far from the airport. We had planned on going to Busch Garden but by the time we got to Tampa we wouldn't have had enough time to enjoy it.

We didn't talk much about my decision to accept the job, since it was a done-deal. I think Rebecca's plan was to find me another job as fast as she could, which would have been fine with me. I didn't want to move to Ft. Myers. I felt like I had to. I didn't have a choice as far as I was concerned, and I was thankful to Mr. Sullivan for finding me a job. It looked like a good place to work and a nice place to live. I was going to make the best of it.

CHAPTER NINE
Fort Myers, Florida

WORKING AS A BOAT mechanic at Randy's place suited me just fine. The only bad part was being away from Rebecca. There was a bar right across the street where the other three mechanics and I would go for a beer most every night after work. We didn't usually have more than one or two and didn't stay more than an hour, if that. It was more of a social get-together to talk shop. We didn't get to visit with each other much during the day even though we worked side-by-side. Every few days, maybe once a week, Randy would join us, which was good.

A few of the boat owners would occasionally stop in after coming off the water and I made a few friends that way. Other than that, I didn't know anyone and had nothing to do after work. I got in the habit of going to the bar, then back to the apartment, where I would eat, maybe watch a little TV and then be in bed before 10:00.

I'd call Rebecca every night and we'd talk for ten or fifteen minutes before we went to sleep. She missed me and I missed her but she had all of her family and friends to look after her. I didn't have anyone. After about three weeks of living alone, the nightmares started to get worse. One night I had a bad one which woke up one of my neighbors.

It was the one about my days on the Chinook and our supposed allies, the South Vietnamese. Things were never too good between Americans and the ARVNs. They were supposed to be the ones doing most of the fighting but it didn't work out that way, at least not while I was there. Maybe it was that way back when our guys were military advisors, but once our combat troops hit the ground in 1965 it was all us.

There were reports of South Vietnamese soldiers getting off helicopters, like mine, and shooting the crew as they did. One of my jobs as crew chief was to have my gun locked and loaded and ready to fire if one tried that on our ship. There were lots of times when we had to force them to jump off our craft at gunpoint because if they didn't get off we'd either have to leave and take them back with us or get shot at while waiting for them to get off. We wanted them off as fast as possible.

So this nightmare has me watching ARVNs who are refusing to get out because some enemy fire was hitting the sides of our Chinook. The pilot is yelling at me to get them off. I'm yelling at them to get off. The gunners are looking the other way, trying to shoot the people who are shooting at us, and four or five of the ARVNs open fire on us. They hit the pilot, the co-pilot and the gunners before I can kill them. My buddies are still alive, but they're dying and they're all saying, "George, you were supposed to protect us. Why didn't you? Why didn't you?" I'm crying telling them there was nothing I could do, there were too many of them, but that I had killed them all. Then they close their eyes and die, their last words being…"but George, you were supposed to protect us," and I woke up crying.

That never happened to me but something similar to that did. One night when I was still a mechanic with the wheels and tracks, before I transferred to the Chinook, some of our guys died because of what one of our supposed allies did. It was during a time when we were trying to train the ARVNs to handle the artillery and fight for themselves so we could get out of Vietnam altogether. This was after Nixon had been in office for over a year and was reducing the number of troops on the ground as much as he could as fast as he could to appease the American public while still trying to win the war.

One night, while I'm trying to sleep, we start getting incoming artillery rounds. We run for our bunkers, but the shelling goes on and on for what seems like an hour, and it is coming from behind us, from where our own artillery base was. We knew something was wrong but we had no idea what it was.

Come to find out, an ARVN crew had changed the coordinates and was purposefully hitting our compound. When someone finally discovered what was going on, the ARVNs were killed, but not before we lost aircraft, buildings and soldiers. The Viet Cong were just regular people, fighting to rid Americans from their land. They didn't wear uniforms and could be the cleaning men and women during the day and then go out and fire mortars at us at night, after they found out where everything was on base. Or they could be soldiers in the South Vietnamese Army. That was a huge part of the problem. We didn't know who the enemy was unless he, or she, wore an NVA uniform or was firing a gun at us.

There was nothing we could do. Nobody wore name tags. We couldn't speak the language and oftentimes we didn't trust whoever it was that was translating for us. All we could do was protect each other and try not to get killed. Sometimes in my dreams I'd be having a conversation with some smiling Vietnamese person and then, in an instant, the person would morf into some deadly killer trying to cut my head off.

I didn't mention it to Rebecca at first, hoping that it was a one-time thing, but when it happened again a few days later, I did. The manager came and talked to me about the problem. I kept all of the windows closed after that, no matter what the weather was like outside.

After talking things over with her, we agreed that I should find a dog. I did, at the animal shelter. We thought that maybe the nightmares had gotten worse because I was lonely and that maybe the companionship of a pet would help. She wasn't finding any jobs for me and was talking about taking a semester off from school, her last semester before she got her AA, and moving down in January. We decided that there was no reason to wait and that I should get the dog right away.

I picked out a female cross between a Golden Retriever and something else that weighed about 50 pounds. She wasn't a puppy but she was still young, maybe a year old or so. She didn't bark much, which was good. The apartment owners didn't care about her trashing the apartment, but a barking dog, especially while I was at work, wouldn't have been acceptable. Dogs hadn't been allowed in the apartments before but since they planned to tear the building down and build a high-rise it didn't make any difference. We named her Bailey.

With the dog, I couldn't stay as long at the bar after work. I had to walk Bailey. Rebecca chose the name. On weekends, I'd take Bailey to the beach. She loved the water and would chase balls until my arms would tire out. She was tireless.

Things were going well at work. All the guys were good to work with and I didn't have any trouble doing the work. Whenever I didn't know something about an engine I hadn't worked on before, the other guys would help out. It wasn't like one was trying to out-do the other.

The days turned into weeks and the weeks into months. Before I knew it, my 90 day probationary period was over and it was Thanksgiving. We had the long weekend off. I flew home after work on Wednesday and arrived back in McHenry late that night. Rebecca was up, waiting with open arms.

Rebecca and I were happiest when we were together. Married life was good for both of us. The thought never entered our minds, at least it never entered my mind, that maybe this wasn't going to work. We were going to make it work.

We had Thanksgiving dinner at her parents' house and my parents joined us. Rebecca and I sat close to one another all day long, holding hands like we were still the newly-wed couple that we were.

That weekend we talked about how we didn't want to keep living in different places. Since she hadn't found me another job, and since I was happy with the job I had, the only option was for her to move down to Ft. Myers to be with me.

I was making enough money for her to come down and do nothing but go to school. She could finish up down there within six months so long as she didn't lose too many credits by transferring.

If she agreed to move down to Ft. Myers, she could do that as soon as the semester ended. We could stay at the apartment for a couple of months before we had to be out. That would give us some time to find a place. I was hoping that's what she would decide to do, but I left it up to her.

Sunday rolled around and it was time for me to go. She still hadn't made a decision. She planned to talk to a counselor at school and find out, for sure, how many courses would transfer and then decide. If Lee County refused to accept too many of her courses, it wouldn't make much sense for her to transfer and lose all those credit hours she'd worked so hard to get. If Lee County accepted enough of her credits, it sounded like she'd make the move.

The flight back to Florida was a lonesome journey. The drive from the airport to my apartment was worse. I missed being with her and kept asking myself if the job and the money were worth it. I kept reminding myself that I didn't have a choice. I didn't have any other job offers. Besides, I liked Ft. Myers and winter had already arrived in Maryland.

Ft. Myers is in the southwest part of Florida. I-75 makes a 90 degree turn at Ft. Myers and goes 80 some miles due east to somewhere between West Palm Beach and Ft. Lauderdale. Temperatures had been in the 30s in Maryland while I was there but the temperatures were in the high 70s and occasionally into the 80s in Ft. Myers during the day and at night the temperatures would occasionally get down into the 50s. That's when people would start to break out sweaters and sweatshirts.

I was sure that the weather in Florida was a factor in my favor. There was no doubt that Rebecca would like the warm temperatures in Ft. Myers a whole lot better than those freezing cold, bleak, nasty days and nights from December until April in the mountains of Western Maryland. If she didn't agree to move down for good on her own, I planned to fly her down for however long she had between semesters and have her spend as much time in the sun and on the beach as possible. If that didn't convince her, nothing would.

I had left Bailey in a kennel while I was gone, but it was too late to pick her up by the time I got back. I went to bed late that night praying that Rebecca would decide to move down. Despite the fact that I'd just had a great weekend with my wife who loved me, my parents and her parents, who loved me too, or maybe because of it, I was depressed. I had another nightmare that night.

This one was about the children. Most of the kids under the age of four ran around with no clothes on. If they had any clothes on, they were dirty. They had such sad eyes, like they knew their chances of having a life –like what the children of even the poorest people in the United States would have – weren't very good. They were always begging for money. I always gave them whatever change I had in my pocket. Of course, their money was so cheap to us that if I gave them hundreds of their coins, called dong, it amounted to about a penny.

When children ran up to any U.S. soldiers, I never saw a soldier turn them away. Everybody I ever saw always gave them something, even if it wasn't money – food, a trinket or something. This one time, though, in An Khe, while I was on an Armored Personnel Carrier picking up troops, I saw this little kid, who couldn't have been more than three, walk up to a group of about six soldiers who were standing around, waiting for orders to board the vehicle.

I watched as the kid walked right to the middle of the group. He had a little knapsack on his back but I didn't think anything of it. Neither did the soldiers. Just as one of the soldiers was reaching in his pocket for some change, the kid exploded, killing him and all the soldiers. I couldn't believe my eyes. Still can't. The Viet Cong had booby-trapped the kid.

When the bomb went off, I leapt up in bed, just as I had a hundred times before, panting. I couldn't fathom the depth of the hatred or despair that could make someone do that to a little kid. Still can't. They killed their own children just to kill some of us. They mercilessly tortured and slaughtered captured U.S. soldiers and South Vietnamese soldiers, even their countrymen who showed any friendliness to us at all. It was a horror to experience and a nightmare I kept experiencing.

I got a call from Rebecca the next night after I got home from picking up Bailey and taking her for a good long swim in the Gulf, which I enjoyed as much as Bailey did. All but one or two courses would be accepted for transfer. She was coming down in less than three weeks. I went to sleep happy, hoping that would keep away the bad dreams.

The next three weeks went by fast. I drove by the school where Rebecca would be going and looked for places to live close by. I'd heard that traffic got real bad during the winter months when all the snow-birds and winter visitors arrived. The week after Thanksgiving I noticed an increase in the number of cars on the roads. We started to get more boats in for storage and repair too.

As soon as her last class ended, Rebecca flew down to join me. Our plan was to drive back to Maryland and be there by Christmas, since I had the week after off. Provided Rebecca didn't change her mind between now and then, we'd load up our truck and come back down.

During the next two weeks Rebecca spent most of her time looking around for a place to live. Bailey was her constant companion. Rebecca immediately liked her. What was not to like? She was a friendly, happy dog that thought the whole world loved her and she loved everybody she saw. She wasn't much of a watch dog since she never barked and would wag her tail at anyone who came to the door.

The apartment complex was scheduled for demolition in two months. We wanted a house with a back yard where Bailey could run around and be outside during the day. Whatever Rebecca wanted was fine with me. Since we wouldn't have to give the landlord any notice we could move as soon as she found what she was looking for.

Rebecca found a two bedroom, one bath home in a quiet neighborhood called Island Estates, about fifteen minutes south of the downtown area. It was close to her school and not far from the water. We signed a year lease and could move in on January 1. It was only 1100 square feet, but that was enough for us. It had a fenced in back yard and seemed perfect.

Christmas is a nice time of year in Ft. Myers. Every year they have a big celebration they call the Festival of Lights and the whole area around the Edison Mansion is lit up with thousands upon thousands of Christmas lights. We walked through the area several times during those next two weeks. It would be our first Christmas together as husband and wife and we enjoyed being with each other more than ever after being apart for the last three months.

We spent most of the first weekend on the beach. Winter had come early to Western Maryland and the relentless cold had set in. Rebecca liked the warmth of the sun and the beautiful beaches of Sanibel and Captiva Islands. She especially liked walking the beach with Bailey and watching her swim after tennis balls we threw into the Gulf for her to chase.

Everything went according to plan and before we knew it, we were on the road up to Maryland. Moving is never fun. I think everything I owned would have fit in the back seat of the truck but Rebecca had more than I expected, a lot more.

I rented a twelve foot U-Haul trailer to pull behind the truck. We were able to get the beds, furniture and all of Rebecca's clothes into the truck and the trailer. After spending Christmas Day with our families, we headed south early the next morning. Rebecca had become as excited about making the move as I was. She'd never lived anywhere but in McHenry and once she accepted the fact that living in Ft. Myers was the best thing for us, she let go of her doubt and hesitance and enthusiastically accepted the challenges involved.

We settled into the new house without too many problems and within a few weeks things began to settle down. I got the feeling of happiness back that I had known during the first two months of our marriage. Every afternoon we'd take Bailey for a long walk through the neighborhood. We met all of our neighbors. Everyone was friendly. Bailey helped us make friends.

Once classes started, Rebecca turned her attention to her studies and she started to think about where she would work after graduation. She now wanted to be a legal assistant, or paralegal. She decided she didn't want to get into the medical field after all. She wanted to work in a civil law firm. But she also wanted to have a baby. We started talking about raising a family and if we could afford it on my salary alone.

It was a nice time for us. Everything was new and different, especially the weather and going to the beach in January. We were still in love with each other. I'd had a few relatively minor episodes with the nightmares, but nothing major since Rebecca had come down in mid December. I was happy. We were happy. Life was good again.

CHAPTER TEN
Trouble in Paradise

IT ALL CAME APART one day in early April. It happened completely unexpectedly. It was a Friday afternoon, a pay-day. It had been a good day, no problems, and I was in a fine mood. I had four crisp hundred dollar bills in my wallet and was thinking about what Rebecca and I would be doing that night when Randy asked me to help move a few boats. Jeff, the guy who usually took care of that, had gone home sick and boats were backed up.

An hour or so before quitting time I took a twenty foot Carolina Skiff out of the water. After I centered it between the forks and raised it up, and as I was backing up, about to take it to the barn to put it on its rack, this short, middle-aged man with no shirt and dark sunglasses came up from behind and started yelling to me. I couldn't understand what he was saying so I pushed back on the throttle, put it in neutral, put my foot on the brake, and let it idle, so I could hear him better.

He told me that he was in a hurry and I should put the Carolina Skiff down and get his boat out of the water and onto his trailer right then and there. I told him that I'd get to it as soon as I put the Skiff away, which wouldn't take long, but that didn't satisfy him. He wanted me to drop everything right then and there and take care of him.

I couldn't hear everything he was saying over the engine and it didn't seem as if he was understanding me too well, so I put the brake on, hopped off of my machine and explained to him as nicely as I could that I was a mechanic and I usually didn't have much to do with this kind of thing. I told him that it wouldn't take me more than five minutes to put it where it belonged. I told him, again, that I'd take care of him next.

That still didn't satisfy him. I explained that it would take me more time

84

to put the boat back in the water, secure it and start all over again with his boat than it would to just let me finish what I was doing. He moved a little closer to me and raised his voice a little, as if I wasn't understanding him or that I would understand him better if he yelled louder. It was obvious that he had been drinking. His breath had a strong smell of alcohol.

He had a New York accent and was talking to me like I should do whatever he said. I tried to be as nice to him as I could but nothing I said satisfied him. He kept saying he was in a hurry and had to get someplace. I don't remember where he said he had to go. I felt like telling him where he could go, but I didn't. I looked to see if I could find Randy or someone else to talk to this guy, but no one else was around.

After several minutes of that, I took a deep breath and politely asked him to back away and let me do my job. I told him for the fourth time that I would get to it just as soon as I could. I turned my back and hopped up on the fork lift, released the brake, put it in reverse and started to push down on the throttle, but he was still standing there, blocking my path. I couldn't move until he got out of the way and he wasn't getting out of the way. I sat there just looking at him, not saying a word, and he stood there looking at me, not moving.

Finally, I put the brake back on, turned the engine off and said, "I'm going to get my manager. I've told you that I'll get to your boat just as soon as I'm finished with this one, but that isn't good enough for you, so you wait right here and I'll be right back. We'll do whatever he says, how's that?"

Before I could get away, he gets between me and the office and says that he paid a lot of money to keep his boat, which looked like it was relatively new and hadn't been used much, at our marina. It had two large Yamaha four-strokes on the back, and was clearly an expensive rig. He said if I didn't get his boat out of the water in the next five minutes he was going to take his boat and put it somewhere else, at another marina. Then he called me a name…he called me a 'fucking' moron – and he pushed me.

At first, I backed up and didn't say anything, but I was fuming. I tried to walk around him, but he blocked me. He must have sensed that I was afraid of doing anything to him because he was a customer. He could say whatever he wanted to me and I wasn't going to do anything about it. So he pushed me again and said, "Get that damn thing off of your lift and get my boat out of the water –Now! I'm a paying customer and I'll have your miserable minimum-wage job if you don't." He swore at me again and he pushed me again, saying "Now get up there and do it!"

I don't remember much of anything after that.

The next day, I woke up on a hospital bed with my hands and feet tied. I felt pain in the back of my head and my shoulders. My wrists and my feet hurt from the restraints. I had to go to the bathroom. My head hurt, my back hurt, my neck hurt. I'd never been restrained like that, ever. I called out, crying for help but nobody came.

As I lay there, I began to piece together what had happened. I could remember the argument and I had a very vague recollection of being in a fight. I didn't know who they were but I could see myself fighting back. That was as much as I could recall and even that was a blur.

An attendant finally came to the side of my bed. He was a tall, thin, African-American with a gentle voice. He calmly explained to me that he wasn't allowed to take off the restraints but that he would call the police officer and tell him that I was awake and responsive.

He told me that the pain in my head and shoulders was because I had bruises on me when I was brought in. They had cleaned me up as best they could. I could feel the bandages on me. I didn't remember any of that. He told me that I'd been given some heavy sedatives and had been sleeping for over twelve hours.

I was able to move my head from side to side and I could see that I was in a room by myself. The man told me that I'd caused quite a seen during the night, screaming and yelling, tossing and turning, trying to get loose, so they had moved me away from the other patients because of it.

The bed was unlike any hospital bed I'd ever seen before. It had extremely strong metal supports and heavy leather bindings with a protective layer of felt inside to keep me from injuring myself. There was a support for each of my hands and feet. There were two thick, leather straps across my torso too.

He told me that I had raged for quite a while, even after the sedatives kicked in. I'd kept the whole hall awake. He was surprised to find me as calm as I was. He told me he had no idea as to why I was there or if I would be going to jail or not.

Though he said he probably shouldn't be telling me, he read my chart and said that I had been given a heavy dose of thorazine soon after arrival at the hospital. The chart also showed the number of times nurses came by to check on me and that I had been moved twice because of the commotion I had caused. I had absolutely no recollection of any of that.

Other than feeling groggy and in pain, I was pretty much back to my normal self. Since nobody but the police could take the restraints off me, I was basically a prisoner, waiting until the police arrived. Rebecca was outside, trying to get in to see me, but they wouldn't let her in. I was in a ward where I wasn't allowed visitors. I wasn't able to use a phone since my hands were tied.

A cop came in about noon and took me to jail. I didn't know it, but he was the same one who had arrested me the day before. He asked me questions about what happened. I told him what I could remember but it wasn't much. I asked him how the guy was that I'd been in a fight with, but he wouldn't tell me. He said he didn't know.

Once I was processed into jail, given a uniform and placed in a cell, Rebecca was allowed to see me. The guard put me in a small room with a chair and a thick glass window. Rebecca was on the other side. I didn't know what to say. I tried to explain what happened but I couldn't. She was crying, looking at me as if she had been the one I had hit. All she could say was "What happened?" and "How could you."

She was scared, and so was I. I'd never been in trouble with the law before. I kept saying that I was so sorry for what had happened, but that didn't do any good. She kept crying. We sat there, unable to hold hands or touch each other. After half an hour, the guard came and told us that our time was up.

The next morning I was taken before a judge who told me that I was charged with Attempted Murder and Aggravated Battery, both second degree felonies, punishable by up to fifteen years in prison and a fine of up to $10,000. I learned that the man I'd been in the fight with was in critical condition. The judge said that if the man died, additional charges would undoubtedly be lodged against me.

The judge then asked me if I could afford a lawyer. I didn't know what to say. I'd never been in court before. The only thing I could think of was to say that I didn't know any lawyers, other than Mr. Sullivan, but he was from Maryland. She asked me a number of questions about how long I'd been in Florida, if I had a job, where I lived, how much money I made – all kinds of questions unrelated to the charges. In fact, she told me not to tell her anything about what had happened because whatever I said could be used against me.

When she found out I had a job, owned a home in Maryland and I hadn't lived in Florida for more than eight months, she told me that I made too much money or had too many assets, or both, to get a lawyer appointed to represent me. I'd have to find my own lawyer. She set my bond at $50,000 for each charge.

After I told Rebecca what had happened, and listened to her sob uncontrollably for ten minutes, I called Mr. Sullivan at his home in Cumberland, Maryland, even though it was a Sunday, collect. He told me that he didn't handle criminal cases and that I should have asked for a public defender. I explained that the judge had told me I didn't qualify for a court-appointed attorney. Mr. Sullivan said that he'd see what he could do. I gave him our home number and asked him to let Rebecca know whatever he was able to find out. He said he would.

By 4:00, when I hadn't heard back from Mr. Sullivan, I realized that

I wasn't going anyplace. I was thinking that I didn't intentionally hurt the guy. All I did was defend myself. To me, I hadn't done anything wrong. The thought hadn't entered my mind that I might be guilty of committing a serious crime that could send me to prison for a lot of years. I just wanted to get out of jail, go back to work, and back to my wife and our dog. I wasn't a criminal. I wasn't a danger to society. They were going to let me out. I was sure of it.

I blamed the guy I'd gotten in a fight with for everything that had happened. I had no idea what injuries I had inflicted on him but the judge had said he was in critical condition. I prayed he didn't die.

CHAPTER ELEVEN
Attempted Murder

RANDY CAME TO VISIT later that afternoon, shortly after 5:00. He had a look on his face that made me think he was the one in jail, not me. There wasn't a hint of a smile on his face. He asked how I was doing. I told him about the bond and all. He already knew about that and said he wished there was something he could do to get me out of jail, but there wasn't. He said he would help any way he could and that I should have my lawyer call him once I found one.

He asked what Rebecca was going to do if I wasn't able to get out. I hadn't thought about that as I was still thinking that somehow I was going to find a way to get out of jail soon. I told him I didn't know. He offered to help her with moving if she needed any. The more he talked, the more nervous I became. I realized he was thinking that I could be going away for a long time, not just stuck in jail for a week or two. He didn't even mention about when I might be coming back to work or if I had a job waiting for me when I did get out. I didn't ask.

He spoke in a very low voice like he didn't want anyone to hear what he had to say, even though the room was supposedly sound-proof so guys could talk to their attorneys and not have anyone hear the conversations. I hoped I didn't look as bad as he did. He was obviously deeply concerned about what had occurred.

After about twenty minutes, he said something about his insurance and that I might be getting a visit from a lawyer. I thought he meant a lawyer for me. He explained that it would be a lawyer for the marina.

It was then the thought occurred to me that he was more concerned about a lawsuit being filed against the marina than he was about the criminal charges against me, but I told myself not to think that. Randy really was a

89

nice man, I knew that. When I asked him about it, he said that since I was an employee of the marina, on duty, that the marina would more than likely be responsible for my actions. He was absolutely certain that the man would make a claim against the marina for all of his medical expenses and then some. He told me not to talk about the case to anyone in jail and that the lawyer would explain it when he came to see me. I hadn't thought about that aspect of the situation at all.

I asked if he was worried about losing his business. He said he had good insurance but he was afraid the insurance company would try to find a way to avoid paying whatever had to be paid. He told me again not to say anything to anybody until I talked to the lawyer. I asked if there was a chance the insurance company would pay for my lawyer and he said he didn't think so but I could ask. Then he said what I'd been thinking – things would be a whole lot worse if the man died or was really seriously injured, brain-damaged. He had a hard time believing that I wasn't able to give him more details about what happened, but I couldn't.

I asked him if he knew how the man was. He didn't. He said he was going to go to the hospital to see what he could find out. I asked him to call Rebecca and make sure she was alright. He said he would. I felt a whole lot worse after he left than I did before he came.

Since I couldn't remember hardly any of the details about how it happened, I still didn't feel like I'd committed a crime. Apparently I wasn't going to be able to deny that I'd beaten the guy up, but he started it. He pushed me. He called me names. I just reacted. To my way of thinking, I acted in self-defense.

I was having a hard time with the idea that I had done something so bad that I was going to be kept in jail or sent to prison. I didn't go around getting in fights. I hadn't been in a fight my whole life, not even in Vietnam. I didn't know the law and everyone I talked to told to keep my mouth shut until I got an attorney. But I didn't have the money to get an attorney, so I couldn't talk to anyone about anything.

Jail wasn't as bad as I thought it might be. It was bad, just not as bad as I envisioned it. Not that I ever envisioned me being in jail, but I'd seen enough movies and television shows to have some idea of what it was like. It was one large room with about fifty guys in it, with several rows of bunk beds.

Everybody seemed to know what I was in for and gave me a wide berth. I was one of the smaller guys in the cell but they must've thought I was crazy or maybe they'd heard I was a Vietnam Vet and was dangerous. For whatever reason, no one bothered me and I didn't bother anyone else. I recognized a few of the guys from the day I was in front of a judge. They would have heard all about my background and what I was charged with. That must have been how they knew about me, I figured.

Rebecca came to visit that afternoon. She was only allowed to stay for half an hour though. There were only a few rooms for inmates to see family, friends or their lawyers. The lawyers always came first. Before our half hour was up, a guard came in and told us we had to get out because a lawyer was there to see her client and there were no rooms available.

The days went slowly. Every day I expected a call or a message from Mr. Sullivan. He was my only chance, but he was up in Maryland. Rebecca made some phone calls. Once the lawyers found out that we didn't have much money, they turned her down. Mr. Sullivan called Rebecca and told her that he'd made a few phone calls to the attorneys he knew in Lee County but none of them practiced criminal law. He hadn't had any luck yet. He also told her that he had talked to a few criminal defense lawyers in Lee County but they all wanted an awful lot of money, which I didn't have. Nobody could give me any information on how the guy I'd been in a fight with was doing other than he was still in the hospital.

By the fourth day I decided to take things into my own hands. I called one of the bail bondsmen whose name was on the wall next to the communal phone. He came over later that day. The guy's name was Joey and his face brightened when he heard I owned property, even though it was in Maryland. He said he'd look into it and get back to me. He told me that he knew a couple of young attorneys who might be willing to talk to me, especially after I told him that I had a couple of thousand dollars in the bank.

I didn't know what to do. I didn't have enough money to get myself out of jail, I didn't have enough money to hire a lawyer, but I didn't qualify for the services of a public defender. It seemed like most everybody else in the cell with me had public defenders. The ones who had private attorneys seemed to get out of jail real quick. It was only the guys with no money, or really serious charges against them, who were stuck in jail, like me.

One good thing, though it wasn't all that good, really, was that I had a bad nightmare the third night I was there. It was the one about the ARVNs refusing to get out of our Chinook and all of my friends being killed before I could do anything to save them. Apparently, I screamed so loud it woke everybody up. When the guards came in and woke me, I was fine, but people moved their beds away from me. I guess I made a big scene. The other prisoners seemed to steer clear of me even more after that.

Other than that one time, I didn't have too many nightmares, at least not at first. I wasn't comfortable being there and I slept like I did when I was in Vietnam, like something was about to happen at any time, and it usually did. There were always fights going on, some guy hitting on a smaller, weaker prisoner, or racial things. It was one thing or another, and sometimes it was over stupid stuff of no consequence at all. Most every night, and sometimes more than once a night, the lights would come on and guards would rush into the room with night sticks in hand and break up some disturbance or search someone's property. It was always something. I didn't sleep well at all, but when I did fall into a deep sleep I'd have a nightmare and wake everyone else up.

Rebecca became more and more depressed as each day went by, even more so than I was. I had to do my best every time we talked to cheer her up even though I was the one in jail looking at thirty years in prison. After I'd been in jail for almost ten days, a guard called me out on a Saturday, late in the afternoon, to tell me that I had a visitor, a lawyer. I had no idea who it was.

I sat down on the plastic chair and saw a short, balding man in a black suit with a bright pink tie on opposite me, who seemed to be about my age. He had pale, white skin like he didn't get out in the sun much, with no facial hair. He told me his name was Robert Tylor and he'd been given my name by Joey, the bail bondsman.

He said he'd looked at the court file and also checked with the hospital about the condition of the man I'd hit. I let out a huge sigh when he told me that the guy was no longer in critical condition, and he was out of the hospital. Mr. Tylor said that from what he was able to find out, the guy had a broken nose, two black eyes, bruises all over his face and head, and he was still being checked for possible brain damage. Apparently he was out of danger of dying, though, and that was good news for me.

He handed me two sheets of paper. He explained that these were copies of the Florida Statutes I was charged with violating. He thought I'd like to see for myself what they said. He knew about my property in Maryland and that I had some money in the bank. He told me I was in some serious trouble and his usual fee for representing a person charged with two second degree felonies was $50,000, or $25,000 apiece. He said he'd be willing to take my case if I could come up with $25,000 in cash. He wouldn't accept a note secured by the property.

I glanced at the two sheets of paper as he was speaking. He told me they were for me to keep and I could read them later.

I told him I had about having $4,000 in the bank but that my wife, who wasn't working, was going to need that money. I also told him that unless I could get out of jail and go back to work I didn't have any money to pay him. We still owed a lot of money on the house we owned and I doubted that we could borrow any money against it. He said that I might have to sell it. I told him I didn't want to do that.

He said that if I would give him $1500 that he would file a Notice of

Limited Appearance and try to get my bond reduced. He said that Joey was still working on a way to use the land as collateral for my bond. If he could get my bond reduced it would make it easier for Joey to go the bond for me and then I could go back to work and maybe find a way to come up with his fee.

I told him I'd have to talk it over with my wife to see what she thought about that. He said that was understandable, handed me his card as he stood, and told me to give him a call after I'd talked to her.

Rebecca came later that afternoon and I told her all about the visit from Mr. Tylor. Rebecca said she was thinking she'd have to go back to Maryland, get her old job back, and move back in with her parents. She didn't want to live in our house without me and it would save us money on the heating bills and all. She would fix the house up as best she could so that it would sell faster if that became necessary. It made sense, but I didn't want to see that happen. My whole world was falling completely apart.

We talked for an hour. No one else was waiting to use the visitation room and she cried the whole time until the guards came to tell us she had to leave. Before she left, we agreed that I'd use $1500 of our remaining cash to pay Mr. Tylor to get my bond reduced, if he could. She'd take the rest and go to Maryland if I wasn't able to get out and go back to work after the hearing.

I called Mr. Tylor Monday morning and gave him the news. He came to see me late the next day. That same day, before he got there, I received a notice of preliminary hearing in the mail. Apparently the law required that I be taken before a judge after being in jail twenty one days to make certain that there were sufficient grounds for them to continue to keep me in jail pending trial.

Mr. Tylor had me sign a retainer agreement which basically said he was representing me only for the purpose of filing a motion to reduce bond but when I showed him the notice of hearing he agreed to represent me at the preliminary hearing too, since the motion to reduce bond would be heard at the same time. I told him that Rebecca would bring the cash to his office. The agreement wasn't binding until he received the cash.

Mr. Tylor asked me to tell him what I could remember about what happened that day since an attorney/client relationship had been established, anything and now everything I said to him was privileged and confidential. I told him what I could remember, which wasn't much, other than that the man provoked me by pushing and shoving me and calling me names. He seemed displeased that I couldn't provide more details but said that it wasn't critical because I wouldn't be testifying at the hearing anyway. He said that the State would be required to call witnesses and present evidence, not the defense. He could learn all about the case against me at that time.

After I was taken back to my cell, I read the papers he had given me. The first one said:

Florida Statute 782.04, Murder

1. When perpetrated from a premeditated design to effect the death of the person killed or any human being, it is murder in the first degree and constitutes a capital offense, punishable by death;
2. The unlawful killing of a human being perpetrated by any act imminently dangerous to another and evincing a depraved mind regardless of human life, although without any premeditated design to effect the death of any particular individual, is murder in the second degree and constitutes a felony of the first degree, punishable by imprisonment for a term of years not exceeding life in prison;

Florida Statute 777.04, Attempts, solicitation, and conspiracy

1. Any person who attempts to commit an offense prohibited by law and in such attempt does any act toward the commission of such offense, but fails in the perpetration or is intercepted or prevented in the execution thereof, commits the offense of criminal attempt;
2. If the offense attempted is a life felony, or a felony of the first degree, the offense of criminal attempt to commit that crime is a felony of the second degree, punishable by a term of imprisonment not to exceed fifteen years.

The next paper read:

Florida Statute 784.045: Aggravated Battery
  A person commits aggravated battery who, in the course of committing a battery:

1. Intentionally and knowingly causes great bodily harm, permanent disability, or permanent disfigurement.
2. Whoever commits aggravated battery shall be guilty of a felony of the second degree, punishable by a term of imprisonment not to exceed fifteen years.

The crime of battery occurs when one:

1. Actually or intentionally touches or strikes another person against the will of the other person; or
2. Intentionally causes bodily harm to another person;
3. A person who commits the crime of battery is guilty of a misdemeanor of the first degree, punishable by a term of imprisonment not exceeding one year.

Since the man hadn't died and wasn't going to die, it seemed as if I might be alright so long as he didn't have any permanent disability or permanent disfigurement. He had a broken nose. That's not all that serious, I thought. So long as there was no brain damage, maybe things wouldn't be so bad. I was hoping for the best, for him and for me. A charge of battery still meant the possibility of a year in jail, but I didn't intentionally hit him, and I certainly didn't want to kill him. I was defending myself. In my mind, I was innocent of any wrongdoing.

CHAPTER TWELVE
The Preliminary Hearing

ON THE TWENTY FIRST day after I was arrested, I was taken to court in a van along with several other men for my preliminary hearing. I was wearing the orange jumpsuit all county prisoners were issued. It had my inmate numbers on the front and back. My hands were chained behind me and my feet were chained together just far enough so I could move forward with a shuffle. There was a chain that connected the chains on my hands to the chains on my feet. There was also a chain that connected me to the prisoners in front and behind me.

When we were brought in the courthouse, most of us were brought into the same courtroom. We were put in the jury box. Just before we all entered the courtroom, the bailiff took the chains that connected us to each other off. Just before we all sat down, the chains that connected our hands to our feet were taken off next, but he left our handcuffs and the chains on our feet on. Once I was seated, I looked over and saw Mr. Tylor sitting in the back of the courtroom.

After about a dozen or so cases were heard, mine was called. I stood and shuffled towards the table where defendants like me sat, escorted by a bailiff who kept a hand on my elbow. I sat next to Mr. Tylor. I noticed by the name plate on the bench that my judge was Anthony M. Marcolo.

Once I was seated, the judge, who was a short, stout man with black hair, thick glasses and large black frames, said, "You are George Patrick Murphy, I assume?"

I responded, "Yes, sir, I am."

"Good morning, Mr. Murphy. The purpose of this hearing is to determine if there is reasonable cause to believe that you have committed the offenses with which you are charged, which are attempted murder and aggravated battery. Is the State prepared to proceed?"

A tall, thin man, who seemed to be about my age, seated at the table next to us stood and said, "Yes, your Honor, we are."

"You may proceed, Mr. Snyder."

"The State calls Deputy Stewart, your Honor."

I turned and saw the deputy who had taken me from the hospital to the Lee County Jail walk through the double swinging doors that led from the area where the general public sat to the inner courtroom. Rebecca was sitting in the first row right behind me. She was dressed in her Sunday's finest, looking glum. She mustered a smile and held up crossed fingers on both hands. Like me, she was hoping that somehow something good would happen today.

After the Deputy was sworn, he stated his name and began to answer questions asked of him.

"At approximately 18:50 hours on Friday, April 3rd of this year, I received a call from dispatch instructing me to proceed to the Caloosahatchee River Marina where a physical disturbance of some kind was occurring. I was told that Lee County Rescue had been dispatched to the scene and there was at least one, and possibly more injured persons. I happened to be the unit closest to that location and arrived within two minutes of being dispatched. Upon my arrival, I observed a man who I later determined to be the defendant, George Patrick Murphy, fighting with four other men, who I later determined to be the owner of the business and three of his employees. I observed that another man was laying on the ground, bleeding profusely from his nose and mouth.

"I immediately exited my car and ordered the men to cease fighting. The four men backed away from Mr. Murphy, who continued to swing his fists and pursue the men. I pulled my night stick from its holster and ordered Mr. Murphy to cease, but he did not obey my command. Instead, he turned towards me and approached me in a menacing manner. When he got within two feet of me, I hit him once across his right shoulder, which caused him to fall to one knee momentarily.

"Within seconds, however, he began to rise to his feet, yelling obscenities. I swung again, hitting him on top of his head, which I did not intend to do. I was trying to hit him in the back. When I hit him on the head, he fell to the ground and was momentarily unconscious.

"I then put his arms behind his back and placed handcuffs on him. With the assistance of two of the men who had been in an altercation with Mr. Murphy, I placed Mr. Murphy in back of my squad car.

"While I was in the process of subduing Mr. Murphy, Lee County Fire

Rescue arrived. They were attending to the victim, a Mr. Edward Kuhn, who appeared to be unconscious and unresponsive. Before I could attempt to make contact with Mr. Kuhn, and while I was in the process of placing Mr. Murphy in my squad car, they placed him on a stretcher and took him away.

"I then proceeded to take Mr. Murphy to the Lee County Hospital, which was only a few blocks away. I took him directly to the psychiatric ward"

"Let me interrupt you for a moment, Deputy Stewart. Please tell the Court why you took Mr. Murphy to the psychiatric ward of a hospital instead of directly to jail," the attorney for the State asked.

"From my observations of Mr. Murphy's behavior, and from what little information I was able to gather from Mr. Murphy's employer and fellow employees, it seemed to me to be the best thing to do. I didn't want to take him to central booking if he was going to act the way I had seen him act. I felt that he could be a threat to my safety and the safety of jail personnel."

"Was Mr. Murphy conscious when you did so?"

"I don't believe so. He was lying in the back seat of my vehicle, slumped over, making strange noises."

"Strange noises, Deputy? Can you be more specific?"

"Loud and disturbing. It sounded like an animal, like a bear or something. At times, his body shook violently, too. In fact, he kicked the inside of my vehicle so violently that he broke the rear window on the driver's side, which had to be replaced before I could use the vehicle again."

"Please tell the court what happened upon your arrival at the hospital, Deputy."

"I had called ahead and told hospital personnel I was bringing in a man who I believed was in need of immediate psychiatric care and treatment. When I pulled into the circular driveway three male nurses were waiting for me. They took Mr. Murphy from my vehicle and placed him on a stretcher. I removed my handcuffs after they placed secure restraints on him. They wheeled him into the hospital. He was still in a semi-conscious state and there was no problem in doing so."

"What did you do next, Deputy?"

"I parked my vehicle and went into the hospital where I filled out a number of forms."

"I show you what has been marked at Exhibit 1 for identification purposes only and ask you to tell the court what these are."

"These are copies of the forms I filled out at the hospital. Some of the writing on there isn't mine, but the narrative part is."

"What was your next involvement in this case, Deputy?"

"After I made certain that Mr. Murphy was safely in their custody, I returned to the Caloosahatchee River Marina to interview witnesses in order to prepare my report."

"Did you direct hospital personnel to administer thorazine to the Defendant at that time, Deputy?"

"I did not. I do not have the authority to do that, only a medical doctor can do that."

"Did you later find out that thorazine, which is a heavy sedative, had been administered to Mr. Murphy?"

"Yes. After I finished my investigation at the Marina, I returned to the hospital to see if I could take a statement from Mr. Murphy and formally place him under arrest."

"Were you able to do that, Deputy?"

"No. Upon my return to the hospital, which was several hours later, I found Mr. Murphy in an isolated room, lying in a bed, with restraints on. He was not conscious. I asked hospital personnel to call me when he came to. I was scheduled to be off the next day, so I told them to call the police station and have them call me on my cell phone so that I could follow up on this investigation properly."

"Before we go any further regarding Mr. Murphy, please tell the court what you learned upon your return to the Marina that afternoon."

Mr. Tylor stood and said, "I object, your Honor, to any statements made by persons who will not be testifying in court here today. Any such statements are hearsay."

The judge looked over at him and seemed to sneer as he said,

"Your objection is over-ruled, Mr. Tylor. The purpose of this hearing is to determine if there are reasonable grounds to believe that the defendant committed the crimes with which he is charged. This is not a trial. Please proceed, Mr. Snyder."

"You may answer, Deputy, if you recall the question. Do you?"

"Yes, I do. I spoke with Randy Cross, the owner of the Marina, as well as three men who work as mechanics at the Marina, whose names are in my report. I spoke to them only briefly. Most of the information in my report comes from Mr. Cross."

"What did Mr. Cross tell you, Deputy?"

"Mr. Cross told me that Mr. Murphy was an employee of his and had been working for him as a mechanic for over six months. He said that Mr. Murphy had been an excellent employee, that he had never exhibited any violent tendencies in the past and he had no idea what had caused Mr. Murphy to do what he had done that day."

"What did Mr. Cross say that Mr. Murphy had done that day, Deputy?"

"Mr. Cross told me that Mr. Murphy had been asked to operate a fork lift for a few hours that afternoon, taking boats out of the water and putting some boats in the water. Normally, that was not part of Mr. Murphy's job responsibilities. His job was to work on engines. He didn't usually have any contact with customers or with general public.

"Mr. Cross said that he was in his office, finishing up business for the week, when he heard a loud disturbance, raised voices. He looked out and saw Mr. Murphy on the ground on top of the victim, Mr. Kuhn, punching him. He also saw the other three mechanics running from their work area over to where Mr. Murphy and Mr. Kuhn were fighting. He immediately jumped up and ran out to where the men were, after calling 911 and asking that police and rescue personnel be sent to the scene.

"Mr. Cross and the others pulled Mr. Murphy off of Mr. Kuhn, but Mr. Murphy began to fight with them. He said that he and the others were struck several times by Mr. Murphy before I arrived. They were successful in keeping Mr. Murphy away from Mr. Kuhn."

"Did Mr. Cross have any idea what started the altercation between the two men, Deputy?"

"He did not."

"Were any of the other three men able to shed any light on that issue?"

"They were not. They saw the fight taking place and ran over to stop it."

"Please describe for the court what you were able to see of Mr. Kuhn's condition, Deputy."

"I looked over and saw nothing but blood. There was blood all over his face and torso, his shorts, his hair…there was blood on the ground…there was blood everywhere."

"Were you able to talk to Mr. Kuhn that day?"

"I was not. When I returned to the hospital and found Mr. Murphy unconscious or asleep, I went to find Mr. Kuhn. He was in the Emergency Room, being attended to by a team of physicians. I was told that he had sustained multiple wounds to the head and the doctors feared that a serious closed head injury may have resulted. I was told that Mr. Kuhn was still unconscious. I wasn't able to actually see him for myself nor was I able to talk to him at that time."

"What was your next involvement in this case, Deputy Stewart?"

"The next day, late in the morning, I received a phone call from the hospital informing me that Mr. Murphy was awake. I asked his condition and was told that he was coherent and responding appropriately to questions asked of him. They told me that he wanted to have the restraints taken off of him, but hospital personnel refused to do so until I authorized it. I immediately put on my uniform and went to the hospital."

"Please describe for the court the condition of Mr. Murphy upon your arrival."

"He was like a completely different person. After speaking to him for a few minutes, and discussing the case briefly with the staff, I decided that the restraints could be removed and that I could take him to the county jail for processing, which I did. I was able to place the hand-cuffs on him without any difficulty whatsoever. He cooperated with me completely."

"Did you attempt to take a statement from Mr. Murphy at that time?"

"After formally placing him under arrest, and advising him of his rights, I asked him to tell me what happened. He told me that all he could remember was that Mr. Kuhn had pushed him and called him names. He said he didn't remember anything else about the incident."

"He couldn't remember anything else?"

"That's what he told me."

"What was your next involvement in this case, Deputy?"

"After transporting Mr. Murphy to central booking and turning him over to them, I went back to the hospital to check on the condition of Mr. Kuhn."

"What did you find out?"

"Mr. Kuhn was in the critical care unit undergoing some tests at the time. From what I was told, there was still some concern about internal bleeding in the brain and the doctors were monitoring him closely."

"Was there any concern as to whether or not Mr. Kuhn might die as a result of the wounds inflicted upon him by Mr. Murphy, Deputy?"

Again, Mr. Tylor stood and said, "Objection, your Honor. The prosecutor is asking this officer to tell the court what the diagnosis was of medical experts. That is improper. It is a key element of the offense of murder and I don't believe the court should allow this witness to testify on that subject."

The judge looked over at Mr. Tylor and said, curtly, "Mr. Tylor, your objection is noted but it is over-ruled."

"Yes, your Honor, but..."

"You may proceed, Mr. Snyder."

"It was my understanding that medical personnel were concerned about internal bleeding in the cranium and the possibility of a potentially fatal hemorrhage, yes sir."

"Deputy Stewart, what charges did you place against Mr. Murphy at you formally arrested him?"

"I charged Mr. Murphy with Aggravated Battery. I knew, at the very least, that he had caused Mr. Kuhn grievous bodily harm. I also charged him with attempted murder. If Mr. Kuhn died, I would have charged him with second degree murder."

"I have no further questions of this witness, your Honor."

"Before I allow you to cross-examine Deputy Stewart, Mr. Tylor, I have a few questions to ask of the deputy," the Judge said.

"Deputy, I heard you testify that Mr. Murphy did damage to your vehicle. Did you charge Mr. Murphy with destruction of property?"

"I did not, your Honor, I…"

"Why not?"

"I felt that the two felonies were more important than a second degree misdemeanor. The damage done was less than $200 and…"

"I also heard you testify that Mr. Murphy approached you in a menacing fashion immediately prior to the time that you were forced to hit him with your night stick, is that correct, Deputy?"

"Yes, your Honor, it is."

"But you didn't charge him with resisting arrest with violence or even resisting arrest without violence. Why not?"

"Again, your Honor, I felt that the two felonies were sufficient."

"But you do believe that he committed both of those offenses, do you not?"

"I usually don't charge anyone with resisting with violence unless they actually put hands on me or have physical contact with me. He did not obey my command but he did not ever touch me, though he threatened to do so. Under these circumstances, a resisting charge might have been appropriate, but I chose not to do that."

"You understand that it is the State Attorney's responsibility to make such a determination ultimately, correct?"

"Yes sir. I present the facts to them at our internal investigation meeting and they decide what charges to file. I understand that completely."

"Alright, Deputy. Thank you. Mr. Tylor, you may cross-examine this witness if you care to do so. Oh, one more thing. Deputy, Mr. Cross told you that Mr. Murphy had been his employee for six months or so. Did you find out anything about how long he has lived in this community and a prior criminal record he might have?"

"Mr. Cross told me that Mr. Murphy had moved to Lee County from Maryland several months ago in order to take this job. I did not find any record of any prior arrests or convictions, your Honor."

"Thank you, Deputy. That's all I have. Mr. Tylor?"

Mr. Tylor stood and walked over to the podium in the center of the room where the other attorney had been standing, and said, "Good morning,

Deputy Stewart. Isn't it true that Mr. Murphy told you that Mr. Kuhn pushed him and cursed him?"

"That's true. I believed I testified to that, didn't I?"

"Yes, you did. My question to you is whether or not you took into consideration the fact that Mr. Murphy may have been defending himself against the actions of Mr. Kuhn and that Mr. Kuhn was the aggressor, not Mr. Murphy?"

"I took that possibility into consideration, sir, but that's not the reason why I charged him as I did. From what I was told by the witnesses, I determined that even if Mr. Kuhn did start the fight, or was the aggressor as you put it, Mr. Murphy went beyond simply defending himself by pummeling Mr. Kuhn into an unconscious state. All of the witnesses described to me what they saw and what they saw your client doing was hitting Mr. Kuhn repeatedly about the head and shoulders while sitting on top of him. That is inexcusable and constitutes the crime of aggravated battery, no matter what the degree of provocation was, in my opinion."

"Did you talk to Mr. Kuhn about how this incident got started?"

"I did. I went back to the hospital several days later. It might have been a week later. If I can look at my report…"

"By all means, go ahead," Mr. Tylor replied.

"Yes, as my report reflects, I went back the following week. Mr. Kuhn was out of the critical care unit and in a private room. He was scheduled to be discharged that same day, as I recall. He gave me a completely different version of events from what you have suggested may have occurred."

"I'm sorry, Deputy, but I haven't seen that statement and…"

"Also, if I might add, I spoke to him this morning and he told me the same thing, that Mr. Murphy was the aggressor."

"You spoke to him this morning?"

"Yes, he's standing out in the hallway right now."

"Well, I can ask him about what he told you but let me ask you this first, if all that Mr. Kuhn has as a result of the fight in question is a broken nose, and it heals okay, that doesn't constitute a permanent injury or permanent disfigurement, does it?

"That's not up to me, but my understanding of the law is that a broken bone, especially bones or cartilage in the nose, can be disfiguring and cause a permanent injury, which could only be corrected by a surgical procedure. There is still a possibility of permanent brain damage from what I understand but you'll have to ask the medical people about that."

"Thank you, Deputy. That's all I have."

Mr. Tylor slunk back to his chair next to me. He hadn't done much to improve my chances of getting out of jail and it seemed as if he may have made the judge mad by his objections.

"Call your next witness, Mr. Snyder," the judge bellowed.

"The State calls Edward Kuhn, your Honor."

I turned to see the man who had brought such misery to my life. He walked right past me without looking at me, straight to the witness chair. He was dressed in a dark gray business suit with a white, buttoned shirt and a bright red tie. I didn't recognize him and would not have known who he was. I had only a vague recollection of a short, loud-mouthed drunk wearing a bathing suit and sandals.

Once he was seated, the attorney for the State began. "Please state your name."

"My name is Edward Eugene Kuhn."

"And where do you live, Mr. Kuhn."

"I live in a housing complex called 'The Landings' in South Ft. Myers."

"How long have you lived there?"

"I moved to Lee County ten years ago and bought my place three years later. I've been there for seven years."

"And what kind of work do you do?"

"I'm in real estate. I'm a salesman with Re-Bar Realty out on Captiva Island."

"Mr. Kuhn, I direct your attention to the afternoon of April 3, 1979 and I ask you to tell this court what occurred on that date."

"I own a 30 foot Grady White fishing boat that I kept at the Caloosahatchee River Marina or I did up until this happened. I was planning to take my boat out of the Marina, trailer it down to Flamingo, which is an hour or two south of Ft. Myers, and spend the weekend fishing with a few of my buddies. Before I put the boat on the trailer and drove down there, I wanted to make sure that everything was working properly, that the engines started up like they were supposed to and that I wouldn't have any problem once I got there. So I called up the manager, Mr. Randy Cross, and made arrangements for the boat to be in the water at 1:00 that afternoon. The plan was for me to stay out an hour or two and then drive down to Flamingo, where my buddies were to meet me. I got there at 1:00 and Jeff, a man who always takes good care of me, had my boat all ready for me. I got in, the boat started fine, and I took it out for a short ride down the river and out into the Gulf. Well, it was a beautiful day and I went a little further than I had planned, so I got back a little later than expected. When I got back, I tied the boat up at the dock, the same dock where it had been when I arrived earlier that afternoon, and I went looking for Jeff. I didn't see him, so I went into the office and was told he went home sick. Mr. Cross told me to go see George and tell him to take my boat out of the water and put it back on the trailer for me. At this point, I'm running late and I'm worried about getting stuck in 5:00 traffic in downtown Ft. Myers. So I do what Mr. Cross told me to do and I see a man on a forklift who is just about to take a boat out of the later, and I walk up to him and ask him, 'Are you George?' He said that he was, and I told him that his boss told me to tell him to take my boat out of the water and put it on my trailer…"

"Mr. Kuhn, let me stop you there. Do you see the man you are referring to in this courtroom today?"

"I do."

"And if you would, please point him out to us."

He looked over at me, pointed, and said "It's the man in the orange jumpsuit."

"Let the record reflect that the witness has identified the defendant as the man he is referring to as 'George' in his testimony," the Judge said. "You may proceed, Mr. Snyder."

"And then what happened, Mr. Kuhn?"

"The man says to me, in a nasty way, that he's busy and there are several boats ahead of me, that he'll get to it when he can. So I said to him, as politely as I could, that I was in a hurry and I would very much appreciate it if he would take care of me next…"

I leaned over and whispered in Mr. Tylor's ear, "That's a lie! That's not what happened!"

He told me to keep my voice down, that he'd have a chance to ask questions in a few minutes.

The attorney for the State went on, "Let me stop you again, Mr. Kuhn, to ask you this. Did Mr. Murphy, or George as you have called him, have a boat on his forklift at the time of this conversation."

"No, he did not."

Again I leaned over and said, "He's lying! I had just taken a boat out of the water!"

Mr. Tylor put a finger to his mouth and said, "Shhh!"

"And then what happened?"

"I told George that I was in a hurry and that I would very much appreciate it if he would take care of me first. George must have been in a hurry to get home or something. He didn't seem to hear me. If he did he ignored me, and kept going towards this other boat. So I stepped in front of his forklift and yelled, 'May I talk to you, please?' Now that really pissed him off, excuse my language, because he jumped down off of the forklift and started yelling at me to get out of his way, that I could get hurt by getting in front of the forklift like that and that I'd have to wait my turn."

"Had you ever met this man before, Mr. Kuhn?"

"No, I hadn't. I'd been a customer there for over a year and I'd never seen him before. Everyone else had always been so nice to me."

"And then what happened?"

"I told him I'd give him an extra $20 if he'd take care of me next. I explained I was late and in a big hurry."

"And what did Mr. Murphy, or George, say to you in response?"

"He told me to get out of his way and he'd get to it when he got to it. That's when I told him that I was going to report him to his boss. That really set him off. He got red in the face and started yelling at me and telling me to get the hell out of his way. Well, I'm from New York, and nobody talks to me that way, so I said to him, "You get your ass on that forklift and get my boat out of the water! Your boss told me to tell you to do that and that's what you're supposed to do, now do it! He didn't like that. He got in my face and was yelling at me, telling me to go back to New York or wherever I came from and get out of his way, and then he pushed me, trying to get me to move out of the way of the forklift, and…"

I leaned over again and told Mr. Tylor, "That's a lie! That's not what happened at all!"

Again, he told me to be quiet.

"Did you push him back?"

"I did not."

"Did you get out of the way?"

"No, I didn't. I stood my ground."

"And then what happened?"

"He pushed me again, and when he did it for the third time I pushed him back, and then he hit me. It was a sucker punch. I wasn't expecting it and he got me right in the nose. My nose started to bleed and blood was spurting out all over me. I put my hands over my nose to stop the bleeding and I bent over in pain, but he kept on hitting me. The next thing I knew, I was on the ground and he was on top of me, punching me, and that's the last I can remember. I went unconscious and when I came to I was in the hospital."

"How long were you in the hospital, Mr. Kuhn?"

"Eight days. I had some bleeding in my cranium and my brain started to swell. They were afraid I might have a permanent brain injury or that I could die. They wouldn't let me go until all the tests were completed."

"Have you been given a clean bill of health, Mr. Kuhn?"

"I was told to see a neurologist or neurosurgeon, one of the two, and I have an appointment to see one next week."

"And how is your nose?"

"It still hurts. It's still broken, and they say it won't be right for another month or two."

"And did you consent to having Mr. Murphy strike you about the head as you've described?"

"Did I consent? What?"

"It's a legal technicality. Did Mr. Murphy strike you, as you've described, against your will?"

"Yes it was against my will. I didn't want him to almost kill me. I wanted to go fishing."

Mr. Kuhn looked over at me, glaringly, raising his voice as he spoke, directly to me as he continued, "He ruined my weekend, ruined my nose, maybe caused me permanent brain injury, caused me a lot of pain, cost me lot of money, and I want him prosecuted to the full extent of the law!"

"Thank you, Mr. Kuhn. I have no further questions of you."

The judge then said, without looking up, "Any questions of this witness, Mr. Tylor?"

"Yes, your Honor." He walked back to the podium and asked, "Mr. Kuhn, your nose wasn't actually broken, was it?

"Not broken? Are you kidding? It was smashed, and he kept on smashing it, even though all I was doing was covering it up, putting my hands over my nose, yelling at the top of my lungs for help to get this maniac off of me. Not broken? What are you talking about?"

"I mean, the nose really isn't a bone, is it? It's made up of cartilage and…"

"Made up of cartilage? Have you ever had a broken nose? Do you know what it feels like to have your nose broken?"

Mr. Kuhn was growing angrier as he spoke. The judge intervened and said, "Mr. Kuhn. I apologize for any insult occasioned upon you by the questions being asked of you by the attorney for the defendant. He has a right to ask these questions and even though they may seem irrelevant, I must direct you to answer his questions the best you can. You are not permitted to ask questions of him."

The Judge then turned to Mr. Tylor and said, "I think you've asked about enough questions regarding the nose, don't you?"

"One more question, your Honor, if I may. Mr. Kuhn, has anyone told you that your nose will not heal and be as good as it ever was?'

Mr. Kuhn, who was obviously agitated, responded by saying, "I'm supposed to go back to see a specialist in a month to see how it has healed. I won't know until then."

"Have you been in many fights in your life, Mr. Kuhn?"

"I've been in a few. I grew up in a tough part of Brooklyn. You have to stand up for yourself up there or you'll get run over. I can take care of myself alright."

"And wouldn't it be fair to say that you and Mr. Murphy, my client, were engaged in a mutual affray, or that the two of you just got in a fight like you have with other people up in New York in the past on other occasions?"

"I'm a grown man. I don't go around getting in fights. This wasn't a fight. He sucker-punched me and then beat me up. This was no fight. If it was a fair fight I'd of…"

The judge, who was obviously displeased with the questions being asked by Mr. Tylor, interjected, "Mr. Kuhn, that will be all. You have answered the question. Any further questions, Mr. Tylor?"

"No, your Honor."

"Any further witnesses from the State, Mr. Snyder?"

"No, your Honor."

"Will the Defense be calling any witnesses, Mr. Tylor?"

I looked over at him, thinking that I'd have a chance to tell the judge what happened, but Mr. Tylor stood and said, "No, your Honor."

"You are excused, Mr. Kuhn. Thank you for coming to court today. I am sure everyone in this courtroom wishes you a speedy and complete recovery."

As Mr. Kuhn was leaving the courtroom, the judge asked, "Any summation by the State?"

"Briefly, your Honor," Mr. Snyder responded.

"The purpose of this hearing is to make certain that there is a reasonable basis for this Court to believe that the Defendant has committed the crimes with which he's been charged and that his continued incarceration is justified. Clearly, the testimony this Court has heard this morning establishes that there is a reasonable basis to believe that this Defendant committed the crime of Aggravated Battery when he struck Mr. Kuhn in the face, broke his nose and sent him to the hospital for eight days with massive swelling of the brain and a possible traumatic brain injury, the full extent of which injury is not known at this time.

"Regarding the charge of attempted murder, the State of Florida believes that the actions of Mr. Murphy, as described by Deputy Stewart, reflect that but for the intervention of Deputy Stewart and the other men, Mr. Murphy might well have killed Mr. Kuhn that day. From the testimony you have heard here today, even though Mr. Kuhn was unconscious and unable to defend himself, this Defendant continued to pummel him. We believe the evidence is sufficient to allow the charge of attempted murder to proceed. As this Court well knows, this is only the preliminary hearing. The State of Florida asks that you bind Mr. Murphy over for trial based upon the evidence presented this morning."

"You may respond, Mr. Tylor."

"Your Honor, on behalf of Mr. Murphy, I submit that the evidence presented is insufficient to ..."

Judge Marcolo interrupted and said, "Insufficient?" Insufficient in what respect, Mr. Tylor? Excuse me for interrupting but I want to make sure I am following your argument. On what charge do you suggest that the evidence is insufficient? That Mr. Murphy tried to kill Mr. Kuhn or that Mr. Murphy did not batter him and put him in the hospital for eight days with a potentially catastrophic injury to his brain?"

Mr. Tylor was obviously flustered by the judge's comments. He stammered,

"I am referring to the attempted murder charge, your Honor, and I..."

"You understand that the purpose of this hearing is not to determine guilt or innocence, only to establish that there are 'reasonable' grounds to believe that a crime may have been committed and that the defendant, and in this case your client, Mr. Murphy, committed the crime with which he is charged, don't you, Mr. Tylor?" the judge asked, with what seemed to me to be a sneer.

Again, Mr. Tylor was taken aback by the judge's remark and mustered a response of,

"Yes, your Honor, I do, but..."

"So what element of the crime of attempted murder is lacking, Mr. Tylor? I grant you that there is insufficient evidence to establish premeditation, and that has not been suggested by the State. But are you suggesting that this court has not heard enough testimony to believe that there is sufficient evidence to establish, at the very least, that your client might have killed Mr. Kuhn but for the intervention of other people, including Deputy Stewart, and that it would be a question for a jury, not the court, to decide on the issue of his intent? Is that your argument, Mr. Tylor? I want to make sure I'm following you here."

"Yes, your Honor, that is what I am suggesting, on behalf of Mr. Murphy, that..."

"So you want this court to find, as a matter of law, that Mr. Murphy did NOT have the intent to kill Mr. Kuhn when he was pummeling him senseless, is that it, Mr. Tylor?"

Mr. Tylor lowered his eyes to the ground, shuffled the papers he was holding in his hands and on which he had written some notes, and murmured, "Yes, your Honor, it is."

"Excuse me? I didn't hear you, Mr. Tylor. You'll have to speak up. What did you say?"

"I said 'yes,' your Honor, that is my argument."

"Well, I am obligated to allow you to complete your argument, and you may do so now that I understand what it is you are suggesting. Do you have any other argument to make as to the charge of Attempted Murder, Mr. Tylor?"

"No, your Honor, I do not."

"How about the charge of Aggravated Battery? Do you have an argument to make as to that charge?"

"Yes, your Honor, I do. On behalf of Mr. Murphy, I would suggest that from what Mr. Kuhn said in court today, and from what we observed, it would not appear that he has suffered a permanent injury, as all of his wounds would seem to be either healed or healing and..."

"So you want this court to make a finding of fact that the injuries to Mr. Kuhn's brain are not permanent, despite the fact that he is still under the care and treatment of doctors, is that it?"

"The court has heard no testimony from any medical..."

"But the court heard Mr. Kuhn testify that he is to see a neurologist or neurosurgeon, and an orthopedic specialist for his nose as well. I heard that. Didn't you hear that, Mr. Tylor?

"I think the evidence presented establishes that Mr. Kuhn suffered a bloody nose, nothing more, your Honor, taking the evidence in the light most favorable to the Defendant and..."

"Mr. Kuhn testified that he had a broken nose and it was still healing. That's what I heard. Do we need to get a transcript of this hearing, Mr. Tylor? Or is that what you heard, too?"

"That is what he said, your Honor, but..."

"So are you suggesting that when Mr. Murphy punched Mr. Kuhn in the nose, breaking it and causing it to bleed, that was not 'great bodily harm,' is that it?"

"Yes, your Honor. I am suggesting that a broken nose is not a sufficiently bad injury to constitute..."

"But what if it doesn't heal right, Mr. Tylor? What if he needs rhinoplasty or further surgery? What if his sense of smell is permanently affected? What if his nose doesn't return to its normal size? Do you want this court to rule at this time, as a matter of law, that Mr. Kuhn's injury is not sufficiently serious to meet the required element of 'great bodily harm'? Is that your argument?"

Again, Mr. Tylor lowered his eyes and said, meekly, "Yes, your Honor."

"Alright, now I understand your argument. Anything further to advance, Mr. Tylor? Judge Marcolo asked mockingly.

"No, your Honor. I do not."

"The court finds that there is ample evidence presented to establish that the crimes of Attempted Murder and Aggravated Battery were committed by this Defendant. Mr. Murphy shall be bound over for trial. The court has also heard testimony which indicates that there are two other charges the State could file against him, those being resisting arrest and destruction of property, but that is up to the State, not me."

Judge Marcolo opened up his desk calendar and continued, "Since Mr. Murphy is in custody, trial must be set within six months of the date of his arrest which means he must be tried no later than the second day of October. Let's see what I have at the end of September…I have a two week trial calendar beginning on September 20. I will set this case for trial during that time period."

Mr. Tylor turned and began to walk back to his chair when the judge said, "Mr. Tylor, before you leave. I noticed a Motion to Reduce Bond had been filed. Do you want to argue that motion?"

"Yes, your Honor, I do. Mr. Murphy can't get out of jail with the bond set as high as it is and I ask that you reduce it so that…"

"Reduce it? So that he can get out of jail? Is that what you want me to do? The judge asked, in a somewhat lighter and higher-pitched voice.

Mr. Tylor brightened a bit and said, "Yes, sir. It is."

The judge then lowered his voice and said, "Despite the fact that he's only lived in Florida for approximately eight months, has no ties to this community and may pose a danger to this community? You want me to help him get out of jail, is that it?"

"Mr. Murphy has no prior criminal convictions. He is married. He has a job, or at least he did have a job until this happened. I can't say for sure that his job will still be there when he gets out, but…"

"Mr. Tylor, the purpose of bail is to make certain not only that the defendant will appear in court at the time of trial but also to make certain that nothing like this would happen between the time of arrest and the time of trial. Can you guarantee me that your client will appear in court for trial and that he won't commit any crimes if I should reduce his bail so that he can get out of jail, Mr. Tylor?"

"Well, not me personally, your Honor, but…"

"Do you know who the public blames if I let someone who is charged with a violent crime out on bond and that person commits another violent crime, Mr. Tylor?

When Mr. Tylor didn't respond the judge continued, "Do you, Mr. Tylor? Well I'll tell you. It's me, or some other judge, and I don't want to take that responsibility, Mr. Tylor, not in this case or in any other case for that matter. Your Motion to Reduce Bond is denied.

Mr. Tylor turned to walk away but the judge continued, "Not so fast, Mr. Tylor. I see where you filed a Notice of Limited Appearance. Is it your intention to continue to represent Mr. Murphy in this case?"

"I haven't made that decision yet, your Honor. Mr. Murphy needs to pay my retainer fee before I will agree to represent him."

"Well, I am going to direct that you file a notice with this court within the next twenty days telling me if you are in this case or not. If not, Mr. Murphy is to find himself another lawyer."

"Would the Court consider appointing me to represent him, your Honor, if he can't come up with the money?"

"He has assets with which he can hire a lawyer, Mr. Tylor. The State of Florida doesn't need to be paying an attorney to represent Mr. Murphy or anyone else who owns land, a vehicle and has the ability to hire their own attorney. He can sell his house if he has to. You, Mr. Tylor, are to let me know if you are going to represent Mr. Murphy or not, and you are to do so within the next twenty days, understood?"

"Yes, your Honor."

Mr. Tylor, who seemed somewhat eager to get out of the courtroom, whispered to me, "I'll come see you this afternoon. We can talk about what just happened then."

The bailiff came up behind me, put a hand on my shoulder and told me to get up. I was led back to the jury box. I looked over at Rebecca. She was as white as a sheet of paper. I asked her to come visit and she nodded her head.

Twenty minutes later I was in the van on my way back to jail. I had never been in court before, not even for a traffic ticket, and I was stunned by what had occurred. I didn't have anyone to talk to about what had happened but I doubt it would have helped. I was speechless. This judge had as much as said that I was guilty of the charges. If he were the judge to sentence me I'd be going away for a long time. I could only hope that Judge Marcolo would not be the judge to hear my case in September, but it sounded as if he would be. I realized that I was in way more trouble than I had imagined.

CHAPTER THIRTEEN
Rebecca Leaves Me

Mr. TYLOR CAME TO see me later that afternoon. He looked sheepish, as if he'd just had his head handed to him in court, which he had. "I want you to know that I'm not the only attorney who's had a problem with Judge Marcolo. He's well-known for doing things like that to other attorneys. That was the first time he's ever done it to me."

"It seemed as if he didn't like you," I offered.

"He's been known to make attorneys cry."

"In court?"

"Yes. He's made several women quit because of things he's said to them."

"Quit being attorneys?"

"No, I'm talking about his Judicial Assistants, women who work for him in his office."

"Can he get away with that?"

"He's a judge. He can do whatever he wants, but there are some restrictions. If he goes too far he can get in trouble with the Florida Bar Association and the Supreme Court of Florida. There is a committee, the Judicial Qualifications Committee, which handles complaints against judges who go too far. I may order a transcript of that hearing and see how it reads. He was very rude and discourteous to me, don't you think?"

"Yes, I do," I responded. "I thought it was because of me and what I'm accused of doing."

"No, it wasn't about you. It was about him making himself feel superior to everyone else, especially the lawyers."

"But he's going to be the judge at my trial?"

"Yes, he's on the criminal bench for the next two years and unless something happens, he'll be the one to hear your case."

"If it was up to him, I think he'd hang me right now."

"He's a little man. Sitting on that bench, he looks ten feet tall, but when he comes down off that bench, he's only about five feet tall. He's got a Napoleonic complex."

"Was Napoleon a little man?" I asked. I didn't know. I knew the name but I couldn't have told him whether he lived in the 5th century or the 15th century. I had no idea.

"Yes, very little, maybe not even five tall as I understand it, but he commanded the French army, and the entire country, twice. They followed him wherever he said to go."

"Waterloo? That's where it all ended for him, right? Where Napoleon met his Waterloo."

"Right, but that was after he invaded Russia and lost tens of thousands of men to the bitter cold, got exiled and banished from France for years but he came back and they still followed him, even after that. Amazing, isn't it?"

"So I've got a judge who is like Napoleon? What can I do about it?"

"Nothing, really. You're stuck with him."

"Great. So what do I do now?"

"Well, the first thing you've got to do is get some money to pay for an attorney. This judge isn't going to appoint the Public Defender's office to represent you as long as you own a house in Maryland. You heard him say that."

"Right, but it's not all mine and it's not worth all that much anyway," I responded.

"Either that or borrow the money. Do you have anyone you can borrow some money from?"

"No. Besides, lawyers are asking for $25,000, or more, just like you are. My parents don't have that kind of money and neither does anyone else who might be willing to loan me money. Even if you could find me a lawyer who would do it for less, I can't come up with anywhere close to that much money."

"I don't know what to tell you, Mr. Murphy. You heard what the judge said. It's up to him."

"Can't we appeal or something?"

"You could, but that's expensive and besides, you'd probably lose."

"I'd probably lose?"

"Yes. Things like the amount of bond and the sufficiency of evidence are called 'matters of discretion' which means that it's up to the discretion of the court to decide. Appellate courts don't get involved in such things unless they're really egregious."

"And my case isn't?"

"I don't think you'd win on appeal but again, that costs money and you don't have it."

"So I'm screwed. Is that what you're telling me?"

"That's about the size of it."

"And what about you? Are you still my lawyer or not?"

"Not anymore. My job ended this morning. Now, if you can come up with some money, I might be willing to represent you but I'm not making any promises. I don't like going in front of that judge any more than you do."

"Great. That makes me feel even worse."

"If you can get some money together, call me and we'll talk about it." He stood and said, "Sorry I wasn't able to be of more help, but I tried."

"Thanks anyway," I responded, thinking that I had wasted $1500 on him.

"Good luck, Mr. Murphy."

"Yeah, thanks." I said. I sat there alone, after he had left, pondering my bleak future, until a guard came and led me back to my cell.

I kept waiting for Rebecca to show up, but she didn't make it before the visiting hour ended. I called several times but got no answer. I didn't see her until shortly before closing time the next day. As soon as I took one look at her, I knew that things between us had changed. She began the conversation by saying, "George, I can't go on like this."

I responded by saying, "I know how hard this must be for you, and I don't know what to say except I'm sorry. I understand completely if you decide to go back to live with your folks in Maryland until I get this all straightened out."

But then she said, "No, I mean I can't go on like this as your wife. I've talked it over with my parents and I plan on filing for divorce once I get back home."

"Please don't do that, Rebecca! I begged her. "What that man said yesterday wasn't true. He lied. That's not the way it happened."

"What about the police officer? Was he lying, too?"

"I told you I didn't know what happened after he cursed me and pushed me, and I don't, but I need to talk to Randy and the other guys to hear what they have to say about what happened."

"I have talked to Randy and he said he didn't think you even knew who he was. He said you were like a crazy man – like you were insane."

"That's never happened to me in my life, Rebecca, I swear. I don't know what came over me. Not even when I was in 'Nam did I ever lose it like I did that day. I'll never let it happen again, I promise. Please don't do that. You're all I've got."

"How can you be so sure it won't happen again? It's like your nightmares – when you have one of them, it scares me, a lot."

"But with you I've had them less and less. I've gotten better. You know I have."

"You got Bailey to help with that, and she did, but who's to say they won't come back even worse than before? I think you need help, George, serious help, and …" she looked down, hesitated, looked me straight in the eye and said, "Besides, from what I heard yesterday, you may not be getting out of jail for a long time. I can't wait that long, George. I'm only twenty two years old. I want to have children, be happy, have a normal life. I hate coming into this jail. I hate having to tell people where you are and what happened. I can't live like this, George. I don't want to live like this. I won't live like this."

I could see in her eyes that she meant every word. She wasn't crying like she had every day since I'd been in here. She was stone-cold serious.

"You don't have to file for divorce right away, do you? Can't you wait and see what happens? I didn't intend for any of that to happen. I've never hurt anyone in my whole life! Not even in Nam! I never killed anybody. That's not who I am. You know that, Rebecca."

"No, I don't know that, George. I know that you're in jail, charged with attempted murder, and they say you did some awful things to that man. I don't know what to believe but my bags are packed and my father is flying down here tonight. We're headed back north just as soon as we get the furniture and everything packed up."

"What about your school and all your classes?"

"I've talked to my instructors, and my guidance counselor and they're going to let me take my finals early. There are only two weeks left in the semester. I'm going over there in the morning to get that all done."

"What about Bailey?"

"I'll take her with us. She's a good dog and now it's me who'll need the company."

"What about the house?"

"You mean the one down here?"

"Yeah."

"I talked to the landlord and she told me that she had some people who were interested in renting it. As long as she doesn't lose any money she doesn't care. The rent is paid up through the end of next month."

"What about the house up there?"

"I've talked that over with my Dad and we think we'd like to keep it. I might stay there or I might stay with my folks. I'm not sure, but we think it's a good investment. Besides, I can't live with my parents for the rest of my life. Maybe it'd be a good place for me. I like our home, George."

"I like it, too, Rebecca. None of this would've happened if Bill hadn't died."

"But he did and there's nothing we can do about that or about what happened between you and that Mr. Kuhn. I wish it didn't happen but it did and we have to deal with it. This is the only thing that makes sense, George." Then she looked me in the eyes and said, "I loved you, George."

"And I still love you, Rebecca. I do. You mean more to me than anything else in the world."

"You should've thought of that before you hit that man, George. None of this would've happened if you had just walked away."

"I don't know what came over me...maybe I am sick. Maybe I do need help, but can't you stick it out with me, stay in my corner, at least for a little while?"

"George, I'm here. I've been here with you for five months..."

"We haven't even had our first Anniversary," I pleaded.

"And I don't want to have that with you while you're stuck in jail, George." Her eyes began to water and her voice quivered as she spoke.

I realized that there wasn't much I could do. She could stand up and walk away. I couldn't, and I couldn't blame her for walking away, either. That judge sure made it sound like I was going to be in jail, or prison, for a long time. I didn't know what to say. The best I could muster was, "Will you write me?"

She looked down, avoiding my eyes and said, "I'll do the best I can. This is going to be hard on me, George. I was so happy just a few weeks ago and now everything we worked for, everything we did, everything we hoped for... it's just ruined," she cried.

She stood and said, "I'm sorry, George. I've got to go. Talking to you just makes it that much harder. I love you George and I wish you good luck." Then she said good-bye and was gone.

CHAPTER FOURTEEN
Satchmo

A MONTH AFTER I HAD been arrested, a lawyer from the insurance company came to see me. He told me that he wanted to obtain a statement from me about what had happened that day. He knew that I didn't remember much from that day so I wasn't sure exactly what he wanted me to say. At first, it seemed as if he wanted me to say that everything that happened was because of Mr. Kuhn and I did nothing wrong.

Then he turned the questions around and it seemed as if he wanted me to say that I acted on my own, that it was all my fault and that the Marina wasn't responsible for my actions. He asked me if I could say that I had been told what to do under that circumstance by management but I didn't follow those instructions. He asked me to say that I had been well-trained by Randy but I disobeyed instructions when I responded to the hostile behavior of Mr. Kuhn. He wasn't happy when I told him that I never received any instructions on how to deal with customers since I wasn't ever supposed to be dealing with them.

Finally, after an hour or so, he asked me to sign a statement about how I had acted in self-defense he wrote up while we were sitting there, but I refused. I was worried about the criminal charges against me and if anything I told him could be used against me. This attorney was only interested in whether or not the insurance company was going to have to pay any money. I got to thinking that he didn't have Randy's best interests at heart either. I know he didn't give a damn about what was good for me. I didn't like him at all and was glad to see him leave.

A week later, Mr. Sullivan came to see me. He was apologetic about how long it had taken him to get down to see me and explained that he had been in a long trial and couldn't get away any sooner. He had made several calls but had not been able to find anyone who would take the case for less than $20,000.

I told him about Rebecca planning to file for divorce and he offered me his condolences. He said that he, as a divorced man, knew how hard that was and that I was lucky there were no children from the marriage. The break could be clean. The only thing we had was the land. He also told me that the land had probably gone up in value in the year we owned it.

Then he said something that I had been told by the bondsman months before. If I didn't have the land, I'd qualify for the services of the Public Defender's office. Back then, I didn't want to do it because that was ours, mine and Rebecca's. Now that Rebecca had left me, things had changed. I had no money, Rebecca took my vehicle, and all I had left was some tools and the house. I asked him to call Rebecca and figure out how we could get the land out of my name and into her name so that I could honestly say that I didn't have a pot to piss in.

Just hearing me say those things to Mr. Sullivan made me cry inside. Things were going so bad for me that it was a good thing for me not to have anything at all, to be flat-dead busted. He told me that he would look into it right away and that he would prepare a Quit-Claim Deed for me to sign before he went back to Maryland.

Mr. Sullivan returned a few days later, had me sign the Quit-Claim Deed, by which I gave all of my right, title and interest in the property to Rebecca for ten dollars. He had spoken to Rebecca. She had been to see a lawyer who would be filing the divorce papers soon.

Mr. Sullivan knew the attorney who would be representing Rebecca and he said he'd talk to her. He told me that he'd represent me in the divorce for no fee at all. He'd do his best to see that the divorce was final as soon as possible so that I could get an attorney. It was now early June. I'd been in jail for two months and trial was three months away.

Inmates came and went. There were only a few men who had been in there as long as I had been. They were mostly repeat DUI offenders who had been sentenced to six months or more in jail. It was just as noisy as ever, and fights were still going on all the time.

One time, these two inmates were wanting to fight but they couldn't get at each other because they were in different cells. This one guard who worked the night shift got tired of hearing them yell at each other so he let them out. The fight lasted one punch. The one guy got hit in the head and died. The guard got fired but nothing ever happened to the other guy that I know of.

Even after all the months I had been there, I hadn't had any trouble at all, which was hard to do. But murderers are considered the bad-asses in a jail. Child molesters were the lowest. They got beat up, or worse, all the time.

Those guys and the guys who turned State's evidence on their friends had it the worst. There is a code of conduct in jail, or honor among thieves, if you will, and I, as an alleged murderer, was the beneficiary of that tradition.

Of course, if a guy came into the cell and wasn't too masculine, or was sweet on other guys, he had it bad too. Jail house rapes were not uncommon, though I, personally, didn't see any of that. I just heard about it. The weak ones were culled out and put in separate cells, like separating the wolves from the sheep, but sometimes that didn't happen until after some bad incident had occurred.

Jail was no place for a decent man to be. It smelled, and no matter how much they cleaned the place, the smell didn't go away. I got to thinking that men under extreme stress, facing the prospects of time in jail or prison, sweat different and give off a different odor from people on the outside. I didn't know for sure, it was just a theory I developed.

I had nothing to do. After a couple of months, once the jailers saw that I was no threat to anyone and wasn't a crazed killer, they made me a trustee. I got to be one of the prisoners who served the food every morning. I was still in the habit of waking up early, at 5:00, so it didn't bother me at all that I had to be in the kitchen, while everyone else was sleeping, to get breakfast ready.

Another group of trustees took care of lunch and dinner. It was an honor to be a trustee. It meant you got to get out of the cell for several hours every day and walk around like you were a regular human being instead of a caged animal. Lots of guys, most guys, wanted to be trustees, but not many were allowed to and if you messed up, like some did by abusing their privileges, you got sent back to the general population.

When I wasn't serving breakfasts I was reading. I started to read about a month after sitting in jail, staring at the walls for hours on end. Reading was about the only thing I could do in the cell other than watch TV, which was on from 8:00 in the morning until 8:00 at night. There was only one TV in each cell and it was always on whatever channel the guards wanted to watch.

There was never a discussion about what to watch, though there were a whole lot of complaints about whatever was on. The guards made the decision and that was final. They never changed their minds no matter how much guys complained because they knew that if they did, they'd never hear the end of it. Usually, it was CNN or ESPN.

I started to read the newspaper. Every day a few copies of the Fort Myers News Press were delivered to each cell. As a trustee I always got first crack at them. Like most guys, I started with the Sports section. After reading that, I went to the comics, then the horoscope, then the front page. Before too long I was reading everything. I knew I was hooked when I started trying to do the crossword puzzles.

After that, I began reading magazines. I read every U.S. News or Newsweek article that I could get my hands on. I had never, ever, in my entire life read a newspaper or a magazine from cover to cover but I had so much time on my hands and nothing better to do I started to and I liked it. We'd get some time out in the yard for exercise every so often and guys were usually either lifting weights or playing basketball but I never did. I was happier inside in my little corner of an air-conditioned cell, or off in a corner, reading.

I reached a new plateau when I started reading books. I was big on Louis L'amour novels. By the end of July I had found Mickey Spillane and Erle Stanley Gardner and I liked their stories about law and detectives.

Rebecca wrote to me a few times. Not much, just newsy kinds of things, telling me about her grades and what was going on in McHenry. It sounded like a different place with the changes that had been made at the Marina. It was completely different with Bill's son in charge. Apparently people didn't like it as much and he'd raised the prices on the rentals and everything else. I got a laugh when she said that people were complaining about the mechanics. I guess I'd done a pretty good job up there for a guy who didn't have a clue about boat engines when I started.

In mid-August, I received a certified copy of a Final Divorce Decree from Mr. Sullivan. He told me to show it to the court and ask for a public defender to be appointed to represent me. With the help from some of the jail house lawyers in my cell, I was able to get back in front of Judge Marcolo.

He remembered me I think, but I wasn't sure. I'd grown a beard in jail and put on about twenty pounds so I didn't look the same. When I showed him the decree from Maryland and told him I had no money, no car, no land, no nothing, he appointed the public defender's office to represent me, without so much as a word.

A week later, a woman from the Lee County Public Defender's Office came to see me. She was an investigator. Her job was to take down basic information and put the file together for the attorney who would be handling my case. She wasn't sure who the case would be assigned to just yet. After she was able to get all of the materials from the State, through discovery, and obtained whatever she could through her own investigation, the attorney would come see me.

In ten minutes I told her all about my life, including my entire work history, where I'd lived and what I did during my years in the military. I also told her all that I knew about what had happened that day. She was busy, too busy to chat or talk about anything except what was on a form she had to complete. Guards had called out the names of about a dozen guys who she was going to see that day. Several others whose names hadn't been called asked me to tell her to call them out before she left.

Well over eighty percent of the men in my cell had either public defenders or court-appointed lawyers. Most of them complained about never getting to see their attorney. I didn't know what to expect but from what I'd been told, I was afraid that I wouldn't get a very good lawyer to represent me. There was a saying among the inmates that made me laugh. When asked, they'd say, "No, I don't have a lawyer, I have a public defender." I hoped there was no truth in it.

I asked her to contact Randy and the other mechanics and I explained to her that I wanted to know what they would say when asked about how the fight started and what they saw and did. She told me she spent most of her time seeing people like me in jail and didn't get much chance to get out and view crime scenes or meet with witnesses, but she'd put a note in the file and see what she could do. I gave her the names of guys who wanted to see her and she wrote the names down, but she told me she wouldn't be able to see any of them that day.

As the days went by, I grew more and more concerned about what was going to happen when the trial date arrived. It was now late August and trial was rapidly approaching. I hadn't seen an attorney, other than Mr. Sullivan, since my preliminary hearing with Mr. Tylor. I grew more impatient and began to send daily messages to the Public Defender's Office asking for someone to come see me.

About a month before the trial date, a guard told me that my lawyer was there to see me. I had no idea what to expect. When I opened the door to the visitation cubicle, I saw a thin, disheveled looking white man with long, curly brown hair, and a straggly mustache looking back at me. From the way he was seated, he looked to be very tall. I hadn't sat down yet when, in a deep, low voice, he began, "Mr. Murphy, my name is Mike Satchel and I'm your lawyer."

He handed me his card as he continued, "I've reviewed the file, read the transcript of the preliminary hearing and talked to your former boss and the guys you worked with…"

"You talked to Randy and the other guys?" I asked, incredulously.

"Yes. Now here's what I propose to do. I'm going to file a motion with the court to have you examined by a psychiatrist."

"A psychiatrist? I'm depressed, but I'm not crazy," I said.

"Look, do you want to get out of jail or not?"

"Of course I do."

"Well, I think this is your best shot. I think we can beat the Attempted Murder charge, but I don't see how I can get around Agg Battery, and that carries fifteen years. With this judge you'll do some serious time."

"So self-defense won't work?" I asked.

"No, even if he started it, from everything I know, it seems pretty clear that you took it to a whole different level, and the law doesn't allow that. Once he was down, you had to stop hitting him and you didn't. The best I could possibly do would be to get you off with simple battery, which carries a year in county jail and this judge would give you every day of that."

"Is it me or is this judge that way towards everybody."

"He's that way towards everybody, even me, especially me, so don't take it personal." He rasped. "But listen to me, I don't have much time. This judge is going to get really pissed off at me because notice of claiming insanity as a defense was supposed to have been done a while ago, and he'll yell and scream at me, but he'll have to go along with it. It's going to cause this trial to be continued, but I can't help that now."

"Insanity defense...will they put me in a mental hospital if I'm found not guilty?"

"Not unless you're still crazy, but from what I can see and from what I've read you're not, so you'd walk out of court a free man if we win."

"But what if the psychiatrist you send me to says I'm not, or I wasn't insane at the time this happened?"

"Then you're in trouble, but this guy you're going to see is really sympathetic to Veterans, especially Vietnam Veterans. I don't think that's going to happen. I'll bet you have bad nightmares, right?"

"Yes, I have and I still do, but not as much in here. I don't sleep so good in here and it seems as if I'm always sleeping with one eye open, so to speak. How did you know?"

"You're not the first vet I've represented. I've been a PD for five years now. Most guys have who went over there came back with a few skeletons in the closet, so to speak."

"So does that defense work very often?"

"No, and there's no guarantee we'll win this time but I think it's our best chance."

"What happens if we lose?"

"The judge could send you to prison on both charges."

"So I could be going to prison for thirty years?"

"There are some guidelines the judge has to follow. I don't know where you'd fall in, but even with no prior criminal record you'd still end up doing several years in prison, I'm sure."

"So I'd be giving up my right to trial if we go this route you're suggesting?"

He seemed to become a little exasperated with me and the questions I was asking, and said,

"Look, here's how it works. When you claim that you were temporarily insane, and therefore not criminally responsible for your actions, you admit that you did what they have accused you of doing, so yes, you give up your right to challenge the charges being made against you. You're saying that I did what I'm accused of doing but I'm not guilty of those charges because I was temporarily insane. Now, that doesn't mean you give up your right to a trial, it's just that at your trial the jury won't decide guilt or innocence, per se, it will decide if you were insane at the time of the offense or not. If not, then you're not guilty by reason of insanity. Understand?"

"I think so. And you don't think we have a chance of winning at trial otherwise?"

"I'd never say you don't have a chance, but I'd say the odds are heavily against you."

I sat there quietly for a few seconds, mulling over what I'd been told. He continued, "It's your decision. I can't make it for you, but I need to know what you want to do. If you need some time, that's fine, but I'll need to know your answer by the end of the week."

"Today's Tuesday."

"I'll need to know no later than Thursday afternoon, okay? I have to file some papers with the court and I'd rather not wait 'til next week. It's going to be bad enough for me. This judge is going to give me a bunch of shit for being so late with this as it is."

"But I just met you. How could you have done this sooner?"

"The PD's office was appointed to represent you over a month ago. He's not going to be happy, believe me."

"I'm going to have to give this some thought," I said.

"Hey, did you know what you were doing when you hit that guy as many times as you did or not?"

"No, I don't remember hitting him at all," I responded.

"And did you know that it was wrong to hit that man, break his nose and keep on hitting him until he was unconscious?"

"Yes, I knew that. I'd never do that to someone, especially over something as stupid as what he was talking about."

"But you hit him anyway, didn't you?"

"That's what they say. I don't remember it."

"That's the point. I'll argue that at the time all that happened, you didn't know right from wrong, that you didn't know what the consequences of your actions would be, that you were temporarily insane. I think I can sell it. I can make that guy look like the bad guy and you look like the good guy."

"I see where you're going with that…and you think it might work?"

"Yeah, I think it might work."

"I'd be taking a big chance, wouldn't I?" I asked.

"I think it's your best chance. In fact, I think it's your only chance of winning. Otherwise it's just a matter of how much time you want to spend in prison. You're not going to get probation from this judge. I can promise you that."

"Let me think about it."

He stood up and said,

"Let me know by Thursday afternoon, 4:00, okay?"

"I will. Say, how tall are you anyway?"

"Six three, and you?"

"Five foot seven and a half."

"You're a pretty tough guy for bein' only five foot seven and a half feet tall, eh?"

"Not really, I've never been in a fight in my life."

"That's what I'm talking about. I can win this case, Mr. Murphy. Let me know what you decide."

He turned and walked out. I noticed that his shoe laces were untied and his shirt was hanging out the back of his pants. He sure didn't look much like Mr. Sullivan, but that was my lawyer...Mike Satchel.

"Thank you, Mr. Satchel," I said.

"Satchmo. Call me Satchmo. Everybody does." With that, he gave me a wink and was gone.

CHAPTER FIFTEEN
A Court-Appointed Psychiatrist

WHEN I GOT BACK to the cell, one of the guys asked who my lawyer was. I told him it was Michael Satchel and when I did one of the other guys piped up, "You got Satchmo!"

"Is that the guy who looks like he just put a finger in an electrical outlet?" another said.

"That's him," said a third. "He's the best over there, though, or at least he gives a shit. You got lucky."

Yet another guy said, "I like that Doherty guy, too, but I heard he's leaving to go into private practice. All the good ones do."

The first man said, "Satchmo's my lawyer, too. Tell him to call me. I haven't seen him in a month."

Hearing all that stuff made me think maybe I had a good attorney after all but I wasn't all that confident about it. I wasn't insane and I didn't like the idea of having to say that I was. I thought about it and thought about it and finally, on Thursday afternoon at about 2:00, I called over to the PD's office and left a message for Mr. Satchel that I'd go along with his recommendation to go with the insanity defense.

On the following Monday, I received a letter from the PD's office which included a Motion to Continue Trial, A Notice of Intent to Claim Insanity and a Motion for Psychiatric Testing, as well as a Notice of Hearing on the two motions for that Friday.

I was taken off breakfast duty that Friday because I had to go to court. They brought me over with a bunch of other guys and stuck us in the jury box while the court heard several other cases, just like the last time.

There must have been about ten of us and we were all chained together just like before until we got right outside the courtroom. They took off the chains that held us together and left the chains on our hands, but not on our feet this time. Once I sat down, I looked over and saw Satchmo. He was standing with a group of other attorneys, but he stuck out. He was taller than the others and looked just as disheveled as before. His tie hung down a few inches from his chin and I could see that his shoelaces were untied. Then there was his hair. He looked like a comical figure amongst the others in suits and ties and shiny shoes.

They all scurried for their chairs once the back door to the courtroom opened. The bailiff walked in and said, "All rise. The Circuit Court in and for Lee County is now in session. Judge Anthony Marcolo presiding."

The little man in his black robe followed behind the big, burly bailiff, who towered over him. Once the judge sat down, though, he immediately took command of the courtroom.

"Good morning," he muttered in a gruff voice. "The first case on my docket is the case of the State of Florida versus Thomas Cole."

I noticed that Mr. Satchel began to rise, as did one of the guys behind me. Before either one had taken a step, the judge continued, "I've read the file and the motion, and it is denied."

"But Judge, I'd like to be heard," Mr. Satchel complained.

"I've got 32 matters to be heard this morning, Mr. Satchel, and I have no time for it. I'm not reducing your client's bond."

"But Judge, I…"

The judge continued, "The next case to be heard is the State of Florida versus Ernesto Perez."

The man behind me sat back down, as did Mr. Satchel. The judge dealt with that man's case just as quickly, barely taking the time to look up from the file at the man or his attorney. For the next thirty minutes, I sat there and watched the judge deny motion after motion, chastise attorneys left and right and all without so much as a single kind word to anyone, defense attorneys, defendants and even the prosecuting attorneys or clerks. The bailiff was accorded some deference as occasionally he would say, "Mr. Bailiff, would you please…" before telling him what to do.

When it came time for my case to be heard, I had no idea what to expect, other than I was probably going to lose. I didn't even stand up when it was called. I stayed where I was. Mr. Satchel walked to the podium and the judge started in on him.

"Mr. Satchel, this motion should have been filed thirty days ago. You know that. What's your excuse?"

"Sorry, Judge," Mr. Satchel mumbled, "we were appointed to this case recently and…"

The judge quickly rebuked him by saying, "You were appointed over a month ago, sir,"

"And we're extremely busy at the PD's office, as you know. We do the best we can, your Honor."

"I don't seem to have as much of a problem with other attorneys in the Public Defender's Office as I do with you, Mr. Satchel. If this continues, I will have a talk with your employer, do you understand?"

"Yes, your Honor," Mr. Satchel responded, in a somewhat patronizing tone of voice, as if he'd heard this before.

The judge looked up from the papers in front of him somewhat abruptly, peering over his glasses as if he sensed some disrespect in Mr. Satchel's tone of voice. He continued, "I have half a mind to deny this motion," he added. "What says the State? Do you oppose the motion?"

An older woman in a wheelchair situated at the table next to ours responded, "The State is not happy with the timing of the motion either, your Honor, but so long as the Defendant's right to a speedy trial is waived, the State will not oppose the motion."

"Even though we are so close to trial, Mrs. Hoffenberg?" the judge inquired.

"There are a few cases out of the Supreme Court which seems to indicate that where the motion is filed a day or two before trial, or even a week before trial, that the court could, with proper exercise of discretion, deny the motion, but not where, as in this case, trial is still a month away."

The judge appeared to be annoyed by the response he received from the State and continued, "Will your client waive speedy trial, Mr. Satchel?"

When Mr. Satchel didn't respond immediately the judge asked, "Have you even discussed this with your client, Mr. Satchel?"

"Yes, your Honor." he responded.

"And he is in agreement? Knowing it will cause a delay in the trial? Will he waive his right to a speedy trial, Mr. Satchel?"

"Of course, your Honor." Mr. Satchel responded, as if to say that he knew what every other criminal defense lawyer in the country knew about a defendant's right to a trial within a certain amount of time after arrest.

"I don't see a written consent to a continuance from your client, Mr. Satchel, or a written waiver of a speedy trial. Where is your client? Is he here?

"He should be here in court today," Mr. Satchel said. He looked over at the jury box where I sat. He pointed at me, saying "There he is." When he said that, the judge looked over so I stood up."

"I'm here," I said. My voice quivered a bit as I spoke. This judge put the fear of God in people, including me. He held my fate in his hands and I knew that he wouldn't think twice before sending me away for a long time.

"And do you agree to waive your right to a speedy trial so that a psychiatrist can examine you, as your attorney has asked the Court to do?"

"I agree with what my attorney has said, your Honor." I responded.

"Mr. Satchel," the judge continued, "I'm not happy about this, but your motions are granted. Trial in this matter is continued until the third week of January. As you request, I'll appoint Dr. Baldwin to examine him," the judge said almost begrudgingly. Before Mr. Satchel had time to say another word, the judge was on to the next case.

Mr. Satchel looked over at me and winked as he turned to walk out of the courtroom. Ten minutes later I was on my way back to the Lee County Jail. I was going to be in jail for another three months, which wasn't good, and I wasn't happy about that, but I felt like we had won a minor victory. I still wasn't all that sure about how successful the insanity defense would be. I had to trust Mr. Satchel on that, but my confidence level wasn't all that high in him, despite what the other guys in jail with me said about him.

The letters from Rebecca stopped once the divorce was final. In the beginning, shortly after she was back in Maryland, it had been every week. Then it slowed to every other week and now it was over. She was moving on and there was nothing I could do to change that. I still wrote to her, though my letters were growing shorter and more infrequent too. There just wasn't much I could tell her that I hadn't already said. My days in jail weren't all that interesting to write about.

As I grew more depressed, my nightmares started coming back. They got so bad that the complaints from my fellow inmates got me kicked out of the cell I was in again. They moved me to a different wing. I was put in a cell with another guy at the end of the hall.

When I first got there, I didn't know what he'd done to deserve having me put in there with him until that first night. He snored like a freight train. I guess they figured we deserved each other. He wasn't a bad guy, but he had a drinking problem and had been given a year in jail after his third DUI in less than five years.

If I didn't get to sleep first, I wasn't going to get any sleep. I had to wake him up, without him knowing what made him wake up, and then try to beat him back to sleep. And when I started making noises, as I did when I was having a nightmare, he'd get up and shake me because he couldn't sleep when I did. We were a good pair. Even the guards stayed away from us.

A month later, a guard took me to a room at the front of the jail. It had what looked to be a new carpet, a large wooden desk with glass on top, eight black leather, high-back chairs surrounding the desk and it smelled good. It was, by far, nicer than any place else in the jail I'd been and as a trustee I'd been all over the jail. I'd never seen this room before. It was the conference room.

Sitting at the head of the table was an older man in a suit and tie with a full head of curly, gray hair and a full, neatly-cropped gray beard to match. The guard announced my arrival saying, "Dr. Baldwin, this is George Murphy." He closed the door behind me and locked it.

As I walked in, Dr. Baldwin looked up, peering over thick, black-framed glasses, and said in a kindly voice, "Good morning, Mr. Murphy. Sit down over here, please," motioning me to the chair on the right side of the room.

"My neck hurts this morning and it's easier for me to turn my head to the left than it is to turn it to the right for some reason."

I walked around to the other side of the table. When I was about to sit down, he stood and extended his hand saying, "Pleased to meet you, Mr. Murphy. I'm Ed Baldwin."

We shook hands. "Thank you, Dr. Baldwin. I'm pleased to meet you as well."

I suddenly felt nervous. The guard hadn't told me who I was to see and I hadn't prepared myself mentally for this. I knew he was the man appointed by the court to examine me and that he would tell the court whether or not I was, in his opinion, insane at the time of the incident. I didn't know if he was on my side or against me. I wasn't sure how to act or what to say.

"Relax, Mr. Murphy," he said, sensing my nervousness. "I'm here to help you if I can. As I expect you know, I've been appointed to examine you. I've been doing this for many years now and I've seen a number of men just like you who have returned from Vietnam with psychological scars. I've developed a bit of expertise on the subject of what is now referred to as post traumatic stress disorder. You've probably never heard of the term, have you?"

"No, Dr. Baldwin, I can't say that I have," I responded.

"Well, it's a phrase of relatively recent vintage. After World War II, or World War I, or any wars since the beginning of time, soldiers with any kind of psychological symptoms were said to have battle-fatigue, or shell-shock. It's the same condition, just a different name."

The expression on his face changed and became more serious. He lowered his voice and said, "However, just because men have experienced some horrific things during their years as soldiers in battle that does not give them a license to kill or do horrible things. It just explains why otherwise good, decent, patriotic men do things that they would never otherwise do.

"In your case, and I've read your court file and the records kept on you here at the jail, it seems to me that you fit this pattern. I expect that you fall into that category, am I correct?"

"I'd never been in a fight before in my life, Dr. Baldwin. I don't know what came over me that day. I don't even remember half of what happened."

"I'm not surprised," he said. "I saw where you have no prior criminal record, no history of domestic violence or abuse, no record of alcohol or drug problems…a fairly good and consistent work history, married…"

"I had a long spell of alcohol abuse there for a while, Dr. Baldwin, but it never got reported to anyone, and I'm divorced now, for the second time."

"That happen recently?" he asked.

"Within the last two months, while I've been in here, and that was all because of this fight I got into."

"That's unfortunate. It takes a special woman, or man, to understand what you have been through and what you are continuing to go through. I'll bet you've had trouble sleeping at night for a long time now, haven't you?"

I hesitated before answering, because I wasn't sure how to answer, wondering how much he knew, and he continued, "Am I right?" he asked, peering into my eyes, with a hint of a smile.

"Well, whenever I have a nightmare I usually can't get back to sleep at all, and there was a time when I had to take a lot of pills to get to sleep."

"Any problems here in jail, with sleeping, that is?"

"They've put me in a separate cell because of some bad dreams I've had every now and then."

"I saw that in the records. They say you caused quite a commotion in your cell a few times."

"That's what they tell me," I responded somewhat sheepishly. It wasn't something I was proud of.

"You've probably never talked to anyone about it, have you?"

"You mean someone like you – a doctor or psychiatrist?"

"I mean anyone at all, Mr. Murphy."

When I looked in his eyes, they were as black as black could be with no sign of emotion in them. It was like looking at two marbles.

Again, I hesitated, not sure how much to reveal or what to say.

"Mr. Murphy, may I call you George?

"Sure," I responded.

"You are a young man, not even thirty years old yet. I'm an old man. All of my children are older than you. I have a grandson who is almost your age. I'm a psychiatrist and I'm here to help you. You have to let me help you. I can't do all the talking here. I never learn anything when I talk. Have you ever talked to anyone about your bad dreams?"

I lowered my eyes and said, "No, I haven't Dr. Baldwin."

"Not even your wife, your parents, your best friends – no one?"

"No, no one."

"I'm not surprised, George. It is not uncommon. Men who've been through what you've been through, although everyone's experiences are different, are the same in many ways. They think it's a sign of weakness to admit problems, especially psychological ones."

My hands were resting on the edge of the table. He took the hand closest to him and put it between his two hands. "I can't promise you what will happen if and when we go to court but I can tell you that I hope to help you with your problem, son. I want you to tell me about your dreams."

I looked at him, this short, thin, old man I'd never met before, who wanted me to share my deepest and darkest secrets with him. I tried to pull back my hand, but he had a firm grip. "You've got to trust me. I'm a psychiatrist. I'm not here to harm you or do damage to you. What you say to me will be used to justify my findings. If you don't confide in me I won't be able to help you."

I looked at him, still not sure what to do. I hadn't been in the room for five minutes and he was asking me to spill my guts about what had been eating at my insides ever since the plane landed in Cam Ranh Bay so many years ago. I didn't know if I could trust him. My attorney hadn't prepared me for this.

"I'm not here to help the State of Florida put you in prison, George. I'm here to determine if you should be allowed to go free. I am your expert witness. The State of Florida will hire someone else who will, undoubtedly, find that you are as sane as can be and that you are fully and completely responsible for your actions on that day. You've got to give me some ammunition to fight with. I've got to have reasons, good reasons, as to why you should be allowed to go free. Then you have to hope that the jury will agree with me."

"Okay, Dr. Baldwin. I'll try, but this isn't going to be easy. I don't know where to begin."

"George, I've got all day. I'm in no hurry. My only purpose for being here is to help you if I can. I'm not promising you that I can but I'll try. Let's start at the beginning. Tell me about your family, where you were born, what your childhood was like."

I told him about Jeannette, my folks, my love of machines and cars and everything I could think of about my childhood days. Every now and then he'd interject a word or two about his first car, or his love of basketball as a kid, or something to pry a few more details out of me.

I told him about me signing up for the Army and why I did it. He asked me about my grades and how much I knew about Vietnam and the war before I joined. I told him the truth. I didn't know diddly-squat about it. None of us did. He shook his head, knowingly, "You were all just boys, raised on watching John Wayne movies, thinking you were going to be heroes, like Audie Murphy, or the Lone Ranger. You had no idea what you were in for."

He shook his head, sighed, and said, "It's sad. Please, go on. What things did you do in the Army, in Vietnam?"

I told him all about being a mechanic and then a crew chief on a Chinook.

"Why did you sign up for a second tour, George?"

I explained about the promotion, the money, the thrill it was to ride in those huge flying machines, and not wanting to back to Germany.

"You didn't want to go back to Germany? You decided to stay in Vietnam rather than go back to Germany?"

"That's right."

"George, you are crazy," he said with a smile on his face. "Were you having nightmares back then?"

I explained that the nightmares didn't start until I was back in the States and how, though it was awful, I felt that I belonged there. We were all in it together. I told him that even though I was scared to death most of the time, I doubted I'd ever find anything else in my life that was as important, or as engaging, as what I went through in Vietnam, as bad as it was.

"So why'd you get out? Why didn't you do another tour?

"Guys were dying left and right, especially on helicopters. I mean maybe only about half of the pilots made it through and even fewer of the gunners and crew chiefs. I remember one day saying to myself that it was time – that I'd better get out then or I was going back in a body bag. I remember thinking that it was like gambling. I'd had a run of good luck and I figured I was pushing my luck to stay there any longer. That was probably the smartest thing I ever did, get out while I still could."

"But you stayed in the military after that, why?"

I told him how I really didn't mind the military. I thought it was going to be my whole life. They let me work on machines, big machines, and paid me well for it. I told him how being a mechanic in the Army was a whole lot more exciting than changing tires and doing tune-ups on cars at the gas station where my Dad worked.

After I told him about working in Virginia while still in the Army, getting out and going back to Jeanette, working at the gas station, my marriage to Joanna and then losing my job, he stopped me and asked a lot of questions about that guy at the gas station I'd had the major dispute with, the one who caused me to lose that job.

"But you didn't actually come to blows with that man, did you? You never hit him and he never hit you, correct?"

"No, I'm not that way. I was mad, madder than I can ever remember being before this incident but I just walked away."

He wrote for what seemed like a minute or two, looked up and said, "Go on."

I told him about driving the delivery truck, the 18 wheeler, the divorce and getting the job with Bill, about Mr. Sullivan and about marrying Rebecca.

"You were happy at Deep Creek Lake weren't you, George?" He said, smiling.

"I was – those were the happiest days of my life."

"Then what happened? What changed?"

I told him about Bill dying, about Mr. Sullivan finding me a job in Ft. Myers, Randy and the rest, right up to the day of the fight.

"So when did you have your first nightmare, George?"

"You know, it's funny, Dr. Baldwin, but I wonder why I never had a nightmare while I was in Vietnam. I guess it's because I didn't have time to think about what was really going on while it was goin' on. I was too worried about surviving every day, every minute of every day. The first nightmare I had was after I got back to the States. I was this big war hero but I had this nightmare one night that caused me to roll around the floor in the barracks at Ft. Eustis, crying like a baby. All of the other soldiers didn't know what to make of it. I was pretty embarrassed, and ashamed, really, but there was nothing I could do about it. It just happened."

"Do you remember that dream, George?" He asked, softly.

"I do," I responded.

"Tell me about it."

I heaved a deep, long sigh, shrunk down in my chair, and began. I told him all about Tillie and us being blown up by the bomb in the road.

"Did you pull the trigger, George?"

I had never told anyone about that dream. I had never told anyone what really happened. I hated to think about it and didn't want to talk about it. I lowered my head, avoiding his probing eyes. "No, Dr. Baldwin, I didn't."

"What did you do, George?" he asked.

I started to cry. "I let him die…I let him die…I didn't even try to help him. I knew he'd die if I didn't and he did," I lowered my head and sobbed.

Dr. Baldwin put his hand on my shoulder and said in a low, soft voice, "He was going to die anyway, George. You knew that. You knew he was going to die, didn't you, George?"

"Maybe, but I could have tried," I said. I looked up, straight in his eyes and asked, "I should have tried, shouldn't I, Dr. Baldwin? He was my best friend."

"You had an instant to decide what to do, George. You did what you thought was right at that moment. It was a split-second of time in a lifetime of split-second decisions, George. Don't punish yourself anymore for that. From what you've told me, he would have died right there in your arms no matter what you did. You didn't do anything wrong, George. Forgive yourself."

"I can't, Doc. I think about it all the time and dream about it still. It's my worst nightmare, and I have many, but I can't talk about that with anyone… you're the first person I've told about any of this."

"You didn't do anything wrong, George. Forgive yourself for that," he whispered, repeating himself several times.

We sat silently for a minute or two while I regained my composure. When I did, I muttered, "Sorry about that, Doc."

"Don't be. I want you to tell me about all of them, George. But first, tell me, didn't you see someone at the base for any of these problems? After that first night, word must've gotten around. I expect that wasn't the only time you had that experience, was it?

"No, there were others, and yes, I saw a counselor at the base once or twice."

"What did he tell you?"

"He said it was normal and that it should all go away after I'd been back in the States for a while longer. He wasn't worried about it or about me at all."

"That's because it was so prevalent. There were so many young men just like you, George, who were having the same problems. The Army didn't want to acknowledge the problem. They still don't, but go on, tell me about some of the other dreams you remember having."

I told him about the dreams in which the ears grew back a whole body and the dead child running off.

"So some of these dreams were just your imagination, and some involved things that other soldiers told you about, plus those which involved things you really experienced right, George?"

I told him that was right. Many were about things I'd actually seen, like the Vietnamese woman being shot in the head, men being blown up by bombs in the road, a man losing his head to a helicopter blade, the be-headed men I saw, the Buddhist woman who set herself on fire, the exploding child and a dozen other experiences like that.

"And then there are the ones that caused you fear, about things that could have happened but didn't, yes?"

I told him that was right too, like when our allies, soldiers in the South Vietnamese Army, the people we were fighting for, refused to get out of the helicopter and killed all of my crew members, and about the fear I had of being over-run by an all-out assault by the North Vietnamese regulars, and the fear of having my rifle backfire during an assault and other things. I also told him about my fear of rats and snakes eating me while I was sleeping, all of which wasn't far from the truth. I spoke for fifteen or twenty minutes.

The whole time I was talking, he was writing. He'd look up every now and then, ask a question or just murmur a knowing sound like "mmmm," or say, "I understand," or something like that. I told him as much as I could remember about my dreams, and when I thought I was finished, he asked more questions.

"And what about the time after your wife came down to see you, the four months or so before the incident? Those were good months for you, George, weren't they? Any problems to speak of? Any nightmares during that time?"

"Those were great months, Dr. Baldwin. We were in love. We were talking about having children and enjoying a warm winter and being together, taking long walks on the beach with our dog. That was a great time in my life."

"No nightmares?"

I told him they were much less frequent. I also told him what it was like for me before Rebecca moved down and why I got Bailey.

"These days, talking about now, do you find yourself sitting and staring into space, George?"

"Some of the guys have told me that I do. They say I can be looking right at them and not even see them. They say it's like I'm looking at something a mile away."

Dr. Baldwin looked up from his pad and said, "They call that the 'Thousand Yard Stare,' George. You're not the only one who does it."

After what had to be at least three hours, either I ran out of things to say or he ran out of questions. "That's all I can remember right now. There's more, I'm sure, but I can't remember it."

"Before we end, I need you to tell me what happened on the day of this incident you're in jail for. What can you tell me about the incident?"

I told him what I could remember. When he asked what I thought had caused the situation to escalate the way it did, I had no explanation. The guy had been a jerk and he must have pushed the wrong button was all I could say.

"He pushed a button that was deep in your subconscious, George. One that you didn't know was there."

I heaved another of what had been many sighs and said, "I have thought about it and thought about it and I have no explanation for why I let that get out of hand. That is just not the way I am. I had nothing to gain by it, nothing at all. I should have just walked away."

"And I know you wish you did, George, but that's how life is, isn't it? One little thing happens and the next thing you know life has changed, completely, and we can't bring it back. We can't un-do what has been done. You're not a criminal, George. You're a good man."

I lowered my head, wishing his words were true, and muttered, "All of a sudden I'm tired, Dr. Baldwin. I'm tired of talking about it. It makes me cry to think of all that I've lost and all that I'll never have again, over nothing… nothing at all."

"You've been talking for two hours now, George. You should be tired. That's enough. You did just fine today, George. I can help you."

He reached over and patted me on the shoulder.

"Thank you, son, for what you did in the Army. You probably haven't heard that too many times, have you?"

"No, I haven't. I rarely talk about my days as a soldier anymore."

"The whole country was torn up by what happened in Vietnam. The soldiers, our soldiers, were victims in that way, too. Not only did they come back wounded, scarred, crippled and damaged, nobody thanked them for what they had done. Men didn't want to think they had died for nothing, that what they had done in Vietnam had no meaning. So many people in our country felt that we didn't belong there, that what we were doing was wrong, that it led to an enormous internal struggle here, too. Returning soldiers weren't welcomed home. Those who made it home, and many didn't, even those who came without physical wounds, came home with mental problems that were hard to deal with, especially by themselves, without any help from the country that sent them there. It was a tragic period in the history of our country and we're not over it yet."

"Dr. Baldwin, I've given this a lot of thought, and I'm proud to have been a soldier in the United States Army, but I don't think we could have won that war unless we killed every man, woman and child in the entire country. They didn't want us there to stop the communists. Most people didn't care who ran the government, especially those dirt-poor farmers out in the country. I think everybody just wanted our money. Either they wanted our money or they wanted us dead, or both."

"That's probably the saddest part, George. We think of the war from our point of view, from your point as a soldier on the front line, or as the United States being the leader of the free world trying to prevent the spread of communism, but what about them? What about the Vietnamese? We were there to help them keep their country out of the hands of the communists, and we destroyed their land, killed men, women and children who may or may not have been against us, turned their wives, sisters and daughters into prostitutes and told them we were there to help them. What about them? Vietnam was one of the poorest country in the world at the time. It was a land full of rice paddies and little more. They just wanted peace and they got anything but that from us."

"They didn't wear uniforms, Dr. Baldwin, at least not in the south, and we didn't speak their language, none of us did. It was us versus all of them. We didn't know who to trust, so we didn't trust anyone but each other."

Dr. Baldwin stood and said, "George, that's enough. That's all for now. Before you leave, I will need to have you take a few tests. They are standardized tests that people like me use to base their findings on. It's important that you answer the questions as best you can. These are not tests that you can pass or fail. They are more a test of your personality, though the tests do measure your intelligence level as well. Just do the best you can. It will take you about another hour or so to complete them. I don't need to be with you while you take the test."

He walked toward the door and pounded on it several times. Within moments, the lock turned, the door opened and a guard appeared in the doorway.

"Deputy Williams, would you please take Mr. Murphy to a room where he can take these tests. I have some work to do back at my office. I'll come back later today to pick them up, okay?"

The deputy assured him that he would do as asked.

"Give me just another moment with Mr. Murphy," he said. "I'll be finished in about two minutes."

The guard closed the door but didn't lock it. Dr. Baldwin turned to me and said, "I can't promise what will come of this, George, but I will do my best to help you get out of this mess you're in right now."

I stood, walked over to the door and said, "You already have, Dr. Baldwin. It felt good to get that off my chest. I've been carrying all that around inside me for a long time."

I reached out and extended my arms, we embraced, and held each other for several seconds. I gave him one last big hug and said, "Thank you, Dr. Baldwin."

"No, thank you, George, and good luck, son."

He turned, knocked on the door, which opened immediately. I wiped tears from my eyes as I walked out of the room.

CHAPTER SIXTEEN
A Psychiatrist for the State

AFTER MEETING WITH DR. Baldwin, I didn't hear much of anything from anyone for a while. A few weeks later, I received a notice from the court that the State would be allowed to have me examined by a psychiatrist of their choice. I was concerned about talking to someone who probably would be testifying against me at trial. Through all the jail-house lawyers I was learning things about criminal law, like my Fifth Amendment rights. I knew they couldn't make me testify against myself at a criminal trial, but I wasn't sure about what would happen at my trial, since I had asserted an insanity defense. Was I was going to have to tell this guy everything or not?

I called the PD's office and spoke to Mr. Satchel. He explained that since I had entered a plea of not guilty by reason of insanity, I was admitting that I had committed the offenses of aggravated battery and attempted murder, or that the offenses occurred. That meant that I had to tell the State everything about what had happened and answer all the questions asked of me about what had happened and about my insanity defense. He added that Dr. Baldwin had written a very good report on my behalf. I asked him if I could see it and he told me that he'd bring it by next time he came to see me but he'd rather I not see it until after I talked to the psychiatrist for the State.

He warned me, "Remember, George, whoever it is, and I don't know who it will be right now, he or she is not your friend. Be careful about what you say, okay?"

I assured him that I would be.

A week later I was called out of my cell and taken down to the conference room where I had met Dr. Baldwin. I was surprised to see a middle-aged woman in a bright yellow dress. I was expecting another bearded old man. I don't know why, I guess that was just my perception of what all psychiatrists looked like.

She stood when I entered, smiled and said, "Good morning, Mr. Murphy. My name is Joyce Andrews and I am a psychiatrist. I'm pleased to meet you."

I was somewhat taken aback by her friendly manner. She was a pretty woman, with medium length blonde hair and, though she was at least fifteen years older than me, or more, I felt a little funny being with her. I hadn't seen any women at all since Rebecca's last visit. It made me feel a bit strange. I smiled back at her, saying, "I'm pleased to meet you as well, Mrs. Andrews."

"Please call me Dr. Andrews," she said. I prefer it that way."

"Sorry about that. I will," I said.

We sat down, and I think her smile and mannerisms disarmed me. She was wearing perfume and that, too, threw me off. I wasn't used to it. I felt intoxicated, or dizzy. I had been apprehensive about meeting this doctor and I'd been told to be careful about what I said by many of my fellow inmates, because doctors could twist my words to support whatever conclusion they were trying to reach, but my defenses seemed to evaporate. She put on a pair of glasses, which matched her dress. They changed her appearance some, making her look more professional.

"I've read your file and I've read the report of Dr. Baldwin," she began. It seems as if you aren't having any problems at all these days, are you, Mr. Murphy, from a cognitive perspective?"

"Cognitive?"

"By that I mean, daily living, getting along with people, performing your tasks as a trustee – those kinds of things."

"No, I'm not having any problems with those kinds of things," I responded.

"And you haven't had any problems of that nature to speak of since the day of the incident, it appears, is that correct?"

"You mean here in jail?"

"Yes, I do."

"No. I get along okay with everyone. The only problem I've had in here was when they moved me to a private cell because I was making too much noise, because of my nightmares."

"We'll talk about that in a few minutes. And it seems as if everything was going well in your life during the few months you had been here in Ft. Myers working as a boat mechanic. Is that correct?"

"Yes, it was. I was doing well at work, my wife and I were in love with each other and I was happy. Everything was good in my life, until Mr. Kuhn came to the Marina that day, that is."

"And did you have any problems that you'd like to tell me about before you came to Ft. Myers? I'm referring to the years after you got out of the Army and before you moved to Ft. Myers."

"Well, I had a problem with a fellow worker one time up in Jeannette, and I was pretty depressed and unhappy after my first divorce, and…"

"But you didn't see the need to see a psychiatrist or a psychologist at any time, did you?"

"You mean outside of when I was in the Army?"

"Yes, I'm referring to that period of time after you were discharged from the Army."

"No, I never saw a psychiatrist or a psychologist ever before speaking to Dr. Baldwin, not even while I was in the Army. I saw a counselor while I was in the Army but I'm sure he wasn't a psychiatrist or a psychologist. I don't know what he was."

"You don't consider yourself insane now, do you, Mr. Murphy?"

"No, I'm not insane."

"And when you went to work on that day, the day of the incident with Mr. Kahn, you weren't acting strangely or having any mental problems, were you?"

"No, everything was fine."

"So is it fair to say that you really had no mental problems either before or after this incident?"

"Yeah, I think so," I responded. "There was nothing wrong with me before this thing happened and there's nothing wrong with me now. It was just that one day, that one incident. It probably didn't last five minutes – that was the only time in my life that I…"

"Ever got in a fight, Mr. Murphy? Is that right?"

"That's right. I had never been in a fight before…never. I'm not a fighter. I've never hurt anyone in my life."

"So if anyone were to ask you if you had any mental health problems right now, what would you say?" She asked in a sweet and non-threatening voice.

"Right now? I'd have to say that I'm pretty depressed over what happened to me, being in here, my divorce, and what's going on in my life right now, but…"

"But who wouldn't be, right? This is a difficult situation you are in and you'd like to be able to get out of jail and put all of this behind you, like it was a bad dream, wouldn't you?"

"Absolutely."

She spoke so nicely to me, like she understood me. She knew what I was going to say before I said it. Several times I had to remind myself that she was a psychiatrist for the State who was there to examine me.

"But aside from that, how would you describe your current situation, from a mental health point of view?"

"I'd say I'm coping with it as well as I can."

"You don't think you need any mental health counseling now, do you?"

"I don't think so. No, I'd say I'm doing okay dealing with it all. I've never had anything to do with the law before so this is all new to me and it gets confusing at times, like this not guilty by reason of insanity business."

"And you understand that if the judge or a jury finds you were temporarily out of your mind during the five or ten minute period you had the fight with Mr. Kuhn that you will be found not guilty because you were insane at the time, don't you?"

"Yes, Mr. Satchel has explained that to me."

"And you also understand that if the judge or a jury finds you are no longer suffering from any mental illness, or no longer insane, if you will, after being found not guilty by the jury, that you will be able to walk out of this jail as a free man, don't you, Mr. Murphy?"

"That's what I'm told."

"And that fight with Mr. Kuhn, you feel as if you were acting in self-defense, is that it?"

"That's exactly right. He started it." Finally, someone was seeing things from my point of view, not his, I thought to myself.

"And to your way of thinking, all of this was because of Mr. Kuhn and his actions, is that right?"

"Absolutely! I never would have gotten in a fight with that man if it weren't for him pushing me and swearing at me...never." That was exactly how I felt. I was glad to finally have a chance to tell that to someone.

"But you don't remember Randy and the others, including the police officer, coming along to break up the fight, do you?"

"No, I don't. Once the fight started, I don't remember much of anything except for waking up on a hospital bed with chains and leather straps on me."

"He made you mad, didn't he, Mr. Murphy?"

"He did. I've never been so mad in my entire life, Dr. Andrews, and that's the truth."

"He made you so mad that you felt like you could've killed him, didn't he?"

"That's right," I blurted. "I was so mad I couldn't see straight."

"That's about what I gather from what I've read," she said. Then she paused for a minute or so, looking down at her notes. When she looked back up she said, "Now, I've seen the test results from the standardized tests given you by Dr. Baldwin so there's no need for me to have you take them again, but I do want you to tell me about these nightmares you told Mr. Baldwin about. Are you still having them?"

"Well, right now, ever since they moved me into a cell with a guy that snores loud enough to wake up the whole jail, whenever I start to have a nightmare, he shakes me and wakes me up so, I guess the answer is yes, I still get them, but they don't last too long and I'm not causing any problems here in jail any more, at least not as much as I was. I have trouble getting back to sleep sometimes, but other than that, it hasn't been as bad as it has been in the past."

She went on for a few minutes, asking questions about several of the things I had told Dr. Baldwin about my dreams, all of which were apparently in his report that I hadn't seen. She knew about Bailey, about my childhood, and she seemed to know about everything I'd told Dr. Baldwin.

Every question she asked with a smile, even when talking about my deepest, darkest secrets. I don't know why, because I knew better, but I answered all of her questions like I was a kid in a candy store, hoping that the storekeeper would give me some more candy if I acted real nice, as if she was going to write a report that said let George Murphy go free. My brains were scrambled that day.

"You were proud to be in the United States Army, weren't you, Mr. Murphy?"

"I was, for the most part. I enjoyed being in the Army. Vietnam was tough, and I would never go back if I could do it all over again, but I made it through and I'm proud of that."

"You should be. It's not easy being a soldier in a war, I'm sure, but you didn't expect a war to be child's play, did you?"

"No, and that war was worse than any we'd ever been in, I'd say."

"Do you think it was worse than fighting the Germans or the Japanese in World War II? Or worse than World War I, Mr. Murphy? Or the Civil War? Or the Revolutionary War, for that matter?"

"No, I can't say that, but at least those men knew who they were fighting – the enemy at least wore uniforms – I think that was the hardest part for us."

"But you never actually killed anyone, did you, Mr. Murphy?"

"There were times when I held a machine gun on a helicopter, while I was the crew chief, and I shot into the jungle many, many times, not knowing if I hit anything or not, and I did my time as a sentry, carrying my M-16, and I fired it every now and then, but no, I never actually shot anyone that I know of."

"So there were plenty of guys who had it much worse over there, didn't they, Mr. Murphy?"

"Oh, yeah. The grunts had it much worse than me. So did a whole lot of other guys, but it was bad for all of us," I said, shaking my head at the thought of all that I'd seen, done and heard about while in Vietnam.

"And there were hundreds of thousands of foot soldiers, soldiers who marched through the jungles over there, weren't there, Mr. Murphy?"

"All told, there were millions of us there."

"So you'd agree with me that there were hundreds of thousands of soldiers, or grunts as you called them, who had it a lot worse than you did, didn't they, Mr. Murphy?"

When she asked that question, I sensed that maybe I'd been talking too much. I responded by saying, "At least that many." Then she went back to talking like she understood me and knew what I'd been through and put me back at ease.

After half an hour, she stood, extended her hand, smiled and said, "Thank you, Mr. Murphy. I don't have anything further to ask you. I thank you for your cooperation today. It's been a pleasure meeting you."

I stood, shook her hand and said, "Thank you, Dr. Andrews. It's been a pleasure for me, too."

The smile was still on her face as she led me to the door. A guard took me back to my cell. Despite that one moment of doubt, I felt a bit giddy. I felt like maybe things were going to work out alright after all. I was as sure as I could be that she was going to write a report that was favorable to me.

Three weeks later, Mr. Satchel came to see me.

"Did you have a good time with Dr. Andrews, George?"

"Oh, yeah," I said. "She was as nice as could be to me. I liked her."

"Well, she said some very nice things about you, too, George."

"Really?" I asked. "What did she say?"

"Well, she said that you are a very nice man and that you are not suffering from any mental illness at the present time…"

"That's good," I said, excitedly.

"She also said that you weren't suffering from any mental illness at the time of the incident," he added, matching my level of excitement.

I could feel my face fall as the smile turned to a frown. I responded, "That's bad."

"Yes, George, that's bad. I told you to be careful, didn't I?"

"You did."

"What came over you? Did you really tell her that he made you so mad you could have killed him?"

I remembered the exchange. "I didn't actually use those words. Those were her words. She sort of put those words in my mouth the way she asked the question," I offered.

"You didn't help your case when you said that, George."

"I thought she understood me and that she understood the way I felt that day."

"She understood all right. She understood enough to find that you knew the nature and consequences of your actions, that you felt you were justified in using physical force to defend yourself against the insults and a shove given you by Mr. Kuhn, and that you were and you are responsible for your actions."

I lowered my head, realizing how foolish I had been in thinking that she might really give me a favorable report.

Sensing my thoughts, Mr. Satchel said, "But don't feel too bad, George. No matter what you would have told her, she was going to find that you were not insane at the time of the incident."

I looked up and said, "Really?"

"Yes, in the five years she's been doing this, she has yet to find anyone insane."

"No one?" I asked.

"Not one person. That's why the State uses her. They know they are going to get a favorable report."

I pondered that thought for a few seconds and asked, "So what does that mean as far as my case is concerned?"

"It means we're going to trial and that we've got to hope the jury will agree with Dr. Baldwin and not with her."

Mr. Satchel stood and said, "See you in court, George."

Trial was scheduled to begin in less than a month. I'd be spending Christmas behind bars.

CHAPTER SEVENTEEN
Picking a Jury

THE DAYS PASSED SLOWLY as the January trial date approached. My parents came to visit during the week after Christmas. Mr. Sullivan came once, too. My parents brought some clothes for me to wear during the trial. It was hard seeing them. They were so sad about what had happened and so afraid I'd be sent to prison. We all cried, even my father, who I never saw cry in his life, not even when his parents died.

I was taken to court once for a pre-trial hearing before Judge Marcolo. I didn't understand much of what went on. It was all legal jibberish as far as I could tell. I couldn't understand many of the words and they talked about things like jury instructions, how long the trial would take and the scheduling of witnesses.

After the hearing was concluded, I meet with Mr. Satchel for a few minutes in the holding cell, before I was taken back to jail, and he told me that the State was willing to agree to a sentence of five years in prison if I'd abandon the insanity defense and plead guilty to the charge. Mr. Satchel said that I could plead 'no contest' if that would make me feel better. I asked him what he thought I should do.

"I'm a trial lawyer. I love being in trial. That's the best part about being a lawyer as far as I'm concerned. So if you ask me, I'd tell you let's take our chances. We can win this thing, but it's up to you. If we lose, I go have a few drinks and drown my sorrows. You go to prison. You're the one who has to decide, not me."

"How much of it is up to Judge Marcolo? How much will it hurt me to have him as our judge?"

"He'll hurt you if he can. If it were up to him, you might as well start whistling Dixie right now, but it's not. It's up to a jury. In criminal cases the judge can't decide the case, only a jury can do that. In civil cases, a judge can enter what is called a 'summary judgment' if he feels that the evidence is strong enough to allow him to do that."

"And do you think they might believe Dr. Baldwin, not Dr. Andrews?"

"Dr. Baldwin is a good witness but it depends on the jury. Sometimes you'll find that men jurors like Dr. Andrews but the women don't. Sometimes it's the opposite. It just depends on the jury you get. Every jury is different."

"You can't give me an idea of what my chances are? Fifty-fifty?"

"Yeah, I'd say fifty-fifty is a pretty safe bet. I'm sure not going to try to talk you into going to trial. It's your decision, not mine. I'll do the best I can for you by answering whatever questions you have, and I'll do the best I can for you during the trial, that's all I can promise."

I was so depressed, so tired of being in jail, and so angry at myself for letting myself get into this situation in the first place, I just didn't know what to do. I didn't want to be in jail any longer and I sure as hell didn't want to go to prison. Finally, I decided to take my chances in front of a jury.

A week later I was sitting in court, wearing a new blue sports jacket and tan pants with a new white shirt and a blue-tie with gold stripes that my parents had bought for me at a J. C. Penney store. I sat next to Mr. Satchel, waiting for the judge to enter the courtroom. Twenty people were sitting in the back of the room behind me.

A tall, thin man in a black suit and blue tie was sitting at the table opposite us. He was the attorney for the State who was prosecuting me. I'd never seen him before. Every time it had been someone different. He didn't look over at me at all. He didn't say much to Mr. Satchel, either. When I asked Mr. Satchel about him, he said, "Don't worry about it. He's a jerk. I won our last two trials and he's not happy with me. He says I made improper arguments to the jury, that I expressed my personal opinions, which I did, but I didn't do it on purpose and the judge ruled that it didn't affect the outcome, which it didn't. It's just sour grapes on his part, that's all."

Within moments, the back door to the courtroom opened, the bailiff walked in and said, "All rise! The Circuit Court in and for Lee County, Florida, is now in session, Judge Anthony Marcolo presiding.

Once the judge sat down, he began. "You may be seated. Good morning, ladies and gentlemen. Welcome to jury duty in Lee County. The case for your consideration today is a criminal case and it is the case of the State of Florida versus George Patrick Murphy.

He turned towards me and said, "Mr. Murphy, would you rise so the panel will know who you are?"

I stood, looked at the judge and then over at the jury and sat back down.

"Mr. Murphy is represented by attorney Michael Satchel." Mr. Satchel stood up and said "Good morning."

"Representing the State of Florida is William Wadkins, who is an Assistant State Attorney." Mr. Wadkins stood up, nodded, and sat back down.

"Do any of you know Mr. Murphy, Mr. Satchel or Mr. Wadkins?" the judge asked.

No one responded.

"I will assume that means no. Our Court Reporter, who is keeping a record of our proceedings, is Sophie Crow. Our Clerk, who is keeping up with our paperwork and items of evidence, is Sarah McIntosh. Our bailiff, who has assisted you so far this morning and who will assist those of you who are selected to be jurors on this case throughout the trial, is Jack Conners.

"Do any of you know any of them, or me, for that matter?"

When no one responded, the judge continued, "The case for your consideration involves a charge that on the 3rd day of April, 1979, George Patrick Murphy did unlawfully strike one Edward Kuhn, without justification or excuse, and did cause the said Edward Kuhn great bodily harm, in violation of Florida Statute 784.045. This offense is known as Aggravated Battery.

"Mr. Murphy is also charged with attempting to cause the death of Edward Kuhn, without premeditation or design, in violation of Florida Statute 784.04. This latter offense is known as attempted murder.

"Mr. Murphy has admitted that the two offenses occurred, but he has plead not guilty to the charges, claiming that he was insane at the time of the incident. This defense is referred to as being 'Not Guilty by reason of Insanity.'

"To select a jury to hear and decide this case, we're going to call the first thirteen of you to the jury box. You will be called at random. I will ask you some preliminary questions and then the attorneys will have an opportunity to ask you some questions. Our questions are not intended to embarrass you in any way or to try to pry into your private affairs. Our questions are intended to assist the attorneys in selecting the fairest and most impartial jurors that they can for this particular case and this particular set of circumstances.

"After the attorneys question you, they will approach the bench and we will have a bench conference. At that time some of you may be excused from the jury. If for any reason you happen to be excused, please, do not be offended. It is not because we don't think that you would make a good juror, it is just that someone else might be a better juror for this case. You may very well be a better juror on another case going on down the hall or going on upstairs.

"With that understanding, ladies and gentlemen, if the clerk calls your name please stand and follow the bailiff, Mr. Conners, who will show you where you are to sit. If your name is not called, please remain seated.

"We would ask, however, that those of you who are not called pay attention to the questions asked by the Court and the attorneys, since you may be called at a later time if we are unable to select six jurors from the first thirteen prospective jurors.

The clerk called out names and juror numbers. I was half paying attention to what was being said, but Mr. Satchel was feverishly writing down all of the names in boxes he had drawn on a sheet of paper. I was watching peoples' faces and all that was going on around me.

Judge Marcolo began to question the first juror.

"Mr. Moore, you are from the Captiva Island area of Lee County and you have lived here most of your adult life, is that correct? You are married and you and your wife, Maggie, have two children? You presently are working at the Bank of America as an Account Executive, is that correct? Your wife works part-time selling real estate, is that right? You have not been a victim of a crime and you are not related to any members of law enforcement, correct? Do you know of any reason that you could not be a fair and impartial juror in this case?"

The judge proceeded to ask the same or very similar questions of all of the prospective jurors. Almost half of the prospective jurors were retired. There was only one person who seemed to be about my age. He had long hair and was wearing blue jeans and a t-shirt and looked out of place with the other people there. Most were married, most had children, and many had grandchildren.

It seemed as if it was a fairly broad spectrum of people. Several on the panel were Hispanic, a few were black, some Jewish, but most were Caucasians of various Christian faiths. There were housewives, a businessman, a teacher, a bus driver, two construction workers and even a lawyer. A few had prior jury service. Two of them had sat on a criminal jury before and several others had been jurors on civil cases in the past.

"Ladies and gentlemen, there are going to be a number of people called as witnesses in this case and I am going to read a list of those individuals. I ask that if you know any of the people whose names are called, please raise your hand and I will then inquire how you know that particular person.

"Deputy Robin Stewart;

"Dr. Joyce Andrews;

"Dr. Ronald Baldwin;

"Edward Kuhn;

"Randy Cross;

"Tom Sparrow,

"Michael Stone; and

"Andrew Binder.

"Do you know any of the people whose names I have just mentioned?

None of the jurors indicated any knowledge of any of the witnesses. I turned to Mr. Satchel and whispered, "Four of them are the guys I worked with. Are they all going to be witnesses?" He responded that they probably would be but that he didn't know for sure what the State would do. I knew that Randy would be a witness, but I hadn't known about the other three.

After half an hour or so, the judge said, "Thank you, ladies and gentlemen. The attorneys will now have some questions of you. Mr. Wadkins, you may inquire."

Mr. Wadkins stood and said "Thank you, your Honor," and began to ask more personal questions of each juror, following up on the answers given to Judge Marcolo. He seemed to be about the same age as Mr. Satchel but he was clean-cut with short, black hair, no facial hair, and he was neatly dressed. Satchmo presented a different image.

While Mr. Wadkins was questioning the lawyer, who obviously didn't want to be there, I leaned over and told Mr. Satchel that the top button on his shirt was loose. He looked back and said, "I know. I like it like that. It squeezes my neck if I button it."

The lawyer was explaining why he didn't think he could be fair or impartial in this case. I couldn't figure out from what he was saying if the lawyer would be a good juror or a bad juror for me, but it wasn't hard to see that he would rather be back in his office making money than sitting as a juror in my case making $15 per day.

After questioning each of the prospective jurors, Mr. Wadkins began to question the jury as a group. "Does everyone understand that in this case, unlike most every other criminal case, the issue is NOT whether or not Mr. Murphy committed the offenses with which he is charged, which are Aggravated Battery and Attempted Murder, it is whether or not he was not insane at the time the offenses were committed?"

Although the judge had told the jurors that my defense was 'Not Guilty by Reason of Insanity,' a few had quizzical looks on their faces when Mr. Wadkins asked that question and had questions about it for him. Mr. Wadkins was uneasy in answering their questions and the judge interceded, "Ladies and gentlemen of the jury, I will instruct those of you who are chosen to sit on this panel as to the law to be applied in this case. The purpose of this portion of the trial is simply to select six fair and impartial jurors. As I have explained, in this case Mr. Murphy has not challenged the allegations that he committed the acts which gave rise to the two criminal charges made against him. Instead, he claims that he is not criminally responsible for those actions because he was temporarily insane at the time he committed those acts. With that understanding, please do your best to answer the questions asked of you. Next question, Mr. Wadkins."

"Does everyone understand that because the Defendant, Mr. Murphy," and he turned and looked directly at me for the first time as he spoke, "claims that he is not guilty by reason of insanity, the State of Florida has the burden to prove that he was NOT insane at the time of the incident in question, and that it is my job, as the Assistant State Attorney who will prosecute this case on behalf of the State of Florida, to present sufficient evidence to allow you to determine that Mr. Murphy was SANE at the time of committing these two offenses? Do you all understand that?"

Although most of the jurors nodded appropriately, I could see them stirring in their seats. I thought to myself that this whole concept of 'Not Guilty by Reason of Insanity' was probably a new concept for many of them.

The judge seemed to be becoming a bit irritated by Mr. Wadkins' questioning and said, "Again, I remind you, ladies and gentlemen, I will instruct you on the law which you are to follow, not the lawyers." He turned to Mr. Wadkins and said, "and if you would, Mr. Wadkins, confine your questions to whether or not these jurors are suitable for this case and not so much about their understanding of the law."

Mr. Wadkins stammered, "But I…"

"Next question, Mr. Wadkins," the judge said, in a somewhat stern voice.

Mr. Wadkins asked, "Does everyone understand that the term "reasonable doubt" does not mean beyond a shadow of a doubt or beyond any doubt whatsoever, it means beyond a REASONABLE doubt?"

When everyone indicated that they did, he continued, "Do you agree to hold the State of Florida to its burden of proof, which is beyond a reasonable doubt, but not a higher burden?"

Again, the jurors collectively indicated that they understood those principles.

"No one on this panel knows Mr. Murphy, personally, but let me ask you all this, has anyone ever been to the Caloosahatchee River Marina, which is located straight across the river from here?" As he asked the question, Mr. Wadkins pointed out the window in the direction of where the Marina was located.

Juror number 8, Beverly Shannon, who, like Mr. Kuhn, was a real estate salesperson in an office not far from the downtown area, raised her hand and said that she had gone out on a boat from there on one occasion with friends.

"Do you recall seeing the defendant, Mr. Murphy, or anyone else who worked there at that time?"

She indicated that she couldn't remember anyone she had seen that day at all, other than the people she was with.

"Would the fact that you may have seen Mr. Murphy or one or more of the people who might be witnesses in this case on that one occasion at the Marina where this incident occurred make any difference to you or affect your ability to hear and decide this case, Mrs. Shannon?"

When she answered that it would not affect her at all, Mr. Wadkins continued, in his deep baritone voice. "Let me ask you this, do you all agree that you will follow the law as it is given to you by Judge Marcolo even if you don't agree with it?"

Juror number 14, Katherine Evans, raised her hand and said "Are you asking me if I am going to disregard what the judge says and do whatever I think is right?"

"My question is do you agree to follow the law as the judge instructs you and not make up your own theory of what the law should be, that is correct."

"I agree to follow the law. That's my job. I promise to do my job the best I can if I'm chosen to be a juror on this case," she responded.

"And do all the rest of you agree to do the same? Follow the law, even if you don't completely agree with it?"

All nodded accordingly, although a few jurors had a puzzled look on their faces. They didn't know any of the facts and circumstances surrounding the incident yet and they were confused by the prosecutor's questions. Despite that, they all agreed that they would follow the law.

"Do you agree that you will not allow sympathy to affect your ability to hear and decide this case if the Judge instructs you that you are not to do so, and that means either sympathy for or against the victim in this case or for or against Mr. Murphy? Mrs. Feitz, do you understand that?"

"I haven't heard the facts of the case yet, but I agree to follow the law. Yes sir."

"Do you all agree to return a verdict of guilt if sufficient evidence is presented to demonstrate to your satisfaction that Mr. George Patrick Murphy was, in fact and as a matter of law, SANE when, on April 3, 1979, in Ft. Myers, Lee County, Florida, he intentionally struck Mr. Edward Kuhn, without legal justification or excuse, and in doing so caused great bodily harm to Mr. Kuhn, thereby committing the offenses of Aggravated Battery and Attempted Murder?"

When all nodded in agreement, he concluded by saying,

"Thank you, ladies and gentlemen of the jury. I have no further questions of you at this time. I thank you for your candor and for your careful attention to the questions I have asked."

Judge Marcolo then said "Mr. Satchel, you may inquire."

Mr. Satchel rose rather ungracefully from his chair and ambled up to the podium. He put his legal pad down and began, "Good morning, ladies and gentlemen of the jury. As Judge Marcolo told you earlier, my name is Mike Satchel and I represent George Murphy in this case."

Mr. Wadkins had stood behind the podium which was placed directly in front of the jury box and hadn't moved during the entire time he questioned the panel. Mr. Satchel immediately walked to the side of the podium. When he did, Judge Marcolo chided him, "Mr. Satchel, if you would, please remain behind the podium when you address the jury."

"But your Honor, I thought the rule was as long as I stayed within an arms length of the podium that was acceptable," Mr. Satchel replied, which seemed to annoy the judge.

"That may be the rule of procedure when you appear before other judges, Mr. Satchel, but in my courtroom you are to stay behind the podium. Do you understand?"

"Yes, your Honor," Mr. Satchel replied. He put his right hand on the podium and moved a foot closer, and was, technically, behind it, but he still wasn't directly behind it. The judge seemed to notice and let out an audible sigh, but didn't say anything more. It seemed pretty obvious to me that Judge Marcolo didn't care much for Mr. Satchel and I thought to myself that the jury could probably sense that too, which wasn't good for me.

"You all understand that the purpose of this portion of the trial is to select six fair and impartial jurors to hear and decide this case, correct?" Mr. Satchel continued,

Everyone nodded appropriately.

Satchmo had a relaxed, easygoing manner about him, which was in stark contrast to Mr. Wadkins's more business-like presentation. He was very earthy, almost folksy in his mannerisms, and I thought to myself, as I listened to him ask a few personal questions of each juror, that he was doing a pretty good job so far. He acted as if he was meeting them at a cocktail party or, as was more likely the case, a bar. He asked his questions with a smile on his face, too. I hadn't known what to expect, but so far I was impressed.

He continued, "You have been told that this case involves charges that George Murphy, who I will refer to as George, got in a fight with Mr. Edward Kuhn and he tried to kill him in doing so, correct?"

"Objection, your Honor. We have been over all of this already. You told the jury what this case is about. I told this jury what this case is about. This is repetitive. The State does not wish to allow counsel to argue his case to the jury on *voir dire* examination. Besides, the defense is that Mr. Murphy was insane at the time, not that he didn't commit the crimes. "

"Sustained. Next question, Mr. Satchel."

"You all understand that George doesn't deny that he got in a fight with Mr. Kuhn and that his defense is that he is not guilty of the charges because he was temporarily insane at the time of the incident, correct?"

"Objection, your Honor. We've been over this and…"

"Sustained. Mr. Satchel. Please ask questions that pertain to whether or not these thirteen people are qualified to sit as jurors on this panel. Thank you."

I could sense that Judge Marcolo was becoming a bit impatient with Mr. Satchel.

"Do any of you have friends or relatives with mental problems?"

At that, a murmur started in the back of the jury box and erupted into a group laugh. It caused Satchmo to laugh as well. Neither the judge nor Mr. Wadkins saw any humor in it.

Mr. Wadkins stood, but before he could say anything, Mr. Satchel continued, "Let me re-phrase that. Do any of you have friends or relatives who have ever been hospitalized for mental problems?"

The jurors' smiles faded and two raised their hands.

"Yes, Mr. Green?"

"I have a nephew who's been in and out of jails and hospitals. They can't quite figure out what his problem is, but he has some kind of mental problems, that's for sure."

"And you, Mrs. Silverman?"

"My sister is getting older and…well, she's not able to take care of herself anymore. They say it's dementia. Is that the kind of thing you want to know?"

"Yes, ma'am. It is."

Another person raised a hand and asked, "Do you want to know about seeing a psychiatrist or a psychologist on a regular basis? Is that what you're asking? I'm not sure what you mean by mental problems," he said.

"Yes, I want to know about that. I don't want you or anyone to tell me anything too personal. I'm wanting to know if any of you have family or friends with mental problems that require them or have required them in the past to seek professional help. I'm asking for a show of hands."

At that, almost half of the jurors raised their hands.

"How about any of you? Again, without telling me anything about it, just raise your hands, please."

Some jurors squirmed in their seats. They didn't like the question but two or three raised their hands. Mr. Satchel wrote on his note pad for a few seconds, then looked up, "Thank you. How about military service? How many of you are veterans?"

Half the men raised their hands.

"Vietnam veterans?" Mr. Satchel continued.

About half of those took their hands down.

"World War II vets?"

Two of the older men on the panel raised their hands.

"Any vets from the Korean War?"

One man raised his hand. He had his hand up for all three questions.

"You are retired from the military, Mr. Militana, correct?"

"After almost 40 years. I went in as an eighteen year old kid in 1941 and retired just last year," he responded proudly.

"You saw a lot of men with battle fatigue, 'shell-shock,' or what is now called 'post-traumatic stress disorder' didn't you, sir?"

"It's not easy being in battle. Everybody gets stressed when someone points a gun at them. I'm not someone who has too much sympathy for that kind of stuff. I marched with General George Patton. He'd put those kind of guys right at the front and I agreed with him. That's what I'd have done, too. "

"Thank you for sharing that with us, Mr. Militana. Anybody else feel that way about men who complain of mental difficulties arising from being in battle or in the military at a time of war?"

Mr. Satchel turned to the only juror who was about my age, Wally Saunders. "How about you, Mr. Saunders? Any military service?"

"Not me," he responded. "I had a high lottery number so I wasn't called, but if I was drafted, I'd have gone to Canada, or maybe an island in the Caribbean."

He laughed as he said that, but nobody laughed with him.

Another juror spoke up and said, somberly, "I lost a brother because of Vietnam. He wasn't killed over there but when he came home he wasn't the same. He got into drinking too much and taking drugs and was dead within five years. I blame that on what happened to him in Vietnam."

"Thank you, Ms. Zane, or is it Mrs.?"

"Mrs., thank you."

"Anyone else?"

There was a stir amongst the prospective jurors, and another hand was raised.

"If you're talking about men coming back from Vietnam having mental problems, I know a whole bunch of people like that." another man offered. Someone behind him said, "Me, too."

Mr. Wadkins apparently knew that this was a 'Satchmo' tactic, that he liked to endear himself to a jury, and would basically try to argue the case right from the get-go. He also knew that Judge Marcolo didn't like Mr. Satchel much and wouldn't tolerate that. He wanted to stop Mr. Satchel before he got too far into his argument. He had found a way to get the jury to open up to him some.

Mr. Wadkins stood. "Your Honor. I object to this line of questioning. We'll be here all day if Mr. Satchel is allowed to talk about soldiers returning from Vietnam with mental problems."

"Your objection is over-ruled, Mr. Wadkins, but I'm not going to allow too many more questions along these lines, Mr. Satchel. The purpose of *voir dire* examination is to select six fair and impartial jurors. I won't allow you to pry too deeply into their personal background and affairs and this is only relevant only if it would affect their ability to be fair and impartial in this case."

Turning to the jury the judge said, "Ladies and gentlemen of the jury, I will instruct you on the law to be followed in this case at the appropriate point in the trial with regard to the issue of the insanity defense. The purpose of this portion of the trial is to determine if you can be a fair and impartial juror in this case. To that limited extent, the questions asked of you so far have been proper. You may continue, Mr. Satchel."

"Let me re-phrase the question slightly. Would you all agree with me that it is not uncommon for men to return from war and have mental problems as a result of their experiences?"

"I object, your Honor," Mr. Wadkins pleaded.

With an audible sigh, Judge Marcolo said, "I will allow the question. Your objection is over-ruled, Mr. Wadkins."

Mr. Satchel looked at the jury but received no response.

"Does anyone disagree with that statement...that it is not unusual for men who fought in Vietnam, or Korea or WWII, to return with mental problems resulting from their service in the military?"

No one raised their hands, but one offered, "The term mental problems covers a lot of territory, doesn't it?"

"Yes, it does and..."

"Your Honor, I object," Mr. Wadkins said disdainfully, "Mr. Satchel's questions are so vague. The term 'mental problem' could mean anything."

Judge Marcolo said, "I'm going to sustain the objection at this time. Mr. Satchel, unless you can ask a question which will go to the issue of whether or not a prospective juror can be fair and impartial in this case because of some specific prior experience in his or her life, I'm not going to allow you to continue with this line of questioning."

At that, Mr. Satchel turned to the jurors and said, "Let me ask you all this question…as you have heard, Mr. Murphy has claimed that he is not guilty because he was temporarily insane. What you haven't heard is that he is a Vietnam Veteran and he says it is because of what happened to him over there. My question is this, do you know of any reason why you could not be fair and impartial in this case under that circumstance? Other than Mr. Militana, who has already explained his thinking on that point, is there anyone else?

No one raised a hand or responded.

"So if Mr. Murphy can prove that he was temporarily insane at the time of the incident in question, and that his condition arose or occurred as a result of things he saw and did while he was a soldier in Vietnam, you will find him not guilty by reason of insanity – is that correct?"

Mr. Wadkins stood and, with a pained expression on his face said, "Your Honor, Mr. Satchel is injecting facts in his questions and I…"

Mr. Satchel kept his eyes on the jurors, who were looking back at him, as Judge Marcolo said, "Over-ruled. I will allow that question but I am nearing the end on this, Mr. Satchel."

No one, other than Mr. Militana, seemed to have a problem with that statement. If they did, they didn't say anything. Mr. Satchel looked at them all for a few seconds, waiting for a response. When he didn't receive one, he turned and said, "I have no further questions, your Honor. Thank you, ladies and gentlemen, for your candor."

"Counsel, approach the bench."

Mr. Wadkins and Mr. Satchel rose and walked up to the bench. I was close enough to hear the judge ask, "Can we do this here or shall I excuse the panel."

"Mr. Wadkins said, "This shouldn't take but a few minutes. I'm fine with doing it here."

"I think we should do this outside of the presence of the prospective jurors, your Honor," Mr. Satchel said.

"Alright, Mr. Satchel, we'll do it your way. You may return to your seats."

As they did so, the judge said, "Ladies and gentlemen, we're going to give you a short break and then when you come back we will continue with the selection process. We won't be long so I'm going to ask you to remain in your seats for a few minutes. You can stand and stretch, use the restrooms if you need to. We have a few things to discuss with the attorneys in my chambers." With that, we will take a ten minute recess."

After the judge left the room, Mr. Satchel said, "You'll need to come along with me." I asked what for. He told me that they were going to do jury strikes. I didn't know what that meant.

"We're going to pick our jury. Anybody you didn't like, other than Mr. Militana?"

"No, they all seemed nice enough," I responded.

"Nobody give you the 'evil eye' or anything? Nobody you just didn't like, for any reason at all?"

"No. That woman who's in real estate might not be so good," I offered, "and I don't want that lawyer on my case, either.

"Yeah, we'll bump her," he responded, "and we won't reach him. He was the last of the prospective jurors."

Mr. Wadkins was already out the door, following Judge Marcolo, but Mr. Satchel didn't seem to be in a hurry. When I said something about it he replied, "They can wait. They can't do anything unless we're there. They don't care much for me, and I don't care for them, either."

"I noticed."

"But the big thing, the only thing that is important, is whether or not the jury likes us. What do you think? he asked.

"I don't know. They seemed to pay attention to you pretty well."

"Yeah, and I got them to laugh. I always try to make a jury laugh, even if it's at me," he said. "Anyone else we want to get rid of?"

When I responded 'no,' he stood and said, "Let's go."

We got into chambers and sat down. The judge said "Gentlemen, the procedure is as follows: the State goes first as to the first six prospective jurors and then I will alternate back and forth as strikes are exercised. First, however, do either of you have any challenges for cause?

"Yes sir," Mr. Satchel began, "Mr. Militana can't be fair and impartial and I ask that he be stricken for cause."

"Why? Just because he likes General Patton? That is not enough," Judge Marcolo responded. "

"But Judge, the man doesn't believe good soldiers can have post traumatic stress disorder…that's my whole defense!" he protested.

Unfazed, Judge Marcolo responded, "You will have to use a peremptory challenge on him, Mr. Satchel. Anyone else?"

"You mean for cause, Judge?"

"Yes."

"No, your Honor."

"What says the State?"

"I don't have any challenges for cause, your Honor, though I'd like to use one on Mr. Saunders if I could think of a good reason why he is legally unfit to serve as a juror, but I can't. He's just a would-be draft-dodger." Mr. Wadkins replied.

"I will deny the request to excuse Mr. Militana for cause. Mr. Wadkins, what say you as to the first six?"

Mr. Wadkins said "The State accepts that panel, your Honor."

"Mr. Satchel?"

"The defense strikes Mr. Militana."

"That puts Mr. Saunders as our sixth prospective juror. What says the State?"

"The State will exercise its first peremptory challenge on Mr. Saunders, your Honor."

"That puts our realtor, Mrs. Shannon, into the sixth chair. What says the defense?"

"We exercise our second strike on her, your Honor."

"That gives us Mrs. Silverman. What says the State?"

"We would accept that panel, your Honor."

"Defense?"

"The defense will accept that panel, your Honor."

"Alright. So that we're clear, I am required to allow back-striking up until the time the jury is sworn, but after this, I won't be happy about it. I'll ask again, State, any peremptory challenges?"

"The State accepts this panel, your Honor."

"Defense?"

"The defense accepts that panel too, your Honor."

"The panel is now Morgan, Phorr, Jordan, Moore, Feitz and Silverman. One last time. Any further challenges? If not, that's your panel."

When both sides had no further challenges, the judge said, "As far as an alternate is concerned, Mrs. Jackson is the next on the list. You both have one peremptory. Do either of you have a challenge as to Mrs. Jackson?"

After neither attorney voiced an objection the judge then said, "Alright, then, we have our jury. I'll be back in the courtroom in a moment. I have a call to make." As he picked up the phone, we turned and walked back into the courtroom to our seats.

CHAPTER EIGHTEEN
The Trial

THE JUDGE RE-ENTERED THE courtroom and said, "As I call your name you may step from the jury box. All of you whose names I have called are excused from this case. You are to return to the general auditorium where you reported this morning. You may be re-assigned to a different case. Those of you who are left in the jury box are selected and designated to be on the jury to try this case."

Once all of the other prospective jurors had left the courtroom, all that remained were the two lawyers, me, the court personnel, the judge and the seven strangers who were going to decide my fate. The judge continued. "Mrs. Jackson, you are the alternate juror in this case. The rest of you are the six jurors who will hear and decide this case. Please stand and raise your right hand. The Clerk will now administer an oath to you."

"Please raise your right hands. Do you solemnly swear and or affirm that you will fairly and truly hear and decide this case based upon the evidence presented to you?" All responded that they would. The jury was sworn before noon.

Judge Marcolo dismissed the jury for lunch, telling them to be back by 1:15. After the judge left the room, Mr. Wadkins and everyone else stood up and left, leaving only me and Mr. Satchel and a second bailiff, who had sat a few rows back of me the entire time, watching over me, apparently. The bailiff said to Mr. Satchel, "I've got to get some lunch, too, and I can't leave Mr. Murphy alone. I'll have to put him back in the holding cell. If you don't need to talk to him for more than a minute or two, I can wait. Otherwise, I'll have to lock the both of you in here and leave you. What do you want to do?"

Satchmo told him that he'd be just a minute. The bailiff then walked to the far corner of the room, out of hearing distance.

Satchmo turned to me and said, "Well, what do you think so far, George?"

"I thought you did a very nice job, Mr. Satchel, but Judge Marcolo and Mr. Wadkins were pretty rough on you weren't they?"

"Yes, they were, but I'm used to that. So what do you think of your jury?" he asked.

"We have a jury with three men and three women on it, plus a woman alternate. I don't know. They're all older than me, but they seem okay. What do you think?"

"I would have liked another woman or two on this case, especially someone like Mrs. Feitz, who is a teacher. I think the women might be more sympathetic about this than the men, but I'm not sure. This case is going to be a battle of the experts. Sometimes they're harder on another woman and sometimes they're happy to see a woman like Dr. Andrews succeed, but I'm happy with the panel." Mr. Satchel said. "It's the best we could do. Sometimes you just have to get lucky with the people on the panel, and I think we did alright."

"Say, George, I'm going to stay in the courtroom, go over my notes and get ready to make an opening statement. I really can't talk too much right now."

"No problem," I said. I stood and walked over to where the bailiff was standing who then, after looking out in the hallway to make sure no jurors were around, put me back in a holding cell where I sat until a little after 1:00 when he came to take me back to the courtroom.

At exactly 1:15, after everyone was re-assembled and in their assigned seats in the courtroom. Judge Marcolo entered, sat down and said, "Mr. Wadkins, you may make your Opening Statement to the jury at this time."

"Mr. Wadkins strode up to the podium, bowed to the judge and began, "May it please the court, ladies and gentlemen of the jury. The State of Florida intends to prove that the Defendant, George Murphy, was sane at the time he struck Edward Kuhn in the nose, breaking it, and proceeded to continue to beat him about the head with his fists until Mr. Murphy's co-workers came to break the fight up.

"However, Mr. Murphy was so angry at Mr. Kuhn, and so anxious to continue fighting with him, that it wasn't until a Deputy Sheriff for the Lee County Sheriff's Office arrived at the scene that order was restored and even then that didn't occur until Deputy Steward hit Mr. Murphy with his night stick, twice, after Mr. Murphy refused to obey the Deputy's lawful commands.

"The State will present the testimony of a psychiatrist, Dr. Joyce Andrews, who will tell you that Mr. Murphy was sane at the time of the incident. She will tell you that he simply lost his temper and flew into a rage.

"You will hear from Mr. Murphy's fellow employees, the four men who attempted to subdue him before the police arrived, who will tell you that he was completely out of control.

"The defense is expected to call a psychiatrist who will testify that Mr. Murphy was temporarily insane as a result of…"

"Your Honor, I object. Mr. Wadkins is about to tell the jury about my defense, not what he is going to present in his case in chief. It sounds as if he's about to get into what the ultimate issue is going to be. That is improper."

"Mr. Satchel, I agree with you. Mr. Wadkins, please confine your statements to what you intend to prove and how you intend to do it. Stay away from any argument and what evidence the defense might present, please. This is not the time for that. You may continue."

"Yes, your Honor. As I was saying, ladies and gentlemen, the State will prove, through eye-witnesses, including the victim, Edward Kuhn, as well as an expert witness, that the Defendant committed the two crimes with which he is charged and his defense that he is not guilty, or not legally responsible for his actions, due to his claimed temporary insanity is without merit. The State intends to call six witnesses and it hopes to conclude its case before we adjourn this afternoon, in less than four hours. I thank you for your careful attention to what I have just said and what you will soon hear."

At that, he strode back to his table.

"Mr. Satchel. Do you wish to make an Opening Statement at this time?"

"I do, your Honor."

"You may proceed."

Mr. Satchel stood and lumbered up to the podium. He put a legal pad on top of the podium and began by reading from his notes, looking up at the jury every so often.

"Good afternoon ladies and gentlemen. As you know, Mr. Murphy doesn't deny that he got in a fight with Mr. Kuhn and, even though Mr. Kuhn started the fight and provoked Mr. Murphy…"

Mr. Wadkins stood up and said, "I object, your Honor. The defense in this case is insanity, not self-defense. This is improper on Opening Statement."

"I agree, Mr. Wadkins. Mr. Satchel, please confine your comments to what you expect to present in defense of Mr. Murphy, not your argument. Save that for Closing Arguments, please."

"But your Honor, I…"

"Mr. Satchel. The Court has ruled. You may continue."

Mr. Satchel seemed flustered. There went his script and he wasn't sure where to pick up after being told that he couldn't say the things he was planning to say about Mr. Kuhn.

He stood quietly for a few seconds, looking at his papers, then said, "The defense will call Dr. Edwin Baldwin, a respected psychiatrist in this community, who will tell you that Mr. Murphy, or George, was out of his mind once that fight started. He's going to tell you how George is a veteran of the Vietnam War and that while in the Army he saw a number of bad things happen. He's going to tell you how George, who was a mechanic and a crew chief on helicopters in the Army, went off to war as a young man...too young, really, and how what he saw and what he did left huge psychological scars on George."

At that, Satchmo walked over and put his arm on my shoulder. When he did, the judge scolded him.

"Mr. Satchel. Please remember my admonitions of this morning regarding not leaving the podium when addressing the jury."

"Yes, your Honor," Mr. Satchel said as he walked slowly back to the podium. "As I was saying, George was just a kid, two days out of high school when he went into the Army. He was in Vietnam a year later. He's a hero, really. He did two tours of duty there. He didn't have to, but he did. When he got out, after completing a six year commitment, he was honorably discharged.

"George had never been in a fight before, or since. This was, as far as anyone knows, the only time in his life he'd been in a fight. Dr. Baldwin is going to tell you that the only reason George acted the way he did that day was due to the provocation by Mr. Kuhn and what happened to him, George, that is, in Vietnam. He's going to tell you that George suffers from Post-Traumatic Stress Disorder. He'll explain to you what that means. He's going to tell you that George was temporarily insane. George is no criminal. Once you've heard all the evidence, I'll have another opportunity to come before you and present my argument as to why you should find George not guilty. For now, that's all I have to say. Thank you for your attention."

Before Mr. Satchel had made it back to his seat, Judge Marcolo said, "Mr. Wadkins, call your first witness."

"The State calls Eugene Kahn."

The back doors to the courtroom opened noisily and everyone turned to watch Mr. Kuhn, dressed in his finest clothes, walk in. He walked right past me, without looking at me, straight to the witness box where he was administered an oath.

Once he was seated, the prosecutor began to ask him questions, just as the other prosecutor had at the Preliminary Hearing. Mr. Kuhn's answers were the same.

After Mr. Kuhn had testified about how it was all my fault and that I had beaten him mercilessly, Mr. Satchel had a chance to ask questions.

"So were you in a hurry that afternoon, Mr. Kuhn? he began.

"Yes, I was. I was supposed to meet my friends down in Flamingo at 5:00 and I wanted to avoid rush hour traffic. Everyone who lives in Lee County can understand that, I'm sure." he said, smiling at the jury. "It was about 4:00 as I recall."

"And were you upset when George didn't take your boat out of the water as soon as you asked him to?"

"I tried to tell him that I was in a hurry, but he wouldn't listen. He started to tell me that he was a mechanic, that this wasn't his job and that he was supposed to get off work at 5:00 and all this, and I really wasn't that interested in his problem. I told him that I was a paying customer and I expected to be treated well."

"And how did George react when you told him that?"

"He got back on his fork lift and started to get this other boat, not mine."

"Are you saying that he didn't already have a boat on his fork lift?"

"That's right. He didn't. He could have picked my boat up and put it on my trailer right then and there and none of this would have happened."

"So what did you do then?"

"I stood in front of the fork lift so he couldn't move without running me over."

"And what did George do?"

"He came down off of the fork lift and attacked me, that's what he did."

"So you never cursed him?"

"Absolutely not!"

"And you didn't push him first?"

"Absolutely not!"

"And he basically cold-cocked you, is that right?"

"He blind-sided me. I never saw the punch coming. If I had I'd of..."

"You'd have what, Mr. Kuhn?"

"I might be the one sitting at that table with you, sir. He never would have landed a punch," he said, glaring over at me as he did.

"You're a pretty tough guy, are you?"

At that point, Mr. Wadkins stood up. He didn't like what he was hearing.

"Your Honor, I object. We aren't here to try the case as to why the fight started. The only question is Mr. Murphy's mental condition at the time of the incident. This is far afield from that."

"I'm going to over-rule your objection, Mr. Wadkins. You may continue, Mr. Satchel. Is there a question pending?"

Mr. Kuhn then blurted, "I can take care of myself."

"So if George says he already had a boat on his lift when you first came up to you, he'd be mistaken?"

"That's right. He'd be mistaken."

"And if George says that you cursed him and called him names when he wouldn't stop what he was doing, put the boat back in the water and take your boat out of the water, he wouldn't be telling the truth."

Mr. Kuhn looked over at me and said, "He'd be lying."

"And if George said you pushed him and started the fight?

"He'd be lying!" he said, raising his voice and looking over at me even more menacingly than before.

Mr. Satchel seemed to come alive. He moved slightly in front of the podium, which he had positioned as close to the witness stand as the judge would allow, keeping one hand on it so as not to raise the ire of Judge Marcolo, and put his face as close to Mr. Kuhn's as he could. He was getting to Mr. Kuhn and showing the jury some of what I had seen that day.

"So how much did this boat cost you, Mr. Kuhn?"

"I bought that boat new. It cost me fifty grand. The engines were almost as much, or more even."

"Those were twin Yamaha four-strokes? 250 horse power?"

"That's right."

"And you were a good customer, weren't you?"

"I paid my bills on time and it wasn't cheap keeping my boat there."

"Couldn't you just back your trailer down the boat ramp and load it yourself?"

"No, you have to use their equipment to get boats in and out of the water."

"You felt like you deserved better treatment, didn't you, Mr. Kuhn?"

"I did deserve better treatment. I didn't deserve what I got. I hope Mr. Murphy there gets what he deserves."

Their voices seemed to rise with each exchange, one getting a little higher than the other. The tempo speeded up, too.

"What he deserves? Did he deserve to be cursed and pushed?"

"I didn't curse him and if I'd hit him he would've been the one on the ground."

Mr. Wadkins stood up and shouted, "I object! Mr. Satchel is badgering this witness the witness." He had to scream to be heard over the two of them. They had raised their voices. The jurors had a look of disbelief on their faces about what was going on in front of them.

"I agree. I sustain your objection and instruct you to get behind the podium, lower your voice, and ask your next question, Mr. Satchel."

Mr. Satchel kept his eyes fixed on Mr. Kuhn as he backed up and stood behind the podium, and asked, "How's your nose, Mr. Kuhn?"

"It's fine now but I went through six months of pain because of him," he responded, pointing his finger at me.

"And how about your head? Any problems with your memory or anything?"

"No, thank God. No thanks to him. I had to undergo two Cat-scans and take other tests – I was in the hospital for eight days because of him. They tell me I'm fine. I lost time from work. Who's going to pay me for that? Him? I don't think so. I wish I could sue him for what he did to me but he's got no money."

"Your Honor, would you please instruct this witness to answer the questions asked of him and not volunteer information as he just did."

"Mr. Kuhn, please just answer the question asked of you, nothing more," the judge said.

"Any injuries that haven't gone away, Mr. Kuhn?"

"None that I know of," he replied, and then added, "yet."

"So did he land a lucky punch, is that it, Mr. Kuhn?"

"Objection!"

"Sustained."

Mr. Satchel turned and started to head back to his chair, then he stopped and said, "Were you ever in the military, Mr. Kuhn?"

Mr. Wadkins stood to object, but before the words came out of his mouth, Mr. Kuhn responded, "No."

And Mr. Satchel said, "I didn't think so," and sat down.

Mr. Kuhn sat there, red-faced with sweat visible on his forehead and cheeks, waiting to be told what to do.

"Any re-direct, Mr. Wadkins?"

"No, your Honor."

"Mr. Kuhn, you may step down. May this witness be excused, gentlemen?"

Both attorneys replied at the same time, "No, your honor."

The judge continued, "Mr. Kuhn. You are free to go today, but you remain under subpoena until this case concludes. There is a chance that you may be re-called as a witness. Do you understand?"

"Yes sir."

He walked right past me, within a foot or two, much closer than he had to, staring at me. I could see the jury watching him. I didn't react. I looked straight back at him. The jury had seen him for what he was really like. Mr. Satchel had gotten under his skin.

The courtroom was quiet as the back doors closed behind Mr. Kuhn. "Call your next witness, Mr. Wadkins," Judge Marcolo said.

"The State calls Randy Cross."

I turned and watched Randy walk into the courtroom. As he walked by, he put his hand on my shoulder and patted it. He was dressed like he'd come from work, which he probably had. It was obvious that he wasn't comfortable in a courtroom.

After Mr. Wadkins had him testify to all the things he had seen and done, Mr. Satchel had the opportunity to question him.

"Had you ever seen George act like that before?"

"No, I hadn't. George had always been the nicest guy to everyone. I never heard him raise his voice before. I was shocked."

"Did it seem like the same person who had been working for you for over six…eight…what was it, ten months?"

"He was starting his eighth month with me. He came to work at the first of September the year before and no, it didn't seem like the same person at all," he said, gravely, looking straight at me. "That wasn't the George I knew."

"Did he look the same? I mean, would you have recognized him if you didn't know who it was?"

"I don't think so. His facial expressions made him look like a completely different person."

And then Mr. Satchel asked, "Did you think he recognized you, Mr. Cross?"

"That's the thing the guys and I talked about afterwards. It was like he didn't know who we were. He was ready to fight us and we hadn't done anything to him."

"How long did this whole thing last?"

"Not even five minutes, if that."

"For those five minutes, do you think George was insane?"

"Objection!" screamed Mr. Wadkins. He didn't want to hear Randy's response, but before the judge could rule on the objection, Randy blurted out, "Yes, I do."

Then the judge said, "Your objection is sustained. I instruct the jury to disregard the answer given by Mr. Cross. You, and you alone, ladies and gentlemen of the jury, are to decide whether or not Mr. Murphy was sane at the time he committed the acts in question. Mr. Cross is a lay person and he is not permitted to offer his opinion on that issue. You may proceed, Mr. Satchel."

"No further questions, your Honor."

"Next witness."

"The State calls Andrew Binder."

While we were waiting for Andy to be seated, I asked Mr. Satchel why Randy wasn't allowed to answer the question of whether I was insane or not. He told me that it was because Randy was being asked to give an opinion on the ultimate issue in the case, which isn't proper. Only the experts could do that. Besides, that was the most important issue in the case and that was for the jury to decide."

"So why'd you ask the question?"

"It's up to the prosecutor to object. If he doesn't object, there's no error. If Randy had said that he didn't think you were insane, it would have helped the State's and hurt our case."

"Did you know what he was going to say before you asked the question?"

"No."

"So why'd you ask the question?"

"Calculated risk – from the way he was answering questions, I felt confident that he'd say yes."

Andy testified to the same basic things that Randy had said. Mr. Satchel didn't ask if he thought I was sane, but he did ask if he thought that I recognized him. There was no objection and he said he didn't think so.

Tom and Mike said the same thing. I heard things I hadn't heard before. I had no idea how hard I had fought them that day. I must've been out of my mind. These were my friends. They weren't trying to hurt me. I didn't remember any of that.

The next witness was the deputy sheriff. He testified about how he arrived at the scene and found me in a state of rage. He admitted hitting me on the head with his billyclub, which he called a night stick, because I was so out of control, though he said he didn't mean to. I could see that the issue was coming down to if I was totally out of control because I was so mad or if I was acting the way I was because of what I went through in Vietnam. The officer must have thought I was a crazy man or else he wouldn't have hit me with his club like he did and he didn't take me straight to jail. I was lucky he didn't pull his gun.

Because of all the objections and quarreling that had gone on, by the time the last witness testified, it was after 4:00. The State wasn't sure that Dr. Andrews could finish her testimony before 5:00 so the judge sent everyone home early.

After the jury was gone, and everyone else except for me, Mr. Satchel and the bailiff who was there to watch me, had left the courtroom, Satchmo asked me how I thought the day had gone. I told him that the afternoon went better than the morning did, and it seemed as if there had been some surprises, like what Randy said and how Mr. Kuhn behaved.

"There always are. No two trials are the same. I think we had a good day, a really good day. The jury saw Mr. Kuhn for what he is, a big jerk, and your buddy Randy helped you out when he said he thought you were insane."

"Even though the judge told them to disregard that?"

"Jurors can't do that. They heard it. They can't forget what they heard. There's a saying in law, 'you can't un-ring a bell.' Once the bell is rung, or once someone says anything, you can't take it back. The only thing the judge could've done would have been to declare a mistrial, which he didn't want to do, but he could have."

"So we've got a chance?"

"Oh, yeah. We've got a good chance."

"Better than fifty-fifty?"

"I wouldn't say that. Tomorrow we have the shrinks. Let's see how that goes."

"Will I have to testify?"

"Not unless I think I need to put you on to win the case and if I do then I will. We'll just have to wait and see."

Then he looked at the clock on the wall, since he didn't wear a watch, and said, "Say, I've got to go. I've got a softball game to play in and it starts in half an hour. I didn't think I was going to be able to make it, but now that we finished early, I can."

"No problem. Don't get hurt," I said. "You're all I've got."

"Unless I'm dead drunk, I'll be here," he said with a smile. Then when he saw what must have been a look of horror on my face he added, "I'm kidding," gave me a wink, and said, "See you tomorrow."

I stood and walked over to the bailiff, who then brought me downstairs to a waiting van. I was the last inmate from court that day and the driver, who was a deputy sheriff, too, was anxious to get home.

That night, I lay in bed and wondered about what had really happened that day with Mr. Kuhn. No matter how many times I thought about it, and I'd thought about it thousands of times, I couldn't remember anything after he pushed me and cursed me. I must've been crazy.

Everybody else over went through what I went through, or worse. I knew I wasn't the only guy having these bad dreams. There must have been thousands of other guys who were having problems like that besides me. What was wrong with me, I wondered. Maybe I was crazy. Maybe I still am, I thought. I lay awake worrying about what the next day would bring. I'd either be getting out of jail or looking at a long time in prison. I didn't sleep much.

CHAPTER NINETEEN
Day Two of Trial

THE NEXT MORNING, I shaved, showered, put on my only other collared shirt with the same tie, jacket and pants as the day before and, after breakfast, sat around waiting to be taken downtown to the courthouse. If the trial lasted another day I'd have to wear the same clothes again. I was told the trial would more than likely be over today.

I had been in jail for over nine months and the thought that I might actually be able to walk out of jail today was hard to believe. I tried not to think about it. I didn't think about what I would do if I was actually allowed to walk out of jail. I was afraid of being sent to prison and the fear of what that would be like weighed heavily on my mind. There was no middle ground. It was win or lose. I was scared.

Time passed even more slowly than usual while I sat in my cell, waiting to be called out. I knew that a guard would come get me at 7:30. They always did things at the same time every day. There was nothing I could do except sit, wait and worry.

Finally, 7:30 arrived and I was taken down to a holding cell where, together with six other guys who had to be in court that day, I sat for half an hour, waiting for the van to take us to court. The van left at 8:00 every day. Court began for some at 8:30. For others, like me, trial began at 9:00, so I was going to sit and wait in a holding cell inside the courthouse until a bailiff came and brought me into the courtroom.

By 8:45, I was seated at my chair at our table. I was the first one there. I sat and watched all the court personnel arrive one by one. The jurors were brought in as a group and put in the jury box at 8:55 by the bailiff. Mr. Wadkins arrived shortly after I did. Mr. Satchel was the last one in, getting in just a minute or two before the judge took the bench. He looked a little hung over to me.

"So how did the game go?" I asked.

"We won. Beat the State Attorneys 14-7. I loved it."

"Are you guys in a league?"

"Yeah."

"Does Mr. Wadkins play?"

"Are you kidding? Look at him. He spends his spare time in the library, for fun. No, he doesn't play."

As I was asking him about what would take place today, the bailiff walked in and said, "All rise. The Circuit Court in and for Lee County, Florida is now in session. Judge Anthony Marcolo presiding."

Once Judge Marcolo was seated, he said, "You may be seated. Let the record reflect that all of our jurors are in place and I thank you all for being punctual. We are ready to begin day two of trial in the case of the State of Florida versus George Patrick Murphy. Mr. Wadkins, call your next witness."

"The State calls Joyce Andrews."

Dr. Andrews, who had been sitting right behind the prosecutor's table, walked through the double-doors, past me, over to the clerk to take the oath. Once she was seated, and settled, she looked to Mr. Wadkins, awaiting his questions.

She was wearing a dark business suit, the kind professional women wear, not the colorful outfit I saw her in. She had black-framed glasses on and her hair was pulled back and tied behind her head. She had a serious expression on her face.

"Please state your name."

"My name is Dr. Joyce Andrews."

"And Dr. Andrews, if you would, please tell us your academic background, beginning with college, including any honors or awards you received while there."

"I graduated from the University of Florida, with honors, in 1962. I then attended graduate school at Florida State University from 1962 until..."

She was going on and on about what she had done and where she had done it. I was listening, but mostly I found myself watching the jury, watching how they were reacting to her, and they were fixed on her. She was an attractive woman and spoke well. Mr. Satchel had told me that she could have that kind of an influence a jury. He was afraid that the three men might be more impressed by her looks and give her testimony more credence than they should. They were all paying close attention.

"…I came back to Ft. Myers after graduating, and opened my own practice at that time."

"So you have been a psychiatrist here in Lee County for the last fourteen years, is that correct?"

"Yes, that's correct."

"And are you a member of any professional societies?"

Dr. Andrews droned on for another few minutes about what professional groups she was a member of. When she finished, Mr. Wadkins continued, "And are you active in any organizations within our community?"

After what seemed like fifteen minutes of her telling the jury what an outstanding person she was, Mr. Wadkins said, "Your Honor. I would tender Dr. Andrews as an expert in the field of psychiatry and ask that she be allowed to express her opinions in this case as an expert."

Mr. Satchel stood and said, "The defense would stipulate that Dr. Andrews is an expert."

"With that stipulation, the Court will find that Dr. Andrews is an expert witness and she shall be permitted to offer expert witness testimony in this case."

"Thank you, your Honor. If you would, Dr. Andrews, please tell us if you had occasion to meet the defendant in this case, George Patrick Murphy."

"I did. I met with Mr. Murphy about a month ago. I was appointed by this Court to examine him on behalf of the State of Florida to determine if he was sane at the time he committed the two crimes with which he is charged, Aggravated Battery and Attempted Murder. Prior to meeting with Mr. Murphy, I reviewed the court file, which included the report prepared by Dr. Baldwin, who is the defendant's expert."

"Now you and I did not speak about this case in detail before that, did we?"

"No, other than to make arrangements for me to conduct my examination, which was a scheduling kind of thing, but not about the facts of the case. In fact, I didn't talk to you at all. I talked to a secretary as I recall."

"And after meeting with Mr. Murphy, did you prepare a report?"

"I did."

"And I show you what has been marked as Exhibit One for identification purposes only, and I ask if that is your report."

"It is."

"Did you administer any tests to Mr. Murphy, Dr. Andrews?"

"I did not. Dr. Baldwin tested him and I relied on those tests. They are standardized tests and I would have given Mr. Murphy the exact same tests, which wasn't necessary, for obvious reasons," she replied.

"And is there anything else that you reviewed that I haven't mentioned, Dr. Andrews?"

"I read a transcript of the preliminary hearing that was provided to me by your office," she responded.

"And as a result of meeting with Mr. Murphy, reviewing the court file, including the transcript you referred to, reviewing the report of Dr. Baldwin and the results of the standardized tests, have you formed an opinion, within a reasonable degree of accuracy within your profession's standards, on the issue of whether or not Mr. Murphy was sane on April 3, 1979 when he became involved in a physical altercation with one Edward Kuhn?"

"I have."

"And if you would, please tell us, what that opinion is?"

Dr. Andrews had been turning her head back and forth from where the prosecutor was standing, asking questions of her, to the jury. Before answering this question, however, she turned her whole body so that she was facing the jury directly and, while looking directly at them, said,

"It is my opinion that Mr. Murphy was completely sane at the time he battered Mr. Kuhn. I have no doubt that he was enraged, and lost control of his temper, and that it was completely out of character for him to act that way. However, I am a psychiatrist," she said gravely, "and I don't use the word insane lightly. People who are truly insane are unable to function in our society and they are hospitalized because they are a danger to themselves and others. Mr. Murphy may have been mad, angry, enraged – whatever you want to call it – but he was not insane. In fact, he told me that Mr. Kuhn made him so angry that he wanted to kill him."

"If you would, Dr. Andrews, can you briefly describe for the jury what kinds of things you would have to see in a person before you could call him or her insane. Or, stated differently, what kinds of things you did not find in Mr. Murphy which prevented you from finding him to be insane on April 3, 1979?"

"Well, Mr. Wadkins," she responded, with a hint of a condescending smile on her face, "as you well know, since we are in a court of law, I structure my thoughts, and my opinions, the way the law defines the term. Although I am not a lawyer, my understanding of the opinion from the United States Supreme Court in the M'Naughten case, which I've read many times, is that the question to be answered is whether he knew right from wrong. Using that standard, there is no doubt in my mind about it. Mr. Murphy knew what he was doing was wrong but he was so angry and so enraged that he allowed those feelings of passion to outweigh his better judgment. He committed acts for which he is legally responsible and he was sane at the time of doing so."

For over an hour, Mr. Wadkins asked Dr. Andrews questions about her examination of me and about her opinions. It was hard to sit through and not be able to say a word in my defense. I felt a sense of relief when he finally said, "Thank you, Dr. Andrews. I have no further questions of you."

I had been frozen in place as I heard her testify. Worse yet, the jury seemed spellbound. They hadn't taken their eyes off her. A few people, none of whom I knew, had come into the courtroom. One of them had a note pad and was taking notes. I thought it was someone from the newspaper or maybe even from the insurance company, I didn't know. No one had made a sound while she spoke. I was thinking to myself that my chances of winning had gone down measurably.

I snapped out of it when Judge Marcolo asked, "Cross examination, Mr. Satchel?"

"Yes sir." Mr. Satchel said, rose slowly to his feet, and slowly made his way to the podium. I had no idea what he would ask or what he could say to un-do what had been done. She appeared supremely confident and self assured.

"Good morning, Dr. Andrews."

"Good morning," she replied somewhat curtly. She knew that his job was to discredit her and they may have danced this little dance before.

"How long did you spend talking to George?"

"I would estimate that I spent about an hour with Mr. Murphy," she replied.

"And how much time did you spend reviewing his file prior to meeting with him, Doctor?"

"A couple of hours, at least."

"And I assume it took an hour or so to write your report?"

"That is correct."

"So including the time you spent reviewing his file, the time you spent with George, writing your report, talking to the prosecutor it was what...four, maybe five hours all together, is that it?"

"It might have been more than that. I think it was a little longer. I definitely spent several hours on this case," she said.

"And let me ask you, who pays your bill when you do these court-appointed examinations, Dr. Andrews?"

She smirked and said, "As you well know, the State of Florida does just as they paid for Dr. Baldwin."

"And how much are you paid?"

She gave Mr. Satchel a look of disdain and said, "I charge $150 per hour for these examinations, which is far below what I charge my private clients."

"And do you charge more for in-court testimony?"

"Yes, I do. I believe every expert witness I know of does."

"And how much do you charge for that?"

"My fee is $250 per hour for in-court testimony, which is the standard rate. Judge Marcolo is required to review and approve my bill, I should add."

"And can you tell me how many hours you have in this case so far, Dr. Andrews?"

"I don't know off the top of my head the exact number, but I've given you an estimate of my time. Isn't that good enough?"

"Do you have your complete file with you there?" he asked, pointing at the file in her lap.

"Yes, but I…"

"Go ahead, take a minute or so if you need to…we can wait."

"Well," she said, as if she was being asked to do something unpleasant. "If you insist."

She looked toward the judge and Mr. Wadkins, hoping that someone would tell her she didn't have to do that. After a minute or two, she said, "It looks as if I have billed for exactly 5.2 hours in this case, which does not include my testimony in court here today, my travel time and the time I spent reviewing my file last night and this morning in preparation for my being here this morning."

"And let me ask you this, Dr. Andrews, do you see yourself as someone who is supposed to be completely fair and impartial? Are you someone who is given free latitude to examine someone and express a fair assessment to the State Attorney's Office, or the judge, regardless of what that opinion is?"

She brightened at the question, and quickly responded, "Absolutely. If I had any doubt in my mind I would have no hesitancy whatsoever in telling the State Attorney, or the judge, or anyone else what my opinion was."

"Even if it meant that someone like George here might avoid criminal prosecution for allegedly committing a crime?"

"Absolutely. I see myself as one who is completely fair and impartial, as I said."

"So tell me, Dr. Andrews, why is it that in all of the cases you have been appointed to examine criminal defendants, you have NEVER found ONE person to be insane?" He raised his voice to emphasize his point.

"Objection!" screamed Mr. Wadkins.

"Counsel approach the bench!" Judge Marcolo said sternly.

The court reporter and the two attorneys scurried up to the bench, I followed behind and stood several feet away. Once the court reporter had her machine in place he said, seethingly, "You ever pull a stunt like that in my courtroom again I'll have your license, do you understand me, Mr. Satchel!"

"Yes sir, but…"

"Don't 'but' me, Mister. You know that was improper. It's like asking a man when he stopped beating his wife, and you know it!" he hesitated for a few seconds and then continued, "You didn't lay the proper predicate. You have no idea how many cases she has been appointed on or what opinions she has expressed, do you?" He asked sternly.

Mr. Satchel didn't respond. I was looking at the jury and I didn't see how they couldn't hear what the judge was saying. It was louder than a stage whisper, that was for sure.

"Do you, Mr. Satchel!" the judge persisted.

"I know that in all the cases I've been involved with and all of the cases I'm aware of she hasn't ever found anyone insane, Judge."

"That's not good enough, Mr. Satchel..."

He paused and steamed a bit, seemingly growing redder in the face as he did.

"I have half a mind to declare a mistrial..."

He turned to Mr. Wadkins. "What do you want me to do, Mr. Wadkins? Do you consider that to be so egregious that you would ask me to declare a mistrial?"

"I think a cautionary instruction is appropriate, your Honor, and I think Mr. Satchel should be sanctioned."

"I agree with that. I'll deal with you later, Mr. Satchel. This may be an ethical violation, in my opinion. At best, it's a cheap shot, but since the State isn't asking for a mistrial, I'll give a cautionary instruction. And don't even think about pulling a stunt like that again, Mr. Satchel," he warned.

"Yes sir," Mr. Satchel replied.

As we were walking back to our table, I looked over at Mr. Satchel and he winked at me. No one else saw it but me. He had done that on purpose.

Once the attorneys and I had returned to our places, and after the court reporter was back in her chair, the judge said, "Ladies and gentlemen of the jury, I have sustained the State's objection to the last question and you are instructed to disregard it completely. Any reports this witness may have prepared in other cases, having no relation whatsoever to this case, are completely irrelevant. You should not make any assumptions, draw any conclusions or have any inferences which may arise from the question, and you are not to speculate on what Dr. Andrews' answer might have been. Mr. Satchel, ask your next question."

"Dr. Andrews, do you recognize, or acknowledge, that there is a mental illness or disease known as 'Post-Traumatic Stress Disorder'?"

"There are those within my profession who have identified the behavior of some people, primarily soldiers returning from Vietnam, as a condition called 'Post Traumatic Stress Disorder,' Mr. Satchel."

"Actually, it doesn't. I asked if you, Dr. Joyce Andrews, recognize that there is a mental illness or disease known as Post Traumatic Stress Disorder. Do you?"

"No, I do not. It is a disorder but it is not a disease or illness, such as Schizophrenia, Neurosis, or Dementia. All of those are mental illnesses and diseases. The condition you refer to as 'Post-Traumatic Stress Disorder' has not yet been accepted by my profession as being a disease or mental illness."

"But it is a mental disorder, true?"

"It could be, depending upon the extent of the problem."

"And it could be a mental infirmity too, yes?"

"It could be, but the problems which people who have experienced stress as a result of a traumatic event vary widely, Mr. Satchel, so even if Mr. Murphy is correctly diagnosed as having Post Traumatic Stress Disorder that does not mean that the problem has risen to a point where it has become a mental illness or infirmity."

"And it could be a mental defect?"

"It could be."

"So are you saying that he may have a problem, and he may have Post Traumatic Stress Disorder, but it isn't bad enough to classify it as a mental disease, disorder or infirmity, is that it?"

"I am saying two things: one, he does not have Post Traumatic Stress Disorder, and two, even if he does, he does not have it to the extent that it will excuse his conduct in this case."

"So let me get this straight – do you agree that he has nightmares which resulted from his service in the United States Army in Vietnam?"

"I do not doubt that he has, on many occasions, had nightmares which occurred because of the experiences he had in Vietnam. That is not the point."

"But you don't think his experiences were bad enough to cause him to have stress?"

"I did not say that either. I do not doubt that his experiences in Vietnam caused him stress."

"Both while he was in Vietnam and for years after?"

"I do not doubt that Mr. Murphy continues to experience a degree of stress as a result of his time in Vietnam."

"Even to this day?"

"Even to this day," she responded.

"So if he has stress, as a result of the traumas he experienced in Vietnam in the past, why do you say that he does not have Post Traumatic Stress Disorder?"

"I did not say that he does not have a degree of stress that is caused by trauma he experienced in the past. I said he does not have it to such an extent that it constitutes a mental infirmity, defect or disorder."

"Not five minutes ago you told this jury that Mr. Murphy did not have Post Traumatic Stress Disorder. Are you changing your mind?"

"I said that he does not have a problem of such significance that it rises to the level of being an infirmity, defect or disorder, so let me make myself perfectly clear. Yes, I am saying he does not have Post Traumatic Stress Disorder.

"And since Dr. Baldwin concluded that he did, you simply disagree with him, is that it?"

"I disagree with Dr. Baldwin's conclusions. That is correct."

"And you agree that it is up to this jury to determine if Mr. Murphy suffers from Post Traumatic Stress Disorder, don't you?"

"Of course. I understand that."

"And you would agree that it is up to this jury to determine if Mr. Murphy has a 'mental defect' as that term is used in the Florida Statutes, correct?"

"That is not entirely correct, Mr. Satchel. Clearly, this jury has the ultimate responsibility to make that determination, but they are lay persons. I am an expert in these matters. I am allowed to offer my expert opinion and Dr. Baldwin will be allowed to offer his expert opinion. The jury will decide who to believe, but as I have told you several times now, it is my opinion that Mr. Murphy does NOT have Post Traumatic Stress Disorder and even if he does, he does not have it to the extent that it constitutes a mental illness, disease or defect as required by the law, so it is not entirely up to the jury to make that determination, though they do have the last word on the subject in this courtroom."

"Can you explain to me and to this jury the difference between a disorder, a defect and an infirmity?"

"The difference between a defect, a disorder or an infirmity is really quite significant," she said, rising up in her chair and straightening her back as she spoke. "I went to school quite a long time to learn them. I don't believe Judge Marcolo wants me to take an hour to try to explain the differences here today, Mr. Satchel. To put it as plainly as I can, your client does not have a mental disorder, a mental infirmity or a mental defect. Can I be any clearer than that?"

"Dr. Andrews, into what category of disorder would 'Post Traumatic Stress Disorder' fall? Wouldn't it be in the category of disorders?"

Seeming somewhat exasperated by the question, she responded, "Post Traumatic Stress Disorder' would fall into the category of an anxiety disorder."

"Tell us of some other anxiety disorders, Dr. Andrews, please."

Hesitating a moment, as if waiting for the judge to tell her that she didn't have to answer the question, she said, "A panic disorder, obsessive-compulsive behavior, agoraphobia, social phobias —it really encompasses a number of generalized anxiety disorders, called GADs in my profession, the overwhelming majority of which would never rise to a level sufficient to excuse criminal conduct, Mr. Satchel. I really don't see where this is relevant."

At that, Judge Marcolo interjected, "With all due respect, Dr. Andrews, please leave the issues of relevance to me and just do your best to answer Mr. Satchel's questions even though you may feel that they are irrelevant. Thank you, Doctor."

"So you don't think that soldiers returning from Vietnam, or Korea, Europe, Japan or anyplace else could actually be so scarred from a psychological or psychiatric point of view that their mental problems could rise to the level of a mental infirmity, defect or disorder, is that it?"

"That is not correct. I acknowledge that there may be times when a soldier comes home from war and has a serious mental illness as a result of his experiences during battle, but I am saying that Mr. Murphy is not one of those soldiers, and I should add the trauma necessary to cause a mental problem does not have to be the result of war. It can be caused by a violent physical assault, a natural catastrophe or something along those lines."

"So you agree that the term 'Post Traumatic Stress Disorder has a place in the field of psychiatry, correct?"

"I do not challenge the basis for the term. It's not a new concept, just a new name. In the past, it was referred to as battle fatigue, shell-shock, and other things. It's not abnormal at all. I think that's my point, sir. It is not unusual for soldiers who have been in war to come home and have unpleasant thoughts, or dreams as a result of those experiences. The term, Post Traumatic Stress Disorder, is a relatively new one, that's all."

"So can we use the term Post Traumatic Stress Disorder to refer to that condition which was previously called battle fatigue or shell shock for the purposes of this discussion?"

"That will be fine," she replied, with a hint of exasperation.

"But you don't think the condition which Mr. Murphy has, which I am referring to as Post Traumatic Stress Disorder, is bad enough that it rises to the level of a mental infirmity, defect or disorder, is that it?"

"For the third, or fourth, time, that is exactly it, Mr. Satchel."

"Why won't you agree with me that it could constitute a mental disorder? It is a disorder! How can you say that having horrible nightmares is not a mental infirmity, defect or disorder? It's not normal, is it? Everybody doesn't have those problems, do they?"

"I object, your Honor." Mr. Wadkins interjected. "Mr. Satchel has asked three or four questions at the same time. Which one does he want the witness to answer? Besides, at this point he is badgering the witness. How many times does she have to say the same thing over and over?"

"Sustained."

"Does every soldier have the horrible nightmares George has experienced, Dr. Andrews?"

"No, Mr. Satchel, they do not, but let me say this to you...in my profession I must make a decision as to whether or not people are truly a danger to themselves or others as a result of a mental infirmity, defect or disorder, and there are many categories of mental illnesses and diseases we haven't discussed, and that person, because of such severe problems, must be institutionalized. I believe that Post Traumatic Stress Disorder, or battle fatigue or shell shock is an irregularity, but unless a person is a danger to himself or others because of that condition, whether it is a mental infirmity, disease or defect or a mental illness or disease, he will not be institutionalized. Does that answer your question?"

"But you are familiar with the Florida Statutes on this subject? 775.027, to be exact, regarding the definition of insanity, are you not?"

"Objection, your Honor. Mr. Satchel is now asking for a legal opinion..."

"Over-ruled. He asked this witness if she is familiar with the statute, that's all at this point."

Realizing that he had achieved a rare victory, he persisted, "Are you familiar with the statute, Dr. Andrews?"

Sighing, she responded, "Yes, Mr. Satchel, I am quite familiar with the statute."

"Then you acknowledge that Florida Statute 775.027 includes the words mental infirmity, disorder or defect, correct?"

"Yes, Mr. Satchel, those words are included in the Statute."

"And you're telling this jury that Post Traumatic Stress Disorder is not a mental infirmity, disorder or defect?"

"No, I..."

"Objection, your Honor. The witness has answered that question five times already."

"Your objection is sustained. Move on, Counselor," Judge Marcolo said.

"So will you agree with me that the nightmares Mr. Murphy has as a result of his service to this country in Vietnam are unusual?"

"I will agree that it is unusual, Mr. Satchel, for a soldier to continue to have the problems your client complains of nearly ten years after the events occurred."

"Will you acknowledge Mr. Murphy's condition to abnormal?"

"I will agree that it is abnormal for a soldier to continue to have the problems your client complains of nearly ten years after the events occurred, yes."

"So you acknowledge that there is a condition known as Post Traumatic Stress Disorder recognized by your profession, but you won't acknowledge that the problems George has, or the condition he is in, is sufficiently bad to constitute an infirmity or defect, even though he continues to have stress which resulted from traumatic events years ago, is that it?"

At that point, it seemed obvious even to me, that he had gotten under her skin. She was clearly flustered. She responded, raising her voice ever so slightly, and said, "Let's cut to the chase, Mr. Satchel. What I am saying is that if every man, woman or child who suffers from some sort of trauma during a war came home and committed crimes, they couldn't all walk free and be absolved of wrongdoing because of what they experienced. My father fought the Japanese on Okinawa and he saw things that Mr. George Murphy never even dreamed of seeing, I can assure you, and there's nothing wrong with my father. Mr. Murphy got angry when Mr. Kuhn said something to him he didn't like. Unrestrained passion or ungovernable temper is not insanity, to quote from the statute or the rules, and your client was not insane when he beat up Mr. Kuhn. I think that says it as clearly as I can say it, Mr. Satchel. Hundreds of thousands of men had it worse, much worse, than Mr. Murphy did and they didn't commit crimes like this, did they?"

Mr. Satchel remained quiet for a few seconds, allowing Dr. Andrews' response to echo throughout the room. I guess he figured that he had done about as well as he could with her, and that he had taken a few pedals off her flower, so to speak, because he then said, in a low voice, "I have no further questions of this witness, your Honor."

He stood there, still looking at Dr. Andrews for a few seconds longer, as the judge asked, "Any re-direct, Mr. Wadkins?"

When Mr. Wadkins said that he didn't have any further questions of Dr. Andrews she stood and walked past Mr. Satchel, glaring at him, glancing at the jury only briefly, as she left.

"Ladies and gentlemen of the jury, we've been at this for over an hour and I'm going to give you a short break. Please return to this courtroom in ten minutes. Mr. Bailiff, if you would, please take our jury out and bring them back in at 10:45. Thank you

CHAPTER TWENTY
My Expert Witness

Once the jury had been escorted from the room and the judge had left the courtroom, too, I turned to Satchmo and said, "I don't think she likes you, Satchmo."

"She doesn't."

"Neither does the judge or Mr. Wadkins it seems."

"They don't. Nobody in this courtroom does, except you and sometimes I'm not so sure about you. See, if I do my job, everybody has to work. If I convinced you to enter a plea of guilty or no contest then nobody has to work. I can either be the grease to make the system work or I can be the monkey-wrench in the system. Today, I'm the monkey-wrench and they don't like that."

"So how's that going to affect me?" I asked.

"We'll see. It all depends upon the jury. Their decision, I think, will depend on what Dr. Baldwin has to say. I've got to go use the bathroom...a little too much beer last night celebrating our victory. I'll be back in five minutes."

I sat alone in the courtroom. He was right. I was probably his only friend in the courtroom, but if I was found guilty he'd lose me, too. But he wasn't alone in that regard. He was definitely my only friend. I had no one else to talk to, no one else in the courtroom pulling for me to win.

I wondered, as I often did, how much different it would have been if I could have hired a high-priced defense lawyer, the kind that get their clients out of jail before trial, instead of a public defender. But I didn't have any money, so that wasn't an option. I was reminded of the expression, I didn't have a lawyer. I had a public defender."

He was all I had and I told myself I should have been happy to have him.

I didn't know it until somebody told me that it wasn't until 1961 that a Public Defender system even existed. Before that, criminal defendants were often sent to prison without any representation at all.

I could only hope that his tactics of challenging everything and offending everybody in the process were working. I thought he was doing a pretty good job. He took the sting out of what Dr. Andrews had testified to when Mr. Wadkins asked her questions and the mood in the courtroom changed dramatically. And he did a great job on Mr. Kuhn, too. The insanity defense was his idea. But my case hinged upon Dr. Baldwin's testimony.

Ten minutes later, the jury returned to the courtroom. Exactly fifteen minutes later, the judge returned. He was obviously displeased to see that Mr. Satchel was not back yet. He sat there, visibly fuming. Two minutes later, Mr. Satchel came hurriedly back into the room, saying, "Sorry, your Honor, I…"

"Now that Mr. Satchel is back from our fifteen minute break, we can begin. Mr. Wadkins, call your next witness."

"The State rests, your Honor."

"Counsel approach."

The two attorneys and the court reporter walked up to the bench. I followed behind.

"What says the defense?"

"Your Honor, on behalf of Mr. Murphy, I would move for a directed verdict. The evidence presented by the State is insufficient, as a matter of law, to establish a prima facie case of Aggravated Battery or Attempted Murder, and the testimony of Dr. Andrews is insufficient to prove that Mr. Murphy was sane at the time of the incident."

"Insufficient?" he asked, incredulously. "Never mind. Your motion is denied. You may return to your seats."

After the court reporter was in her seat and ready to proceed, the judge said, "Ladies and gentlemen, the State of Florida has rested its case. The defense will now present its case in chief. Mr. Satchel, call your first witness."

"The defense calls Dr. Edwin Baldwin."

The bailiff walked out of the courtroom and returned within seconds. Dr. Baldwin was walking right behind him.

After he was sworn and seated, Mr. Satchel asked, "Please state your name."

"Edwin Forrest Baldwin."

"And what is your occupation?"

"I am a psychiatrist."

"And would you please tell…"

"Your Honor," Mr. Wadkins interrupted, "in the interest of time, the

State would stipulate to the qualifications of Dr. Baldwin and that he is an expert witness."

"With all due respect, your Honor, I would prefer that the jury know of Dr. Baldwin's qualifications. They heard all about Dr. Andrews and I think it is only fair that…"

"As you wish, Mr. Satchel. You may proceed."

"Dr. Baldwin, please tell the jury about your educational background and work history."

Dr. Baldwin proceeded to tell the jury about how he had obtained his undergraduate degree at Harvard and then gone on to Emory University in Atlanta for one of several graduate degrees. As I listened attentively to his testimony, I also kept an eye on the jury. There was no doubt that he was well-qualified, but so was Dr. Andrews. I thought that he was more qualified than she was but he was a lot older and had been around a lot longer, had more experience. At this point in the trial, they had heard enough, I thought. They were waiting to hear what he had to say. That was the important part, not the credentials.

The two experts were definitely different. Dr. Andrews was in her mid-forties and he was pushing seventy. With his gray hair and gray beard, gray suit with a red tie, he presented himself as a grandfatherly professor. She looked more like a young up and coming professional compared to him.

When he finished telling about his awards, books, articles and the rest, Mr. Satchel said, "Your Honor, now I would ask that Dr. Baldwin be declared an expert witness."

Before the judge could rule, Mr. Wadkins said, "We so stipulate, again."

"Based upon the stipulation, the court finds that Dr. Baldwin is an expert witness and he shall be allowed to offer expert opinions in this case."

Mr. Satchel then asked, "Did you, Dr. Baldwin, have occasion to meet my client, George Murphy, and examine him to make a determination as to his competency?"

"I did."

"And when was that, Dr. Baldwin?"

"I met with George on November 17 of last year."

"And how long did you meet with him, Dr. Baldwin?"

He looked over at George and said, "We must have talked for almost three hours, didn't we, George?"

I didn't know what to say. I wasn't expecting to answer any questions. He continued, "Yes, I think it was about three hours, maybe a little less."

"And did you prepare a report of your findings and conclusions?"

"I did," he replied.

"And how much time have you spent on this case, prior to today, Dr. Baldwin?"

"I have over a dozen hours invested in this case, so far. George presents a very interesting situation and I felt it necessary to conduct research on the issue of Post Traumatic Stress Disorder."

"How much do you bill for your time, Doctor?"

"For this case, my rate is $150 per hour. For my private clients, it is much higher."

"And do you testify for and on behalf of the State, too, Doctor?"

"Well, I consider that I am testifying on behalf of the State of Florida right now. They're the ones who pay me. It's just that I happen to be testifying on behalf of a defendant in this situation. I am often called upon to testify as a witness for the prosecution, too. I 'call them as I see them,' as they say."

"So when asked to examine a defendant by the State, you've offered testimony in the past that the defendant was not insane, is that correct?"

"Not exactly. If I am asked by the State Attorney's Office to examine a defendant, as Dr. Andrews was in this case, and I render a report finding the defendant NOT to be insane, the case rarely goes to trial. In fact," he said, pausing to look up at the ceiling and stroked his beard a few times, "I don't remember ever testifying under a circumstance like that. My testimony would only hurt the State and the attorney involved would never call me as a witness."

"But that is not the conclusion you reached in this case, is it, Dr. Baldwin?"

"No, it is not, but in this case I've been asked to examine Mr. Murphy by the defense, not by the prosecutor."

"Please tell the jury what opinion you have reached in this case, Dr. Baldwin."

"It is my opinion that at the time George got into that fight with Mr. Kuhn, he was absolutely out of his mind and he was temporarily insane."

"And what was the cause of that condition, Doctor?"

"It was a result of his time in the military. George was in the Army for six years and spent a few of them in Vietnam. He had a bad time while there and he still isn't over it."

"And what, specifically, is the condition which caused that temporary insanity, Doctor?"

"The condition is known as Post Traumatic Stress Disorder."

"And is that a mental infirmity, disorder or defect?"

"It most certainly is an infirmity and it's a defect, too, and Post Traumatic Stress Disorder is, by definition, a disorder, isn't it? That's what it is called…a disorder."

"Is Post Traumatic Stress Disorder a new concept, Doctor?"

"Yes, it is, at least by that name. The illness, or infirmity, has been in existence probably since the beginning of time when men first started fighting with each other in hand-to-hand combat. The earliest reference to the disease comes from the Greeks…"

Dr. Baldwin settled back in his chair, looked at the jury and continued, "In the book, The Iliad, written some five hundred years before Christ, Homer tells the tale of how the Greeks conquered Troy by the use of a large wooden horse which, according to the legend, contained hundreds of Greek soldiers. In the early morning hours, after the Trojans had gone to sleep, thinking that they had won the war, the Greek soldiers came out of the horse, opened the gates of the city and allowed the Greek army to gain entry and eventual victory."

He paused and said, "Incidentally, that is the origin of the expression 'Beware of Greeks bearing gifts,' but I digress."

He continued, "Homer tells of the tallest and most powerful Greek soldier, a man named Ajax the Greater, or Ajax the Great. There was another Ajax mentioned in the story and he was called Ajax the Lesser. Achilles, who was considered to be most-favored by the gods and, except for his heel, invincible in battle, was the fiercest of warriors."

I looked up and saw Judge Marcolo looking at the ceiling, rolling his eyes in angst over this testimony, which didn't have anything to do with my case, but the jury seemed to be enjoying it.

Dr. Baldwin went on, "Ajax's shield was supposedly so big it took the hides of seven oxen to cover it. Can you imagine that?" he asked, knowing that he would get no response from the jury.

"After the war," he continued, "Ajax returned to Athens and fell into disfavor with one of the gods. He is said to have fallen into a sort of stupor, a spell placed upon him by that goddess, Athena. He went out and slaughtered a whole herd of sheep, thinking they were Trojan soldiers. When he came home, realizing what he had done, he was distraught. His wife, Tecmesa, found him in a condition which she described as sitting and looking off into space, as if he had a 'thousand yard stare.' Scholars have interpreted that as being the result of his days in battle.

"It is said to be the earliest recorded reference to the condition I believe George here," he said, pointing at me, "suffered from on the day of the incident. There have been many other literary references to that phrase and, more importantly, to the condition now known as Post Traumatic Stress Disorder, or PTSD."

"Did you conduct any tests on George or, stated differently, did you have George take any tests?"

"I did."

"And how did George do?"

"He was right in the middle, in the average category. If you think of it as being a 'bell-shaped curve,'" he said, demonstrating with his hands, "George would have been in the center, at the top of the curve if you will, from a purely intellectual point of view."

"Did you do personality testing as well?"

"I did."

"And did any abnormalities surface?"

"No, they did not. George is a very nice fellow, with no discernable phobias or mental problems," he responded, and then looked at the jury, lowered his voice and said, "Other than this problem he has with PTSD, of course, which is, as I have said, a result of his days in Vietnam."

"And how does this problem manifest itself, Dr. Baldwin?"

"George has terrible dreams, nightmares. He has had this problem for years, ever since he left Vietnam."

"And if you would, please explain how this problem George has with PTSD affected him on the day he got into the altercation with Mr. Kuhn."

"Well, George has never received any help for this problem. In the Army, they apparently told him it was normal and that it would go away once he was away from the battlefield a while longer. It didn't. He never had anyone to talk to about it, either. It caused or at least contributed to the demise of his first marriage."

Dr. Baldwin then shifted position in his chair and said, thoughtfully, "You see, George had all this emotion pent up inside of him...a rage, if you will, at much of what he saw and did in Vietnam and all that frightened him, still does. He was no more than a boy when he went off to Vietnam, just months after graduating from high school. He never killed anyone over there and, according to him, never got into any fights in his entire life, but in Vietnam he was around violence, threatened with violence and taught how to be violent.

"Mr. Kuhn pushed the wrong button and unleashed these demons that had been buried deep inside George's brain for so long."

"Would you describe that demon you just referred to as being an 'irresistible impulse,' or an impulse George simply couldn't control?"

"Absolutely."

"And at the time of the fight, where George was throwing punches at Mr. Kuhn, do you think, or do you have an opinion I should say, as to whether or not George knew what he was doing?"

"I do and my opinion is that he did not know what he was doing. He was absolutely out of his mind."

"And do you have an opinion as to whether or not George knew that it was wrong to hit Mr. Kuhn as he did."

"Yes I do, and my opinion is that George had no idea what he was doing at the time so he had no idea that what he was doing was wrong. In fact, George didn't remember hitting Mr. Kuhn at all. He could remember the details leading up to the actual physical confrontation but he could not remember anything about what happened after Mr. Kuhn pushed him and cursed him,"

"I object," Mr. Wadkins said, standing as he did so. "Dr. Baldwin is testifying to facts not in evidence. That is contrary to what Mr. Kuhn testified to here yesterday, your Honor."

I had looked over at Mr. Wadkins while Dr. Baldwin was testifying and he had been squirming in his seat, apparently waiting for an opportunity to stop what was coming from his mouth.

"Well, that's what George told me." Dr. Baldwin responded.

"Wait! Wait, Dr. Baldwin, until I have ruled on the objection. Ladies and gentlemen of the jury, Dr. Baldwin is not a fact witness in this case. He was not there when the acts occurred. He is an expert witness offering his opinion on the issue of whether or not the defendant was sane at the time of the incident. Regarding his testimony about the facts surrounding the incident, keep in mind, again, that he was not a witness to said facts. He can, however, base his opinion on what was told to him by others, if he chooses to do so. In this instance, Dr. Baldwin is testifying as to what the defendant, George Murphy, told him. To that extent, the objection is over-ruled. You may proceed, Mr. Satchel."

"Would you say that George's actions were the product of that mental infirmity, disorder or defect?"

"Yes, it is, or I should say, yes, they were."

"And if you would, explain how you were able to find out about these 'demons,' as you have called them."

He responded, gravely, by saying, "George has told me of his terrible dreams, some of which are just awful. He could not make these up."

"Tell us about them, Dr. Baldwin."

"You want me to tell you what George told me about his dreams?"

"Yes, I do."

"If you insist," he responded, and then he went on and on for twenty minutes detailing each and every one of the nightmares I had told him about. There were a few others I thought of later that I hadn't told him about.

As he was testifying, I could see the jurors moving about uneasily in their seats. It was hard for me to listen to his testimony and I could tell that they didn't like having to listen to it either. They looked over at me at times with looks on their faces which were ones of disbelief or horror. I couldn't tell if they were thinking that I was a sick creature, or if they felt pity, or compassion, for me. Dr. Baldwin was giving them a good sense of what it was like for me and what was really going on in my brain.

When he finally finished, I heard the noise of jurors sitting back in their seats. They had been sitting forward, literally on the edge of their seats, listening to Dr. Baldwin talk.

Mr. Satchel asked, "And are all of the opinions you have offered here today within a reasonable degree of accuracy, within the standards established by your profession, Dr. Baldwin?"

"Yes, they are," he responded.

Mr. Satchel then said, "I have no further questions" and sat down next to me.

Mr. Wadkins cross-examined him for twenty minutes, but Dr. Baldwin stuck to his guns and refused to give an inch. The jury seemed not to be paying as much attention to the questioning. They had heard enough. They would look over at me every now and then, as if they were trying to figure out what they thought about me and about whether or not I had been insane at the time. I felt that I was being judged right then and there.

When Mr. Wadkins finally gave up and said he had no further questions, the judge said, "Ladies and gentlemen, it is now quarter to twelve. We will take our lunch break at this time. Please return to the jury room no later than a quarter to one. We will continue with the trial promptly at one o'clock. Thank you."

After the jury had left the room, Judge Marcolo asked Mr. Satchel if he would be calling any other witnesses. Mr. Satchel surprised me when he answered that he would not be calling any other witnesses except, possibly, me. The judge then rose, saying that he wanted the trial to conclude today if at all possible, and left the courtroom.

I looked over at Mr. Satchel and asked, "You think I should take the stand?"

"It's up to you, George. The decision about whether a defendant should testify is probably the most important decision in a criminal case, at least it is most of the time, I think, and I try to leave that up to the defendant."

"You think I know what is best? I've never been in a situation like this. I have no idea what to do."

"Yeah, but you'll be the one serving the time if we lose. I'd rather you be the one to make the decision than me."

I didn't have a clue, but before I had a chance to ask another question, the bailiff walked over and asked if I was ready to go. He wanted to get some lunch. Mr. Satchel told him that we'd be spending the lunch hour in the courtroom, if that was all right. The bailiff said that he'd lock us in, so that I couldn't get out. We said that would be fine.

When he had left, I asked, "So what do you think?"

"I'd say this…right now it's a battle of the two experts. The jury has to choose between what Dr. Andrews told them and what Dr. Baldwin said. What do I think they're going to do? I don't know. It could go either way. I think your testimony will make the difference. It could hurt and it could help. There's no telling how it's going to go over until we see how it goes but by then it's too late to change our minds. We've got to do that now, right now."

"That's a lot of help."

"Okay, George, let me put it to you like this. The jury is judging you. They've heard enough evidence to convict you, but they have also heard enough evidence to acquit you, too. It could go either way. But in my opinion, the jury always wants to hear from the defendant. In this case, they want to know more about you. They want to hear you say that you didn't know what you were doing that day. The only reason not to testify, I think, is if we're afraid you're going to say something wrong, or get tripped up on something, or if the jury isn't going to like you. I don't think that's what's going to happen. I think you'll do fine, but I could be wrong. It's up to you, but if you want to know my opinion, I think you should take the stand."

"If we lose?"

"You're going to prison for a long time with this judge."

"If I win?"

"You may be walking out of the Lee County jail this afternoon."

"There's no middle ground?"

"No. This is a win or lose situation. The State has offered you a five year sentence. They might agree to a three to five year sentence, but that hasn't been offered yet. I don't see them doing anything less here, knowing Wadkins the way I do. Besides, this judge might not accept that deal anyway."

"He has the right to reject a plea bargain?"

"Yes."

I looked at him and saw this guy who looked like he had stuck his finger in an electric outlet, who had infuriated a judge who had absolutely no use for me several times during the trial, and wondered if I would risk spending years in prison on his advice.

I put my face in my hands and pondered what the future held for me. I was tired of being in jail and wanted out. I'd heard nothing but terrible things about prisons and knew I wanted no part of that. I had no one else to turn to, no one else to trust. Satchmo was all I had.

"I think you're going to do just fine, George. I think this jury is going to like you," he offered.

I let go a loud sigh and said, "Let's do it."

He proceeded to tell me what to expect. We went over the questions he would ask me and how I should respond. He told me to look at the jury and remember that I was trying to convince them, not Mr. Wadkins.

"He won't believe anything you say, even if you tell him the world is round. He is out to convict you. That's his job."

Then he told me what to expect when Mr. Wadkins had the opportunity to cross-examine me.

"That will be the whole case, George, how you do on cross-examination. You're going to have to tell them everything."

"Everything? I can't do that. I've never told anyone everything, not even Dr. Baldwin."

"Today, if you want to walk out of here a free man, you're going to have to tell everything."

"I'll do the best I can," I muttered, thinking of the things I'd have to reveal.

"He's going to try to take your heart out, George. Be ready. Don't let him. And whatever you do, don't get in a yelling match with him or lose your temper. If you do, you're cooked. Remember what happened with Mr. Kuhn. Got it?"

"I understand," I responded.

"Remember, also, that the jury will be listening to every word you speak. They will be watching every move you make, and they will be deciding whether you are guilty or innocent, so keep that in mind at all times. Don't let them see a bad side. Know that they are watching you every time you do anything and act accordingly."

Then he told me that he needed to get ready for closing arguments and go over the instructions to be given the jury. I sat there, awaiting my date with destiny, wondering what my fate would be.

CHAPTER TWENTY ONE
My Testimony

W HEN THE LUNCH HOUR ended, doors to the courtroom began opening shortly before 1:00 and soon all of the various courtroom personnel returned, including some spectators. When the judge was back on the bench, after the jury was in their seats, Mr. Satchel announced that he was calling me as a witness."

"Be sure to look at the jury," Satchmo whispered as I stood up.

I walked up to the witness stand, like everybody else had done, raised my right hand, swore to tell the truth, and sat down, feeling somewhat numb.

Satchmo took me through the easy things like my name, where I was born, what I'd done in my life and everything leading up to April 3, 1979 when the incident occurred. I told him and the jury everything I could remember about what had happened that day. He didn't ask me about my dreams, other than ask if everything Dr. Baldwin had testified to was true. I told him it was.

His last question to me was, "And you'd NEVER been in a fight before, in your whole life, not even while you were in the Army, is that right, George?"

I responded that it was true. I'd never been in a fist fight before. I explained that I'd held a gun many times and shot it in the direction of an enemy I hardly ever saw while a crew chief on a helicopter. I told him that there were also many times while I was on guard-duty that I'd fired my gun, although most of the time it was just shooting into heavy brush.

When he said that he had no further questions, Mr. Wadkins stood up and walked slowly towards the podium. I knew what I was in for. I knew I was about to get into a fight but I wasn't going to be able to throw a punch. It would be all defense and blocks. He came out swinging.

192

"You got mad that day, didn't you, Mr. Murphy?"

I wasn't sure how to respond, so I said, "Yes, I guess I did but, as I said, I don't remember much about it."

"But he made you mad, didn't he? Mr. Kuhn cursed you and pushed you, right? He made you mad when he did that, right?"

"Yeah, I guess so."

I looked over at Mr. Satchel and he was pointing a finger at the jury, doing the best he could not to let anyone see him doing it, telling me to look at the jury. He had a look of concern on his face, like I was messing up or something.

"And you'd never been in a fight before, is that it, Mr. Murphy?

He asked the question in this 'sing-song' kind of voice, like he didn't believe me.

"That's right. I hadn't."

"So have you ever been mad in your life before, Mr. Murphy?"

He was trying to make me look foolish, that was obvious. This wasn't going too well so far.

"Well, sure I've gotten mad before. Everyone does every now and then, don't they?" I looked over at the jury and tried to muster a laugh, but no one was smiling back at me.

"And did you tell Dr. Andrews that he made you so mad that you could have killed him? Is that what you said?"

"I don't remember saying that to her. I've never hurt anyone in my life. I wasn't trying to kill that man."

"So is that what you told her or not? You heard her testify here in court this morning that you told her that, didn't you?"

"I heard her say that, but I was just answering her questions. I didn't mean to say…"

"So did you use those words, Mr. Murphy, or is Dr. Andrews mistaken? Which is it?"

"Objection, your Honor!" Mr. Satchel screamed.

Mr. Wadkins was on the attack and the objection stopped him. I took a deep breath when the focus of everyone's stares shifted over to him, not me.

"What is the basis for the objection, Mr. Satchel."

"My client hadn't finished with his answer, your Honor. I would ask the Court to instruct Mr. Wadkins to allow my client to finish his answer before asking another question."

The judge turned to Mr. Wadkins and said, "Please allow the witness to complete his answer before asking the next question, Mr. Wadkins. You may proceed."

"So did you want to say anything further, Mr. Murphy? Did I cut you off?"

I didn't know what to say, but I mumbled something about that wasn't what I meant to say and that I had no intention of killing Mr. Kuhn.

"But you may have used those words, is that it?"

"I don't remember saying that. I remember saying that I got mad when he cursed me and pushed me. I did say that to her."

"So mad that you could have killed him, right, Mr. Murphy?"

I could feel my defenses crumbling. I didn't know how to respond. I looked over at Mr. Satchel, but there was nothing he could do to help. I looked over at the jury and said, "I didn't mean to hurt that man. I don't know what came over me. I just wanted to go home and be with my wife. I didn't want to get in a fight and go to jail."

"And you don't want to go to jail or prison now, do you, Mr. Murphy?"

"No, I don't."

"And you want this jury to find that you are not guilty of the crimes of Aggravated Battery and Attempted Murder due to the fact that you were temporarily insane at the time, don't you?"

"I believe I was temporarily insane, Mr. Wadkins."

"And you know that if this jury finds that you were temporarily insane at the time of the incident you'll go free, don't you?"

"That's what I'm told."

"That's because there's nothing wrong with you now, is there, Mr. Murphy?"

"No. I'm fine now. I'm like I've been my whole life."

"And you were fine the day after the incident, weren't you? When you woke up in the hospital?"

"I couldn't move. I had to go to the bathroom and they wouldn't let me. I was in pain. I was tied up and they had to wait for the police to get there to untie me. Other than that, I was back to my normal self. Yes, sir."

"And Mr. Kuhn was in pain, too, wasn't he, Mr. Murphy? He was in the hospital too, wasn't he?"

"That's what I was told."

"And he was in the hospital for eight days, wasn't he, Mr. Murphy?"

Mr. Wadkins was raising his voice every now and then, but mostly he was asking his questions like he knew what my answers would be and like he didn't believe a word I was saying. I hesitated for a few seconds, trying to figure out how to respond.

"Wasn't he, Mr. Murphy?"

"Yes, I guess he was," I answered.

"And he had a craniotomy. Do you know what that is, Mr. Murphy?"

"No, I don't. Not really."

"They drill a hole in your head and let blood out. Doesn't sound like fun, does it, Mr. Murphy?"

"No, it doesn't," I said softly.

"And he had a broken nose, too, didn't he? You broke his nose, didn't you, Mr. Murphy?"

"Objection, your Honor. Mr. Wadkins is asking two questions at the same time."

"Over-ruled. You may answer, Mr. Murphy."

"That's what he said."

"You did great bodily harm to him, didn't you, Mr. Murphy?"

"Objection."

"Over-ruled."

"I don't know what that means," I muttered.

"You don't know what the term 'great bodily harm' means, Mr. Murphy? What part of that don't you understand? The word 'great' maybe?"

"I guess that's what I meant. It's a legal term. Compared to what? I don't know what it means. I don't."

"But you put him in a hospital for eight days and he had a broken nose, a closed head injury necessitating a craniotomy. He was unconscious for several hours, too."

When I didn't respond, Mr. Wadkins said, "You beat the hell out of him, didn't you, Mr. Murphy?"

"Objection."

"Sustained. Next question."

"You would have kept on hitting him if your co-workers hadn't stopped you, wouldn't you, Mr. Murphy?"

"I don't remember even seeing Randy and the other guys that day. I would never have fought with them. They were my friends."

I felt like a boxer who had been knocked down and was struggling to get to my feet. I blurted out, again, "I must have been out of my mind that day. I never would have fought with them – never."

I took a deep breath. I felt like I had finally given a decent answer. I was like the boxer who had gotten to his feet and was running away, trying to regain my balance before being hit again.

"But you did, didn't you," Mr. Wadkins continued, staying on the offensive, screaming at me in his clear, staccato voice.

I lowered my head and said, "That's what they all said I did."

"So you're not contesting that you did what everyone says you did, are you? You beat up Mr. Kuhn, causing him great bodily harm, putting him in the hospital, and nearly killing him. You fought with your friends. You were ready to fight with the police officer. You did all those things, didn't you?"

When I didn't respond right away, he continued, "Or are you denying that you did any of those things, Mr. Murphy? Which is it?"

"Objection."

"Over-ruled."

"I'm not denying what they all said I did," I responded. "I just have no idea why it happened. It's just not like me. I would never do those things they said I did…never."

"But you were mad, Mr. Murphy, right? You were mad."

"I was mad, that's true."

"And since you'd never been in a fight before, according to what you've told this jury, you didn't know how you'd respond when provoked, did you? It had never happened before, right?."

"Oh, people have made me mad before, I've told you that. I'd never been in a fight before. That's what I said."

"So you didn't know how to respond to what you considered a physical attack on you, did you?"

"No, I guess not."

"So what you did was to fight back, wasn't it, Mr. Murphy? You fought back, didn't you?"

"Yes, I guess I did."

"You defended yourself, didn't you, Mr. Murphy?"

My brains were spinning. This sounded like what I'd been saying way back in the beginning, that I acted in self-defense, so I said, "Yes, that's right. I was defending myself. I didn't start that fight."

"You acted in self-defense. Is that it?"

"I think so. He started it."

"And you just kept hitting him and hitting him," Mr. Wadkins threw a punch in the air with his left hand, then his right, and back and forth, "until he stopped moving, didn't you, Mr. Murphy?"

I lowered my head. I knew that I was supposed to look over at the jury, but I was confused by the questions. I said, "That's what they say I did."

"Even after he stopped fighting back, you kept hitting him and hitting him, didn't you, Mr. Murphy?"

"That's what they say. I don't remember."

Mr. Wadkins straightened, turned his face to the jury, with a look of satisfaction on his face, as if he'd proven me out to be a crazed man who had beaten poor Mr. Kuhn nearly to death.

"You're lucky you didn't kill Mr. Kuhn, aren't you, Mr. Murphy?"

"I'm glad he didn't die. I'm sorry for what happened." I offered.

Mr. Wadkins looked down at his papers, hesitated for a few seconds, allowing my last answer to resonate throughout the courtroom, as if there was an echo. I could hear the words, "I'm glad he didn't die...I'm sorry for what happened..." repeating themselves in the moments of silence.

"Let's talk about these 'bad dreams' you've had, Mr. Murphy. You say they didn't begin until you were back in the United States, out of Vietnam, correct?"

I let out a sigh, like I'd been through round two of a fight and round three was about to begin.

"That's right," I responded.

"And the only person you ever saw about these 'bad dreams' was a counselor in the military, is that right?"

"That's right."

His tone of voice was mocking, like I was a complete idiot, as he asked, "So you didn't have the money to get professional help or what? Why didn't you get professional help, Mr. Murphy?"

I didn't know how to respond. Why hadn't I? My brain was moving fast. I knew that if I said I didn't think it was that important, it would be bad, but if I said it was the money, he'd attack me from another direction.

I responded, "It really wasn't something I could talk about."

"A lot of soldiers have the same kinds of problems, don't they, Mr. Murphy?"

"I don't know. I've never talked to any other soldiers about it, other than that counselor a couple of times."

"You're not telling this jury that you had it worse than the men on the ground, the soldiers slogging through the rice paddies, sleeping on the ground in the rain, are you?"

"No, I'm not. There were lots of guys who had it much worse than me. That's for sure," I responded.

"And you don't think that any soldier, Vietnam vet or otherwise, should be allowed to go around beating up people and then claim it was due to..." and he slowed down his speech, articulating each word with a kind of dramatic flair, as if it were some bull-shit words made up by a bunch of psychiatrists like Dr. Baldwin, Post-Traumatic-Stress-Disorder, do you, Mr. Murphy?"

This was it. He was basically asking me if my entire defense was ridiculous. If I agreed with that, I might as well sit back down and accept the fact that I was going to prison for a long, long time. My case would be over.

I took a deep breath and responded, "I'm not saying that I had it worse than other guys, but I am saying that me being in Vietnam like I was affected me in ways I didn't understand and still don't. I'd never told anyone the things I told Dr. Baldwin, not my first wife, not my second wife, not my parents, not my best friends…not my lawyer…no one. I'm not a killer and I'm not someone who goes around beating up people. I don't know why this thing happened with Mr. Kuhn. I really don't. I wish it had never happened."

I hesitated, took another breath, and looked over at the jury, "I lost my wife, who I loved more than anyone else before, my job, my freedom, my home, all of my money. I've lost everything I've ever had, everything I ever wanted…"

I broke down and started to cry, thinking about it all.

"And you wish it had…"

"Objection! He hasn't finished his answer yet, your Honor."

"Have you finished your answer, Mr. Murphy, or not," the judge asked.

"No, I haven't, your Honor. I just need a minute…," I mumbled, wiping away the tears, and then I went on, "The only thing I ever wanted to be since I was a little kid was a mechanic, to work on cars. The military let me do that. The only reason I went into the Army was because we thought that if I didn't I'd be drafted and could end up as a soldier in a rice paddy. Then I wanted to find a wife…a good wife…those days on the road, alone, were hard on me. My bad dreams were always the worst when I was alone, that's why I got a dog last year."

I told them about Bailey and about how the nightmares were getting better, or at least there were fewer of them, since I'd been with Rebecca, and how they had to move me to a new cell at the jail because of my nightmares. I was starting to tell him about how my cell mate had to wake me up whenever I started to have one, when Mr. Wadkins started to ask another question.

Mr. Satchel stood up and said, in a loud voice, "He's still not finished answering the question, your Honor!"

"Let him finish his answer, Mr. Wadkins."

"I don't remember the question at this point, your Honor. I think he has gone way past answering my question and…"

"Let him finish." The judge said.

I talked and talked until finally I had said all I could think to say. Mr. Wadkins then asked, "Are you finished?"

I said I was. "So if they were that bad, why didn't you seek professional help, Mr. Murphy?"

"I guess I just couldn't to talk to anyone about it," I offered. "I still can't. This is the first time I ever have talked about them, other than to Dr. Baldwin and Dr. Andrews."

"You couldn't talk about them or you didn't want to talk to anyone about it?" He asked incredulously. "You lost jobs, a wife, had to move out of your parents' home, had bad nightmares and you couldn't talk to anyone about it?"

"I've never told anyone about any of my bad dreams before I talked to Dr. Baldwin," I replied.

"So when you knew that if you could prove that you were temporarily INSANE you could get out of jail, that's when you spilled your guts, is that it?"

"Objection!"

"Sustained. Please re-phrase your question, Mr. Wadkins."

"So these bad dreams make you crazy, do they, Mr. Murphy?"

He put both hands up in the air and shook them around as he said the word crazy.

He was trying to regain the offensive. I think when I spoke for so long that the jury started to listen to me and not to him as much. I paused, trying to figure out how I could express what I really thought about these dreams.

"I don't understand why I have them. I know that there are other guys out there with worse problems than me, I'm sure, but I do know that I wish they'd go away. You have no idea what it's like to wake up on the floor of an Army barrack crying like a baby with all the other soldiers looking at you like you're a sissy, or a weakling, or worse yet, a coward. You have no idea what it's like to go to sleep at night with a woman you love, praying that one of those nightmares doesn't happen, or praying that the woman won't leave you when it does. You have no idea what it's like to wake up in the middle of the night in a panic, sweating like a pig, trying to figure out where you are, praying that you aren't about to be killed by men wearing black pajamas with bayonets in their hands charging at you. You have no idea what it's like to try to go to sleep with bombs bursting all around you, not sure if the next one has got your name on it or not…"

I put my hands in my face and started to cry, again.

Mr. Wadkins could see his case slipping away. He couldn't ignore my tears, but he couldn't acknowledge them either, so he asked, "And it's because of these bad dreams, for which you never sought ANY professional counseling, that you flew into a rage and beat Mr. Kuhn to a pulp, within a whisker of death, is that it, Mr. Murphy?"

I didn't answer him. He turned his back on me and said, somewhat disgustedly, "I have no further questions of this man, your Honor."

Mr. Satchel stood up, remaining at the table and said, in a low voice, "Tell the jury, in your own words, about your dreams, George." Then he sat down.

I took another deep breath, looked at the jury and began. I told them all about the first dream I ever had, the one about the young Vietnamese child falling off the back of the truck. I told them about the dream of being over-run when my rifle backfired. I told them about the woman prisoner who'd been shot right in front of my eyes, and about the truck exploding after hitting a bomb right in front of me and Reno, and about my fellow soldiers being beheaded while I was on guard duty, and being over-run by a VC attack while I was on guard duty, about having my buddies killed by supposedly friendly South Vietnamese soldiers who refused to get off a helicopter, and all the rest.

Then I told them about some of the dreams I'd had where I was the one killing women and children who were standing close to a VC soldier with a machine gun, or how I shot a Vietnamese baby with a back pack on his back which I was sure was a bomb, only to find out that it wasn't, or how we bombed an entire village to extinction after having a few mortars land near our base, and other stories I hadn't told Dr. Baldwin.

Fifteen minutes later, though I was exhausted, I told them about Tillie. I cried several times as I told that story. I wasn't a doctor. I didn't know for sure what anyone could do to save him, but I didn't try. I cried as I told them how I felt for all these years that I might have been able to save his life. I still blamed myself for him dying. I was slumped over in the chair, my head in my hands, tears streaming down my face when I finished.

Mr. Satchel whispered, "No further questions, your Honor. The defense rests."

CHAPTER TWENTY TWO
The Verdict

AFTER THE STATE INDICATED that it had no rebuttal evidence to present, the judge gave the jury an afternoon break. Once they were out of the courtroom, the two lawyers and the judge talked about what instructions were to be given to the jury and some other things. He allowed the attorneys only twenty minutes apiece to give their closing arguments. Satchmo had asked for an hour. The State Attorney didn't seem too happy about it, either, but it was almost 3:00 and the judge said he wanted to get the case to the jury with enough time so that they might return a verdict before 5:00.

When the bailiff brought the jury back, closing arguments began. The State went first, since we had called a witness other than me. Otherwise Satchmo would have gone first.

Mr. Wadkins began, "Ladies and gentlemen of the jury, I want to begin by thanking you for your service in this matter. I am sure that you have other places you would rather be but because of you and others like you, we have the best system of justice in the world. Regardless of your verdict in this case, justice will be served. I am sure Judge Marcolo and all who are in court with us here today join me in thanking you for your promptness in being here when you were supposed to be here, and your attentiveness to all that has gone on over the last two days.

"The case you have heard and are to decide is an unusual case in that it involves a defense of insanity. Mr. Murphy does not deny that he beat Mr. Kuhn, breaking his nose, rendering him unconscious and putting him in the hospital for eight days. No, Mr. Murphy says he doesn't remember it, but he told Dr. Andrews that Mr. Kuhn made him so mad that he 'could have killed him.'

"You heard the testimony of his employer and co-workers and the testimony of the deputy sheriff who arrived at the scene within minutes of the call. Mr. Murphy was a crazed man. The deputy had to physically subdue him by hitting him with his nightstick. Mr. Murphy told you that he acted in self defense, and that he was 'mad' because Mr. Kuhn pushed him and cursed him, which Mr. Kuhn denies.

"Now, the important thing to remember, I submit to you, ladies and gentlemen, is that even if Mr. Kuhn did antagonize Mr. Murphy, which is NOT a point that the State of Florida concedes, but even if he did, that did not give Mr. Murphy the right to beat him senseless and then continue to beat him until other people interceded. There can be no doubt that Mr. Murphy committed the crimes he is charged with. The only issue is whether or not he was sane and it is the State of Florida's burden to prove that he was sane at the time he committed those offenses.

"To prove that Mr. Murphy was sane, the State had him examined by a psychiatrist, Dr. Joyce Andrews. You heard her testify. She explained to you, repeatedly, why it is her opinion that Mr. Murphy wasn't insane, he was angry. There is a difference.

Perhaps more importantly, however, you heard Mr. Murphy testify. Keep in mind there is no doubt whatsoever about Mr. Murphy's sanity now, five minutes before the incident or the day after the incident. The only time period at issue is the five minutes or so that the fight took place.

"Mr. Murphy claims that for those five minutes, he was 'temporarily' insane.

"Ladies and gentlemen, Mr. Murphy got mad. He allowed his passions to get the better of him. Judge Marcolo will instruct you on the law which you are to follow and I ask that you pay very careful attention to that part of the jury instructions in which Judge Marcolo talks about passion and rage NOT being a justification or excuse for criminal behavior.

"For the defense, you heard the testimony of Dr. Baldwin. I am sure you were all as interested as I was to learn about Ajax the Great, the Iliad and the history of the Trojan War, but I am also sure that you brought your common sense into this courtroom with you and you will use that common sense in deciding this case.

"Does it make sense to you that soldiers returning from Vietnam could avoid criminal prosecution by claiming a condition called 'Post Traumatic Stress Disorder' caused them do it and it EXCUSES their behavior? What is that? A 'get out of jail free' card, like in Monopoly? Is there anyone in this courtroom who thinks that war is a pleasant place to be? Of course he saw and heard bad things during that war. What soldier didn't?

"More importantly, as Dr. Andrews told you, it isn't a mental defect, and it isn't an infirmity. Now, I can't deny that PTSD is called a disorder, but as Dr. Andrews explained, he doesn't have it to such a level that it is a disabling condition. Now, we all know or have read about or seen people in the movies or on TV who are insane. That is a term of art within the psychiatric profession that is not used lightly. People who are insane are put in mental hospitals. On behalf of the State of Florida, I submit to you that Mr. Murphy was not insane on the day of the incident. He committed two serious crimes and he belongs in a jail."

Mr. Satchel stood and said, "I object, your Honor!"

"Sustained. Ladies and gentlemen of the jury, you are not to concern yourself with the punishment aspect of this case, only the issue of whether or not Mr. Murphy was sane at the time of the incident in question. Please disregard Mr. Wadkins reference to the possibility of jail. You may continue, Mr. Wadkins."

"The point is, Mr. Murphy was sane during those five minutes that he beat Mr. Kuhn senseless. His actions may have been caused by rage, extreme anger or unbridled passion, but they did not occur because he was insane due to a mental defect, infirmity or disorder.

"Ladies and gentlemen, I will have one more opportunity to address you. After Mr. Satchel gives his closing argument, I will have time to rebut, or contradict, whatever he tells you that I don't agree with. I will close for now and reserve time to address you again when he is finished. Thank you."

"Mr. Satchel, you may present your closing argument at this time."

"Yes, your Honor," he said as he strode to the podium, standing taller and showing more confidence than at any time during the entire trial.

"Good afternoon, ladies and gentlemen. I, too, together with George, thank you for your service in this case. As you know, the issue for you to decide is whether or not George was temporarily insane at the time he got in a fight with Edward Kuhn. Basically, you are judging George. You are to decide who to believe and what to believe. George is the only person on trial here today, not Mr. Kuhn and not the two psychiatrists. Your verdict will either be in favor of George or against him. There is no middle ground.

"You've heard the testimony of two psychiatrists. They disagree. You may feel that one was better qualified than the other or that one was more persuasive than the other, but you could rely on the testimony of either one in making your decision in this case. Both are well-qualified. They've both received fine educations and they have both accomplished a lot during their lifetimes.

"However, the testimony that was most important to you, I would think, in your deciding this case came from George's mouth about half an hour ago. You heard him answer difficult and probing questions asked of him by this prosecutor. You know his whole life story. Is he a criminal? That's for you to decide.

"Now, Judge Marcolo is going to tell you what the law is when it comes to the legal issue of insanity. That is called a jury instruction. He's going to tell you that you must find and determine if Mr. Murphy suffered from a mental disorder, infirmity or defect at the time of the incident and if you find that he did suffer from a mental disorder, infirmity or defect, you must decide if, because of that 'disorder, infirmity or defect, Mr. Murphy did not understand and appreciate that what he was doing was wrong. Or, stated differently, he didn't know right from wrong when he was doing the things he did.

"You heard from four men who worked with George. They told you that they hardly recognized George. It didn't seem to them that George recognized them either. George wasn't himself. That wasn't him.

"He was suffering from a condition called Post Traumatic Stress Disorder that you've heard so much about here these past two days. Can there be anyone here who doubts that men come home from war with terrible thoughts in their heads as a result of things they saw and did? So what is that condition called? Battle fatigue? Combat stress? Shell-shock? What? And what difference does it make? Men come home from war with things going on in their heads that sometimes affect how they behave. Who's going to dispute that?

"And no one will argue that everyone who comes home from war has a license to commit crimes. That's not what we're talking about here today. It's about George Murphy. It's about whether or not, because of the mental problems he has as a result of his service in the United States Army in Vietnam, George is legally responsible for what he did on April 3, 1979 at the Marina.

"George isn't asking you to find him not guilty because he's a veteran or because he's a nice guy, which he is. He's asking you to find him not guilty because he was temporarily insane at the time he did those things. He did not know right from wrong. He does not even know what he did. He can't remember a thing after being pushed and cursed. He doesn't remember fighting with his friends. He doesn't remember being subdued and arrested by the deputy. He was, in truth, out of his mind and…temporarily insane as a result of a mental illness or infirmity known as Post Traumatic Stress Disorder.

"Please remember all the things that Dr. Baldwin told you, not just about Ajax the Great and the Trojan War, but about the bad nightmares George has experienced and continues to experience. Remember how he's been put in a separate cell because of the ruckus he makes when he has one of those nightmares. Keep in mind who he is, what he's done and why he is having those problems, and after you retire to deliberate your verdict, and after you've selected a foreperson, check the box that says 'Not Guilty by Reason of Insanity.' Thank you."

He hesitated, looked at each juror for a few seconds, and walked back to his seat next to me.

"Mr. Wadkins, rebuttal?"

"Yes, your Honor. Mr. Satchel just told you that Mr. Murphy is not a criminal. We KNOW he committed criminal acts, that makes him a criminal, doesn't it? The only question for you to decide is if he is legally responsible for the criminal acts which he committed.

"You are required to follow the law. Judge Marcolo is about to instruct you on what that law is. He will tell you that you are not to allow sympathy or compassion for Mr. Murphy to enter your mind. This is your civic duty. You have taken an oath and sworn that you will faithfully fulfill that civic duty. It is a solemn trust.

"The law is clear and unequivocal. The State has met its burden of proof. You have heard enough evidence from Dr. Andrews, the witnesses and Mr. Murphy himself to know that he became enraged by something Mr. Kuhn did and he did not control that anger.

"On behalf of the State of Florida and Lee County, I ask that you return the only true verdict which the evidence allows and the law permits and that is a verdict of guilty, finding Mr. George Murphy legally responsible for his actions of April 3, 1979. Thank you."

Judge Marcolo turned to the jury and said, "Members of the jury, I thank you for your attention during this trial. Please pay attention to the instructions I am about to give you.

"George Patrick Murphy has been accused by the State of Florida of committing the crimes of Aggravated Battery and Attempted Murder. Mr. Murphy has entered a plea claiming that he is not guilty of those crimes due to him being insane at the time those two offenses occurred.

As the Judge was explaining the law to the jury, I looked over at them and saw them staring intently at him. I heard the familiar sound of doors locking. The bailiff had locked the doors to the courtroom when the judge began to instruct the jury. Apparently, Judge Marcolo did not want the jury to be distracted as he read to them. The trial would soon be over. There was nothing for me to do but await their decision.

I was listening, just like the jury was, as the judge gave them their instructions, but I could not see how the jury could remember everything he was telling them. I couldn't. It was hard to understand it all. I heard the important things, like, "Before you can find the Defendant guilty of the two charges, the State of Florida has the burden to prove that Mr. Murphy was sane at the time of commission of the acts and it must do so beyond a reasonable doubt. For ten minutes, Judge Marcolo gave them instructions on the law they were to follow.

"A person is considered to be insane when:

1. He had a mental infirmity, disease or defect; and
2. Because of this condition
   a. He did not know what he was doing or its consequences;
      or
   b. Although he knew what he was doing and its consequences, he did not know it was wrong.

"In determining the issue of insanity, you may consider the testimony of expert and non-expert witnesses. The question you must answer is not whether the defendant is insane today, or has ever been insane, but simply if the defendant was insane at the time the crimes alleged were committed."

I grimaced as I heard him say, "Unrestrained passion or ungovernable temper is not insanity, even though the normal judgment of the person is overcome by passion or temper.

Whenever the words 'reasonable doubt' are used you must consider the following:

"A reasonable doubt is not a mere possible doubt, a speculative, imaginary or forced doubt. Such a doubt must not influence you to return a verdict of not guilty if you have an abiding conviction of guilt. On the other hand, if, after carefully considering, comparing and weighing all the evidence, there is not an abiding conviction of guilt or, if, having a conviction, it is one which is not stable but one which wavers and vacillates, then the issue of sanity is not proved beyond every reasonable doubt and you must find the defendant not guilty because the doubt is reasonable.

"However, if you have no reasonable doubt as to the defendant's sanity on April 3, 1979, you should find the defendant guilty.

"It is up to you to decide what evidence is reliable. You should use your common sense in deciding what the best evidence is, and which evidence should not be relied upon in consideration of your verdict. You may find some of the evidence not reliable, or less reliable than other evidence.

"In this case, you have heard the testimony of expert witnesses. Expert witnesses are like other witnesses with one exception. The law permits an expert witness to give his opinion. However, an expert's opinion is only reliable when given on a subject about which you believe him to be an expert. Like other witnesses, you may believe or disbelieve all or any part of an expert's testimony.

"The constitution requires that the State proves its accusations against the defendant. It is not necessary for the defendant to disprove anything. Nor is the defendant required to prove his claim of insanity. It is up to the State to prove the defendant's guilt by evidence, and in this case the State must prove that George Murphy was sane at the time the offenses were committed.

"There are some general rules that apply to your discussions during your deliberations. You must follow these rules in order to return a lawful verdict:

1. You must follow the law as it is set out in these instructions. If you fail to follow the law, your verdict will be a miscarriage of justice. There is no reason for failing to follow the law in this case. All of us are depending upon you to make a wise and legal decision in this matter;

2. This case must not be decided for or against anyone because you feel sorry for anyone, or are angry at anyone;

3. Remember, the lawyers are not on trial. Your feelings about them should not influence your decision in this case;

4. Your duty is to determine if the defendant's sanity has been proven or not, in accord with the law. It is my job to determine a proper sentence if the defendant is found guilty;

5. Whatever verdict you render must be unanimous, that is, each juror must agree to the same verdict;

6. Your verdict should not be influenced by feelings of prejudice, bias, or sympathy. Your verdict must be based on the evidence, and on the law contained in these instructions;

"You will be given a verdict form. In this case, you will be required to answer two questions contained within that verdict, which read as follows

"We, the jury, find as follows, as to the defendant, George Patrick Murphy:

    a. As to the charge of Attempted Murder, we find the defendant:
       Guilty   _____
       Not Guilty by reason of insanity   _____

    b. As to the charge of Aggravated Battery, we find the defendant:
       Guilty   _____
       Not Guilty by reason of insanity   _____

"Your verdicts must be consistent with each other.

"You will be taken to the jury room by the bailiff. The first thing you should do is elect a foreperson. The foreperson presides over your deliberations, like a chairman of a meeting. It is the foreperson's job to sign and date the verdict form when all of you have agreed on a verdict in this case. The foreperson will bring the verdict back to the courtroom when you return.

"In closing, let me remind you that it is important that you follow the law spelled out in these instructions in deciding your verdict. There are no other laws that apply to this case. Even if you do not like the laws that must be applied, you must use them. For two centuries we have agreed to a constitution and to live by the law. No one of us has the right to violate rules we all share.

"Please rise and follow our bailiff to the jury room where you will now deliberate and decide the outcome of this case. Our alternate, is now excused, and she will not be able to be with you as you deliberate and decide this case."

The jury rose, except for the alternate, and followed the bailiff out of the courtroom.

Once they were gone, the judge left the courtroom and Satchmo wandered around, talking to the clerk, the court reporter, the bailiff and anyone else who had watched the trial. When he returned he told me that he liked to ask questions of everybody and find out who they thought the foreperson will be, how long they thought the jury would be out, what they thought of the trial, things like that.

"What do you think?" I asked.

"About what?"

"All of those things you just mentioned."

"Well, the foreman is going to be one of the three women, or at least I think so. As to how long they're going to be out, that depends. If you are going to win, I think it will be a quick verdict. The longer they're out, the worse it will be for you, but it could mean we convinced one or more of the jurors and it's a hung jury."

"What happens if it's a hung jury?"

"They try you all over again."

"I don't want that."

"No, we want a fast verdict. That's what I think."

"And that means what? Less than an hour?"

"That's right, less than an hour."

He then got up and sauntered over to talk to Mr. Wadkins, as if it were another day at the office. I sat there with my stomach churning, pondering what my fate would be. I prayed.

The knock on the door forty five minutes later sounded like a rifle shot.

The bailiff hurried toward the jury room. Mr. Satchel told me that the knock didn't necessarily mean that the jury had a verdict as they could have had a question. He hoped it meant that they had reached a verdict.

Within seconds, the bailiff re-entered the courtroom and announced "We have a verdict."

He walked into Judge Marcolo's chambers to inform him. As he was doing that, Mr. Satchel turned to me and said, "Here we go. Good luck, man!" and he shook my hand. I was too nervous to respond.

After the attorneys and their clients were seated, and the court reporter and the clerk were in their places, Judge Marcolo entered the room. As he did he said "Keep your seats. I understand we have a verdict. Mr. Bailiff, please bring in our jury."

I watched as the jurors paraded single file back into the courtroom. Several of them looked at me. Satchmo leaned over and whispered, "That's a good sign, man. They're looking at you."

Once the jury was back in the room, Judge Marcolo said, "Will the defendant please rise."

Mr. Satchel and I stood up. Everyone else stood up, too. Judge Marcolo then said, "Ladies and gentlemen of the jury, have you reached a verdict?"

"We have, your Honor," one of the women jurors responded.

"Madame Forewoman, if you would, please hand your verdict to the bailiff."

The bailiff took the verdict from her and delivered it to the judge, who took a few seconds to review it. The courtroom was completely silent.

My heart was thumping. I thought to myself that it was so loud Mr. Satchel and the others might be able to hear it. I looked over at the jurors, but they were looking straight at the judge. I knew that the verdict meant the difference between going to prison or getting out. I no longer had a home to go to, though my parents would probably take me back. They hadn't been down to see me except that one time over Christmas. My Dad was still real sick and my mother could never leave his side. Where would I go if I got out? What would I do? All these thoughts raced through my mind in a matter of seconds.

The expression on Judge Marcolo's face gave no clue as to the outcome. He looked stern all the time and I knew he didn't like me or Mr. Satchel. He gave the verdict back to the bailiff, who handed it to the clerk, and said, "Madame Clerk, please publish the verdict."

My knees were shaking. My hands were perspiring. I don't think I had felt this nervous when riding on a helicopter taking enemy fire. I'm sure I wasn't or I couldn't have done my job. I had never been more nervous in my life.

The clerk read:

"In the case of the State of Florida versus George Patrick Murphy, we, the jury find as follows:

As to the charge of Attempted Murder, we find the defendant Not Guilty by reason of insanity."

Satchmo put his arm around my shoulder and whispered, "Congratulations, man!"

The clerk continued,

"As to the charge of Aggravated Battery, we find the defendant 'Not Guilty by reason of insanity."

I let out a huge sigh and looked over at the jurors, crying as I did. A few of them looked back, impassively. The others continued to listen to the judge, awaiting instructions. I wanted to go thank all of them, but I realized they had just done their jobs and were ready to go home.

The judge asked Mr. Wadkins if he wanted to have the jury polled and he said he didn't. I stood there smiling for the first time in a long time, and crying. I turned to Mr. Satchel, gave him a bear hug and said, "Thanks, man. You did a great job."

The judge was thanking the jurors for their service and telling them that they could leave. After they were gone, as we were still standing there, he turned towards me, without any sign of emotion and said, "The jury having returned a verdict of not guilty by reason of insanity, the court must now consider the issue of Mr. Murphy's competence at this time. Mr. Wadkins, do you wish for me to have Mr. Murphy undergo further psychiatric testing to determine his sanity at this time?"

I looked over at Mr. Wadkins, who hadn't looked at me once since I had gotten off the witness stand, at least not that I ever noticed, and listened as he said, "No, your Honor. The State has no basis to believe that Mr. Murphy is not sane today."

"With that, the Court hereby declares that this trial is concluded. Based upon the verdict returned by our jury, you are to be forthwith released from custody, Mr. Murphy. My bailiff will see to it that you are processed out of jail as soon as possible. You shall remain in custody until you are properly discharged. Mr. Satchel, I want to see you in my chambers in fifteen minutes."

Without saying another word, he stood, turned and walked out of the courtroom. I knew that I would soon be a free man. What would I do? Where would I go?

*　　　*　　　*

An hour later, I was walking out of the Lee County Jail. I still had on the clothes I wore for the trial. I had been given a paper bag with the clothes I had been wearing on the day of the incident, plus my wallet, my keys and whatever else I had in my pockets at the time. There was no one there to meet me and I had no idea where I was going or how I was going to get there.

I opened my wallet and was relieved to find the four hundred dollar bills still inside. As I was standing there, wondering what direction to walk in, Satchmo came walking down the sidewalk toward me.

"What are you doing here?" I asked.

"I've got to see another client. His trial starts next week."

"What's the charge?"

"Armed Robbery."

"What's your defense?"

"Identification issue. They've got a real weak eye-witness and a problem with the confession. We'll probably lose at trial, but it's a good case for an appeal. I'd love to see Marcolo reversed."

"What did he say to you after the trial ended today?"

"He read me the riot act for how I handled your case."

"He wasn't at all complimentary?"

"Nope. He gives me shit every time, no matter what, but he treats everybody that way. It doesn't bother me. The main thing is we won!" and he gave me a high-five.

"So what about you?" he asked. "Where are you headed?"

"I think I'll go down to Key West and see if I can find a job down there. With all the boats they must have, I'm sure there will be somebody looking for a good mechanic."

"Not back up to Maryland?"

"Maybe in the spring. We'll see. I really don't know. Like I told that Mr. Wadkins, I lost everything…my wife, my job, my apartment, my house, everything I had…hell, I even lost my dog. I've got nothing. I've got to start all over."

"You got some money to get you there?"

I told him about the $400 was still in my wallet. "That'll hold me for a little while," I said.

"Want a beer?" he asked.

"No, thanks. I'd better get to Key West before I start drinking. I haven't had anything but water and Kool Aid for nine months. If you can tell me where the bus station is, I'd appreciate that."

"Better yet, I'll give you a ride."

"What about your client?"

"He can wait."

Satchmo dropped me off at the Greyhound Bus Station and we said our good byes. As he backed up and started to slowly drive off, he rolled down the window and said, "You're a lucky man, George Murphy. Today the gods smiled on you. Good luck, man," and he winked.

I stood watching him drive away until I couldn't see his car anymore. I was lucky not to be spending most of the rest of my life in a jail or prison and I had him to thank for it. I thought about calling my parents, Mr. Sullivan, Randy or Rebecca, and telling them the news, but decided all that could wait. I was 29 years old with little more than the clothes on my back and some money in my pocket to show for it. I had no idea what lay ahead for me.

For now, I just wanted to get away and try to sort it out. There was no way to make sense of it all. I was going to just 'be' for a while, not look forward or back. Just live in the present. A sandy beach and warm sun seemed like a good a place to do that. Maybe, just maybe, the demons in my head had been exorcised. I had let them all out. I was a free man again.

THE END

Epilogue

Wikipedia defines the term "Thousand Yard Stare" to mean "the unfocused gaze of a battle-weary soldier. The stare is a characteristic combat stress reaction which may be a precursor to, or symptom of, post-traumatic stress disorder." As of the time of this writing, there are still a few among us who remember the horrors of the first World War, which involved the use of poisonous gasses and trench warfare. Many more of us, though I am not one of them, lived through the atrocities of World War II, which included concentration camps, massive aerial bombings of innocents in Europe, devastatingly costly beach invasions in the Pacific and in Europe, ghastly fire-fights and titanic battles between warships and submarines in the oceans and seas all over the world, ending, of course, with the detonation of two atomic bombs that killed hundreds of thousands of people, all of which left psychological and physical scars on survivors.

Many combatants were subjected to torture and deprivation and came away with mental disorders as a result of what is called the "Forgotten War" in Korea in the early '50s. The effects of the Vietnam War during the '60s and early '70s, including such things as exposure to Agent Orange, drug abuse, alienation and a permanent disorientation, not to mention great internal strife, still plague our country. Nowadays, Gulf War I of 1991, Gulf War II in 2002 and now Afghanistan have sent and continue to send tens of thousands home with an assortment of injuries, maladies, frustrations, disillusionment and ailments, including Post Traumatic Stress Disorder.

Approximately 10,000 soldiers have died in Iraq and Afghanistan in the last eight years and there are 57,939 names on "The Wall" in Washington, D.C., but the number of veterans who returned suffering from PTSD, side effects from exposure to Agent Orange or other abnormalities, both physical and psychological, is incalculably higher, since so many deny or refuse to reveal such problems.

For most of us in the Boomer generation, myself included, the undeclared war in Vietnam remains most vivid in our collective memories and, if asked, it would continue to be the event which overshadows anything else that has occurred or will occur in our lifetime, more so than the killings of JFK, Martin Luther King, Bobby Kennedy, landing on the moon, the Gulf Wars in Kuwait and Iran, Afghanistan, Iraq and Pakistan, 9-11 or anything else. The condition now known as Post Traumatic Stress Disorder is not something that arose during that 1959-1975 period of time, but the term did come into existence as an aftermath of the Vietnam War. It was called something else in prior years, things like shell-shock or battle-fatigue.

In fact, just as Dr. Baldwin testified in this book, the earliest written record of the symptom is thought to come from the play *Ajax* by Sophocles in which Ajax, considered by many to be one of the greatest of the Greek warriors during the Trojan War, second only to Achilles, is beguiled by the goddess Athena and loses his honor and then his mind. His wife, Tecmessa, strives in vain to find comfort and support for her mentally diminished husband from his soldiers and friends. In some translations, she describes Ajax sitting in a stupor with a "thousand yard stare."

There can be little doubt that many, if not most, soldiers who have either endured, committed or observed atrocities during war have been bedeviled by the recollection of those horrors long after the battles ended. For some that recollection can be haunting and disabling. This book is about one such soldier, a man I call friend, and his personal battle with the problem.

In the process of writing this book, I conducted research on various issues and read several books about the Vietnam War and Post Traumatic Stress Disorder (PTSD). I read Stanley Karnow's book *Vietnam: A History* (Viking, 1983), and I included some of the factual statements found therein in this book. I acknowledge and thank Mr. Karnow for his contribution to our collective understanding of that complicated and confused period of our history, which comes from mostly from a political and historical perspective as he was a journalist covering the war in its earliest stages and had personal experiences to draw upon.

I also read *Chickenhawk* (Penquin, 1983), which is an account of the war written by a combatant, Robert Mason, who was, in 1965, a helicopter pilot in the First Air Cavalry Division, the world's first combat airmobile unit. Mr. Mason's book provided a gripping account of what that was like from the perspective of a pilot and, more importantly to this book, from the perspective of one who suffered afterwards from what he experienced while there.

Upon reading his book, I located Mr. Mason, who lives in High Springs, Florida, not far from Cedar Key and Gainesville, and met him. At his suggestion, I then read the sequel which he wrote, called *Back in the World*, about his return from Vietnam and his problems with Post Traumatic Stress Disorder.

I then read a book written by his wife, Patience, who wrote from the point of view of a spouse of a veteran who suffers from PTSD, entitled *Recovering from the War: A Guide for all Veterans, Family Members, Friends and Therapists,* (Patience Press, 1990). She has lectured extensively on the subject across the United States and has appeared on national television on many occasions. I thank both Bob and Patience Mason for the insight I was able to glean from their books about the war and the issue of PTSD.

I also read a moving account of the war written by Ronald J. Glasser, entitled *365 Days* (George Braziller, 1971), which chronicles the war from the point of view of not only the soldiers but also the nurses, doctors, medics, helicopter pilots and others. Mr. Glasser was and is a medical doctor and he provides graphic details of how horrific that conflict was from the point of view of the ones who cared for and treated wounded and dying soldiers. It provided me with more than an ample amount of factual accounts of human suffering to give me a basis for understanding how those who survived the ordeal of serving 365 days in Vietnam would come away with scars on their bodies and their minds that could never easily be forgotten or removed.

Another book I read and found extremely illuminating was *A Hard Rain Fell,* (Sourcebooks, 2002) by John Ketwig who, like George, was a mechanic in Vietnam from 1968 until 1969. He explained in graphic detail how servicemen other than the front-line grunts in the jungle experienced things which caused them to suffer from PTSD.

The nightmares experienced by George in this book are, I fully expect, much like the real-life experiences of many soldiers returning from that war. Many similar stories can be found in the books written by Bob Mason, John Ketwig and the others mentioned above.

I read several opinions issued by the United States Supreme Court in the case of Gary Bradford Cone, a decorated Vietnam War hero, regarding the legal issue of whether or not Post Traumatic Stress Disorder (PTSD) could be a defense to a crime or used as a mitigating factor at the time of sentencing. At the time of writing, Mr. Cone remains under a death sentence in Tennessee for a crime committed in 1978, though his case has been before the Supreme Court of the United States on three occasions, the most recent being in December of 2008.

As with my other books, I have attempted to present the issue of PTSD from a legal perspective, since I am a lawyer and that is what I know best. Those legal issues are presented as accurately as possible. PTSD remains a serious concern for many veterans, including those returning from Iraq and Afghanistan today, as well as soldiers from the Vietnam era, Korea, and for that matter, anyone, not soldiers, who experienced a trauma of such significance to scar the psyche, since PTSD can come from other accidents or unfortunate occurrences, too, like being a victim of a rape, armed robbery, a car accident, an injury causing permanent paralysis and other such things

A Veterans Administration survey released in 1988 estimated that some five hundred thousand of the three million U.S. troops who served in Vietnam suffered from Post-Traumatic Stress Disorder—a higher percentage than those affected by shell-shock in World War I and battle-fatigue in World War II. Symptoms of the problem, which sometimes appear ten to fifteen years later, range from panic and rage to anxiety, depression and emotional paralysis. Incidents of divorce, suicide, drug addiction, crime and alcoholism significantly exceed those who had not served in Vietnam.

I began this book with a relatively simple premise, which was to tell a story about my friend, George, and what he had experienced in Vietnam and how he continues to be haunted by his experiences while there. One day, well over a year into the project, George asked me if I was a veteran and how much I knew about what went on in Vietnam from a soldier's perspective. I told him that I had opposed the war, like the majority of people in this country did at the time, but I had been declared 1-A after taking the required physical examination and I had been eligible for induction.

However, on December 2, 1969, a lottery was conducted and my birth date, July 14, 1947, was the 331st date drawn. I was spared since the quotas were filled well before then by the hundreds of thousands of men who were drafted and required to serve, whether they wanted to or not. What I knew about Vietnam came from newspapers, books, television specials, movies, friends and clients.

I had few close friends who were lost in that conflict, but I had been in law school in Washington, D.C. during the years 1969 and 1973 and I experienced first-hand all that went on with the marches, the protests, the rallies, the songs, the speeches, the tear gas, the police batons on demonstrators and all the rest. I had, like the entire country, been inundated with the issue. It cast a pallor over everyone and everything, and included a student strike in 1970 after four students died at Kent State University, shot by National Guardsmen, which shut down the entire national educational community, which may have done something to hasten the end of the war. Nixon continued to unsuccessfully look for an 'honorable' way to end the war until 1975 when we finally withdrew.

The trial of George's case in this fictional tale took place in 1980. In 1981 John W. Hinckley attempted to kill President Ronald Reagan. When a jury acquitted him of all charges the following year, based upon the insanity defense, there was much public hue and cry. Laws regarding the defense were changed.

Since 1981, the law in the State of Florida is that the defendant, not the State, must prove that he or she was insane, instead of the other way around as it was before the Hinckley acquittal. Also, the standard of proof has changed slightly, making it more difficult to prove insanity.

For lawyers and legal scholars, arguments have centered around the M'Naghten rule, which arose out of an 1832 case in England when a criminal defendant who sought to kill the Prime Minister was acquitted by reason of insanity for shooting and killing someone else, thinking it was the Prime Minister. The M'Naghten test is basically as stated in this book. There is also an irresistible impulse test, known as the Durham rule, which is used in some other states. There are many variations on the theme, and sentencing options can be quite different from state to state as well.

In Mr. Hinckley's case, to my knowledge, he remains confined at the St. Elizabeth's Mental Hospital in Washington, D. C. but beginning in 2006 he has been allowed many extended visits outside the hospital. The Secret Service knows when he is to be released and where he could be found at all times. It is expected that someday Mr. Hinckley will be freed when psychiatrists determine he is no longer insane, or no longer suffering from a mental infirmity, defect or disorder, though that may not be how the law reads in Washington, D.C. That is how the law reads in the State of Florida.

The bigger picture in this book is, of course, the issue of Post Traumatic Stress Disorder. As I was finishing this book in late 2009, Max Cleland, formerly a United States Senator from the State of Georgia, who lost both legs and an arm when a fellow U.S. Marine accidentally dropped a live grenade and Senator Cleland was injured trying to prevent injury to others by grabbing the grenade and throwing it away from where he and other soldiers stood, authored a book after losing his bid for re-election in 2002. In his book he talks about suffering from PTSD. One of the lead stories of the year 2009 concerns the violent and sometimes criminal behavior of veterans returning from deployment in Iraq and Afghanistan.

In real life, George did not actually beat someone to a pulp as described herein, but he could have. An incident happened that was quite similar to the event described and George did lose control. He is thankful that it did not escalate to the point it did in this book, but he told me that it easily could have. He was restrained and put in a mental hospital pursuant to what is known as the "Baker Act" before things worsened. He lost his job because of it but he remains thankful that nothing worse occurred.

Under Florida law, anyone who poses an immediate threat to the life and safety of himself or others due to a mental illness can be involuntarily hospitalized pursuant to the Baker Act, and that is what happened to George that day. George continues to receive psychiatric and psychological counseling for his problems to this date.

I hope you found this book to be both thought-provoking and interesting. I also hope that you enjoyed the time spent reading it.

Pierce Kelley

About the Author

PIERCE KELLEY is a lawyer and educator turned author who received his undergraduate degree from Tulane University, New Orleans, Louisiana in 1969. He received his Doctorate of Jurisprudence (JD) from the George Washington University, Washington, D.C. in 1973. Following his admission to the Florida Bar, Pierce began his legal career as an Assistant Public Defender in Clearwater, Florida. In 1979 he moved to West Virginia and became the managing attorney of a Legal Services office in a rural five county area in the northeast corner of the state called the Potomac Highlands. In 1985, Pierce returned to Miami, where he was raised, and served as an Assistant Federal Public Defender for the Southern District of Florida.

Since 1986 Pierce has worked exclusively in the area of civil law, concentrating on personal injury, consumer and family law matters. He has served as lead counsel in over 100 jury trials and has successfully argued before the Supreme Court of Florida and the Supreme Court of Appeals for the State of West Virginia. He is currently an active member of the Florida Bar and an inactive member of the West Virginia Bar Association. He is admitted to practice in the United States District Courts for the Southern, Middle and Northern Districts of Florida, the 11th Circuit Court of Appeals and the United States Supreme Court, though he has yet to do so. He is now a sole practitioner in Cedar Key, Florida.

Pierce began writing in 1989 when a freak accident in a softball game caused him a broken ankle. While convalescing, he wrote *A Parent's Guide to Coaching Tennis*, which was recognized by the United States Tennis Association as being *the* perfect introduction and primer for parents of beginning players. Over a span of 50 years, Mr. Kelley was a nationally-ranked player as a junior, in the open Men's Division, and as a senior. He was also the president of the Youth Tennis Foundation of Florida from 1987 until 2007.

In 2000, Pierce authored his second book, *Civil Litigation: A Case Study*, while teaching paralegal students as an Adjunct Professor at St. Petersburg

College in St. Petersburg, Florida. He taught at various colleges and universities as an Adjunct for over 25 years.

Pierce completed his first novel, *A Very Fine Line*, in 2006. Since then six more have followed, which are *Fistfight at the L and M Saloon*, *A Plenary Indulgence*, *Bocas del Toro*, *Asleep at the Wheel*, *A Tinker's Damn!*, and *A Foreseeable Risk*. He has also written *Pieces to the Puzzle*, which is a collection of personal essays, and *Kennedy Homes: An American Tragedy*, which is an account of a major Fair Housing case Mr. Kelley was involved in during the years 2004 and 2007. *Thousand Yard Stare* is his eighth published novel.